Born in Hampshire, **Jan**[illegible] [illegible]areer in London as a music public[illegible] [illegible]g with bands such as Status Quo and Thin Lizzy, before training as a journalist with Mirror Group Newspapers. Since then, she's worked extensively in ITV as a writer/producer/director on news, current affairs, outside broadcasts and documentaries on subjects as diverse as ballet, football and barbershop singing. She was a finalist at the New York Television Festival for her documentary about the plight of Romanian orphans. She is now Head of Features at ITV (Westcountry), commissioning all feature programming for the station.

Jane lives in Torquay, Devon with her husband Iain (alias best-selling romantic novelist Emma Blair). In her spare time, she plays the piano, enjoys theatre, gardening, photography and escaping to France. For more information on her books, please visit her website at: www.janeblanchard.com

ALSO BY JANE BLANCHARD

In Cahoots!

Nailing Harry

Getting It!

Fanning Old Flames

JANE BLANCHARD

TIME WARNER
BOOKS

TIME WARNER BOOKS

First published in Great Britain as a paperback original in
August 2005 by Time Warner Books

All characters in this publication are fictitious and any resemblance to real persons, living or dead, is purely coincidental.

A CIP catalogue record for this book
is available from the British Library.

ISBN 0 7515 3365 3

Typeset by M Rules
Printed and bound in Great Britain
by Clays Ltd, St Ives plc

Time Warner Books
An imprint of
Time Warner Book Group UK
Brettenham House
Lancaster Place
London WC2E 7EN

www.twbg.co.uk
www.janeblanchard.com

For Tim, Chris, Elise and Laurence

Acknowledgements

Huge thanks to my wonderful husband Iain, for so patiently putting up with me disappearing into my office to write this book. And also for nudging and cajoling me at just the right moments. Thanks also to my son Mark who patiently sorts out my computer glitches and has created my website. Sincere thanks to my agent Pat White and to all the lovely folk at Time Warner. And finally thanks to all my loyal and patient friends who forgive my lack of communication when I'm writing and who are convinced they're all in my books. You're not, folks, but maybe next time . . .

Chapter 1

It all started with a phone call.

'A day at a health farm?' The words struck instant terror into Maggie's heart. She could immediately visualise a room full of Caprice, Elle and Naomi-like figures mocking her saggy stomach and whispering, 'Tummy tuck, darling. I'll give you a number. There's a marvellous chap on Harley Street. I could fast-track you in there next week.' The nightmare quickly moved on to her being rushed off to hospital after collapsing over an exercise bike.

'I . . . I . . . don't think I'd have the courage . . .' she started, gazing round the kitchen with its pile of washing up waiting to be done. The sinkful of plates and pans might have made the shortlist for the Turner Prize but they weren't going to provide any inspiration for an excuse.

'Nonsense.' Pam's voice came firmly down the line. 'It'll be heaps of fun. And anyway, I want to *celebrate* being forty, not roll over and begin a slow death. Besides, I want to share it with you.'

Maggie knew from Pam's tone that she wasn't going to take no for an answer. She couldn't even wriggle out of it with the excuse of clashing dates. The voucher that Pam had been given by her work colleagues to mark that mid-life milestone could be taken any time to suit. And clearly Pam was determined the date was going to suit them both.

'It's really kind of you, but . . .' she tried again. But there was no budging Pam.

'Listen, Maggs, you give me a list of dates you're available and I'll just book one of them. OK. Bye.' The phone clicked off.

Maggie replaced the receiver and thought for a moment. A health farm? It sounded like organised torture. Armies of Lycra-clad beauties admiring themselves in mirrors while being pampered by equally beautiful women in white coats with white marble complexions. Root canal work could have been a tempting alternative.

She wandered over to the sink to begin the dishes. As she reached to turn on the tap, she noticed her hands, skin tired and wrinkled, nails dry and flaking. Liver spots were probably only a matter of days away. She was ashamed to realise she couldn't remember the last time she'd bothered with nail varnish, apart from an emergency attempt to stop a ladder in her tights with a timely blob.

Bloody typical of Pam, she muttered to herself. She'll be in her element having what she'll see as a wonderfully pampering day out, and I'll be dreading the ordeal of having perfect strangers gazing at my flabby thighs.

Funny how opposites attract. She and Pam had been best friends since Weltham Grammar School days, although even then they were just as dissimilar. Pam, the taller of the two, was the first girl in the class to go blonde: a full-on platinum job bought with her Saturday girl discount at Boots and shoved on the minute she got home. She'd then survived a run-in with the headmistress the following Monday – *and* kept her hair colour after her mother waded into the fight – which ensured her place up there amongst the great school icons.

Pam always seemed to be ahead of the game. The first in the class to wear heels and lipstick, produce a packet of ten Embassy tipped and then brazenly light up behind the bike sheds. She had style from the word go, even interpreting the school uniform to give it a modern twist. Tie worn loose, shirt collar fashionably turned up, school jumper knotted casually over her shoulders. As well as being tall and thin, she walked like a catwalk model, so even the regulation pleated skirt somehow looked impossibly trendy on Pam.

Maggie, on the other hand, had never quite mastered the art of putting clothes together. Being somewhat heavy in the hip department, she spent her entire teens trying to find ways of disguising them. The search for a minimising pair of jeans became the start of a lifetime mission. Not having Pam's courage, she knew that colouring her dull brown wiry hair any colour other than mousy wasn't an option. And besides, the embarrassment! Someone might have noticed! Or, even worse, said something.

Make-up had also been a bit of a mystery never really solved. Maggie gave up poking herself regularly in the eye with an eyeliner brush and settled for mascara that, no matter how she applied it, always dried in clumps. While Pam sported immaculate scarlet painted talons that always survived an entire weekend, somehow

Maggie always had a couple of chunks missing from her nail varnish before she'd even left her house. These days, with two feuding teenaged children, a lazy husband and no dishwasher, there was no time for a social life, let alone shoving Rouge Noir or Ruby Sorbet on her fingertips.

As she started scrubbing the plates, she racked her brains to think of a really convincing reason not to go to the health farm with Pam. She could plead lack of a decent track suit, but she knew Pam would cart her off to the shops and insist she treated herself. Or, worse still, buy it for her. She'd have to come up with something. The thought of some perfect stranger massaging her saggy neck and offering tactful tips about laughter lines was no joke.

For a few seconds, she contemplated asking the kids to help with the dishes, but she could already hear a row brewing up between them in the sitting room. By the time she'd finished the last of the pans, the squabbling was at fever pitch. As always, it was over the same thing.

'OK, who's got the remote control?' she demanded wearily, standing in the doorway. Beth and George were sitting on the sofas opposite each other, snarling like a couple of feral cats.

'Stupid question,' shrieked Beth. 'He's just a bully. We've had bloody bloody football for the last ten minutes and it's supposed to be my turn now.'

'Well, I can't stand your stupid girlie programmes. All that fashion and soap rubbish,' George retorted. 'And anyway it's a crucial match for Southampton. Win this one and they could be in with a serious crack at winning the league.'

'I don't care,' Beth mocked him. 'Football's all the same. Hours and hours of kicking a ball up and down a bit of grass. All the matches are the same. All the outfits are the same. Even the bloody ball looks the same.'

'Same with your soap drivel,' he sneered. 'They're always either in the pub or in the café and everyone's either rowing or kissing.'

Beth picked up a cushion and threw it at him.

'In case you haven't noticed, dolt brain,' she shouted, 'that's exactly what happens in football. They're either kicking or kissing each other.'

'OK, if they're exactly the same, then shut your stupid face and watch the footie.' George heaved the cushion back at Beth. She burst into noisy sobs, but as Maggie noted wryly there was a complete absence of tears. A roar went up from the capacity crowd at St Mary's.

'Now look, you bitch, they've just scored and I missed it because of your stupid whingeing.'

'That's enough,' Maggie finally shouted above the din. 'Calm down, the pair of you, and stop swearing. Your dad will be home in a minute and he'll go berserk if he hears all this. I'll have that remote control. Now.'

Beth got up from the sofa, glared at George and then stalked out of the room.

'Go and phone one of your sad little friends,' George called after her. 'Go and spend a couple of hours having an in-depth discussion about your boy bands.'

There was a faint response which sounded suspiciously Like 'F off yourself' as Beth clumped upstairs noisily to her room.

Maggie held out her hand for the remote control.

'But Mum . . .'

'No buts,' she announced. 'For chrissake, go and watch

the bloody football in your room and give me some peace.'

George opened his mouth to bark back at his mother but the sound of the front door slamming shut silenced him immediately. Without another word, he handed his mother the remote control and headed for his bedroom.

Maggie sighed. With Beth aged thirteen and George turned fifteen, there were an awful lot of hormones washing around. She just wished they could get on occasionally.

She turned to confront a very stroppy-looking Garth, standing in the doorway, his dark eyes blazing.

'Had a good day, love?' she asked, pretending not to notice the black mood that was coming off her husband in tidal waves.

'No I bloody haven't,' he announced crossly, parking himself firmly on the sofa and kicking off his boots. 'Fanbelt's gone again on the effing van. What's for supper?'

'Chilli,' Maggie replied, with forced jollity.

'I suppose that'll do,' he said ungraciously. 'And I'll have it in here. There's a really important match on tonight and I don't want to miss it.'

Football was king in their house. Garth, who'd entertained dreams of playing in the premier league and possibly for England, had been spotted as a schoolboy player. He'd been signed up by Southampton in his teens but never even made it to the subs' bench, thanks to an Achilles tendon injury. Physically, he still had a footballer's body, tall and muscular with strong legs and arms, but mentally he'd never quite got over a career so brutally cut short. These days, sporting a black beard and a shock of curly black hair now speckled with grey, he could only speculate about what might have been. Occasionally, after a beer too many, he'd let slip just how bitter and cheated he felt about the Beautiful Game. And that running his own gardening business would never – could never – compensate for the fame and riches he might have earned.

Maggie knew from long experience never to discuss it with him. She went straight back into the kitchen to resuscitate the rest of the chilli con carne, glad of the respite. She knew she was partly to blame for their all being so lazy around the house. She should have laid down ground rules years ago but it was difficult when your husband, instead of supporting you, set such a poor example. No one lifted a finger unless she made a fuss. The only advantage to that was that at least the kitchen provided an escape zone from the constant bickering. No one ventured in there, just in case they were asked to do some chores. If the coast was clear, though, they all snack-raided the fridge.

By the time she'd heated up the chilli and cooked some more rice, she could hear renewed sounds of arguing. When she appeared at the sitting room door with a tray for Garth, the Battle for the Remote had resumed. George, hearing the football on again, had ventured back downstairs, hotly pursued by Beth who was now noisily proclaiming that it was all unfair and that men thought they could rule the world, a sentiment that Maggie privately agreed with.

'Can't you get these kids to shut up?' Garth growled as he snapped the ring pull on his beer and took a glug.

'Not if you insist on watching the footie,' said Maggie resignedly. 'Come on, Beth, be a love and go and have an early night. You look really tired. We'll go into town tomorrow and I'll treat you to that nice jumper in Warehouse you fancied.'

George whipped round angrily. 'Hey, that's not fair. Why does she get a present?'

'Because *you've* got the footie.' Oh, God, this was wearying. Perhaps Pam was right. A day at a health farm might actually be a good idea. She could just imagine Garth's reaction. He'd dismiss it as a load of kooky nonsense or condemn it as a blatant rip-off probably run by eunuchs. In a single sentence, he would spoil what pleasure there might have been in a day of being pampered head to foot.

But hang on a minute, she wasn't going, was she, because she was too terrified of being intimidated by all those perfect creatures in her mental picture. Sometimes, she reflected, out-of-season Siberia could seem an attractive destination when Garth and the kids were in full flow.

By Monday morning, even a winter break in Antarctica might have taken on a rosy glow. The post produced a frightening number of bills that were going to push their overdraft to the max and probably beyond. Garth's black mood of a few nights before resumed when he saw the size of his mobile phone account. But, Maggie reasoned with him, running a gardening services business and therefore being outside all day meant he conducted most of his business on it. Why he should be so cross when (a) it was tax deductible and (b) it was he who had run up the calls? Maggie could only put it down to male time of the month.

He casually threw the last item in the pile, an ominously large envelope, across the kitchen table towards her. It was addressed to her in vaguely familiar writing. She ripped open the envelope to find a glossy brochure inside.

> Welcome to Juicy Lucy's Health Farm, a magical retreat from the maelstrom of life, a cool arbour in the frenzied forest of twenty-first-century living, an oasis in the desert that is your office. As welcoming as a lay-by in a traffic jam, an armchair at a bus stop or merely an upgrade on a cheap long haul. Come and be pampered by our fully qualified staff. People from all walks of life enjoy Juicy Lucy's. Our regular guests include top models, pop stars, City movers and shakers, media moguls, and professional sportsmen and women, all seeking that magical world of spiritual and physical well-being that J Lu can provide . . .

Oh, God, Maggie groaned to herself, J Lu. How naff's that? She retrieved a piece of writing paper stuck inside the brochure with Pam's distinctive loopy writing on it.

I've booked us in for Saturday week. Got Beth to check on your kitchen calendar. No more excuses. Love Pam xx

Chapter 2

Maggie sat at the kitchen table, clutching a mug of coffee as she reread Juicy Lucy's terrifying brochure. It was full of Gwyneth and Cameron lookalikes, all impossibly glamorous in whiter than white bathrobes or ridiculously skimpy leotards. Relaxing by the 'pool inspired by a Greek temple', working out in the 'space-age gym' or lunching in the 'seductively cool Arbour Restaurant' – presumably all hiding out from the frenzied forest that was apparently twenty-first-century living.

She flipped on to the treatment pages where Gwynnie and Cam were now relaxing on couches, being massaged by stick-thin blondes in pristine white coats. Everyone sported huge French-manicured nails and fixed grins. Presumably they weeded out the miserable ones with the stubby fingers. Even with mud slapped on their faces, or their heads poking out of some steam bath contraption, Gwynnie and Cam managed to combine a look of ecstasy with pure glamour.

Despite the wall to wall smiles, the treatments sounded incredibly painful. Salt body scrub sounded more like a punishment. Detoxifying algae wrap? Surely that was what top models picked at over lunch? And as for reiki, wasn't that some yoghurt drink served up in Indian restaurants? And what the hell was a Hopi Ear Candle?

Meanwhile, in the Arbour Restaurant, the calories were clearly counted to within an inch of their lives. 'All our menus are colour coded so that you can keep up your dietary regime,' crooned the blurb. 'Even if you're no wheat, no fat, low fat, no carbs, low carbs, high protein, Atkins, Hay, no dairy, vegetarian, vegan or a combination of any of these, we promise you a delicious meal in an atmosphere of total relaxation.'

You'd need to have cracked the Enigma code to get through that menu, Maggie decided. A large photograph of a group of footballers' wives lookalikes looking rapaciously at a plate of tastefully arranged radicchio leaves made her feel strangely hungry. A quick bowl of cornflakes would do the trick. Bet that's on the banned list at Juicy Lucy's, she mused. Right now, they're probably all tucking into a nourishing saucer of toasted sunflower seeds and a no-calorie organic grapefruit, grown lovingly by a caring farmer who'd offered it victim support before picking it.

She glanced up at the kitchen clock and hastily shoved the brochure into her handbag. No time for cornflakes. It was time to go to work. As she picked up her coat and car keys, she felt a pang of regret at leaving the house. It was always so peaceful when Garth and the kids weren't there, she thought guiltily. But there was no question of her being a full time housewife. Her job as a not brilliantly paid secretary at an estate agency was an economic necessity.

'Fantastic. Brilliant. You'll absolutely adore it.' That wasn't the verdict Maggie had wanted to hear when Juicy Lucy's brochure was snatched from her grasp. It hadn't been Garth's reaction either. He'd made some fatuous comment about hoping he wouldn't recognise her when she came back.

'What a fab friend your mate Pam must be,' chorused the entire office at the Weltham branch of Farley & Co.

Maggie realised she was going to appear ungrateful if she didn't summon up at least some vague enthusiasm. Nancy, Jean and Barbara, the three negotiators she worked for, clearly thought Pam's offer was fantastically generous. And of course it was. Except that a glance in any mirror would remind her that her mop of unruly brown hair, sallow skin and body rapidly going south didn't remotely match up to the goddesses in the brochure. And then there was the vexed question of what to wear. Some snazzy Dash track suit was right out of the frame, especially as Garth's gardening business wasn't having its best year.

'I'd love to spend all day in a bathrobe, eat lovely food and put my feet up,' announced Jean, repinning her blonde chignon, which was already in terminal descent. 'Better than touring people round Bleak House. Oh, shit,' she glanced at the clock, 'that reminds me. Got to get out there again. Viewing number twenty-eight, if I'm not mistaken.'

She picked up her briefcase and a bunch of keys and headed for the door. Bleak House was a nickname for No. 37 Church Park on the far side of Weltham. On the face of it a fine example of an early Victorian villa complete with original features such as marble fireplaces, dado rails and servant pulls, in reality it came complete with a range of not very well hidden extras including dry rot, wet rot and woodworm. The Farley & Co. surveyor also suspected there were now bats in the roof space. The bargain price lured many a hopeful over its damp and rotting doorstep, but always the subsequent survey gave it *nul points*. It had been on the market for nearly eighteen months – almost a record, even for Farley & Co. The owners, a bad-tempered brother and sister who'd inherited it from their father, were not in a hurry to sell. He'd died in the sitting room and not been discovered for several months, a fact that neatly encapsulated their relationship with him and their attitude to the house. In other words, they couldn't bring themselves to give a toss.

Trips around Bleak House with prospective buyers were strictly rota-ed between Nancy, Jean and Barbara, who were convinced that the general stench in the house originated from the owner's sad demise.

Most properties on Farley & Co.'s books tended to stick. The agency rarely got the sparkling end of the market; usually the dregs that the smarter and trendier agencies in town didn't want to touch. Bleak House was a typical example, an inheritance sale that was over-priced and under-loved.

Another Farley & Co. property in for the long run was an absolute dog of a bungalow bordering on Weltham's worst sink estate, owned by a terrifying woman called Mrs Daniels, who came equipped with beaky nose and grey hair scraped back into a bun. She was soon nicknamed Mrs Danvers, in honour of Daphne du Maurier's famously daunting housekeeper in *Rebecca*, and so the bungalow inevitably became known as Manderley. If she'd sorted out the damp, painted the whole place magnolia and dropped the price by seven or eight thousand, she'd have had a queue at the door. But everyone was too frightened of Mrs Danvers to dare to suggest that a lick of paint might be a good idea. So Manderley stuck fast, along with Bleak House.

Maggie switched on her ancient computer and waited patiently for it to boot up. Farley & Co. didn't believe in upgrading anything. If it ain't bust, don't fix it, was the company ethos. They were the only estate agency in Weltham not to have a website. Nor did they issue property details with colour pictures, like all their rivals.

'Black and white's perfectly good enough,' Matthew Farley had pronounced firmly when Barbara once had the temerity to suggest that they were lagging behind the pack. 'You don't need gimmicks to sell houses. Properties ultimately sell themselves. A good agent, the right price and a reputation. That's all that's needed. And as for all this worldwide web nonsense, it won't last. Just a phase. Mark my words.'

Matthew Farley, early sixties, thinning grey hair, whiffy armpits and ancient pinstriped suits with travelling shoulder pads, knew it all. And he always had done. Anyone who questioned him got the same response. 'How long have I been in this business? Forty years. Yes, forty years. And how long – do I need to ask you – have *you* been in this business? Yes, that's right. Forty minutes.'

Everyone pitied his wife Betty, a downtrodden, careworn little woman with the beginnings of a stoop, probably thanks to years of cowering in the presence of Mr Know-It-All. Fortunately the staff at Farley & Co. were able to cope quite happily without his forty years' experience for most of the time, as he commuted between his three branches. But the bad news was that he never announced his travel plans in advance, so no branch ever quite knew when he might turn up. Accordingly, they'd all fallen into a routine of tipping each other off. The moment he left the Weltham branch, Maggie automatically telephoned the other two to warn them that he was back on the road. There had been one week last year when no one knew where he was. It was only late on Friday afternoon that it dawned on the entire company that he'd taken a week's holiday, yet managed to keep them on their toes simply by not telling them.

As Maggie's computer finally staggered into action, she glanced through the viewings diary for the next couple of weeks. None coming up for Manderley, unfortunately. That meant Mrs Danvers would be straight on the case again, hissing down the phone.

She was just about to make some coffee when Jean came back in from viewing number twenty-eight at Bleak House.

'Crumbs, that was quick,' said Maggie, as she filled the ancient kettle and tried not to notice decades of furring on the inside.

Jean plonked herself down behind her desk, slammed the keys down on the desk and roared with laughter.

'Did the usual, talked up the potential of the place as we walked to the door,' she reported. 'But then the front step gave way. The wood had completely rotted. By some miracle, the chap was still interested and started talking about a surveyor. That is, until he touched one of the window frames and the wood was so soft his finger left a huge dent.'

Maggie started spooning out the coffee. 'Even the House Doctors would pronounce Bleak House dead on arrival,' she said wryly. 'It's terminal, that place. Carol Smillie and Carol Vorderman wouldn't even touch it with a nail file.'

'At least a telly programme couldn't convey the smell,'

said Jean philosophically. 'I'm going to put a note in the file. None of us must wear stilettos or kitten heels around that place in future. There's a risk of them going through the floorboards. It's flat shoes there from now on.'

'And probably duckboards,' added Barbara. 'How's the stench?'

'Worse than ever,' replied Jean, wrinkling her nose. 'Maybe an oxygen mask as well, then.'

They all started laughing. The shrill ring of the phone cut through the giggles.

'Bet that's Danvers,' said Jean, trying to rearrange her face into a straight line. 'We haven't had a whinge from her for all of two days.' She picked up the phone.

'Hello, Mrs Danv— Daniels. How are you?'

There was a pause while Mrs Danvers went into her usual tirade. Jean held the phone out towards the others so they could pick up the sound of her banging on about Manderley, why wasn't it sold, why wasn't anyone viewing and just what did they do all day long.

'Of course, Mrs Dan . . . iels,' Jean finally resumed. 'You are totally at liberty to find another agent if you feel we're not doing a good job.'

The others broke into huge grins and gave her massive thumbs-up signs.

'Could this mean the end of the Road to Manderley?' Barbara whispered. 'Oh, God, I'd so miss that peeling paint and the rising damp. It always makes this place feel so – er – posh.'

She gestured round the scruffy office. New desks, chairs, carpets, lamps and computers wouldn't have gone amiss. But there was no chance of that, with Mr Farley's tightfisted grip on the helm.

'Of course, Mrs Dan . . . iels,' Jean continued smoothly.

'I'll ask Mr Farley to ring you personally. Of course . . . of course . . . consider it done.'

She replaced the phone. 'Talking of which,' she continued to the other three, 'where *is* the old skinflint today?'

'Well, bit early to say. We haven't heard from the other offices yet,' Maggie reported. 'Do you think he'll ring old Danvers and butter her up?'

'Doubt it,' said Jean. 'Despite his much trumpeted forty years in the business, he wouldn't want to get his hands dirty. Besides, it's all our fault. We've only been here for forty minutes. And never forget that.'

They all sipped their coffee.

'Let's celebrate the hopeful departure of Danvers,' Jean continued cheerfully, 'by having another look at your Juicy Lucy thing.'

They all pored over the brochure once more, trying to celebrity-spot amongst the white-clad goddesses in the photographs.

'Which treatments are you going to have?' Jean asked Maggie.

Maggie looked blank. She hadn't given it a thought.

Jean continued: 'I'd go for the full aromatherapy facial, the aqua jet massage and the reiki. Oh, and look, there are loads of fitness classes. Pilates, that's what I'd go for.'

'Pilates? What the hell's that?' Maggie was ashamed of her ignorance.

'Oh, it's quite trendy nowadays,' said Jean. 'It's about posture, breathing and a bit of yoga thrown in.'

'Really? I've seen the word but didn't know what it was. I thought it had something to do with Pontius Pilate,' said Maggie, now laughing at her own embarrassment. 'Some kind of counselling or confessional for troubled souls.'

They all roared with laughter. Jean, the comedienne amongst them, couldn't resist getting down on the floor to demonstrate some of the movements.

'It's like this, you hold your stomach in, press it down into the floor. Great for pelvic floor, girls. And then count slowly . . . one . . . two . . . three . . .'

'Seconds out,' growled a familiar voice. They all whipped round in the direction of the door to confront a snarling Matthew Farley.

'What the bloody hell's going on here?' he shouted, puce with anger. Maggie bit her lip. She should have known from the silence of the other branches that he might turn up at any time. It was all her fault, for bringing in that stupid brochure.

Jean was still on the floor struggling to get up in as dignified a fashion as possible when Mr Farley launched into his inevitable attack.

'Outrageous behaviour. Does anyone have an explanation?' He glowered at them over his half-spectacles.

'I'm sorry, Mr Farley.' Jean was still trying to get up. 'We were just—'

'I thought not,' he interrupted her. 'How long have I been in this business? Forty years. Yes, forty years. And how long have *you* been in this business? Forty minutes.'

Oh, God, here we go again, thought Maggie, mentally bracing herself.

'Forty years of trading as one of the most successful estate agencies along the south coast . . .' he hissed.

'Not *that* successful,' came a booming voice from behind him. In all the drama, no one had noticed Mrs

Danvers coming into the office. Now she punctuated her arrival by slamming the door shut behind her, causing the front windows to rattle ominously.

Satisfied that everyone's attention was riveted on her, Mrs Danvers, dressed in a tweed cape and matching hat with a large feather in it and brandishing a huge golfing umbrella as though it were a Kalashnikov, proceeded to look daggers at them all. She then settled on Mr Farley as the object of her venom.

'Not *that* successful,' she repeated. 'How long are you going to take to sell my property? Will it be in my lifetime or shall I just go ahead and bequeath it to the nation here and now?'

Mr Farley immediately went into Uriah Heep mode, assuming a grovelling stance and clasping his hands sympathetically, whilst rolling his eyes in the direction of his four staff as if they were some kind of pond life.

'Mrs . . .?'

'Daniels,' she boomed.

'Mrs Daniels, it will be my personal pleasure to visit your property and reassess your needs and how we can be of service to you. I would like to assure you that I have forty years of experience in selling property—'

'Forty years? But I want a quick sale. I don't want to wait that long,' she boomed.

Maggie and the others had difficulty in suppressing a giggle.

'You might have been forty years in the business,' Mrs Danvers continued, now in full flight, 'but you can't seem to sell my house. Come to that, you couldn't sell me a tin of paint.'

Pity, they all thought. That's just what Manderley needed.

Mrs Danvers stalked out of the office, with Mr Farley in hot pursuit, wringing his hands and begging her to reconsider.

'Unlike Farley to be nice to customers,' said Jean, who was now vertical and dusting herself down after her contact with the filthy, threadbare office carpet.

'We're not doing very well,' said Nancy pointedly. 'The past few months' figures have been dire. I think even Mr-Forty-Years-in-the-Business is worried.'

'Oh well, at least we've got him off to Manderley for a while,' said Maggie, dialling one of the other offices. 'Hi, Sarah . . . yes, it's me. He's just left us, on his way to visit a property. Any time in the next hour, I should think. He's in a filthy mood . . . well, Jean on the floor demonstrating Pilates might have been a factor . . . no, don't even ask . . . Bye.'

So, Farley & Co. were on the skids. That was a bit worrying. Maggie ringed the Juicy Lucy date in her diary. She was suddenly beginning to look forward to the day at the health farm after all.

Chapter 3

Pam had insisted on making the whole day her treat, even down to picking Maggie up in her car, a smart red soft-top Renault Mégane. Maggie was secretly relieved that no one at Juicy Lucy's would ever see the embarrassment that was her beaten up old Ford Fiesta with its hidden extras like noisy exhaust and permanent slow puncture.

Pam looked dramatic as ever in a pale turquoise track suit, clearly expensive suede trainers and co-ordinating kit bag. She'd swept her blonde hair up on top of her head with an artfully tied scarf. She had clearly taken note of the clientele in the brochure and was attempting (very successfully, Maggie thought) to look like one of those 'I'm sure I recognise you from somewhere' celebrities.

Maggie's heart immediately sank when she realised that her cheapie track suit by Tesco wasn't in the same class. But Pam, to her credit, hugged her friend warmly and told her she'd never seen her looking so terrific.

'Don't know why we bothered to get dressed up,' Pam reassured her as they roared off out of Maggie's road. 'We'll soon be in those lovely fluffy bathrobes with everything scraped off our faces. We'll come back feeling like new women.'

Just over an hour later, the Renault was scrunching on the gravel of Juicy Lucy's huge carriage driveway. Maggie gazed across the magnificent grounds surrounding the house, the sight almost making her catch her breath. Majestic sweeping oaks, sycamores and limes as far as the eye could see had turned to amber, gold and deep russet.

How someone could dream up a name as naff as Juicy Lucy's for the exquisite Georgian mansion was anybody's guess. Pam and Maggie walked up the wide granite steps, past huge stone pots bearing standard bay trees and box cut into spheres, and admired the massive stone window boxes filled with purple winter pansies, winter-flowering heathers and silvery ivy.

They pushed their way through the double glass doors and into the chandeliered foyer. Everywhere, it seemed, there were deep sofas and chairs, sumptuous cushions, curtains with massive swags and tails, all in different combinations of royal blue and pale primrose. Huge urns of white lilies filled the air with their scent while pan pipes played gently in the background. A group of women in white bathrobes were slumped across a group of sofas in a far corner, looking as though they were about to nod off.

A girl in her early twenties who introduced herself as Leanne started tapping away on a computer as she processed their bookings. Maggie couldn't help gazing at her wonderful porcelain skin and then wondering what the therapist would make of her own rather blotchy, tired version.

'So,' said Leanne finally when she'd typed in the equivalent of a short novel, 'we've phased your treatments so that you can use all the facilities here together today.' She spoke in a smooth, rather toneless way, presumably to help guests attain a confused stupor as quickly as possible. 'So – your totally holistic rebalancing aromatherapy facial including luxury face pack for mature and dehydrated skin – that's both of you at eleven. OK?'

Maggie shuddered. So it was that obvious! Mature and dehydrated. She'd left the booking of treatments to Pam in the end on the basis that she'd sort it out.

'Then,' Leanne continued in a monotone, hypnotically fluttering impossibly perfect long lashes, 'I'd suggest lunch before you to go to your aqua jet massage, deluxe manicure including a free gift of Juicy Lucy's own award-winning nail file and two coats of coloured polish of your choice, Chinese reflexology and Indian head massage. We then recommend a relax-unwind in our meditation suite, Another Plane, complete with soothing music for a sensation of total mental liberation.'

They both nodded inanely. It all sounded frantic to Maggie, not relaxing at all. Also, what the hell was an 'award-winning nail file'? Did they hold ceremonies like the Oscars or the Baftas for manicure sets?

'By starting your treatments at eleven,' Leanne continued, as she tapped away at that bestseller, 'you can attend one of our extensive range of fitness classes to suit all ages and levels of ability beforehand if you wish. You will still have time for a swim, a visit to the gym where our fully qualified instructors will give you a top to toe fitness analysis and maybe a power walk round the grounds, which can be accompanied by one of our personal trainers if you so desire, in between all your various treatments.'

They nodded again.

'Oh, and before you begin your day, we like to give our guests a fully guided tour, so Simon . . .' She beckoned a young man in his early twenties. 'Simon, may I introduce Mrs Margaret Fraser and Mrs Pamela White? Enjoy your day here at J Lu's.'

Simon, surprisingly, had terrible zits, two of which were about to burst. Maggie felt better already. But just like Leanne, he could talk the smooth talk. 'OK, ladies, I'd like to welcome you to Juicy Lucy's and hope that your stay with us is relaxing, fulfilling and energising. First of all, I'd like to show you the fitness suite and introduce you to François, who is our gym instructor for the day.'

'No, sorry.' Pam interrupted him rather vehemently. 'First of all, we'd like coffee.'

'Coffee?' Simon was completely fazed.

'Yes,' said Pam. 'Coffee. We've had a bit of a drive to get here and I don't know about you, Maggs, but I'm gagging for a cup. Nice big latte if possible.'

'But coffee is a stimulant,' said Simon, horrified. 'We really try to steer our guests away from—'

'Well, not these two,' said Pam. 'Just steer us towards a good cup of caffeine and then we're all yours.'

'I'll have to find out if we do coffee,' he replied, incredulous. He loped off as if he'd been asked to nip out for fags for the Queen during the opening of Parliament.

Five minutes later, Pam and Maggie were installed on sofas overlooking the glorious parkland, clutching cups of the frowned-upon substance.

'I think it's fab being forty,' said Pam, leaning back against the huge silk cushions. 'We can start being cantankerous.'

'Really?' The thought hadn't crossed Maggie's mind.

Pam continued: 'Well, you remember how we used to tremble at school just at the very mention of the horrible Miss Small? What a cow she was, banging the desk with a ruler all the time and shouting about Latin conjugations? Except of course her little favourites like creepy Dora Fielding and swotty Freddie Chapple. We certainly weren't amongst that select little band.'

Everyone at Weltham Grammar – except the select little band – hated Miss Small with a vengeance. She would have given the ancient Roman tyrants a run for their denarii. Plain, drab and ruthless, she could have averted Caesar's Gallic wars with a mere bang of her ruler.

'I still cringe,' Pam went on, 'when I think how we used to run around like humble grovelling little minions, absolutely terrified of her. Well, maybe it's because she'd turned forty. So the way I look at it, now it's our turn. We can be stroppy like Miss bloody Small. In fact, I'm beginning to think this growing old thing could be quite fun.'

'How do you mean?' said Maggie suspiciously. This wasn't normal territory for the perennially elegant Pam.

'Oh, you know, when you're old people expect you to be stroppy. And of course, all sorts of perks kick in.'

'Like what?' Maggie could imagine only a world involving catheters and colostomy bags.

'Safe sex. Meals on wheels. Selective deafness. Jaffa Cakes. Railcards. Snoozing in the afternoon. Free teeth and hearing aids. Tea dances. Nostalgia.'

Maggie took a sip of coffee and gently replaced the delicate china cup in its saucer, terrified she'd break it.

'Funny, I thought you'd hate hitting forty,' she said. 'I thought you'd never want to mention it.'

'Me too,' said Pam, tossing her blonde head back and

laughing. 'I was absolutely panic-stricken for ages. I even used to cry about it, but just lately I've realised that I'm suddenly kind of freed up. Tom's away a lot and Mark's at university. I've suddenly got much less washing and cooking to do. It's terribly liberating.'

Pam's husband Tom served with the Royal Navy and was currently on a long posting in Gibraltar. They'd married in their early twenties and Pam, to her own surprise, had adjusted quickly to life as a Navy wife. She liked having him home but she also loved having her own space. And their son Mark had gone off to university in London the previous month so now there was even more freedom. Although Pam missed him terribly, she felt slightly guilty that she so much enjoyed having the house to herself.

'Take today for example,' Pam continued, warming to her theme. 'A few months ago I might not have been able to come because either Tom was home on leave or I had to lend Mark the car to go to his Saturday job. Now I can do what I fancy.'

Sounds wonderful, Maggie thought to herself. She wondered what the kids were up to. Rowing over the remote yet again, she guessed. And Garth was probably being his usual, unshaven stroppy self. Still, she had been surprised and relieved at how relatively uncomplaining he was about her not being home today, a Saturday, to attend his every beck and call.

'Mind you,' Pam had not yet finished her treatise on being forty, 'I don't think I'm quite ready for Saga holidays and Scholl sandals yet. I'm still in Oasis and Warehouse, thank you very much. Anyway, I've been meaning to ask you. Why didn't you celebrate your fortieth?'

Maggie immediately felt a familiar stab of pain. As

with nearly all her birthdays, Garth and the kids had completely forgotten. They'd done their usual trick of rushing out and buying cards on the day itself, but it was never the same. And with Garth's business not doing quite so well, a meal in a restaurant hadn't been an option.

'Just didn't, really,' she said, not quite meeting Pam's intense gaze. 'Didn't seem worth celebrating. Unlike you, I've got several years of pain ahead of me before the kids leave home. Ask me when I'm fifty – might be able to join your escape committee then.'

'Well then, I'm extra pleased that we're celebrating today,' said Pam, who was clearly already relaxed in the surroundings and determined to have a good time. 'And as for lunch, we're going to have the full-on carb, fat, wheat and dairy, plus a death-defying bottle of champagne. And no buts. Now, it's time for your exercise bike, Miss de Mille.'

Soon they were pedalling away under the gaze of François, a rather ugly muscle-bound Frenchman who clearly thought he was a Gallic love god, judging from the way he swaggered around the gym, admiring himself in the huge mirrors.

'I'm sorry you didn't celebrate your fortieth.' Pam resumed a subject that Maggie would have sooner left alone. 'Garth's never struck me as the demonstrative type, but surely he could have come up with something.'

Maggie suddenly realised her eyes were full of tears. She tipped her head back slightly, hoping none would descend. The last thing she wanted was to spoil Pam's day, but the sheer bliss of getting away from Garth's black moods and having time for herself suddenly hit her like an invisible hammer.

Pam caught her blinking back the tears in the mirror in front of them. 'Sorry, hon. I didn't mean to upset you.'

'No, it's OK, really it is,' she replied, releasing a hand from the bike handle to divert a stray teardrop. 'He's not the most thoughtful person on the planet. And he's having a rough time with the business just now. It's all gone rather quiet. One or two old dears who were good and regular clients have died. So money's a bit short and the kids are going through that stroppy stage.'

'Well, sod the lot of them,' Pam announced. 'We're having a day to ourselves. Just forget them all and let's get pampered.'

Maggie was the first to flag, feeling her hamstrings tugging and her breath shortening. As she got off the bike, her legs nearly gave way under her. François shot them both another disapproving look before suddenly turning his gaze to two young model-like creatures who had just entered the gym. When they picked up dumb-bells and started examining the muscle tone in their arms and legs in the mirror, he was straight over, like a dog on heat, to talk them through the equipment.

'Didn't do that for us,' Pam observed with a grin as they sipped cups of water and caught their breath. 'See, that's age for you. If we were twenty years younger he'd have made a bee line for us.'

'Twenty? Seems like a lifetime ago.' Maggie sighed as she regained her breath, remembering the halcyon days of *Howard's Way*, shoulder pads and Spandau Ballet.

'Do you remember me going out with Randy Old Luke?' Pam was clearly in a reminiscent mood. 'Or rather I thought I was. Didn't realise I was sharing him with half the town as well. And you. Who were you seeing then?'

Maggie pondered for a moment. She hadn't thought

back to those days for a very long time. 'Must have been Rick, I think. He was a bit of a love rat too. I remember trying to captivate him in a black mini dress with a huge red belt and red boots. It didn't work.'

'I wonder what happened to them,' Pam mused. 'It's funny looking back on a time when I hadn't met Tom and you hadn't met Garth and our kids didn't exist.'

'Sometimes it seems like paradise,' said Maggie, half to herself. 'Oh, don't get me wrong, I love my kids, but I wish they wouldn't squabble all the time.'

'Oh well, let's forget them all for a while,' said Pam, consulting her watch. 'It's time for our "totally holistic rebalancing aromatherapy facial including luxury face pack for mature and dehydrated skin".' She mimicked Leanne's monotone patter. 'You never know, it might just put the clock back.'

Chapter 4

Zitty Simon the tour manager clearly doubled as maître d' in the Arbour Restaurant. With a flourish, he showed them to a table in a corner with another beautiful view of the parkland, and then presented them with dark green leather-bound menus.

'Oh, and a wine list please,' said Pam. Simon flinched momentarily and then remembered he was dealing with the Caffeine Two. Silly me, he chided himself, of course they'd need another drug to get them through the afternoon. Pam, who loved to be the centre of a bit of drama, glanced briefly at the list, snapped it shut and ordered champagne.

Moments later, Simon re-emerged looking distinctly embarrassed as he lugged a champagne bucket across the restaurant. A ripple of envy went round the room as the rest of the bathrobed diners reluctantly sipped their mineral water or carrot juice.

'What's the most calorie laden, fattiest, most scrumptiously naughty item on the menu?' Pam asked.

Simon winced as he glanced down the list. 'The mushroom stroganoff has soured cream in it,' he whispered, hoping that the other diners couldn't hear such foul language falling from his mouth. 'Or the hot pepper quiche does have a pastry base – although it's terribly thin and it's made mostly with sundried tomatoes and spinach.'

Maggie could sense the nearby tables listening in on their choice. 'Quiche for me,' she announced. 'That sounds delicious.'

'And I'll go for the mushroom stroganoff,' Pam added. 'And some rolls and butter, please.'

Simon turned to head in the direction of the kitchen.

'Oh, and Simon,' Pam shot him a cheeky grin, 'make sure they're white rolls, please.'

An audible gasp rose from all the nearby tables, as forks laden with slivers of raw carrot and cabbage in a fat-free vinaigrette were momentarily suspended in mid-air.

Pam sat back in her seat and admired the view. 'God, this is the life, isn't it, Maggs?' she pronounced. 'Reminds me of the first time I drank champagne. It was when I was going out with Dave – remember that idiot with the old Morris Traveller?'

Maggie nodded. How could anyone forget David Gregg? With a mop of unruly black hair and thick black-framed glasses, he looked like a mad professor. But he had a line in chat that should have made him a politician. If Dave didn't know it, he just made it up. After a while, everyone rumbled him, but he was always popular and very entertaining.

'He told me that car had been owned by the royal family.' Pam laughed. 'Said it had been driven by George the Fifth who'd used it for picnics in the grounds of Sandringham. And then he produced the champagne as if to recreate a piece of its history. Actually, looking back on it, I think it was probably Lambrusco by any other bottle. Eventually my dad informed me that George the Fifth would have had to have been exhumed in order to drive around in a Morris Traveller. But I was naïve enough to believe it at the time.'

'What happened to Dave?' Maggie asked as she sipped her champagne.

'Last heard on the knock,' Pam replied. 'You know, knocking on the door and relieving old ladies of their junk, buffing it up, and selling it at a vast profit. He was always a bit of a wide boy.'

'He'll probably pop up on telly one day on one of those antiques programmes,' said Maggie.

Pam nodded in agreement. 'He certainly had the chat. If he'd had a mahogany tan, a pinstriped suit and a wardrobe full of whacky half-moon specs, he could have beaten David Dickinson off with a stick. I always sensed he'd be really successful.'

'Why did you split up?'

Pam laughed sarcastically. 'Don't you remember? He put an ad in the local paper's lonely hearts column describing himself as a "tall, dark and handsome adventurer who was tired of pretty girls and looking for something more meaningful". The silly idiot stupidly put in his home number. One of his so-called mates spotted it and then basically told everyone. So most of our old class rang him up to take the mick out of him. Including me. Except that I also told him to piss off.'

'He was an adventurer all right,' said Maggie, laughing. 'But you were well shot of him in the long run. Even that nasty little swot Freddie Chapple laughed at you. And normally he wouldn't say boo to a goose. God, he was an odd little creep with those Harry Potter glasses, wasn't he? Top in maths, top in science and bottom in social chitchat.'

'He's probably running MI6 now,' Pam joked. 'Just the type to do it. Billy No Mates gets to the top but no one really knows who he is.'

'Well, what's the verdict?' asked Pam, reinspecting her new bright red nails before starting up the car.

'Utterly fantastic,' said Maggie. 'I haven't enjoyed myself so much in years. I can't ever remember being so pampered.'

'Just what you deserve,' Pam replied. 'Don't worry, one day *your* kids will leave home and then we can do more of this.'

'Fat chance,' said Maggie wistfully. 'It's at least five years before they're both at university, give or take gap years. Then it'll be just me and Garth.'

'Hmmm. You're not happy with Garth, are you?'

Maggie wasn't quite expecting that. She took a sharp intake of breath. Wasn't she? She never had time to think. She was too busy keeping the peace.

'Well,' she stumbled a little over her reply, 'we're going through a difficult patch with the kids just now. It will get better,' she finished more confidently, 'especially if his business picks up a bit.'

'Hmmm,' said Pam. 'I've watched you transform today back into the Maggie I knew at school. You were really tense this morning but look at you now, all relaxed and glowing. And now you've got to go back to the war zone.'

Maggie knew, although they'd never really discussed it, that Pam was not Garth's greatest fan. She rarely visited their house, for which Maggie was eternally grateful. The squabbling battleground atmosphere wasn't conducive to welcoming visitors. And Pam and Garth were like chalk and cheese, really. Pam always radiated warmth and fun, qualities that Garth regarded as a frivolous waste of time. Maggie suspected he actually enjoyed being dour because it cemented his position as head of the household. He and Pam would never have got on, so there had never seemed any point in trying to begin with. By the same token, Maggie never bothered to regale Garth with funny anecdotes from work about Bleak House or the ghastly Mrs Danvers. He just wouldn't have appreciated them. He'd have regarded today's luxurious experience at Juicy Lucy's as an unnecessary waste of time. And money too, if it hadn't been free.

When Pam finally pulled up outside Maggie's dreary semi, Maggie detected tears gathering in her friend's eyes.

'Thanks for making my day so special, Maggs,' she said simply.

'A huge treat for which I can never thank you enough,' Maggie replied.

'Also I want to make a small confession,' Pam continued, looking a bit boot-faced. 'You know all that crap I came out with today about how brilliant it was to be forty and how I could be bolshy and cantankerous from now on?'

'Hmmm.' Maggie nodded.

'I lied. I've been absolutely dreading the big four-o, really dreading it. But today made it a bit more bearable – thanks to you, Maggs.'

'I knew all along. You weren't kidding anyone. Don't worry about being forty. At least we've got all our own hair and teeth.'

'Yeah, for now,' said Pam, trying to force a smile. She turned and gave Maggie a hug. Then she sat in the car for a few moments, watching as Maggie walked up her garden path. Even from the road, she could hear Beth and George slugging it out over something or other, followed by Garth's voice booming over at them to shut up.

Poor Maggie, she whispered to herself, and here am I moaning on about a date on the calendar.

Chapter 5

Heading back to work after the weekend, Maggie was looking forward to giving the Farley & Co. girls a blow-by-blow account of her day at Juicy Lucy's. And perhaps showing off her still unchipped nails while she regaled them with an account of all the glorious treatments. She was delighted that she could, for once, tell them something interesting as opposed to tales of squabbling kids and games of Hunt the Remote.

But as she pushed open the dusty glass door of Farley & Co., she immediately sensed that something was wrong. It was almost as though she'd stepped into a different world. Nancy and Jean were already at their desks looking boot-faced, while Barbara was busily banging down coffee cups.

'Here,' she said, putting Maggie's mug on her desk. 'I've made them all extra strong. You're going to need it.'

'Why, what's up?' said Maggie nervously. 'Look, I'm sorry I'm a bit late, but the parking was terrible this morning and the kids missed the school bus so I had to drop them off. Is old Danvers on the warpath again? Or the Bleak House Two?'

She scanned their faces. She'd never seen any of them

look quite like this. They all wore the same strange expression of fear and shock, gripping their coffee cups as if they were life support machines. Still no one spoke.

Eventually Barbara managed to utter: 'Pick up that letter on your desk and read it. Bad news, I'm afraid.'

Maggie was suddenly aware of a white envelope on her desk and feverishly began opening it. In her haste, she cut her finger on the paper, getting blood all over its contents. In between the smears of red, she scanned the letter and gave an audible gasp of horror. Farley & Co. was no more. It had been bought out by another estate agency, and they were all being made redundant with immediate effect. No thank you or expression of appreciation for all their hard work, no hint of redundancy money, no glimmer of hope, not so much as a tick of a gold watch.

'Bloody hell,' she said in disbelief. Like the others, she went into stunned silence, gripping her coffee, her mind racing. What on earth was she going to do? This couldn't have happened at a worse time. Just how big was the overdraft? With Christmas not far away, and Garth's business on the skids, how on earth were they going to manage?

Jean finally broke the silence. 'Well, at least we won't have to put up with Mr Forty-Years-in-the-Business any more,' she announced with forced jollity. 'Didn't stand him in good stead in the end, did it? Forty years down the effing plughole.'

'What on earth happened, then?' Maggie asked them all. 'I mean, I know we're not the whizziest estate agency in town.' She glanced forlornly at the familiar chipped old desks, wonky chairs and creaking display board in the window. 'But we've been like it for years and years.'

'That's probably the problem,' said Jean. 'Just look at all the others. Jazzy websites, colour brochures and viewings without smarmy old Farley putting them off with his Uriah Heep act and dancing around them like an old tart.'

'Let's face it, would *you* buy a house off him?' Barbara chipped in. 'I'd rather rent a broom cupboard. I think Jean's right. We just haven't moved with the times. He wouldn't invest, wouldn't listen, knew it all. Look at this place.' She paused and gestured round the office. 'It's hardly inspirational loft living, is it? I would imagine the Changing Rooms team would come in here and go, "Oh, sod it, this one's terminal. We'll find somewhere else."'

'So what happens now?' asked Maggie, knots forming somewhere in her stomach.

'Well, I know what I'm going to do,' said Nancy firmly. 'I'm going to nip round to the bakers and buy us the largest, most scrumptiferous jam doughnuts I can find. I think we all need a sugar shot.'

She picked up her purse and marched out of the door. Suddenly two phones started ringing. Maggie answered the first call. 'No comment,' she announced and slammed the phone down.

'The *Weltham Gazette*,' she explained to the others. Jean picked up the next one. There was a pause as the person on the other end was clearly ranting down the phone.

'No idea, Mrs Danv— Danviels . . . I mean Daniels . . . no, I don't work here any more. Yes I am here, but seeing as I am probably not being paid to take this call, you can go to hell . . . fine, in that case we'll probably bump into each other down there . . . unless of course I see you first. In which case, I may have to kill you . . . but of course we'd both be dead on arrival.' She banged down the phone and laughed triumphantly.

'Coo-er,' she said, 'I'm beginning to enjoy this.' The phone immediately rang again. Jean snatched it up.

'Yes, that's what I said. Hell . . . H-E-L-L. Oh, please do report me to Mr Farley. Except that you'll probably find him in pieces because I'll have beaten you to it. Goodbye, Mrs Danvers. It's been a business doing pleasure with you.'

Jean sat back in her chair and laughed. 'That was *almost* worth it,' she announced.

For the next few minutes, calls came in thick and fast, mostly from the staff in the other two branches of Farley & Co., who'd all received the same letter plus calls from journalists at the *Weltham Gazette* and Weltham FM, all sniffing round for a job losses story. But where was Mr Farley in all this?

'Notable by his absence,' said Barbara on yet another frantic branch call. 'No, we haven't seen hide or hair of him. Ironic, isn't it? The one time I'd actually like to see him, so I could rake his horrible face all over with my fingernails and tell him what a complete arse he is.'

Nancy came back grinning with a huge bag of doughnuts, still warm from the fryer.

'The rumour on the street is that old man Farley hasn't paid his tax or been doing his paperwork properly,' she announced. 'That's why he's gone tits up. Patsy in the bakery thinks the bank were about to foreclose on him so he sold up. So much for forty years in the business.'

'But surely he can't just do that without . . .' The realisation was hitting Maggie. She suddenly felt quite wobbly.

'He just did,' said Nancy. 'What we've got to find out is who the new owner is, what he intends to do with the business and whether we'll be kept on.'

Barbara put the phone down from yet another call.

'The other offices are clubbing together to go to a solicitor for advice,' she announced. 'I think we should join them.'

They all nodded their agreement.

'Meanwhile, I don't know about you but the shock is just hitting me now,' she continued, 'so let's leave the phones for a minute and attack those doughnuts.'

They all moved their chairs to form a huddle round Maggie's desk in the corner and sat down with fresh cups of coffee and the cakes.

'Food is such a comfort in times of stress,' Jean mused, as she mopped a stray bit of jam from her mouth. 'I've always thought that rationing during the war was so extra specially cruel. Such a double whammy.'

'Nobody got fat though,' replied Nancy, sugar all round her lips. 'They were probably a lot healthier.'

The old glass front door gave its familiar rattle. They all turned round hastily to see a young man in a dark navy pinstriped suit, pink silk shirt and matching handkerchief appear brandishing a clipboard. Without any attempt to introduce himself, he immediately began glancing around the office, and making notes. They hastily wiped the jam and sugar off their mouths as he shot them a withering look. There was an agonising moment of silence, with no one quite sure whether to challenge him. Perhaps he was the tax man, the VAT man or the bank manager, come to size up his spoils.

The phone rang. Everyone just stared at it.

'Isn't one of you going to get off your fat backside and answer it?' snapped Pinstripe. Jean jumped up to oblige, frantically licking the sticky bits off her fingers.

'Can see exactly why this place went to rack and ruin,' he mused as he continued his survey, 'with you lot sitting in a corner stuffing your faces.'

‘Can I help you?’ Nancy tried to take some control of the proceedings.

‘I really don’t think so,’ Pinstripe announced pompously, without even making eye contact with her. He just carried on with his notes.

Meanwhile, Jean was clearly getting an earful down the phone from the Bleak House siblings, who had just heard the news about the company.

‘No, I don’t know what’s happening . . . clearly you know more about it than we do. No . . . please do feel free to go to another company . . . yes, this one appears to be dead.’

She replaced the receiver and they all sat in further silence, wondering what this young city type was up to but sensing he was bad news.

Suddenly he replaced the top on an expensive-looking fountain pen with an emphatic click, shut the file on his clipboard and headed for the door. As he reached for the handle, he turned back towards them.

‘Oh, I suppose I’d better tell you,’ he announced condescendingly, ‘I’m Damien Smythe, operations manager of Home Truths. We’ve just bought out Farley & Co. We’ll be gutting the offices as from tonight and refurbishing them in our company livery. Most of the teams are in place but there are still a few vacancies. You are, of course, welcome to apply.’

He shot them a look of pure disdain, as if to add ‘if you feel you must’.

‘Oh, and don’t worry about the small number of properties on your books.’ He emphasised the word ‘small’ in a sarcastic fashion. ‘I retrieved the keys and all the details from the safe yesterday.’ The door rattled shut.

Jean went over to the window to watch him climb into a silver Porsche parked ostentatiously on double yellow lines across the street. She was even more furious to see a parking warden admiring the car and cheerfully waving him off without giving him a ticket.

'Smart bastard,' she almost spat after him as he roared off up the street. 'So what do we do now? Ring all the clients or go the pub?'

Nancy replaced her phone after another call. 'Just heard that the other two offices have decided to down tools and all go out for lunch. We're invited. Meeting at twelve at the Amalfi.'

Everyone nodded approval.

'I'd just like to ring one or two of our nicer people,' said Barbara. 'You know, like the Haydens we're trying to sell for. They're lovely. And that sweet old couple with the drunken son and all those manky cats.'

'You can't,' Nancy announced, holding up the phone. 'It's just gone dead. We've been cut off. Don't suppose old man Farley paid the bill.'

'Well, that's it then, I suppose,' said Maggie, reluctantly picking up her bag. 'Not much else we can do now.'

They spent a few minutes clearing their desks of their personal belongings. Jean made a point of emptying the stationery cupboard and dividing the contents up between four carrier bags.

And finally, as a last symbolic act of defiance, they deliberately left the dusty old glass door wide open.

Chapter 6

The Amalfi was a smart Italian restaurant in the next town, about ten miles from Weltham. They decided not to take their cars. 'We must be able to drink lots of consoling Chianti,' Nancy had pointed out. Clearly the other offices had had the same idea, as half a dozen taxis converged on the restaurant within minutes of each other, each depositing its cargo of grim-faced people.

As it was early on a Monday lunchtime, they had the place to themselves, and the occasion quickly took on the atmosphere of a private wake. At first there were long faces, but as the wine flowed the laughter gradually took over.

Maggie, whose mind was now whizzing frantically about the money situation, was relieved to see the prices weren't astronomic. Everyone else was obviously thinking along the same lines, and it was quickly agreed amongst the twenty or so staff that 'in the circumstances' they'd all plump for the fixed price lunch menu, plus lots of cheap house wine.

'It's ironic that we've never had a proper get-together like this before,' said a girl from one of the other branches who'd just introduced herself to Maggie. 'We've spent years tipping each other off about old man Farley's visits but never actually met.'

Maggie surveyed the room. Like the three negotiators she'd worked for, most of the staff were younger than her. She tried to console herself by telling herself that they probably had bigger mortgages than she did. She took a great gulp of red wine and felt immediately better. This will be a thing of the past, she thought, gazing through the bottom of her glass at the picture of the Amalfi coast on the table mat, and felt immediately worse again.

The waiters had quite a job getting orders out of people as there was much conversation of the 'haven't seen you for ages', 'love that hair colour', and 'yes, Faliraki was fantastic as ever' kind. Eventually Philip, the senior negotiator at the biggest branch, banged the table with a spoon to restore calm. He then found himself taking control of the proceedings by suggesting that each branch recount what happened this morning so they could all get some sort of group understanding of the situation.

Nancy, as senior negotiator in Maggie's branch, gave her account of the morning's drama, including the arrival of Pinstripe with his clipboard. It seemed that his description matched a 'client' who'd time-wasted at the two other branches the previous week.

'The chap I dealt with was deeply unpleasant,' Philip told the now hushed throng. 'You know the type, kept changing his mind about what he was looking for, i.e. nothing, and kept glancing round the office. I got the distinct impression that he was also earwigging the other conversations going on.'

'If it's the same chap,' Sam from the other branch chipped in, 'I had the gut feeling that he was from another agency trying to poach some of our clients. He spent ages achieving nothing and now I come to think about it, yes, he did spend time looking around. Most people want to view the properties, not measure up the office.'

There was a buzz of agreement in the restaurant. Philip quietened them down again.

'Well, I think our suspicions are probably more or less right. Now, I think we need to decide what we're going to do about this. If we all went to the same solicitor, it would make sense and save us a lot of money. After all, we're all pursuing the same bastard. So can I gauge what people think about that?'

Everyone put up a hand in support. Then the formal nature of the proceedings fell away as the waiters descended on the tables with plates of parma ham and melon or asparagus soup. Two of the girls, clearly still in shock from the morning bombshell, couldn't remember what they'd ordered just minutes before and burst into tears.

Philip rose to his feet to dispel the sudden gloom. 'Hey, let's enjoy getting together and supporting each other. We're all in the same boat so let's fight him all the way. I think we should drink a toast to our not-very-dear departed boss.'

Everyone stood up and raised their glasses.

'Here's to the old bastard,' Philip announced. 'Forty years in the business and he finally went bust.'

'The old bastard . . .' The toast was repeated around the room. In a more positive mood, they all sat down to attack the first course.

Conversation at the tables continued, the most frequently asked question being, 'What will you do now?'

Maggie was surprised to hear quite a few people announcing that they had had enough of dealing with stroppy people looking for palaces at hovel prices and already concluding that 'this was the kick up the arse I soooo needed'. Two of the staff at Sam's branch said they'd had fleas in the office all summer but old man Farley had refused to do anything about it. They announced they were looking forward to finding jobs in 'swanky offices where you don't have to wear fingerless gloves in winter and insect repellent in summer'.

Over the main course, the mood reverted to bitterness. 'I'd personally like to string the bastard up,' announced Sam, attacking his pizza as though it were Farley's face. 'When I think how we froze or sweltered in that crummy office to save that old bastard money. No bonuses, no works outings, not even a thank you. And then we watched it all go down the tubes.'

'Absolutely,' Nancy agreed. 'All the other agencies in Weltham have full colour brochures and websites. Nice company car to whizz the better-heeled clients around and give them a bit of VIP treatment. And what did we have to offer? A glimpse of life in the fifties. I'm surprised the History Channel didn't come round and do a documentary on us.'

The anger started to rise so Philip once again rose to his feet and banged a spoon for silence.

'OK, calm down, everyone. We're all furious and this couldn't have come at a worse time. Especially for me.' Philip's wife was about to have their first baby so he got a huge sympathy vote.

'We've agreed on a group action,' he continued. 'But there are other – perhaps more amusing – things we could do.'

An air of expectancy went round the restaurant, followed by an almost simultaneous slurp of wine.

'For a start, I could ring up the *Weltham Gazette* and see if they'd send round a photographer to take a group shot of us,' he said with a sly grin. 'At least we'd all have a memento of a long overdue staff party.'

Everyone nodded their agreement and managed to laugh.

'And of course we could go round and pay old man Farley a visit. The photographer might like to come along too. What do you think?'

A huge cheer went up.

'Revenge is a dish best served cold,' said Philip, who was rather enjoying his sudden leadership. 'And here it comes. Pudding, everyone.'

They tucked into tiramisu or raspberry panna cotta amid an air of expectancy. By the time the cappuccinos and lattes had arrived, a photographer from the *Gazette* was there, camera loaded, ready to line them all up for a picture.

Maggie found herself now absurdly excited. The wine had hit the spot, especially as she only ever drank wine at lunchtime on Christmas Day. She couldn't believe she was relishing the idea of turning up at Matthew Farley's house for a protest; she, Mrs Meek-and-Mild who never made a fuss but just kept her head below the level of the flying plates and then quietly swept up the virtual debris afterwards.

Soon, the entire staff of Farley & Co. were bundling into taxis and heading off in the direction of the ex-boss's house, a couple of miles away. Everyone was now wearing rather fixed manic grins from too much wine, and regretting they didn't have time to make placards with suitable insults on them.

Matthew Farley's house looked just like an extension of his offices. Shabby and run down, it had a faded glory about it, with the emphasis on the 'faded' rather than the 'glory'. The garden was mildewy with autumnal neglect, forlorn berries still clinging to shrubs, a few sad little blackening fruits left hanging on a pear tree while the rest decomposed on the ground, a couple of stone urns and a few hanging baskets around an old wooden porch filled with long dead flowers.

'Forty years in the business and he couldn't even run to a power washer,' Sam remarked as he took in the driveway, covered in green slime.

Once again Philip took control. 'I'll go up and knock on the door. If he answers, then I suggest everyone forms a semicircle round the porch so you can hear what he has to say.'

Unfortunately the sound of taxis arriving had tipped off whoever was in the house. As Philip started to make his way up the driveway, the downstairs curtains were miraculously closing, as if all by themselves.

'Might not be paying us redundancy, but I see that he can afford corded curtain tracks,' Barbara noted bitterly.

By the time Philip's hand had reached the knocker, the upstairs curtains were closing in the same rather sinister way. The protesters realised that they were beaten. Predictably, no one answered the door. After a few more attempts, Philip bent down and opened the letter box.

'Mr Farley,' he yelled through the gap. 'We know you're in there. You owe us an explanation. Please come out and face the music.'

Silence. Philip tried again. 'Farley? We have some important questions to ask you.' Silence.

Nancy pushed past him. 'Oi, you tight-fisted bastard,'

she shouted. 'Come out here now and say sorry. Better still, come out with our redundancy money.'

Everyone cheered and clapped. Then, without a word of discussion, they formed a line to shout whatever message – or in some cases abuse – they fancied through the letter box. It was incredibly therapeutic, as was the impromptu tour round the back garden by some of the negotiators who couldn't resist doing their job of sizing up the property and pricing it up for a six-week sale. The biggest cheer, though, was reserved for Sam.

'Forty years in the business,' he mocked. 'Forty years to go tits up. Congratulations! So you didn't know it all after all, Mr Know-It-All.'

He turned to walk away and then suddenly turned back, as if hit by a flash of inspiration.

'By the way,' he called through the letter box. 'Crap house!'

He then bowed to the tumultuous applause and howls of laughter.

Chapter 7

Wednesday, and day two of life in the redundancy lane. Maggie felt guilty that she was savouring the peace of being at home alone. Garth had been up at the crack of dawn to go off to a horticultural trade show in Birmingham and the kids had even managed to make it on time for the school bus. So here she was, still not dressed and stretched out on a sofa with a steaming mug of coffee. For the umpteenth time, she flipped through all the Sky channels just for the hell of it.

She gazed out of the window at the threatening dark grey autumn sky. Thanks to a storm that had raged through the night, the trees had finally shed the last of their leaves and were looking self-consciously bare. Rather like me, she thought, nothing to wear and nowhere to go.

Enforced leisure did have its compensations. Daytime telly always seemed an unattainable luxury when she was working but already she'd practically overdosed on property programmes. Yesterday alone, she'd watched several episodes of *Hot Property*, *Property Ladder*, *To Buy Or Not To Buy* and *A Place in the Sun*. They were all so bright and whizzy that they made Farley & Co. look like something out of the Dark Ages. She'd have loved dealing with 'this beautiful Tuscan refuge in need of just a little TLC' or 'your dream Spanish home overlooking a championship golf course'. She thought of the dank horrors of Manderley and Bleak House and wondered what Sarah Beeny would have made of them. Not a lot, she decided. And Hot Property they certainly were not either. The only thing they were fit for was some alternative kind of property show, perhaps called *Serial Demolition* or *Celebrity Bulldozer*.

Her thoughts were interrupted by the telephone. It was a very excited Nancy telling her that the report and pictures of their protest outside old man Farley's house were apparently going to be in the *Weltham Gazette* that day. Nancy went on to inform her that she was off to an interview that afternoon with a rival chain of estate agents. Clearly the grass hadn't started growing under her feet. She seemed really excited and confident about it.

They said their goodbyes and Maggie replaced the phone. She stared at it for a few moments, drained her coffee, and was suddenly overwhelmed by a huge bout of depression about the whole situation. Here was Nancy already up and running and chasing her next job, while she, Maggie, was slumped at home in her scruffy old dressing gown, without even the motivation to get in the shower.

She went back to the TV. There were no more property programmes on that morning so she had a quick waft through the shopping channels, pausing to watch two men in white tuxedos painting a wall bright pink to prove that their 'revolutionary new paint roller system' didn't splat and a very animated woman trying to flog some extremely bling bling jewellery.

Maggie had spent the last two days promising herself she'd not even begin to consider all the economies they'd have to make until she could find another job. But Nancy's prospective interview, coupled with an overdose of 'wannahave' television, had made her wake up to the inescapable fact that her small but regular salary had gone. Garth flew into a purple rage every time she mentioned their finances. And everything, but everything, seemed to involve spending money. There'd never be any bling bling jewellery for her now, even if she wanted some.

She glanced back at the TV. The Sky subscription might have to go, especially if it got down to a question of putting food on the table. She didn't even want to imagine how Garth might be persuaded to give up his essential diet of nonstop football. Probably only if he was in the last ravages of starvation. Football was everything to him, and yet it had proved a double-edged sword. Maggie was sure that, for him, football was rather like a running sore that would never heal. He loved the game, watched it obsessively, yet it was a constant and torturous reminder of what might have been. The more he watched, the more bitter he became about his injury and how it had denied him the recognition and riches that were now an accepted part of a professional footballer's life. Not scraping along running a gardening business from a dreary semi on the wrong side of town.

She pulled herself up short, resolved to get dressed, do a supermarket run and pick up a copy of the *Gazette*. Then she could read the article *and* scan the job ads.

She was just about to step into the shower when the phone rang again. It was Pam, calling from work.

'Maggs, you're in the paper!' she squealed excitedly.

'We never get that kind of excitement in the thrilling world of council environmental services.'

'I haven't seen it yet,' Maggie confessed. She was certain that ever glamorous, ever immaculate Pam would be appalled to know that here she was at midday, unwashed and still in her dressing gown.

'Well you should,' Pam continued excitedly, 'because there's another story on the same page that should interest you. A lot. Go out and buy it and then ring me back.'

Maggie dutifully agreed. Her curiosity jolted her into action. Abandoning the idea of a shower, she tried to tame her wiry hair with a quick comb, and then threw on the Juicy Lucy track suit. Within half an hour, she was sitting in the local Costa coffee shop, the *Gazette* in one hand, a large latte in the other, with a huge almond Danish pastry waiting to be devoured. This would, of course, be the day she bumped into someone she knew, while she was looking scruffy and comfort-eating for Britain.

'Hi, Maggie,' a posh voice trilled from across the café. It was Marina, the office manager from one of the other Farley & Co. branches. Maggie's heart sank. She'd never liked Marina. She was a bit too snooty and self-righteous for Maggie's taste. Typically, she came over immediately and plonked herself down without asking. She shot Maggie a piercing look which said, Oh dear, no make-up, scruffy hair, shoving calories into your face and wearing that cheap track suit. Not dressing for success, are we, darling!

'How are you?' Marina actually asked, not really requiring an answer. Her immaculate navy suit with brass buttons and cream braiding, matching navy and cream court shoes and handbag said it all. As did the two strings of pearls round her neck. The office always referred to her as Her Maj because she affected a regal air and wore clothes that would have admitted her to any unveiling, frigate naming or envelope opening that you could think of.

'Oh, quite enjoying my enforced leisure,' said Maggie, summoning a smile and trying to sound convincing. 'I heard we're all in the paper so I just popped out to get a copy.'

Yes, and took the opportunity to junk food binge at the same time, Her Maj didn't need to say.

'Yes, I suppose it was a pity about Farley's collapse,' she continued, without sounding the remotest bit upset, 'but I think we all saw it coming. I'm afraid I didn't attend the Amalfi lunch. Protests aren't really my thing, yah.'

Maggie tried to avoid eye contact, conscious of her wild hair sticking out all over the place. 'So what are your plans, then?' she asked.

'Oh, having a *well*-deserved break,' Marina brayed. 'Gerald, my husband, is insisting I should take time off and look after him a little more. Which, of course, means I'll probably pamper and spoil him rotten. And with more time to spare, we can give lots of house parties.'

Marina pronounced it 'hice'. Maggie had to stifle a giggle with a small cough.

'Oh, lovely,' she replied, dabbing her mouth with a napkin and unable to imagine anything more ghastly. 'You're lucky not having to get a job, then.'

'Well,' Marina inspected immaculate pale pink nails and a selection of gold and diamond rings, 'I never really fitted into Farleys. Gerald's been saying for ages that he doesn't want me working but you know how we gels like our independence. So actually, Farleys' collapse did me a huge favour, in a roundabout sort of way.'

She pronounced it 'rindabite' and promptly started to honk with laughter. Maggie braved a direct look into her face. All you need is a Hermès headscarf, a Barbour and a shooting stick, and you could sign up with the Windsors, she thought to herself.

'Oh well, enjoy your new-found leisure,' said Maggie, trying to give her the cue to get up and go. Mercifully she did, but not before placing a bejewelled hand patronisingly on Maggie's, and wishing her luck. Maggie watched her negotiate the tables and walk regally to the door, as though she were gliding down the nave of Westminster Abbey, acknowledging imaginary subjects with a leather-gloved wave.

A sudden squall of wind and rain suddenly whipped up in the street outside, sending a flurry of dead leaves into a mini tornado. Maggie looked on with mild amusement as Marina paused in the doorway, produced a scarf from her bag and tied it, HRH style, under her chin before sashaying purposefully up the road.

Stuck-up cow, Maggie wanted to utter aloud as she watched. She could just imagine lucky old Gerald coming home to burgundy suede slippers (because Prince Charles wears ones like that), a glass of claret already chambréed (correct vintage already checked out) and a recipe gleaned from the pages of *Majesty* magazine just coming out of the Aga to be served up on gilt-edged plates. I bet they even hire a butler just to show off, when friends come round to the *hice* parties, Maggie thought bitchily.

In defiance, she took a huge bite out of her Danish, which promptly deposited flakes of pastry and almond all over her face. She read the newspaper report and looked at the photograph of Farley & Co. staff. An interesting memento, she concluded, but the piece didn't really reflect the rebellious yet upbeat mood of the day. She picked up a napkin and tried to remove the sticky bits from round her mouth. Trust me to bump into Marina of all people. Typical of Her Maj to catch her out on a day when she was looking her absolute worst.

She turned back to the newspaper. Wasn't there something else Pam had told her to look out for? She scanned the page, mystified. Around the picture and report on the Farley revolt there was the usual reflection of local life: parish councillors puffed up with their own importance trying to sound like White House senators, a selection of court cases featuring Weltham's low life, and a still-at-large handbag snatcher notching up another couple of victories.

Then she spotted it: *Home Truths Taking Over Farleys.* It was only a couple of column inches but enough to inform Maggie that a new estate agency called Home Truths had bought out Farley & Co. and that they would be completely gutting and refitting all three branches within two weeks. 'All our negotiating teams are in place,' a spokesman was quoted as saying, 'and we're just looking for a couple of admin staff at each branch to complete the line-up.'

What have I got to lose, Maggie thought, as she folded up the newspaper and put it in her bag. Her way back to the car park took her past the Farley office and she decided to see what was going on. Conscious of her appearance, she fished out some sunglasses, left a few coins as a tip on the table and made a swift exit.

The wind was whipping up with a vengeance now and

the sky had turned an ugly threatening dark grey. There had been gale warnings on the news that morning, along with predictions of possible traffic chaos. Rain had started to lash down so Maggie decided it would have to be a very quick glance through her incongruous sunglasses, and then a run for it to the car park.

She made her way along the street, the rain already penetrating her track suit and making the material heavy, cold and clingy. A hot bath when she got home, she promised herself.

Keeping deliberately to the opposite side of the street, she took shelter for a moment in a doorway and gazed across at the estate agency formerly known as Farleys. In just two days, the new owners had gutted the place. From her vantage point, she could see through the polythene screening that they had done a complete rip-out job. The office had been reduced to an empty shell. All the tatty desks, the partition walls, the creaking window displays, even the rattling front door had gone. She wondered if anyone had nicked all the old computers after they had helpfully left the door open on Monday morning. Clearly it wasn't a matter of concern for the new incumbents. A fascia board was already in place and just visible through the polythene. It bore what was presumably the company's logo, a grinning turkey drawn in bright blue and yellow, and proclaimed:

HOME TRUTHS
The No Frills Estate Agent

Maggie gazed at the board for a full minute. She wondered what the 'no frills' bit meant. Farleys hadn't exactly been 'with frills'. No website, no colour brochures. Just a dingy old office with antiquated equipment and a stubborn boss. Judging by the speed with which the old office had been gutted, this new lot looked like they meant business. There was an air of expectancy about the place, a sense that they were going to give their competitors a real run for their money.

As a gutter unloaded its excess rain water on to her head, Maggie made the snap decision to apply for one of the jobs. She made a mental note of the website mentioned on the fascia board and then ran to the car park, her trainers squelching through the puddles. She was now soaked to the skin, yet strangely excited at a new challenge. Yes, she'd get a job. She'd show Garth, the kids, even prove to herself, that she could do it.

Chapter 8

The Home Truths website promised an 'estate agent with a difference' but didn't elaborate. The sparse details gave the impression that it was a young go-ahead company that wouldn't suffer fools gladly. Back home after a restorative bath with the remains of the Givenchy foam she'd received last Christmas and had eked out all year, Maggie found that her brief rush of confidence had disappeared again. Down the plughole just like the expensive bubbles.

She filled in the online application form for an administrator's job and clicked 'send' before she could stop herself. Well, that's me made a complete fool of myself, she thought, as she peeled some potatoes for tonight's dinner. Garth would be home late from Birmingham so she'd decided to make a cottage pie which could be reheated at whatever time he got in. She browned the mince in a pan and began chopping up a large onion. As the hopelessness of her situation came back to her, tears began to well up in her eyes. She wiped them and instantly made them worse with the smell of the onion on her fingers. Soon, she was sitting sobbing uncontrollably at the table.

Losing her job, the kids arguing all the time, Garth's business floundering: it suddenly all weighed down on her. She put her head in her hands and cried so violently that her whole body shook. Her sobs came from so deep within that they actually shocked her.

'It's not fair,' she told the kitchen cupboards, after drying her eyes with a bit of kitchen paper. 'I prop up everyone but nobody gives a toss about me.'

The cupboards couldn't come up with an answer.

'What's to become of me? What am I going to do?' she continued aloud, wiping her still streaming eyes. 'I'm dreading the kids coming home, I'm even more dreading my husband coming home in one of his filthy tempers. I'm out of work and I'm useless. It's my own fault for staying in the same job for too long.'

She thought of the ghastly Marina, swanning around in her horseshoe-patterned headscarf giving 'hice parties' and not having to work. OK, so she was mocked behind her back at work, but maybe life wasn't so bad if there was someone to look after you, probably in some posh country 'hice'. She thought of her glorious day at Juicy Lucy's where, just for once, she'd felt like somebody, as opposed to somebody's wife, mother or dogsbody, for a few precious hours. Her fingers touched her face as she remembered how incredibly smooth and luscious it felt after the facial, how the water bed massage had made her feel so completely relaxed. It had been the most fantastic glimpse of a lifestyle and a mental well-being that she'd never experienced before. And now it had all collapsed around her.

'Shit,' she told the cupboards. Again they couldn't come up with an answer. 'Oh, you lot are just an open and shut case.' She laughed in a slightly manic fashion at her own joke.

Then Maggie did something she'd never thought she'd do. She climbed up on a chair to reach the top shelf of the larder, to see if there was any booze left from last Christmas. Not being much of a drinker, she always stuffed whatever was left over to the back of the baking tin cupboard to 'shove it in the Christmas cake next year'. She hadn't yet made this year's cake so there should be something left. Ah yes, the dregs of the bottle of cream sherry that her ancient auntie always sent every Christmas and a tiny bit of Bombay Sapphire gin. She admired the blue glass of the gin bottle for a few seconds before remembering that there was no tonic water in the house. So she poured the last of the sherry into a small glass. It barely made a couple of fingers' worth but it gave her an instant and much needed jolt. She wiped her eyes for a final time and examined the bottle.

At that moment Beth and George, home from school, burst through the front door, shattering the calm. Already they were at it hammer and tongs over who was going to watch what on the TV.

'Aren't you a bit big for the Tweenies?' George taunted Beth. 'Or maybe your brain's shrunk.'

'I don't think you're in a position to talk,' Beth retorted. 'I caught you redhanded watching Bob the Builder the other day . . . oh, Mum!' Beth stopped in her tracks. She had just taken in the scene. Her mother red-eyed, seated at the table with a pile of used tissues and an empty bottle of sherry in front of her.

'Oh, God, Mum. You're an alcoholic. That's disgusting,' Beth exploded.

'I'm not surprised,' George countered, always quick to exploit any situation. 'You see what you've done to her?'

he railed at his sister. 'You've driven Mum to this with all your girlie hissy fits.'

Beth stalked upstairs, muttering loudly, 'My mother's an alcoholic, that's all I need,' and banged her bedroom door heavily.

'Brilliant.' George smiled, rubbing his hands together. '*Star Trek – The New Generation* all to myself on widescreen! Thanks, Mum. But don't have too many of those. Old people shouldn't get drunk, you know. Doesn't suit them.'

With that, he was straight into the sitting room leaving Maggie with the mince now burning nicely on to the bottom of the pan. 'Why are my children so vile?' she quizzed the kitchen cupboards once more. Because you let them, the cupboards seemed to answer. Maggie turned off the gas and slumped back in the chair. She didn't have the energy to tackle the kids at the moment, but later on she must try to get a grip on the situation.

She was just mustering up the energy to rescue the dinner when the phone rang. It was Garth to say that some main roads out of Birmingham were blocked by fallen trees, causing traffic chaos. So he'd be staying the night rather than risk getting stuck somewhere.

'No "How are you?" or "How was your day?"' she informed the cupboards, rather bitterly. Not that there was much to tell. Got up, watched telly, went out, bumped into Marina, got caught out eating junk and looking a mess, came home, applied for a job, drank sherry, got accused of being an alcoholic. No, not much of a day at all, really.

She examined the empty sherry bottle, enjoying the lavish description of its taste, and then it dawned on her how absurdly delighted she was that Garth wasn't coming home. A whole evening without his black moods, curt responses and constant carpings. Total bliss! She suddenly experienced a potent mixture of guilt laced with ecstatic liberation.

'Marriage shouldn't be like this,' she told the cupboards. 'I'm supposed to long for the sound of his footsteps in the hall. Love, honour and obey. Concoct beautiful candlelit suppers with a bit of Mozart playing in the background. Or sit around together, the perfect nuclear family, eating a perfectly balanced and delicious meal with everyone joining in a meaningful discussion about their day. However,' she paused to chip the burnt mince off the bottom of the pan and crumble in a couple of stock cubes, 'I'd better stop talking to the cupboards or the kids will think I'm mad as well as drunk. So this is me, cupboards, signing off.'

The cupboards stared back at her. Pity there's not more of that sherry left, she thought to herself, cheering up by the minute.

An hour later, the three of them were sitting round the kitchen table eating the cottage pie in stony silence. Perhaps the thought that their mother was heading down the slippery slope to acute alcoholism had given Beth and George a bit of a shock.

'We can share out all of the pie,' she told them. 'Your dad's not coming back tonight. The storm's brought down a lot of trees and blocked some of the roads out of Birmingham.'

The kids could barely disguise their relief. It quite shocked Maggie that their reaction, so upfront, had been the same as hers.

'Now there are a couple of things I want to say,' said Maggie firmly, still prickling from being accused of being drunk. 'One, I am fed up with you two squabbling all the time. It's wearing me down big time. And two, I am not an alcoholic. I lost my job this week. It wasn't a good job or a well-paid job but it put the food on this table and helped your father pay the bills. I am unlikely to get any redundancy pay, so things are going to be very tight until I can get something else.'

She couldn't quite bring herself to add 'and your father would drive me to drink, if only I could afford it'. Instead she said: 'I didn't drink a whole bottle of sherry. It was a tiny bit left over from last Christmas.'

George opened his mouth but she cut him short. 'Frankly, the two of you have not been behaving very well lately. You're both old enough to understand what I'm saying. If you carry on the way you are doing, you'll drive me to an early grave. Now that might suit you both, and to be honest, the way I'm feeling at the moment, it would probably suit me too.'

She paused as she took in their shocked faces. They'd never heard her speak like this before.

Beth recovered first. 'Mum, your cottage pie was lovely.'

'The best I've tasted all day,' said George. He got up from his chair and gave her a hug. Beth followed suit.

'We'll do the dishes,' she said, handing a tea towel to her brother with a forceful look.

Maggie looked at them, incredulous. Soft hot tears started to trickle down her cheeks. She almost didn't notice them and made no attempt to wipe them away.

'You go and watch the telly and we'll bring you a cup of tea,' said George. Maggie got up like a robot and walked into the sitting room. She sat down, dazed at what she had witnessed. Suddenly her kids had demonstrated that they were perfectly capable of behaving like normal human beings. The tears continued, hot and relentless. She couldn't stop them now.

By the time George appeared round the door with a big mug of steaming hot tea, she had cried so much her eyelids had become red and puffy. He handed her the mug and hurriedly disappeared again. He was obviously embarrassed to see her crying.

She flicked through the channels via her now rather blurred vision and decided to catch up on the news. Another terrorist attack, another soap star booking into the Priory, hints of a possible postal strike and a hike in interest rates. Today's storms hadn't done the damage that the weathermen had predicted but they had at least cleared the way for bright if chilly weather tomorrow.

Maggie's attention flickered for a minute. So the storms weren't that bad. Well, of course it was a general picture rather than a local one. Perhaps Garth had had a few beers too many and used the weather as an excuse for not driving back. Sensible at least. Losing his driving licence would be the final straw.

She switched off the TV and wandered back into the kitchen. Beth and George were noisily putting away the plates but she caught the gist of the conversation – '. . . putting up with him all these years, it's not surprising . . .' – before they saw her and promptly shut up.

'Thanks, you two,' she said gratefully. She went over and kissed them lightly on their foreheads. For once, they didn't flinch or moan at her for being soppy.

'Thanks for giving me the best evening I've had in ages,' she continued. 'I always knew you could behave if you wanted to. Please can you be like this again? No more arguing over the TV and irritating each other? Please?'

She could feel the tears welling up again. God knows what her eyes would look like in the morning. The short walk from the sitting room to the kitchen had been a struggle. Her legs had become leaden with fatigue. It was as if her whole body had had enough and it was time to go to bed.

She climbed the stairs slowly, made a quick trip to the bathroom and slid under the duvet, grateful to be alone. Strangely, she was too tired to sleep and just lay gazing at the ceiling, trying to shut down her brain.

Conversations, thoughts and scenes from the day drifted through her head in a random fashion: Marina trying to ape the Queen in her headscarf, the kids allowing her to kiss them without whingeing, peering through the polythene at the gutting of Farleys, Beth's shocked face when she discovered her sitting with an empty sherry bottle, and her guilty relief at Garth's not coming home. As she slipped into a half-slumber, it occurred to her that Garth hadn't even bothered to tell her where he was staying . . . nor had she enquired. It didn't matter really as he had a mobile . . . if she rang now, he'd bite her head off . . . shame to ruin the relative peace of the day . . .

Chapter 9

Maggie was woken the following morning by the telephone. She glanced at the alarm clock. Ten past ten. She panicked and sat bolt upright. Had the kids made the bus, or was that the school ringing to report them for playing truant? She snatched up the receiver as she hastily rubbed her eyes. Ouch, they were sore. She could feel they were swollen without needing a mirror.

'Damien Smythe here from Home Truths,' came a rather clipped voice. 'Maggie Fraser around?'

'Yes, that's me,' she said, waking up to the sound of her own name, but totally missing the first bit.

'Interview. This afternoon. Three o'clock. Royal Hotel. Can you make it?'

'Er, yes, I, er,' Maggie floundered. Then it dawned on her. 'Yes, fine.'

'See you then.' He rang off immediately.

With her blurred vision, it took Maggie three attempts to get the phone back on its cradle. She then leapt out of bed like a scalded cat, snatched up her dressing gown, shoved her feet into slippers and staggered out on to the landing. That was a rude awakening.

'Beth? George? Are you two up?'

No response. She padded down the landing towards their bedrooms. Both doors were ajar. Beth's room was in its usual state, clothes strewn everywhere, half-read magazines competing with a jumble of make-up, cheap jewellery and a selection of odd shoes. She caught sight of a pizza delivery box peeping out from under the bed along with several mugs in which the dregs of the coffee had converted into mould and were coming along nicely. George's room, a temple to the worship of Southampton Football Club, was bedecked entirely in red and white. Old match programmes, posters half peeling off the walls where the Blu-tack had given up the ghost, and another selection of dirty plates and cups, also busily cultivating vegetation. Ground Force could have tackled its first indoor garden.

Maggie sighed. She couldn't face wading through that lot. She wandered into the bathroom to clean her teeth and caught sight of her face in the mirror. Her eyelids were actually so swollen that her eyes were just slits. Her cheeks were red raw from the tears and too much tissue wiping. It was like looking at a snapshot of herself aged seventy-five and counting. She ran the cold tap, rinsed a flannel and dabbed it on her eyes, hoping for a miracle. The cold water was immediately soothing but a miracle would take much longer.

She staggered downstairs, relieved to find that the kids had obviously got themselves up and off to school. At least that was something. A trail of breakfast things revealed that they had actually bothered to make themselves some tea and toast. On the kitchen table, there was a large piece of white paper. On it was scrawled a note from Beth. *Mum. We got up OK. Have a nice day. Luv B and G xxxx*

She sank into a chair and put her head in her hands. 'Kids, who'd have 'em,' she muttered aloud. Then she pulled herself up short. No more talking to the cupboards, she resolved. Look what trouble you got me into yesterday.

The phone rang again. Its sudden shrillness against the rare silence in the house made her jump.

'Damien Smythe here again. Change of plan. Two thirty instead. OK?'

'Yes, fine,' she said automatically, trying to remember what the original plan was, let alone the change. Her brain finally kicked into gear. Of course, the Home Truths job application. She realised with a stab of panic that she'd forgotten where the interview was to be.

'Where do I . . .' she stopped. He'd already gone.

'Oh, shit,' she said aloud. 'Now come on, Maggie, think clearly. It won't be at the office as it's covered in polythene and being invaded by builders. Where would a company hold interviews if it doesn't have any premises yet? Answer, a hotel. Yes, that's it. He mentioned a hotel. But which one?'

She found a copy of the Yellow Pages and drew up a shortlist. Several she rejected on the grounds of being far too downmarket and two that had the reputation of being local knocking shops. She decided to start at the top, in order of star ratings. Within minutes, she'd ruled out the Holiday Inn, and a couple of Best Westerns. Next was the Royal. Hang on, that rang a bell. Had he said the Royal? She decided to call anyway. Yes, said a bored receptionist, Home Truths had reserved a suite for several days for interviews and presentations. Much relieved, Maggie put down the phone and glanced up at the hall mirror. Ghastly, truly ghastly. She could imagine the Royal's snooty receptionists redirecting her to the nearest rehab centre, muttering 'sad, mad and dangerous to know'.

She ran a bath and lay in it with a cold flannel over her eyes, in the hope of reducing some of the swelling. Meanwhile she rehearsed some interview answers to questions she might expect. Realising she hadn't been for a job interview in more than a decade, all she really had to draw on were episodes of *The Office*. The David Brent style of interrogation probably wasn't applicable.

Why did you apply for this job? Answer: Because I don't have one. No, that was not good enough. How about 'I know the business, know the area well'? That was marginally better.

What special abilities and qualities would you bring to the job? Answer: Tea making and extreme tolerance of stroppy clients. True, but not the right answer. How about 'Good telephone manner (not managed this morning, sadly), attention to detail (couldn't even catch the name of the hotel) and smart appearance (not today but has been known to look better)'? She'd have to work on that one.

Where do you see yourself in five years' time? Answer: Older, greyer and fatter. Or how about: Looking devastatingly slim, three foreign holidays a year, Pierce Brosnan lookalike in tow, kids in high-flying jobs . . . oh, the wish list was endless. No, that wouldn't do either. How about 'Consolidating and capitalising on all my experience with a job and salary to match'?

Any questions? Answer: It's my favourite radio programme too. No, far too cheeky. Probably best to ask about when they'd make a decision, pension stuff, holiday and sick pay. Or was that too presumptuous?

A glance at her goose-bumped arm prompted Maggie

to realise she'd been in the bath far too long. She got out, wrapped herself in a towel and glanced in the mirror. Eyes still closed until further notice. Cucumber, she suddenly remembered. Normandie Keith and all the top models swore by it. She hated the slimy feel of it but today she might just have to grin and bear it. She rushed down to the kitchen and found a tiny stump left in a corner of the salad drawer. She carved two minuscule slices and sat at the kitchen table, her head tipped back, pathetically trying to keep them in place in her eye sockets.

Two minutes into her new beauty routine, the phone rang again. This time she picked up a pen and paper before answering it, just in case. It was Pam, calling from work to see how she was.

'Doing a balancing act,' Maggie told her, explaining about the cucumber slices. 'I've got an interview this afternoon and I look like shit.'

Pam immediately sensed an emergency. 'Tell you what,' she announced in a voice that did not admit a refusal, 'I'm on flexitime and I've clocked up quite a lot of extra hours lately with Tom away. Why don't I take a long lunch break and come round? I've got some eye soother stuff in my bag.'

Maggie began a futile protest. 'No, Pam, that's very sweet of you, but—'

'I'm on my way,' Pam cut in and put the phone down.

Maggie was suddenly overcome with panic. The house looked a mess and Pam's was always so immaculate. She scurried around, washing up the kids' breakfast things. Then she gave the worktops a good wipe down and buffed up the taps. Shiny taps, she once read in some lifestyle magazine, gave any kitchen the wow factor.

She then had a whip round the sitting room, clearing up old newspapers and TV listings magazines, shoving all the videos and empty cases into a cupboard and plumping up the cushions. Then she fled upstairs to try to make herself look reasonably decent before Pam arrived.

'Oh, dear,' said Pam as she crossed the doorstep and took in Maggie's swollen eyes. 'I'm surprised your mains burst didn't relaunch the ark. Now don't start crying again.' She held up a warning finger, and fished in a very large handbag.

'Aha,' she announced, waving a small tube of green liquid. 'Cool eye soother – we'll get your peepers looking good by two thirty. But first, lunch!'

She plonked her bag down on the kitchen table and produced plastic boxes containing ready made salad and cold chicken.

'Did a quick ram raid on Marks and Sparks, so here we are,' she announced triumphantly. 'No spicy stuff, though. We don't want you being remembered for your chicken tikka dog breath, do we! Now while I'm arranging this stuff on plates, you tell me about this job so we can decide what you should wear.'

Maggie groaned inwardly. Pam was always so good at this and she was so hopeless.

'Well, it all seems a bit fast and furious,' she said. 'The man who rang spoke like machine-gun fire. And all the website says so far is that it's a no frills estate agency.'

'Hmmm,' said Pam. 'That's a difficult one. Best to assume it's the other extreme from dreary old Farleys. In which case, you must come over as not really part of the former regime. So – smart, with a hint of quirky.'

'I don't really think I can manage smart, let alone quirky,' said Maggie defeatedly.

'We need a look that says, "I am efficient and reliable, but I have a raunchy past which I can draw on when it suits me",' Pam continued, warming to her theme. *What Not To Wear* was obviously her required bedside reading.

'So we pass these swollen eyes off as "a fun night out on the tequila slammers but I'm up and bouncing around and it's business as usual this morning"?' Maggie managed to joke.

'Exactly!' Pam clapped her hands. She was delighted to see Maggie beginning to rise out of her gloom. She made her sit still while she expertly applied the eye soother to Maggie's red and swollen lids. She then dived into the bag once more and produced a bottle of Chardonnay.

'One glass might just brighten you up,' she announced as she glanced at the kitchen clock. 'And neither of us will be driving for at least another hour so that's OK.'

Maggie told her about the sherry incident the previous night, Garth's being stuck in Birmingham and how the kids ended up being nice for once.

'About bloody time too,' said Pam knowingly. 'Time they stopped taking you for granted. And Garth, for that matter.'

Maggie nodded dumbly. She knew Pam's feelings on the subject of her husband. She'd probably felt she could come round to the house during the day because Garth would be – or should have been – at work.

They tucked into the chicken and salad. The wine tasted delicious and Maggie would have been hugely tempted to have another glass to give herself some Dutch courage if fear of being over the limit hadn't stopped her.

Finally came the moment Maggie had dreaded. They went upstairs to sort out what she was going to wear.

Pam started rifling through her wardrobe with the expertise of a Harvey Nicks shopping adviser. Maggie sat on the edge of her bed, dreading what she would come up with.

To her surprise, Pam picked out a rather conservative long black cardigan which Maggie had never worn much and a pair of tweedy maroon wide-legged trousers. Then she added a white cotton T-shirt to go underneath the cardigan. Next she was rummaging through Maggie's handbags until she found what she was looking for.

'This is fabulous,' she announced, brandishing a deep red carpet bag that Maggie had forgotten about. 'Put that lot on.'

While Maggie scrambled into the clothes, hoping her underwear didn't look too scruffy, Pam was raiding her jewellery box. Not that there was much in it. But Pam seemed to have made some triumphant discovery. She produced a string of huge deep-ruby-coloured beads that Maggie had been egged on to buy at one of those girlies' jewellery parties but then never worn. The beads pulled the whole outfit together. Maggie broke out into a huge smile. She couldn't believe how good she looked, and it had all been sitting there in her wardrobe.

Pam looked at her watch. 'Just time to do your make-up,' she said, 'and then you're off.'

She whipped out a huge transparent make-up bag that unravelled into compartments. Soon Maggie was being transformed into a 'last night party girl, today power woman' look. With some skilful eye shadow and mascara, Maggie's eyes looked well on the way to recovery. Pam finished off the look with a burgundy lipstick that Maggie would never have had the courage to choose.

'Gosh, you're clever,' she exclaimed when Pam had finished. 'I wish I could do that. My sense of style died a couple of decades ago.'

Pam did a mock bow in response. 'If your sense of style died, honey, it was when you and Jack broke up. You were never the same girl after that.'

Maggie shot her a wistful look. That one syllable always sent her reeling. Pam was right. The name Jack still sent a shiver down her spine. It evoked so many memories. She'd thought he was the love of her life but somehow it had all slipped through her fingers. She'd never forgotten the night she realised it was all over. Her tears then had seemed to last weeks and weeks and the dull ache for much longer. Twenty years on and the mere mention of his name could still cause pain.

'Long time ago,' she pronounced, wishing like mad to change the subject.

'Time to go,' said Pam cheerfully. 'I'll be back at work awaiting your call on how it went. And actually, Maggs, none of this actually matters. You look great. Never mind the interview, look in the mirror.'

Totally buoyed up by a glass of wine, a delicious lunch and words of wisdom from her best friend, Maggie sailed into town, hardly remembering the journey. She parked in the Royal Hotel's car park and spent a few minutes adjusting her make-up in the rear-view mirror. She then walked confidently into the hotel foyer at 2.25 p.m.

The hotel receptionist directed her to a suite on the sixth floor. Suddenly her confidence began to falter. As the lift headed skywards, the answers she'd tried to prepare in the bath started to jumble around in her head.

Why did you apply for this job? Because I make great tea. *What special qualities and abilities do you bring to the job?* I always warm the pot first. *Where do you see yourself in five years' time?* Tea buyer for the whole group.

The doors opened and she found herself directly opposite the suite. No more thinking time left. She walked through the doors to find a bored girl she judged to be in her early twenties sitting at a small desk with a list. The room was decorated in a soulless cream with pale blue curtains and a couple of tired-looking sofas in a blue and cream floral pattern.

'Name?' the bored girl enquired, not looking up.

'Fraser. Maggie Fraser.' God, it sounded so boringly ordinary.

'Go straight on in.' The girl motioned to a door to her right as she ticked Maggie's name off.

Maggie walked into the next room. Behind a large desk in the middle of another interminable blue and cream room sat two men in dark suits. Amongst piles of paperwork they both had name plates stuck in front of them. Damien Smythe she recognised as Mr Porsche with the clipboard who'd turned up at Farleys last Monday. The other was a Polish name she couldn't quite read.

'Ah, Fraser. Maggie. Take a seat.' Damien Smythe indicated one with a flick of his hand. Neither he nor his colleague looked up, nor did he bother to make any introductions. Presumably the name plates were there to save them the trouble. Maggie sat down, trying to remember not to cross her legs or slouch in the chair.

'Right,' said Damien Smythe, finally making eye contact and shooting her a rather derisory look. 'I'll be blunt. Didn't really want to take on any of Farleys' old staff, to be quite frank with you. Far too much dead wood. Home Truths is a very different operation. None of this smarmy client worship rubbish. We aim to shift properties and if it means insulting people, then insult them we will. If it's a crap house, we'll say so. The sellers will hate us for describing their bijou little apartment as "hardly room to park your arse". But the buyers will love us because they'll know exactly what they're getting, i.e. "a glorified broom cupboard but you can get absolutely legless in some great pubs just down the street".'

Maggie nodded dumbly. She had no idea why she was nodding. It all sounded perfectly ghastly.

'Now I don't care about all this PC crap,' Damien Smythe continued. 'To be brutal, you're a bit old for our team. I'm looking for bright young sparky people who've got a bit of attitude. You don't fit the bill.'

'So why did you bother phoning me?' Maggie snapped at him. She was shocked to realise it was her voice speaking, but her brain was not engaging. She'd obviously blown it in her first utterance.

'Good question,' Damien shot back, suddenly more interested. 'Can't imagine why I did. How old are you anyway? Can't be bothered to read through this junk.' He indicated a couple of pieces of paper, presumably her application, as if they were greasy old chip wrappings.

'I'm thirty-two plus VAT,' she announced firmly. Where on earth had that come from? To her astonishment, Damien and his fellow suit burst out laughing.

'Like it, like it,' Damien declared. 'OK, I'm going to break my own rules here. You've got local knowledge of the market. You might be useful. I'll offer you a trial. Start Monday for a week. See how it goes. Nine a.m.'

He went back to his paperwork. All of a sudden, Maggie realised she'd been dismissed. She picked up her bag, muttered a goodbye and left the room in a daze. What happened to 'my special abilities and qualities', 'reasons for applying' and 'five years' time'? Clearly a more relevant question might have been, '"Where do you see yourself in a week's time?' In the Priory, she conceded.

Chapter 10

Ref/3257 Dreary two-bedroom Victorian terrace, in need of gutting, thanks to previous owner's incontinent dog. Kitchen – yuck, you don't want to go there. Rear yard. No parking. Suit single, non-driving sex god able to function on takeaway food.

Ref/3258 Once a pretty cottage, now a tip thanks to the Bohemian lifestyle of its owner. Three bedrooms, all cupboard sized. Would suit cat swingers. Make us a silly offer as the owner's desperate to go travelling.

Ref/3259 Suburban bliss promised in this 1950s bung. Comes complete with full-on damp in every room, guaranteed tastefree avocado bathroom suite, Formica breakfast bar and oh, wonder of wonders, a serving hatch. Plenty of plugs for your karaoke machine, plasma screen telly, or Dansette record player. All you need to complete your dream are a few bubble lamps around the place, caravanette in the drive and lots of flashing Santas on the roof at Christmas.

Maggie couldn't believe what she was reading. So this was what Home Truths meant when they said 'no frills'. She had to admit the descriptions were terribly funny but what on earth did the owners make of them? Come to that, what prospective buyer would want to view a 'gently sagging house with lovely countryside views. Just as well as the interior's shite'?

Maggie's first morning at Home Truths had been the stuff of a Hammer horror movie – real edge-of-your-seat scary stuff. The branch manager was a statuesque brunette called Vanessa Templeton, a terrifying mixture of Sloane Ranger and old style hospital matron. Maggie judged her to be in her early thirties and very expensively dressed. She certainly possessed the required 'attitude' that Damien Smythe had mentioned. When Maggie ventured to ask why the property reference numbers started with 3257, Vanessa shot her a haughty look.

'No new business ever starts up with number one,' she said sarcastically. 'That would give the game away. We need to look established before we start.'

Maggie kept her head down and her mouth shut, after that. She'd been given a staff manual to read and then told to familiarise herself with the properties for sale. Home Truths had clearly done their homework in advance. They already seemed to have a considerable number of properties on their books.

'You'll meet the two negotiators this afternoon,' Vanessa pronounced. 'They're out viewing new properties all morning so you'll need to get those details into the system before the end of the afternoon. OK yah?'

'Yes, fine,' said Maggie. She got through the staff manual fairly quickly. There were very few rules and even fewer perks, it seemed. Four weeks' holiday, three paid sick days a year, hours appeared to be on a martini contract basis – any time, any place, anywhere. The rules included unashamed emphasis on nudging clients towards 'our inhouse financial adviser' whoever he or she was.

Maggie went back to the property details and the suburban bliss of the 1950s bung complete with nostalgic damp and avocado. It looked strangely familiar. And then it dawned on her. It was Manderley, home of the dreaded Mrs Danvers. Maggie wondered, with a wry smile, how old Danvers would take to the new description of her house. There'd be no Mr Farley to schmooze her into submission now.

She pondered on what old man Farley would think of the Home Truths mission statement. She could almost hear his voice, still claiming to know best, natch, after forty years in – and now out of – the business! She had to admit, though, they'd done wonders with the tatty old office. It was all state of the art desks and computers plus the bright blue and yellow livery and the horrendous grinning turkey logo splashed everywhere.

As the morning wore on, news of the unorthodox Home Truths approach to house selling was spreading like wildfire around town. Various people trickled into the office, some of whom Maggie guessed – and in a few cases knew full well – had no intention of moving. Here they all were, asking for details of houses they had absolutely no intention of buying. They just wanted to read and laugh at the outrageous bumph. They'd soon be able to peruse it all in the privacy of their own homes when the website went online later that day.

Maggie soon realised that Vanessa had been well taught at the Damien Smythe School of Social Disgraces. She had the same clipped, take-it-or-leave-it telephone manner, plus a confidence that came in Lamborghini-loads. Maggie wondered if she, too, were required to adopt the same sort of tone on the phone. Luckily the phone hadn't rung all that much so far.

She had just finished reading all the property details when there was the sound of the door bursting open and a familiar figure stood in the doorway. Mrs Danvers, complete with waterproof cape and tartan pork pie hat, was waving a piece of paper in one hand and a battered old umbrella in the other. She spotted Maggie and marched straight over for the kill.

'You! I should have guessed!' she snorted. 'You couldn't shift it when it was Farleys and you're resorting to this sort of cheap tactic to sell it now. I'll have you know, there's nothing wrong with my bathroom suite. And as for a karaoke machine' – she pronounced it 'croak' – 'whatever that is, you must have mixed it up with somewhere else. I demand to see the manager.'

'That's me,' said Vanessa, who'd emerged from her glass-partitioned room at the rear of the office, clearly fascinated by the exchange.

'You!' Mrs Danvers wheeled herself round and almost spat at Vanessa. 'What would *you* know about selling property?'

'Perfect timing, Mrs Daniels,' she said smoothly. 'I was just about to ring you to say that we have arranged three viewings for your property this afternoon. That is, of course, if it's convenient.'

Danvers visibly faltered for a second or two, greed registering in her eyes at the contemplation of a long-awaited sale. She then mustered her forces once more.

'Well, that's more than the other lot managed in a month,' she rasped in Maggie's direction. 'But I'm still not happy. What will my standing in the town be when they read that rubbish?' She briskly tapped the paper she'd been waving against the nearest desk.

'Well, it would go up if you had that ghastly bathroom ripped out for a start,' said Vanessa without flinching. Maggie audibly gasped.

'And you could lower the price to something a bit more realistic,' Vanessa continued firmly. 'When people make an offer, they factor in the work they'd need to do. And let's face it, Mrs Daniels, your place is really a rip-out job, isn't it?'

Danvers started to splutter, rendered speechless for probably the first time in her life. She turned and stalked out of the office, muttering, 'Oh, send 'em round, then. But I'll be having a word with your boss about the tone of your voice, young lady.'

Vanessa openly laughed as she watched Mrs Danvers's departing frame. 'Stupid cow,' she scoffed, as soon as the door banged shut. 'If she dropped the price by ten grand, someone would snap it up. You've dealt with her before, I take it.'

Maggie nodded. She went on to explain to Vanessa how they'd nicknamed her Danvers and the house Manderley. But the second the words dropped from her lips, she regretted it.

'Brilliant.' Vanessa seized upon it. 'I'll rework the details to incorporate that, if no one takes a sniff at it this afternoon.' She paused and started to honk with laughter. 'Let's hope they don't take a literal sniff, not with all that ghastly damp. Bleugh, it's simply revolting.' She wrinkled her nose in disgust.

'Wouldn't she sue if we called her Mrs Danvers?' said Maggie, realising she sounded rather pathetic.

'Oh, nonsense,' Vanessa retorted. 'If you come to Home Truths to shift your disgusting hovel, it's all part of the service. We're all about results, not hurt feelings. She won't feel bitter once all that lovely bunce is bouncing around in her bank account.'

She began to sashay into her office. Then she turned back as a thought struck her.

'Where's she moving to?' she demanded. 'Does she have a place lined up?'

'Not sure,' Maggie answered. 'To be honest, we never discussed it with her, because it never occurred to us it would ever sell. I think she'd want to stay in the area. Don't think she's ever lived anywhere else.'

'In that case,' said Vanessa, clapping her hands in triumph, 'I'll lob her a few details. Our dreary two bed with the disgusting kitchen might just suit. Or there's another fifties nightmare on the outskirts of town that's just crying out for the bulldozer. Corby Crescent. Take a look. Let me know what you think And while you're at it, print off all the most horrendous ones that might suit the old bag.'

Maggie started scrolling through the properties once again. She soon found 33 Corby Crescent. 'Pity it wasn't built over a collapsing mine shaft, but regrettably we're all stuck with it,' announced the blurb. She couldn't see Danvers getting excited about that. She began the print run.

Just before lunch, another of the Home Truths whizz kids arrived. A sharp-suited evacuee from Canary Wharf, he made his entrance and immediately installed himself at the desk opposite Maggie. She recognised him as the other suit at her interview.

'Hi there,' he announced amid a noisy routine of

designer briefcase unclicking and laptop unveiling. He whacked a glass name holder in front of him bearing the words 'Stefan Lempinsky' and the tag 'financial adviser' on the desk, waved cursorily at Maggie and got stuck into a series of Gordon-Gekko-from-*Wall-Street*-type phone calls. 'The fixed rate . . . not a good deal . . . doesn't anyone pay attention around here . . . no, he doesn't want to reveal his earnings . . . oh, you mean Tax Haven Tony . . . not looking good, buddy boy . . . yeah, I can get you a deal on that . . . don't touch it, matey, commission's shite . . .' Relentlessly, he droned on.

Maggie took an instant dislike to him. She hoped the two negotiators who'd be in after lunch might be more friendly – and a bit less ruthless. She was wearing her interview outfit again today which gave her a little bit of much needed confidence. But clearly, judging by the Mondi/Armani/Yves St Laurent peacock parade going on at Home Truths, she'd need some more fashion help from Pam to get her through the week.

The bright blue and yellow livery all over the walls plus the tension of the first day in a job were combining to give her a headache, so she was desperately grateful when Vanessa announced she could take a lunch break. She put on her mac, turned up the collar and scuttled down the street, now glistening with fine drizzle. She headed for the smart coffee house where she'd bumped into Marina. After a cursory check to establish that it was a Hermès-headscarf-free zone, she ordered a ciabatta roll with mozzarella and tomato and a large latte and then sat herself in a corner, trying to make some sense of the morning's events. So far, she decided, Vanessa was a serious snob with attitude. A sort of Margot Leadbetter from *The Good Life* crossed with Glenn Close, the bunny boiler in *Fatal Attraction*. As for Stefan, he was straight out of the Damien Smythe lookalike agency. Same rudeness, same superiority complex. She couldn't imagine anyone wanting him to arrange a lottery ticket, let alone a mortgage. It was almost as if they were all acting. By the time she'd drained the last of the latte, she'd resolved to stick it for a week and then find something else pretty damn quick.

The first of the negotiators arrived straight after lunch. To Maggie's relief, Fiona Ashworth appeared to be relatively normal. Late twenties, tiny, with a huge mop of blonde curls and wearing a very short black skirt suit, she exuded warmth and personality. She introduced herself to Maggie, handed over some audio tapes of property details for her to transcribe and actually used the words 'thank you'. At last some real work thought Maggie, rather than all the nosy time-wasters of the morning.

She was just getting stuck into typing up the details when the second negotiator came in through the door. A familiar figure stood staring at Maggie in horror and undisguised disbelief.

'Maggie.'

'Marina.'

'What are you doing here?'

'I could say the same.'

Marina covered her confusion by making a huge fuss about shaking the rain off her umbrella in the doorway and taking off the inevitable Hermès headscarf.

Vanessa appeared at her office door, a smirk from ear to ear. 'Of course, I forgot. You two know each other from the Dark Ages. Oh well, that saves introductions.' She promptly disappeared again.

'Fancy bumping into you again.' Maggie couldn't

resist, now that she'd got over the shock. 'And to think only last week you were planning on giving up work if I remember rightly. You were going to spoil that husband of yours.'

'Well, of course I didn't want to give the game away,' said Marina, trying to appear coy. She must have hurriedly cancelled all those 'hice' parties.

Maggie couldn't believe that Marina would fit into the Home Truths ethos of insulting the world in order to clinch the deal. But it wasn't her problem.

Marina handed over her tapes from the morning's viewings, just as Fiona had done.

'There you are, my dear,' she announced condescendingly. 'Try to make some sense of it, would you?' She then fished out a quilted Chanel bag and began retouching her make-up in an ostentatious fashion.

Maggie couldn't resist having a quick listen to Marina's tapes just to see what she'd come up with. 'Simply ghastly house with rotten windows and the smell of dead dog everywhere,' she was intoning. 'Absolutely no room for entertaining properly and only two small bedrooms with very low ceilings. Quite bizarre.'

The next one was clearly much more to Marina's taste. 'Graceful, stylish spacious apartment within eighteenth-century country mansion. Two gorgeous bedrooms, both en suite, plus guest suite. Twenty-four-hour concierge.' Huh, thought Maggie. What she means is it would suit someone who's never seen a pizza delivery box.

She went back to her typing. The afternoon had certainly livened up. She could see Vanessa and Marina coming to blows quite soon. Headscarves and shooting sticks at dawn.

Chapter 11

'Pam's coming over tonight,' Maggie announced. She'd had to pick her moment, ladling out a plate of Hungarian goulash so she wouldn't have to make eye contact with Garth. He was always nastier to her when the kids weren't around to witness it. As bad luck would have it, Beth had gone to youth club and George was staying with a friend after football practice. She felt strangely vulnerable, being alone with him.

She watched Garth's hands flinch as he took his plate. He winced as his fingers made contact with it. 'Bloody thing's hot,' he snapped. 'Why didn't you warn me? And why does *she* have to come round?'

Maggie mentally counted to three before she answered. A trick she'd read about in an article entitled 'Living With A Difficult Man' . . . if you don't have the guts to leave the rotten bastard, the feature implied. Counting to three apparently stopped you opening mouth without properly engaging brain, therefore possibly subjecting yourself to further abuse.

'She's going to help me sort out what to wear to work this week,' she replied quietly.

'How fucking ridiculous,' Garth snorted. Perhaps she

ought to count to thirty-three next time. 'That is so bloody typical. Last week you lost your job, this week you can't even dress yourself. What is it with women that they have to hang around together in packs like buses all the bloody time?'

Maggie paused, to avoid responding. Garth simply glared at her.

'If you recall,' she said eventually, 'your mother always emphasised the importance of serving food on hot plates.' As well as being an interfering old cow who'd given birth to a pig.

'Well, she was absolutely right there.' The pig continued to snort. 'Hot plates are fine, but yours are plucked from the mouth of a frigging volcano. Well, I'll go down the pub when *Pam* arrives.' He always pronounced her name sarcastically.

They finished their meal in silence. Maggie had begun loading up the dishes in the sink when the doorbell rang.

'Oh, nee nah, nee nah, that'll be the style police,' Garth declared. 'That's me out of here for a pint.' He headed straight for the hall, where he grabbed his jacket as he opened the door to Pam.

'Heard the sirens announcing your arrival,' he announced, deliberately without humour. 'So I'm off out. Bye.' The door slammed shut behind him.

Maggie emerged from the kitchen, wiping her hands on a tea towel.

'Stay where you are,' said Pam cheerfully, taking off her bright yellow PVC mac and matching rain hat and hanging them up in the hall. On Pam, they looked terrifically stylish, Maggie noted enviously. If she'd worn that, everyone would have assumed she was collecting for the nearest lifeboat. They went into the kitchen and

Maggie hastily cleared the rest of the dinner things from the table. Pam plonked down a suspiciously large handbag and produced a bottle of Chardonnay from it.

'You need this,' she announced, taking in Maggie's hunched shoulders and general despair. She started searching the kitchen cupboards for glasses.

'Over there.' Maggie indicated wearily. 'Sorry he's so rude. It's not really his fault. There's not much work around at the moment and he's worried sick about it.'

'Fair enough,' said Pam, now wrestling with a corkscrew, 'but that doesn't give him licence to be so stroppy. I bet he's not even bothered to ask about your first day in the new job.'

Maggie gazed down at the table. It was true, but then she hadn't noticed the omission either. She was so used to Garth's ways that it hadn't occurred to her that he'd even be vaguely interested.

Pam poured out huge glasses of wine.

'Now,' she said when they'd taken a couple of sips, 'tell me all about this job.'

Maggie found herself cheering up by the minute as she recounted the crazy philosophy at Home Truths and the sheer enjoyment of seeing Mrs Danvers given her comeuppance. She speculated on how long Marina would last, up against the imperious Vanessa.

'Brilliant.' Pam clapped her hands in delight. 'It might be a bumpy ride, but it sounds heaps more fun than Farleys.'

'I feel as though I'm a time traveller,' Maggie continued. 'As if I've been catapulted from Dickensian England to the twenty-first century. All in a day. Even the computers work properly, the chairs are really comfy, the desks don't wobble—'

'That's normal office life,' Pam cut in. 'Even at the council, we all insist on fresh ground coffee and decent juice. You just got too used to the cheap and not very cheerful Farley way of doing things. Bit like living with Garth.'

Maggie lowered her eyes and took another sip of wine. 'Oh, Garth's all right really,' she said. 'He's had a bad year. A couple of his regular clients died recently and everyone's tightening their purse strings. Farleys' crashing just wasn't very brilliant timing. I think he's more worried than he lets on.'

She began twisting the tablecloth around her fingers in a state of quiet desperation. Pam deliberately changed the subject.

'This new job's good news for you,' she pronounced. 'I know it's all strange and a bit off the wall, but I haven't seen you look so animated about anything in ages. It's given you a kick up the arse, Maggs, and you know it.'

Maggie looked at her, puzzled.

Pam continued: 'Just now, when you were describing your day, I saw a glimpse of you, the old Maggie, the fun one from school. The devil may care girl I skipped lessons with. Not that you were a rebel or a serious party animal or anything, but you lived life to the full. You kind of embraced it all, with your arms flung wide open. But now you sit with them folded in a defensive way.'

Maggie glanced down. Admittedly she was sitting with her arms crossed, but she had to put them somewhere. She took another sip of wine. This was starting to become uncomfortable.

'I saw a glimpse of the old Maggie when we went to Juicy Lucy's, too,' Pam continued. 'It took nearly the whole day to get there, but by the end you had actually come to terms with being pampered and spoilt a bit. And don't deny it. I was there. Go on. Admit it.'

Maggie hung her head. 'You've been reading too many self-help books,' she replied with a forced grin. 'I'm all right really. Garth and I are all right really. We're just having a bit of a blip.'

'Bit of a big blip, I'd say,' said Pam, tapping her nose. 'I'm sure he hates me because he knows I know.'

'Knows you know what?'

'Knows I know that he's a complete arse,' said Pam, before she could stop herself.

Maggie didn't even flinch. 'OK maybe things aren't that brilliant,' she conceded, her finger circling the top of her wine glass, 'but we've been married for nearly seventeen years. We can't maintain the hearts, flowers and violins stuff for ever.'

'Fair enough,' said Pam, 'but was there any of it to start with?'

'Can't honestly remember,' Maggie confessed, her tongue now loosening thanks to the wine. 'How is it with you and Tom? Must be difficult with him away a lot.'

Pam swept up a few stray tendrils of blonde hair with her slim fingers and then examined her rings. 'I'd say we're not "in lurve" now but we really do love each other. If I'm honest, being a Navy wife suits me. I look forward to him coming home. I get very upset when he has to go, but I also like having my own life while he's away. It's the shifting balance of power thingy that's difficult. When he's away, I make all the decisions. When he comes home, he expects to take over. But we basically like each other as well as love each other, and that's what's important. Do you like Garth?'

Maggie half laughed, half sobbed. 'No, not much at the

moment, but fortunately I'm too busy to think about it.'

Pam put her elbows on the table, cupped her face in her hands and looked Maggie straight in the eye. 'Don't you wonder what life might have been like with Jack?'

Oh, no, not again. Maggie could feel an unpleasant shiver go right down her spine, as if to her toes. She glanced at her hands. Her knuckles were white from being clenched. She took another slug of wine for comfort.

'There was never going to be any life with Jack,' she said in a voice as firm as she could muster. 'That night we were supposed to be getting back together, the night he never showed up, was the worst night of my life. No show, no phone call, no letter, no apology, nothing. Just silence. So I'm sorry, but there was never going to be any life with Jack.'

The sheer physical pain of loss, the buckets of tears for months and months afterwards, the constant scanning of faces and crowds, hoping subconsciously for a glimpse of his soft tanned face, china blue eyes and mop of wavy brown hair. The shudder of disappointment every time the phone rang and it wasn't him. The anticipation of picking up the post, to find only the gas bill, yet another piece of junk mail, a letter from Mum or a jolly postcard from a girlfriend. The throaty roar of every old MGB's exhaust, TV reruns of *Casablanca*, *From Here to Eternity* and all their other favourite old films, everything Frank Sinatra and Ella Fitzgerald had ever recorded, a long green dress he'd sworn made her look more beautiful than Ingrid Bergman. These were the symptoms of the terminal illness that was called simply 'Jack'.

'I loved Jack very much,' she said, suddenly fighting hot tears, 'but it's no good loving someone who failed to show up. At least Garth is here. He might not be Mr Congeniality but at least he's stuck it out with me.'

She got up to get a piece of kitchen towel to wipe her eyes.

'I know I married Garth on the rebound,' she said slowly, as she sat down again. 'There – I've said it aloud for the very first time. Admitted it, not just to myself, but to you. And I know he's a male chauvinist pig, but he didn't get a very good bargain either. I don't think he got a very loving wife and I often feel guilty about that. He doesn't know about Jack and all that emotional baggage. He doesn't know that I couldn't ever have made the same commitment to him that I would have done to Jack. So in a way, I've cheated him by not giving him one hundred per cent. What he thinks of me, I have no idea these days. But I needed a different relationship after Jack. I needed to make a different kind of commitment, one that didn't have the potential to hurt. If it was a rebound marriage, so be it. But no matter what Garth ever does to me, he will never have the capacity to hurt me in the way that Jack did. There – I've said it.'

She blew her noise noisily into the kitchen paper and chucked the screwed up sheet in the bin.

Pam sat open-mouthed at this sudden confession. Now it made sense why Maggie had stuck with Garth. She had never realised that Maggie felt such guilt at her lack of emotion where he was concerned.

'I realise,' she began apologetically, 'how lucky I am with Tom.'

'Yes you are,' said Maggie firmly. 'You made an active choice to marry him. You married for love, lust and sheer joy at the prospect of living with him for the rest of your life. I married for the companionship of a man who would be incapable of hurting me. It was a good enough reason then, and it's probably still a good enough reason now. Except that I feel I have short-changed him in a way. Now, let's change the subject and sort out my horrible wardrobe.'

They polished off the last of the wine and went upstairs.

Next day brought a new kind of drama to Home Truths. Vanessa, dressed in a pale blue suede suit that must have cost the earth, had been reading through Marina's property descriptions. And she was not happy.

'Just not pithy enough,' she proclaimed to Maggie and Fiona, tapping the file with her Mont Blanc pen. 'All too bloody polite. We want controversial, we want risqué, we do not want bland "gorgeous this" and "stylish that". We want to shift these properties, not stockpile them. Anyway, where is Marina?'

'Phoned in to say she'll be a little late,' said Fiona, who was clearly relieved that her own outrageous property particulars had passed the Vanessa test.

'Why so?' intoned Vanessa, drawing herself up to her full height, blue suede kitten heels included.

'Something about collecting her husband's suit from the tailors,' said Fiona.

'Can't he do that for himself?' Vanessa retorted. 'What does he do all day?'

'I think she said he's something big in cement,' Fiona replied.

'Well, let's hope it doesn't set,' came the tart reply.

Maggie chuckled quietly to herself. In the time she'd known Marina, she'd never known what her husband did, assuming it to be something appropriate for a member of the landed gentry. Marina had dropped vague hints at times about stockbroking but Maggie had never asked, on the basis of not wanting to give Marina the satisfaction of knowing that she was curious. So, cement, eh? Suddenly Her Maj's image was starting to crumble.

Today Maggie was wearing outfit two, as chosen by Pam. Again she'd somehow put together two or three old items that Maggie had regarded as sale mistakes, teamed them up with a scarf she'd never worn, and suddenly she looked much more businesslike. Maggie was beginning to feel ashamed of how dowdy she'd been looking for such a long time. The tired old skirts and dreary blouses had probably suited the Farley décor but they wouldn't fit into the image that Home Truths clearly wanted to create. She knew she'd have to shape up both mentally and physically if she were going to be invited to stay on.

Out in the new little kitchen at the back of the office, Maggie reflected some more on whether she really wanted to work there. As she loaded the shiny new Italian coffee maker and put out silver-rimmed white cups and saucers on a tray, she admitted to herself that the first day had been a real culture shock. She wondered why on earth she and Marina had been taken on in this new and very different set-up. She'd already convinced herself that she'd been hired by mistake. She'd somehow conveyed at the interview a much trendier forty-year-old with an attitude that she didn't actually possess. Perhaps Marina had clinched it because of her Hermès headscarves and her endless name and place dropping routine.

Marina finally showed up an hour and a half late, flicking rain off a Burberry mackintosh and unravelling yet another headscarf. It was obvious from her body language that she wasn't expecting any kind of showdown.

'Good of you to join us,' said Vanessa, standing imperiously in her office doorway.

Marina, completely missing the sarcasm in her voice, nodded in agreement.

'Just had to collect my husband's dinner suit,' she announced. 'We're at the Hunt Ball tonight. He bought this marvellous suit in Milan last spring. You know how wonderfully the Italians cut their suits. But I think I've done a bit too much Delia lately and he's added a few pounds.'

She began to laugh horsily. Vanessa didn't respond in kind.

'Well, we could lose a few pounds off your pay for being an hour late, or you can make up the time at the weekend,' she announced, stony-faced. 'Take your choice.'

Maggie and Fiona made silent eye contact across the office, waiting for the balloon to go up. They were not disappointed.

'Oh, that's not possible,' Marina exclaimed, completely unabashed. 'We're having a hice party for some stockbroking friends of my husband. They have this simply marvellous country house in Gloucester, you know, totally redesigned by Nicky Haslam, and—'

'—and so I'll take half a day off your annual leave then,' Vanessa announced. 'By the way, details on those houses you viewed yesterday. Not sharp enough. The words "gorgeous" and "splendid" are banned words here. It's all about attitude and the Home Truths attitude is "tell it like it is". Pity you can't harness the attitude that lets you waltz in late to writing some decent eye-grabbing copy.'

Vanessa then pointedly handed Marina's file over to Maggie. 'I'm sure Maggie will sort this out for you and beef it up a bit,' she continued. 'Meanwhile I'm sending you round to Mrs Danvers's place to tell her why, despite three viewings of ghastly Manderley yesterday afternoon, no one was interested, and how, if she wants to keep the place on our books, she either needs to get the decorators in or drop the price by at least ten grand. And then when you come back you'll revamp the details to include the words "Danvers" and "Manderley".'

Under all her ostentatiously applied Kanebo make-up, Marina went white. Without another word, she donned her mac and headscarf, picked up her bag and headed off to Manderley.

The second the door shut, Vanessa burst out laughing. 'Serves you right for wearing a fake Burberry mac,' she proclaimed to Marina's departing back. 'And as for *hice* parties . . .'

Maggie was stunned. Marina had never struck her as a fake. She'd never questioned all Marina's posturing about being part of Weltham's cocktail and canapé set, or the odd mentions of Jennifer's Diary, *Horse and Hound*, Henley, Ascot and Cowes. And now the news that her husband was in cement rather than 'something in the city' . Suddenly there were cracks appearing all over Marina's carefully crafted image.

Chapter 12

To her credit, Marina must have done the business because Mrs Danvers agreed to drop the asking price of Manderley by ten thousand, as Vanessa had demanded. Within twenty-four hours, there was a cash buyer ready to proceed on the purchase.

The news seemed to unleash another flurry of activity. Maggie started to feel a teensy bit of sympathy for Mrs Danvers, who was now being subjected to the full-on Home Truths experience. Vanessa ordered details of every vaguely suitable property to be despatched round to Manderley by courier on the basis that now she had a buyer, she needed a new home. Meanwhile, Stefan was on the phone to her hourly, trying to sweet talk her into a mortgage on the basis of 'just in case your dream home is a teensy bit higher than your budget'. Maggie noted that the word 'mortgage' was never actually mentioned. Phrases like 'exciting new phase in your life', 'here to help you through that financial jungle' and 'support you through this stressful time' were trotted out. They made it sound like she needed a visit to Juicy Lucy's.

However, as Maggie expected, the effect of all the schmoozing was immediate. The door burst open, along with a swirl of November rain and soggy leaves, to reveal the permanently furious Mrs Danvers, in a large tartan cape and a turban, brandishing the inevitable umbrella and wearing a look blacker than the storm clouds gathering overhead.

'Look at this,' she spluttered, chucking down a pile of Home Truths particulars on the nearest desk. Half of them made it to their destination, but the rest quickly slid off and scattered all over the floor. Maggie got up from her desk to retrieve them.

'These,' Mrs Danvers announced, prodding the ones still on the desk with the tip of her umbrella and showering everything in a three foot range with muddy raindrops, 'are positively pornographic.'

Maggie had a pretty shrewd idea what she was referring to. She'd just rescued the details on the 'budget sized semi with lounge dinette. Tiny bedroom would only suit couple planning missionary position sex'. And another shocker: 'This small cottage was the scene for one long shagfest but now they've split up, hence rock bottom offers invited for your very own Heartbreak Hotel. Only for the stout-hearted.'

She turned away to stifle a giggle. Pam was right. This place certainly had its moments. Just as she was wondering how Home Truths would tackle the current scene, Damien Smythe swept through the door, having parked the silver Porsche up on the pavement right outside as usual.

'Mrs Danv . . . iels,' he corrected himself. Clearly the account of Manderley and its intimidating owner had reached his ears. 'Our most valued client.' He kissed her hand with great aplomb. 'Congratulations on a successful sale. This calls for champagne.'

Vanessa, today in black and white Chanel jacket and black pencil skirt, appeared as if by magic with a bottle of Moët and glasses. There was clearly a drinks fridge in her office, equipped for such occasions.

So that's how they unnerve angry customers, Maggie observed. She was fascinated at the speed with which they all turned on the charm. It had the feel of a very practised routine. But how would indomitable old Danvers react? Maggie thought she'd whack them all over the head with her brolly and march out. But instead, to her amazement, Danvers caved in completely, turning into a simpering schoolgirl, coy eyes downcast and lashes a-flutter.

'Well, I . . .' she groped for words, 'don't know what to say.' The umbrella slid from her grasp as her anger evaporated. Maggie was almost disappointed that she'd surrendered so quickly.

'There's no need to say anything,' Damien smoothed on, drawing her up a chair. 'We are just so delighted to have found you a buyer so quickly. And after such an appallingly long time stuck with the, er, other agency. Of course we're all here to help you celebrate – and more important,' he paused to kiss her hand once more, 'find you the perfect home at the perfect price.'

Maggie thought she was going to be sick. Danvers was now sitting down, patting her hair and being positively coquettish, as the cork popped and the pale yellow liquid swished into the glasses. If this carried on, Damien would be grabbing an imaginary mike and crooning 'Take the ribbon from your hair' as he released the scraped back grey bun, kissed the old bat passionately and then whisked her off in the Porsche to some super seduction sesh at a local hotel.

'I haven't had champagne in years.' Mrs Danvers beamed at Vanessa and Damien. 'We didn't get this kind of treatment at Farleys.' She shot a look of triumph in Maggie's direction.

Maggie remembered Pam's advice from Monday night about maintaining a healthy bit of attitude. Make your mark she'd said. Chip in when you can.

'Huh, neither did we,' she said, as boldly as she could manage. 'Not with that disgusting old skinflint in charge.'

Vanessa and Damien both turned and beamed at her. Damien added a conspiratorial wink. Strewth, thought Maggie, big Brownie points for slagging off your previous employer.

The episode concluded with Damien sweeping a now half-pissed and slurring Mrs Danvers into his Porsche for some viewings. At this rate, she'd be snapping up Shagfest Cottage or the Missionary Semi by the end of the day. Maggie mentally shook her head in disbelief. She couldn't wait to relay all this to Pam. It was like being a bit part player in a new soap called *Emmerdale Funny Farm*.

She went out into the kitchen to start washing up the champagne glasses. Fiona came out to help.

'Damien is such a tart,' Fiona commented as they dried and polished the glasses. 'Too smooth to move. That's what we all called him at the last place. Damien Smooth.'

Maggie laughed. She was beginning to like Fiona, even though she envied her ability to wear such short skirts.

'Have you noticed how he never gets a parking ticket on that bloody Porsche?' Fiona continued.

'Yes, I had,' Maggie replied as she carefully put the long-stemmed glasses away.

'Apparently he's done a deal with the local traffic warden. He's selling his house soon and Damien's promised him mates' rates. Sharp cookie, eh?'

'Yes, he certainly is,' said Maggie. 'I find him a bit scary. He seems to live his whole life by doing deals.'

'Yes,' said Fiona. 'It's one long adrenalin rush. Crash and burn, that's Damien. He'd even try to barter on a packet of fags if he could. You'll get used to it.'

'I'm not so sure about that,' said Maggie, suddenly feeling the need to unburden her guilty secret. She made a snap decision to trust Fiona. 'I think they hired me by mistake,' she confessed. 'I made some snappy remark at the interview quite out of character and gave the impression I was a bolshy type. I'm only here on a week's trial.'

Fiona threw her head back and laughed. 'No, no,' she said. 'I can tell he really rates you. You turn up, get on with things and don't whinge. He likes that. But strictly *entre nous*, I think your friend Marina's going to get the plastic elbow.'

'Plastic elbow?'

'Well, she's hardly qualifying for the gold one yet,' said Fiona. Clearly the champagne had loosened her tongue too. 'Damien originally thought she had the required attitude, but he's realised he was mistaken.'

'The only attitude Marina has,' said Maggie, 'is about herself. Stuck up and snooty.'

'She has no reason to be,' Fiona confided, feeling a mutual trust. 'I checked out her address the other day when I was out on a viewing and I don't think a three bedroom detached on an Eighties estate is exactly sufficient reason to ponce about pretending to belong to the landed gentry.'

'But doesn't she live somewhere called Ashleigh Manor?'

Fiona roared with laughter. 'The house might be called Ashleigh Manor, but her proper address as known to her postman is 57 Ashleigh Manor Road. All a question of perspective. Slightly different ring to it, eh?'

Maggie's head started buzzing. All that posh talk over the years about hunt balls, point to points, shooting parties, cocktails, canapés and canoodling up to the local MP. All that faffing on about the dreaded weekend 'hice' parties, marquees on the lawn and hiring caterers. She'd swallowed it all. And worse, she'd never even enquired where 'Ashleigh Manor' was. An appalling omission for someone who worked in an estate agency.

But Fiona had saved the best bit for last. 'I went to take details of a house yesterday that just happened to be owned by a "friend" of hers. We got talking and we made the connection, i.e. that we both knew Marina. She told me an outrageous story about a black tie do she'd once been invited to at Marina's house. Apparently everyone turned up in DJs and ballgowns to cram round a tiny table in a dining room the size of a broom cupboard.'

Maggie was busily updating the website with their latest little gem – 'Nothing to say about this sad little terrace house with its dreary kitchen and no parking. Best bit is its private leafy garden. Just the job if you're a Readers' Wives type' – when the Porsche rolled up on the pavement. Vanessa emerged from her office door and Stefan suddenly shut down his laptop. It was as if they'd synchronised watches for a controlled explosion. All eyes were suddenly on Marina, who was flashing her Kanebo compact around as she sat at her desk powdering her nose.

'Time to go, Marina,' said Damien coldly as he came in through the door. 'Get your coat on and scram.'

Maggie felt the hairs on the back of her neck stand to attention. This was going to be ugly. She was also horribly aware that it was now Friday, and the last day of her trial. Was she about to learn her fate too?

'Oh, gosh, yes,' said Marina, glancing ostentatiously at her Gucci watch. 'Must get over to measure up Mr Hancock's place.'

'No,' said Damien. 'Fiona's sorting it. You're going nowhere, except out of that door. Now.'

Marina went white and started shaking. It was a horrible sight. Maggie turned away in embarrassment. Clearly Home Truths did the hiring and firing the no-frills way as well.

Suddenly Maggie became aware of the tick tick tick of a diesel engine outside. She looked up and saw that a taxi had pulled up right behind Damien's Porsche. It was clearly waiting to take its unwilling occupant home. All part of a well-honed routine, just like the champagne shower on old Danvers.

'I think I'm owed an explanation,' Marina finally managed, her Kanebo-ed bottom lip wobbling for all to see.

'Sure,' said Damien. 'You're crap. You're fired. Your cab's outside. Simple.'

With that, he strode over to the door and opened it. Without another word, the hunched figure of Marina, clutching her possibly rumbled fake Burberry raincoat and bag, scuttled out.

There was an embarrassing silence for probably just a

couple of seconds. It seemed like hours. Maggie could feel her heart pounding and was sure they all could hear it too.

'And as for you . . .' Damien, still standing at the open door, now turned his attention to her. She felt the colour drain from her face, and her hands gripped the edge of her desk so hard that her knuckles turned white. Oh, please God, let there not be a second taxi waiting outside. She strained her ears for sounds of another diesel engine ticking over. The thought of losing her job twice in a fortnight was too much to bear. She tried to decipher his body language clues while studiously avoiding eye contact for fear of what she might discover.

'I'm giving you her job. Three months' trial. See how you shape up.'

The Porsche roared off up the street. Maggie sat stunned and speechless at her desk. Fiona went over and gave her a congratulatory hug. Vanessa nodded approval and disappeared back into the cloud of Chanel No. 5 in her office.

That evening a still shocked Maggie drove home in a complete daze. She pulled up outside the house and switched off the car engine. Garth's pick-up was already parked on the driveway. Before she plunged back into the war zone, she wanted to share her good news with Pam. She fished out her mobile and rang her.

'I'm thrilled to bits and I'm scared stupid,' she told an ecstatic Pam. 'I'm still shaking.'

'This is the beginning of a new you,' said Pam, 'or rather the rebirth of the old you that I used to know.'

Chapter 13

The scene at home was all too familiar. Garth was in his usual armchair, face as black as thunder, slurping from a can of lager as he watched two obscure European football teams thrashing it out in some equally obscure championship qualifier. Maggie knew immediately he was in one of his 'that should have been me' moods and left well alone.

In the kitchen she was greeted with cereal bowls piled high in the sink following an after-school snack-attack on the cornflakes boxes. The kids had obviously retreated to their rooms, unable to squabble about the remote control as their father was home.

Without a word, Maggie wearily hung up her coat and began preparing the evening meal. It was a full twenty minutes after she'd peeled potatoes and carrots, shoved a ready-made steak and ale pie in the oven and begun laying the table that Garth drifted into the kitchen, heading for the fridge and another lager.

'What's up with you?' he demanded, glaring at her.

'Nothing at all,' she replied without looking at him as she laid out knives, forks and plates. 'I've had a long and tiring week at work and I've come home to the usual scenes of devastation. Just don't fancy playing war games tonight, actually.' She wheeled round and shot him a defiant look.

Garth flinched momentarily before continuing his journey to the fridge. He collected another can and left the kitchen without a word. Maggie found herself pulling a face at his departing back. Attitude, attitude, attitude, she whispered to herself. A bit more of the big A would probably improve her lot at home as well as at work. After accidentally getting herself not only kept on at Home Truths but promoted thanks to a few uncharacteristic barbs, she wondered if the same tactics would succeed at home. Buoyed up by the events of the day, she was experiencing a sense of self-worth for the first time in years.

'I am *not* going to let them undermine me,' she muttered as she tested the carrots in the steamer. 'I am not going to roll over when they all start on at me.'

Ten minutes later, a rare silence descended round the table as the Fraser family sat down to eat. Clearly hunger had, for once, overtaken the desire to harangue each other. Even Beth and George were too ravenous to argue.

Garth finally opened his mouth to speak. Maggie braced herself for the usual diatribe about her cooking, and then, before he could utter a word, she decided she'd had enough. For the second time that evening, Garth flinched at the look on her face.

'Well, I'd just like to thank you all for being so concerned about my welfare this week, my first week in a new and very taxing job,' she began, determined not to let her voice wobble. 'Not a single one of you has asked how I got on, so I'd like to take this opportunity of thanking you all most sincerely for your interest.'

She paused and glanced around the table. George rolled his eyes to the ceiling as if to say here she goes again. Beth, who was busily cutting her carrots into tiny pieces, didn't appear to be listening. Garth, wearing his usual thunderous look took another swig from his lager can. No accusations from Beth that *he* was a raving alcoholic, she noticed.

'Well, I've had a most successful week in my new job,' she went on. 'It's been a real challenge, working with some very tough but very professional people. And the best news of all . . .' she paused this time, hoping for a reaction; there was none, 'is that I have not only passed my week's trial but I've been promoted. Of course I would like to celebrate with a glass of wine, but I don't want my children accusing me of being drunk in charge of a kitchen. But perhaps you would raise your water glasses and drink to my unexpected success. That is, if any of you have been listening to what I've said.'

There was a pause. Clearly nobody had been listening at all. I'm not going to cry, Maggie willed herself. I am not going to get upset.

'Well, here's to me and my unexpected success,' she announced. 'And here's to you three, you ungrateful sodding bastards.'

Three faces turned sharply in her direction, as if there'd been a rifle shot. Bastards? Who on earth was she talking about?

'Sorry, Mum.' Beth came to her senses. 'Was miles away. Who are these – er – people?'

'You three,' she said sweetly. 'I just knew I could count on your support.'

Garth entered the fray. 'What are you gabbling on about, woman?' he growled at her.

'Sorry, Garth. I mistakenly thought you'd be pleased. As I said, I've passed my week's trial and been promoted.'

He took a slug of lager. 'Oh, good,' he said grudgingly. 'Well, bully for you. Unfortunately I've had a bloody awful day. Brenda's tied up the figures for the year and it's bad news.'

Brenda was the freelance book-keeper who'd been doing Garth's gardening business accounts for years. For a book-keeper, she looked remarkably like a casting director's idea of a typical barmaid: hair bleached and backcombed. a seemingly endless collection of dangly earrings and large tits worn permanently on display. Maggie had never been a fan of Brenda's but she'd smiled to herself when she'd overheard the kids referring to her as Bet Lynch and laughing at the bouffant hairdo.

'How bad?'

'Twenty-five per cent down on last year,' Garth thundered, 'give or take a few mowings.'

Maggie drew a deep breath and looked him straight in the eye. 'Well then, it's a good job I've landed this promotion.'

Beth seized the moment to score points over her brother. 'I think that's fantastic, Mum. That's made up for Dad's losses then.' She beamed triumphantly at George, who was now scowling at everyone.

Garth, who was seriously miffed that his moment of drama had been effectively wiped out, got up to visit the fridge once more.

'Tut tut. Too much to drink, Dad,' George chipped in. 'You'll end up on the road to ruin. Oh, actually, you already are.'

Garth wheeled round from the fridge. Everyone

expected him to lash out at George. But instead, he pointed an angry finger in Maggie's direction.

'This,' he spluttered furiously, a muscle twitching in his neck, 'is your fault. I've read in the papers about that stupid place you're working. The whole town's up in arms about how rude they all are. Well, all I can say is that it's rubbed off on you. You come in here, sounding off about your "promotion" – what did you do to get that? Win the prize for being the stroppiest employee of the week? I can tell you now, I don't intend to come home to all this grief every night.'

Maggie looked at him as firmly as she could, concealing her shaking hands under the table.

Unexpectedly George waded in to her rescue. 'Hang on a minute, Dad. You always slag Mum off. Now she's done something good, you should be pleased. Especially as it gets you out of a hole with the business.'

Garth realised he'd been suddenly outnumbered. 'All right, all right,' he conceded grudgingly. 'Well done on the job.' He ripped off the ring pull on his lager. As he lifted the already foaming can to his lips, he stopped as a thought suddenly occurred to him.

'Bloody hell. I nearly forgot,' he announced, forcing a smile. 'It's the Big Dig garden show in Birmingham tomorrow. Might give me a few new ideas.'

'Oh, good.' Beth jumped in. 'Mum, we could go out shopping and celebrate your new job.'

This was Beth-speak for 'Let's go out and you can buy me things'. Maggie half nodded, relieved that the tension had been dispelled.

Not to be outdone, George announced that he'd like to go to Birmingham with his father as Saints were playing away at Birmingham City.

'Not a chance,' said Garth briskly. 'It's ticket only. Anyway, you kids need to crack on with your homework.' He looked expectantly at Maggie, hoping for her approval rather than any more of that ridiculous attitude she'd picked up this week.

'Fine by me,' she said. She'd been praying he'd go so she could have some relative peace for a day. She'd come across some leaflets about the gardening show a couple of weeks ago whilst turning out his trouser pockets to put on a wash. Garth often pulled this little stunt, pretending it was a spur-of-the-moment decision to go away somewhere rather than telling her beforehand. She'd long since guessed it was so he could go on his own rather than be cajoled into taking everyone. By making it allegedly a last-minute thing, he ensured that everyone's plans for the day in question would already be in place and he could argue the case for people sticking to them. She didn't blame him for wanting a bit of peace away from her. She felt the same about him.

Much later that night, Garth exacted his revenge. After the debacle over the supper table, he'd stomped off to the pub for the rest of the evening. Maggie, exhausted with everything, and relieved to have some peace, took herself off early to bed. She knew she actually wanted to have a damn good cry but she was far too tired for tears. Her head sank into the pillows and she fell straight away into a deep sleep.

So she never heard the front door click shut, the footsteps up the stairs, the bedroom door opening. All she knew was that suddenly her nightdress was being pulled up, her arms were being pinned to the bed and the smell of strong beer and cigarettes was everywhere.

Her struggle against consciousness was shortlived. She was suddenly wide awake, the full weight of Garth's body on top of her, his beard prickling against her face. And then he was entering her, relentlessly forcing himself inside. She wanted to scream out at him to stop, to push him away, but her voice and her arms seemed to have no power in them at all. She lay there helpless, silent, secret tears coursing down her cheeks.

Garth was muttering as he thrust himself further and further inside her, but these were not the mutterings of lovemaking, more the mutterings of marital entitlement, of screwing her because that was part of the deal. She knew she was dry and unyielding but it wasn't her fault. She could hardly feel aroused when she'd just been woken from a deep sleep. She tried to think erotic thoughts in the hope that the dry pain would go away, but it didn't.

Eventually Garth reached his climax. There were no moans of ecstasy, no closeness after ejaculation, no cuddles and loving touches. He released her arms, rolled off her and turned his back on her. Moments later, she could hear him snoring.

Maggie lay on her back, trying to make out the pattern on the curtains, as the pain gradually subsided. She wanted to sob, but she couldn't even do that. She didn't have the strength to roll over and curl up into some comforting foetal position. It was as though Garth had sapped the last of the strength from her body and then pushed her aside, like some discarded toy. She felt dirty, unloved and ashamed.

Maggie and Pam managed to meet up for lunch in Weltham town centre on Saturday. Maggie had given Beth fifty quid on a hush-hush basis and propelled her in the direction of Top Shop, River Island and Warehouse for a couple of hours so she could have a good natter with Pam. They crammed into a tiny French bistro, so full of rained-on shoppers that the windows were steaming up a treat.

'So how do you feel then, the new Mrs Negotiator?' Pam queried, noting the bags under Maggie's eyes.

'Oh, highs and lows,' Maggie admitted. 'One minute I'm chuffed to bits and really excited about it. The next, I'm absolutely racked with doubt and scared witless. I didn't sleep a wink last night.'

She couldn't quite bring herself to tell Pam exactly why she didn't sleep a wink last night. It was somehow letting the side down. She felt too ashamed at the thought of admitting, not just to Pam but to herself, that her sex life had reached a new all time low. Probably misplaced loyalty to Garth, but it was too much information.

'Pity we can't fit in a day at Juicy Lucy's to calm you down,' said Pam cheerfully. 'Oh, let's have a bottle of wine and something naughty to celebrate instead.'

They consulted the menu, which was mostly in French. Languages were not Maggie's best subject at school. 'We'll both have the cassoulet and a bottle of Côtes du Rhône,' Pam announced to a hovering waiter, to spare Maggie's blushes. 'And we'll complete the damage later on,' she added to Maggie, 'with the raspberry crème brûlée. Now, tell me about this new job.'

Maggie outlined roughly what a negotiator did. Pam listened carefully and then observed that Maggie could do it standing on her head.

'You're biased. But the problem at Home Truths is,' Maggie explained, stopping momentarily as the cassoulet arrived, 'this attitude thing. You've seen the reports in the paper. Half the town's up in arms at the shocking descriptions of the properties, the other's going round with smug looks on their faces because they've shifted their houses in record time. I've only been there a week but we passed on more offers in that time than I think we did in six months when it was Farleys.'

'Isn't that exciting, being part of something so successful?' said Pam. 'We're not exactly NASA control at the council. Apart from the welcome hiss of the coffee machine, the only other excitement is when someone reads out Jonathan Cainer's horoscopes and we all start daydreaming.'

Maggie forked her cassoulet round her plate. 'I'm just scared,' she said slowly. 'Scared of failing. Scared of not being bolshy enough.'

'Why not take a leaf out of Garth's book?' said Pam. 'Just think how unpleasant he is and when you have a stroppy client deal with it in the same way that he would. It's only acting. After all, going to work is only acting really. For example, when I answer the phone and cheerfully say, "Environmental Services, how can I help you?" I don't really mean it, especially when we get all the nutters on the phone. I'd quite like to say, "Would you mind sodding off while I drink my coffee and finish this magazine," but I don't. It's all acting.'

Maggie had never thought of it like that. She took another mouthful of the cassoulet. It was deliciously warming, its comfort almost making her shiver.

'I suppose it boils down to the confidence thing,' Maggie admitted, trying to put last night's nightmare out of her mind. 'Too many years of caving in to Garth's tempers and trying to keep the kids quiet and out of his way. Instead of tackling it, the easier way is to keep your head down.'

Once again, she fought the temptation to spill the beans on last night. Maybe it didn't happen. Maybe she just dreamt it. But no, the soreness from Garth's pounding was a sharp reminder.

Pam shot her a piercing look. 'Got it in one, Maggs. You've got into the convenient rut of "anything for a quiet life". It works in the short term, but long term . . . well, you know the consequences. You've just told me yourself.'

Maggie nodded sadly. 'Trouble is, it's gone on like that for too long. Last night I let rip and there was almost an outcry of, "How dare you get stroppy? That's my territory." It's very difficult to change tack.'

'I realise that. The other night when I came round, Garth swept out practically breathing fire and brimstone. He reminded me of Darth Vader. All he needed was a black leather cloak, a helmet, gauntlets and a bad case of asthma to get the part in the remake. Your Garth Vader has already got the required attitude of wanting to rule the world. You just need to harness a bit of that attitude yourself. Get those gauntlets on, girl, and shove people around a bit.'

Maggie started to laugh somewhat hysterically. Her hysteria finally gave way to neurotic giggles which in turn became roars of laughter. The pair of them ended up wiping their eyes with their napkins. Other diners were looking across at them, wondering what they'd been missing. Pam had always been amusing, even when they were at school.

'So if he's Darth,' Maggie managed when they'd finally recovered their composure, 'what does that make me? R2D2?'

'No, you're bloody Cinderella,' was Pam's immediate reply, 'cleaning out the effing grate all the time, while everyone else goes to the ball. It's time you took a leaf out of poor Cinders's book and gatecrashed.'

Maggie took another sip of wine. Pam was right. Pam was right about most things. To Maggie, she just seemed to have more control over every aspect of her life. Happily married to Tom, perfectly able to cope during his long absences away at sea, justifiably proud of son Mark who'd worked hard at school and now achieved a university place; fulfilled in her job, surrounded by friends and always immaculately turned out. Pam was to Mulberry what Maggie was to Woman at War on Want. Maggie betted her friend's sex life was in good working order too, with lots of loving cuddles and kisses.

'Take today,' Pam continued, sensing this was the moment to push home her point. 'Garth's sodded off to Birmingham. Mind you, that's a relief to us all. So what have you done? Given Beth fifty quid to spend on clothes. Lovely and very generous. She's a teenager who can't exist without the latest gear. But what about you? I bet you aren't planning a whip around the shops to pick up a new outfit to start your new job next week.'

Maggie shook her head. It hadn't even crossed her mind.

'No, I thought not,' said Pam firmly. 'Well, after we've finished here, we're going shopping. And before you protest, I promise a new you at minimal expense.' She hailed a passing waiter. 'Two raspberry brûlées, please.'

She turned back to Maggie. 'Now, this will be your last pudding for a while,' she continued. 'No more comfort eating after today. I know that there's a slimmer Maggie in there, trying to get out, if you don't mind my saying.

You had a fabulous figure when you were going out with Jack.' Maggie winced slightly at the sound of his name. 'Oh, sorry . . . all I'm trying to say is don't let Darth Vader drive you to the biscuit tin. Use the Force. Not the HobNobs.'

Maggie hung her head. The home truths were coming thick and fast. And she knew Pam was right. She'd let herself go over the years. As the pounds piled on, the sizes got bigger. To start with, there were the excuses like having babies, being too tired to exercise, sitting down all day at work. Size 12 led to 14 as surely as 14 crept to 16, and now 18 was, frankly, a bit of a squeeze. The joy of clothes shopping had long since disappeared, along with her waist line.

'Right,' announced Pam, settling the bill and waving away Maggie's offer of notes. 'You've given Beth fifty quid to waste on disco gear she'll wear once. We'll spend exactly the same amount of money on you and I guarantee we can come up with some good, well-cut classics.'

She tapped her nose conspiratorially. Maggie looked mystified, and also terrified at the thought of parting with another fifty pounds she didn't honestly have. But she knew better than to protest when Pam was in this kind of mood.

They walked briskly up the street for several hundred yards, then round a couple of corners and into a tiny cobbled mews. A French patisserie, a shoe shop and a clothes shop met Maggie's surprised gaze.

'Never knew these existed,' she said as they negotiated the cobbles, still slippery from the recent shower. 'Pathetic, since I work for an estate agency.'

'You should get out more.' Pam laughed. 'You've been

too office-bound. This is one of the best-kept secrets in town.'

They passed through the door of the clothes shop to the tinkle of a bell.

'Hi, Sue.' Pam greeted the owner, an elegant woman whom Maggie judged to be in her sixties with beautiful coiffed short grey hair and a perfect English Rose complexion. 'We need a couple of smart outfits for my friend Maggie here, who's just landed a great job and needs a new look.'

'Hmmm,' murmured Sue as she turned to the racks. 'I'm sure we can find something. What kind of job? Wackv or restrained?'

'Oh, definitely wacky,' Pam replied. Then she turned to Maggie. 'Don't panic. All the clothes are not quite new so the prices aren't quite so new either.'

Sue clearly knew her stock well. Within seconds she'd pulled out several skirts, trousers, jackets and tops and nodded Maggie in the direction of a changing cubicle at the back of the shop. As Maggie kept emerging from behind the curtains, Pam and Sue descended on her like Trinny and Susannah, adjusting a collar, turning back a cuff, smoothing a revere, discussing shapes, cuts and co-ordination like seasoned fashionistas. They could have been sitting right next to the catwalk at a Paris fashion show. To her own amazement, Maggie quite enjoyed the experience, especially when she allowed herself a glance in the mirror. No more silent martyr look. She found herself gazing at a woman who meant business. Her pleasure was only marred by the dread of wondering how much it was all going to cost.

When she finally emerged through the curtains in her own clothes, to her horror Sue was packing several items into a couple of carrier bags and Pam was slapping fifty pounds down on the counter.

'Give it me back when you get your pay rise,' she said in a voice that did not invite a reply.

Back on the high street, heading towards the bistro to wait for Beth, Pam gave Maggie a little more detail. 'Sue's shop only opened about three months ago,' she said, 'but it's already doing a roaring trade. Lots of the town's posh totty can quietly unload their mistakes or clear out their wardrobes. And Sue also buys in lots of designer end-of-lines. She used to work with me at the council and wanted to do something like this for years.'

'What made her take the plunge?' Maggie was keen to know. It seemed very courageous.

'Caught her bastard husband playing away. He'd always held her back. Refused to let her do anything much except dump meals on the table at set hours. So the minute the marriage ended, Sue shoved two fingers up to her old life. She took early retirement from the council and started the shop. All she regrets is not doing the whole thing twenty years ago.'

The lesson wasn't lost on Maggie.

'Blimey, Mum, what have you been up to?' asked Beth, clocking the bags immediately.

Before Maggie could reply, Pam cut in. 'Your mum never treats herself. Like most mums, she always puts you first. Like some mums, she doesn't get much gratitude for what she does. But now she's been clever enough to land a brilliant job, she needs to look and feel the part. And she could do with a bit of a boost, quite frankly.'

Beth stood in stunned silence for a moment before she came to her senses.

'Good for you, Mum,' she said. 'You deserve it.' She hugged Maggie and kissed her on the cheek. Clearly Pam's speech had hit its target.

Pam glanced at Maggie. Her eyes had gone all glittery with emotion, and she turned away to wipe a stray tear. Pam suspected it was the first sign of affection she had received in ages.

Chapter 14

Maggie couldn't believe how quickly the days whizzed by at work, now she was out and about with clients, taking instruction on new properties, and then whizzing back to the office to write up her notes. After a nervous start, she was beginning to find her feet. She felt instinctively that Vanessa liked her and was therefore being kind. She'd been asked to pep up a few of her property descriptions to Home Truths' outrageous standards, but not in the way that Vanessa had dealt with Marina. Maggie remembered her chucking the files across the office in Marina's direction, and shuddered thankfully.

By the end of the first week, Vanessa had actually dubbed one set of particulars as brilliant. Maggie thought she'd gone to heaven. The house in question was so utterly neat and prissy you could have eaten your dinner off any surface of your choice. Maggie had come up with a line about the semi's being 'strictly for control freaks. Only Delia Smith/Martha Stewart domestic goddess types need bother viewing. Mere clean, ordinary mortals may want to scream.'

She'd also won praise for 'swanky, ostentatious

architect-designed bling bling bungalow. Master bedroom has en suite and dressing room big enough to suit typical wardrobe of footballer's wife. Lovely roll top work surfaces in kitchen that won't ruin your nail extensions, should you ever get round to learning to cook. Enough room in drive to do a 360 in your Mercedes convertible. Lawn big enough for posh marquee/football practice. If you've got it and want to flaunt it, then this is the property for you. Within ten minutes' drive of nearest Toni and Guy and also top-rated beauty salon that offers botox.'

'It's funny,' she remarked to Fiona one morning over a snatched coffee, 'how everyone describes new swanky homes as being "architect-designed". I mean, who else would you want to design a house? A librarian? A roadsweeper?'

Fiona, dressed in yet another pelmet pretending to be a skirt, laughed her head off. 'Daft, isn't it,' she said, 'but we all fall into that trap. Bit like all that lifestyle hints they put in show houses. You know, the straw hat with ribbons and flowers on a little girl's bed, the breakfast scene of coffee pot and toast rack complete with fake slices but no crumbs in the kitchen. And if it's a really cheapo estate, they take all the doors off to create a bit more space, and put in glass-topped tables and cut-down beds to make the rooms look much bigger. Then there are all the dreamy photographs of beautiful children in perfectly co-ordinating frames, the repro antique furniture in the office to suggest that Dad is a brainy professor, and the dining room laid out with terribly expensive tableware for at least five courses to imply that Mum gives Nigella Lawson a run for her muffins. It's only when the poor sods move in that they realise there are (a) no wardrobes, (b) no room to put them and (c) no way of getting them up the tiny staircase anyway.'

Maggie laughed. Farleys had never attracted any new estates. Their image had been far too crusty for that kind of property. They'd ended up with the turkey end of the market. Yet here was Home Truths with its grinning turkey, shifting properties by the dozen. Even the sale of Manderley was progressing nicely and Mrs Danvers had been persuaded to snap up the 'filthy lounge dinette that would be a power washer's paradise. Be Zena, Warrior Princess and wield your cleaning weapon on this little scrote.' Everyone knew that Mrs D wouldn't dream of cleaning it up. Black mould on the walls and a threadbare carpet were de rigueur at Manderley, so all she was doing was merely downsizing from one hovel to another. Cruising around in Damien's Porsche had clearly done the trick.

The only property that hadn't attracted any interest whatsoever since the takeover was Bleak House, which was still knocking potential buyers out with its pungent smell. Vanessa had visited it and pronounced it 'worse than totally ghastly'. Damien had phoned the son and daughter of the man who'd died there, and told them a few of his own home truths with all the sensitivity of a sleep-deprived Rottweiler.

'For chrissake, if you two have finished the grief bit, could you get some industrial cleaners round there in hard hats and gas masks pretty damn quick before we're all finally overpowered,' he roared down the phone. 'I can't have my staff risking their lives taking people round the place, not with all the Health and Safety regs these days. Wouldn't look good in the local paper, "Home Truths Staff Overpowered by House", would it?'

Maggie had to suppress a giggle when she overheard that one. Clearly the siblings weren't going to get the Porsche persuasion treatment from Damien.

'Er, Damien,' she said tentatively, surprised at her own courage. 'I've never been to Bleak House. Could I go round and see what I could do?'

She immediately regretted what she'd said. What on earth made her open her mouth? So far, things had been going well and this could just rot it all up. She could fall flat on her face and lose the job. She could fall flat on her face from the smell as well, judging by all accounts.

Damien looked up from his laptop. 'Yes, bloody good idea. Give us a fresh take on it. Fresh, ha ha! As if! I'll get the keys out of the safe right now.'

And so Maggie found herself behind the wheel of her car, heading for Bleak House and wondering whether to stop off at the shops to invest in some nose clips and smelling salts. Within twenty minutes she'd pulled up outside the house and was gazing through the rotting wooden gates.

It was an old Early Victorian vicarage which, in its day, must have been quite an imposing house. Now it looked as though Miss Havisham had only just been persuaded into residential care. The slates on the roof were all higgledy-piggledy, the window frames were clearly rotting and the grey net curtains were reduced to hanging fragments. Ivy growing up the side of the house had virtually obscured two of the upstairs windows. One of the chimneys had partly fallen down, its bricks smashed and strewn across a green slimy pathway. What had once been a garden was now a jungle of brambles. The stone wall surrounding the house was crumbling quietly, under a tangle of ivy and convolvulus.

She picked her way carefully up the path and put the key in the lock. The front door was so warped from damp – there'd probably been no heating in the house for years – that she had to kick it open. It squealed, as if in protest . . .

. . . and then it hit her.

The famous pong that everyone had complained about rolled out and smacked her in the face. She gasped, instinctively turning her head away to take a gulp of air.

I must go in, she told herself firmly. I must make a success of this. She took two huge breaths to calm herself down and stepped inside, a hanky over her mouth and the remains of a bottle of perfume she'd found at the bottom of her handbag clutched firmly in her other hand.

She'd been warned to take a torch as there was no longer any electricity supply. One look at the rotting staircase with its fragments of mouldy carpet told her that it was too dangerous to go upstairs. She made her way into the first room off the hall, which she guessed would have been the sitting room. She gazed up at the ceiling, still clinging on for dear life. The central rose had partly come away, together with most of the picture rails, which were now festooned with grey dusty cobwebs and several generations of dead spiders. The floor squeaked ominously and all the walls had huge cracks. What furniture was left had simply rotted away. The fabric on an old sofa and two armchairs had virtually disappeared, leaving lumps of greeny grey filling scattered over the seats and across the floor. It looked as though even the rats had finally given it up as a bad job. The kitchen was in a similar state, except that there were piles of screwed-up newspapers everywhere and a filthy old black stove in a corner. The build-up of grease on it and on the surrounding walls had long since caked into a hard, solid mass. Old pans covered in cobwebs and God knows what else were heaped up on the floor.

Maggie suddenly thought of the old man, dying here. Abandoned by his family, feeling too ill to keep the place clean and finally lying down to die amongst all the cobwebs, alone and unloved. So uncared for that he wasn't discovered for several months. She felt tears pricking her eyes. How sad that someone could be so totally alone in death. And this was his legacy, a house that was once probably warm, comfortable and filled with laughter, before it inadvertently became his grave. She thought about what state his body must have been in when he was discovered. The thought made her feel sick. She stumbled outside and gulped some fresh air. Then she firmly locked the door and whispered the old man a sad goodbye.

Now she understood why all the previous negotiators had hated coming here. It was worse than the scariest horror film. She felt her body untensing again after the sheer horror of being in there. The hackles on her neck relaxed, her shoulders eased and her stomach stopped churning. She gave herself five minutes to calm down before starting up the car and heading back to the office. What on earth could she write about that place that would clinch some sort of sale? And, worse still, how could she negotiate with the son and daughter who had allowed their father to die in such squalor? She knew the future success of her job depended on it. She'd put herself up for this; somehow she had to deliver. Suddenly she had a brilliant idea.

She pulled into a lay-by and fished out her mobile phone.

They were all waiting expectantly when she got back to the office. Fiona, Vanessa and even Damien were looking forward to her verdict, amusement written large on their faces. Maggie deliberately took her time, shaking out her raincoat and umbrella and smoothing out her 'new' jacket before she sat down at her desk.

'Well?' they chorused, unable to wait a moment longer.

'Well, what?' she teased, surprised at her own confidence.

'Well, what did you think?'

'Isn't it ghastly!'

'Bet you thought you'd never breathe again!'

'Yes to all of that.' She smiled at them. And then she could hold out no longer. 'But Bleak House is probably worth a fortune.'

The grins disappeared immediately. 'Whaaaaat?'

'It's sitting on a goldmine.'

They looked puzzled.

'We're not talking Klondyke or anything like that. But there's a builder who's just this week started buying up all the land around it. He's hoping eventually to build a massive estate – part of that government low cost affordable housing scheme. Bleak House is sitting right in the middle of it. So it's prime building land. The owners could name their price as long as they bide their time a little longer.'

Silence, and then 'Phew, brilliant, well done' echoed round the office. Damien was the first to come to his senses. Straight into his too-smooth-to-move routine, he flicked his wrist at Vanessa as if summoning a waitress in some top Italian restaurant and called for champagne.

Out came a tray of long-stemmed glasses, the cork popped from a bottle of Moët, and soon they were toasting Maggie's success.

Maggie was still in a state of shock herself. It had been a shot in the dark, ringing Pam at the council offices. The best she'd been hoping for was that Pam might know of a new leisure centre opening up in the area, or some other amenity that would make the prospect of renovating the house a bit more attractive to a prospective buyer. Or the off chance that some road scheme in the future might mean the dreadful place could be demolished and the old man's ghost finally laid to rest. When Pam had rung her back, triumphant with the tip-off from her boss, Maggie could hardly believe her ears.

'The only pity,' Maggie remarked, after she'd enjoyed the first sip of bubbly, 'is that the son and daughter are so vile. They don't deserve it, frankly. Left that poor old man to die completely alone, and now they're poised to mop up big time on the house sale. Seems unfair.'

This concept was clearly alien territory to Damien, who only dealt in property, not feelings. As far as he was concerned, this was another big tick for Home Truths. Emotions didn't come into it. He downed the rest of his champagne, gave Maggie another approving nod, mouthed the word 'bonus' to her and then roared off down the street in his silver Porsche.

'You've lost weight,' exclaimed Pam, the minute she came through the door. She brushed airily past a glowering Garth to give Maggie a congratulatory hug in the kitchen.

'I'm off to the pub,' Garth grunted, not bothering to disguise his dislike of Pam. He was beginning to blame Maggie's new attitude problem on Pam as well as on that stupid estate agency ethic.

'You look fantastic, Maggs,' Pam continued, ignoring him. 'Those clothes are hanging off you. We may have to go back and buy you some more.'

Maggie looked horrified for a second. She and Garth had just had a row about the amount of money he was spending in the pub. 'I'll make some coffee,' she announced, deliberately changing the subject. 'I think I've probably shed a few pounds because I'm out and about a bit now instead of stuck behind a desk all day.'

'Well, hold the coffee,' said Pam, 'because we're celebrating with champagne.' She suddenly brandished a bottle which she'd dug out of her huge leather shoulder bag. 'Can't let a little coup like you pulled off today go uncelebrated.' She tore off the foil and started untwisting the wire that secured the cork.

'I still can't quite believe this is all happening,' said Maggie, after they'd clinked glasses and sat down at the kitchen table. She didn't have the heart to say she'd already had champagne at the office. 'One minute I'm being made redundant from the most boring job in the world. Next I accidentally land another job because they mistakenly think I'm really feisty. Then suddenly I'm promoted for no reason at all, and today I'm being given a bonus. When am I going to wake up?'

'You *have* woken up,' said Pam wisely. 'That's exactly what you've done. You've rediscovered yourself. You're no longer the putdown you used to be. Look at you: lost weight, great outfit, much more confidence, holding your head up high. Bet old Garth Vader is finding things a bit tougher around here. He's had his power rug whipped from under his feet.'

'Well, I wouldn't go that far,' Maggie temporised, 'but he's not liking it. I still don't quite know what's happened. By a series of complete flukes, I seem to be successful at something. Just hope I don't let it slip through my fingers.'

'You won't,' Pam replied, as she refilled their glasses. 'It's not as though you haven't been there before. You've forgotten how gutsy you were at school. Do you remember how you got us all to blow into the back row Bunsen burners in the physics lab? And it made the front row go bang?'

Maggie shook her head. It didn't sound like her at all.

'Or when we went on that school trip to London and we chucked our boaters in the Thames because we hated them so much?'

'Oh, yes.' Maggie smiled. 'I do remember that. Along with the rollicking I got at home. I got grounded for a week so I had to sneak out of the back door when Mum and Dad were watching *Coronation Street* . . .' She stopped hurriedly. The memory suddenly became painful.

'. . . to meet Jack for a snog down the back lane,' Pam finished for her. 'You brought it up this time, not me. Don't you ever wonder what he's doing, where he lives, what happened that night?'

Maggie took a gulp of champagne in a vain attempt to erase the memory. She didn't like talking about him but tonight she couldn't stop herself. Probably the effect of the earlier champagne at the office as well.

'I don't think a day goes by when I don't think about him in some way or other,' she said sadly, twisting her glass and gazing at the tiny bubbles. 'It's usually triggered by a piece of music or a film or some guy in the street who vaguely walks like him. Jack's basically blighted my life. I wish I could hate him but I don't. I'm probably still in love with him. But I'm only in love with a memory. I'm not in love with the Jack who just disappeared off the face of the earth. He can go to hell, as far as I'm concerned.'

Chapter 15

Maggie didn't see much of Pam for the next fortnight. Tom was home from sea for a very short spell of leave and they'd planned a trip up to see Mark at university. Maggie deliberately left her friend in peace, knowing her time with Tom was very precious. She couldn't help feeling a twinge of jealousy at their obvious closeness and how excited Pam was at the thought of having him home. She also allowed herself a moment of self-pity for not having any other real friends apart from Pam. Work colleagues weren't the same.

Despite the promising start at Home Truths, and the lucky coup regarding Bleak House, Maggie knew she had an awful lot to learn. It was easy to write ghastly things about horrible houses and over-the-top descriptions of the posh end of the market, but the vast majority of properties fell in between the two. They were basically just boring. That, then, was the challenge: injecting some life into the tedious mass in the middle. And of course she was still on trial.

It had also dawned on Maggie how out of touch with life she'd become over the years. Stuck behind a wobbly desk at Farleys dealing with fuddy duddies like Mrs

Danvers and then going home to Garth's moans and groans, she hadn't exactly been surrounded by an intellectual feeding ground. Nor did she have any social life to speak of that might have helped to bridge the gap. Surrounded by sophisticates like Vanessa, Damien, Stefan, and even Fiona – who despite her 'about to go clubbing' wardrobe clearly had an excellent brain on her St Tropez tanned shoulders – Maggie felt intellectually embarrassed, and desperately untrendy. She'd not read the latest books, and didn't know what was in the charts. She couldn't remember the last time she'd been to the cinema, but was pretty sure it was to see *Four Weddings And A Funeral*. At least she'd sorted out the clothes problem, thanks to Pam. And she'd been back to Sue's shop on her own, surprised at her own confidence. Sue had helped her get another couple of outfits together, funded recklessly by the anticipation of her bonus.

One evening at home, when the kids had finally gone to bed and Garth's snoring could be heard virtually bouncing off the bedroom walls, she'd sat in the kitchen with a large cup of coffee and come to some decisions.

The job, she decided, was the best thing that had happened to her in years. She was desperate not only to keep it, but to make a real success of it. She couldn't rely on fluky bits of luck for ever. If that meant boning up on other people's lives and lifestyles, then that's what she needed to do. She'd make more effort to find out what was going on in the world.

Radio 4 in the car going to work. That would be a start. Buying the novel that everyone was currently raving about. Quizzing the kids on what was in the charts – or even, God forbid, joining them in front of *Top of the Pops* or MTV once in a while. Making sure she read a proper newspaper every day and perhaps a couple of extra ones at weekends.

Then she could start contributing to those conversations at Home Truths that she so often felt left out of. Her current ploy was to leap up and make the coffee when a discussion started up about whether that government minister should have stormed out of *Newsnight* last night, why Daniel Day Lewis doesn't make more films or whether *The Life of Pi* should have won the Booker.

Unlike the staff at Farleys, where the level of discussion resembled that of a glorified coffee morning and was largely lifted from the pages of *Chat* magazine, Vanessa, Fiona, Damien and Stefan would happily debate the state of the FTSE, endowment mis-selling, stock market trends, bulls and bears until the cows came home. Then they'd move on effortlessly to talk of Tuscany, the new Bordeaux which promised to be a good investment, and the Sir Terry Frost retrospective at the Tate.

Maggie knew she needed to talk the talk if she were going to survive long term.

Next day she put the plan into action. Bye-bye Terry Wogan on Radio 2, hello Radio 4's *Today* programme. By the time she'd got to work she'd had to admit she'd very much enjoyed John Humphrys's sparring with the home secretary on the new measures concerning community policing.

At lunchtime, she went out and bought a copy of the *Daily Mail*, *Marie Claire* magazine and the latest Patricia Cornwell thriller. Then she picked up a caesar salad baguette and a strawberry smoothie and headed back to the office, smiling at herself for feeling suddenly quite trendy. She'd decided to begin her self-indoctrination programme during her lunchtimes.

Peer approval began almost immediately. Vanessa nodded knowingly as she caught sight of the Patricia Cornwell. 'It's brilliant,' she muttered as she sashayed past. 'Try her book about Jack the Ripper next. Controversial, but simply unputdownable.'

Over the baguette, Maggie managed to read most of the *Daily Mail*, including the Money Mail pages. To her relief, not only did she understand them, but she'd read enough to grasp the scandal of endowment mis-selling through the case studies that were outlined. Shortfall on mortgages was now thought to be affecting millions of people, some of whom were inevitably walking through the doors of Home Truths. No wonder Stefan avoided using the word 'mortgage' when advising clients. Or, rather, pushing them into borrowing more than they had intended to clinch the deal on that dream house. It was all beginning to click into place. Maggie felt an overwhelming shame at not realising all this before.

She was just putting the paper away and getting back to her desk for the afternoon onslaught when the front door opened and then, caught by the wind, banged loudly shut. The middle-aged man who'd just come in stuttered an apology and sat down in front of her desk. Tall, thin and balding, with pale, pockmarked skin. he must have terrible eyesight because he'd managed to pick the most unflattering glasses on the planet. They had heavy black rims that did nothing for him. He gave her a nervous smile as he fiddled with his raincoat, which had got soaked in squally showers.

There was something about him that looked familiar. Maggie couldn't work out what it was: not the hair (or lack of it), not the skin, not even the ghastly glasses. No, it was his teeth: rather crooked, as if there were too many for his mouth. Probably some bit part actor off the telly, hiding behind the glasses, she concluded.

The man started to mention a house advertised in the window. It was one of Fiona's properties in a quiet part of Weltham, 'a minuscule terrace with a dark leafy garden so private it would suit overweight naturists'.

The man pointedly made no reference to anyone's getting their kit off. 'Would they take a lower offer?' he stuttered.

'Yes, I think they would,' Maggie replied confidently. She knew from the file that there had already been more than twenty viewings without a glimpse of a wad. 'Have you viewed it, Mr er . . .'

'Chapple.' That rang a bell. Maggie started scanning his face for clues. 'No, not yet. Don't need to, really. My parents lived there years ago.'

Another clue, and another bell rang. Who the hell was he?

'Well, it might have changed a bit inside,' she tried helpfully. No wedding ring, she noted, so perhaps no wife to consult. Clearly no one had accompanied him to the optician's. Maybe no friends either.

'That doesn't matter. I'd like to make an offer,' he replied firmly.

Maggie got out a form to start taking a few details. 'So, Mr Chapple, your first name please?'

'Freddie. And Chapple spelt C-H-A-P-P-L-E.'

Then it dawned on her. Freddie Chapple, the class swot. The one with the Harry Potter glasses and the conversational skills of a hermit. Top in all the science subjects and bottom in chat-up.

'Good God,' she exclaimed, 'we were at school together. I'm Maggie – I was Maggie Berry when we were at Weltham Grammar. Remember?'

Freddie looked confused for a few seconds. Then he gave Maggie a piercing look. Oh, shit, she thought, I've become so fat and frumpy, even old Freddie 'No Mates' Chapple doesn't recognise me.

'Gosh, er, what a surprise,' he replied at last. 'Well, I never expected to bump into you.'

Maggie found herself laughing nervously. Thank God, Vanessa had gone off to a management meeting this afternoon and wasn't witnessing this painful scenario.

'Well, Weltham *is* our home town, after all,' she said, 'although it's surprising how few people I bump into. I only really keep in touch with Pam these days. Do you remember Pam – Pam Gibson? She's married now. He's in the Navy and they have a son who's just gone to university.'

Somehow Pam's life was much more fascinating to recount than her own, she thought to herself bitterly. Me? I'm married to a pig called Garth and we have two currently stroppy, adolescent children. He runs an unsuccessful gardening business and I may look like I'm doing OK, but, believe me, it's all a fluke. I've also gone to seed, but thankfully most of it is hidden beneath this desk.

'And you?' Freddie enquired politely, peering through his horrendous specs. 'I guess you and Jack must have kids too.'

Maggie felt the colour drain from her face.

'Jack?' she managed, wondering how to get out of this conversation as fast as possible.

'Oh, I'm so sorry if I got that wrong,' said Freddie, immediately apologetic. His face turned bright red with embarrassment, which didn't do wonders for all the pockmarks. Maggie remembered what terrible acne he'd had at school. 'I've always had a habit of putting my foot in it, haven't I?' he continued apologetically. 'Even when we were at school, I always managed to say the wrong thing. Sorry, I thought you and Jack Haley ended up together. I was certain of it.'

'No. I married a chap called Garth. Nothing to do with school. We've got two kids, Beth and George.' She paused, hoping they could move on to the offer on the house. But Freddie's conversational skills clearly hadn't improved with age.

'Sorry I got that so wrong. I thought . . . I think we all thought when you and Jack went off to London together, that was it. Then I heard he was in America and I just assumed you were, too.'

'America?' She heard her voice wobble. 'Jack went to America?' Her throat was suddenly dry.

'Yes. Don't know much more than that. Became some sort of computer whizz kid, I think.'

Maggie couldn't stop herself. 'He did computer studies at university. It was always his great love.' Much more than me, she managed not to say aloud.

'Gosh, and there I was thinking you two had gone off into the sunset.' Freddie, tactless as ever, just couldn't leave it alone.

Fortunately that last remark did the trick. The tears that Maggie could feel starting to form dried immediately. 'No, only him. He went off into the sunset and off the edge of the planet for all I know,' she announced crossly. 'Now, let's get on with this house.'

They began filling in the form and Jack wasn't mentioned again.

Maggie could hear Garth harrumphing in the hallway. He'd only been up ten minutes and he was already in a rage over something. Maggie turned away from the toast she was buttering to watch him coming into the kitchen angrily waving a newspaper.

'What is this country coming to?' he yelled unnecessarily. 'Even the bloody paper boy can't get it right.'

He plonked himself down at the kitchen table so heavily that all the cups bounced in their saucers. 'I've had the *Star* delivered for the past ten years but today what do I get? The bloody *Daily Mail*. I don't want all that female stuff and political crap. I want my football and my—'

'Daily tits? Daily bit of sleaze?' Maggie queried. She couldn't stop herself and immediately regretted it.

'You and your flippin' attitude,' he snapped back at her. 'You've changed since you started that stupid job. And not for the better.'

He shot her a threatening look. She hoped it didn't mean another rough sex session that night. She'd been trying very hard to blot out the last unpleasant experience by pretending it hadn't happened to her. That she'd somehow seen it in a film.

'It's partly my fault,' she replied, trying to keep her voice firm. 'I went into the newsagent's yesterday to order a delivery of the *Mail* every morning and I think they must have got mixed up and cancelled your *Star*.'

Garth looked as if he were about to implode. 'What the fuck do you want with a right-wing piece of rubbish like that? Why do you need to read a bloody newspaper anyway?'

Something snapped inside Maggie. 'Actually,' she retorted, surprised at her own anger, 'I realise I have been stagnating all these years. My new job – which you'd better not knock because it's putting the food on this table – has made me realise how out of touch I am with the world. It's about time I improved my mind. Get it back to how it was when I was at school. When I think back I was quite intelligent in those days. Now all I'm fit for, according to you, is buttering your bloody toast and ironing your shirts. I don't wish to live in the world of the *Daily Star*, thank you very much. I'd like to read the news from a paper of my choice. So today I will correct the error at the newspaper shop and we can then retreat to our different viewpoints.'

'Good idea,' Garth snarled at her. He flicked the plate with his toast across the table in her direction. Unfortunately it veered to one side and shot on to the floor, shattering into several large pieces.

Garth promptly got up and walked out.

That evening Garth wasn't home for dinner. A curt message on their answering machine when Maggie got home indicated he had other plans but he was clearly still in the same black mood. Maggie heaved a sigh of relief at the prospect of some peace, and threw herself into making the kids' favourite meal of gammon steaks with pineapple slices and piles of French fries. When the three of them sat down round the table, it struck Maggie how much more relaxed they were without their father sitting there like a smouldering volcano, liable to erupt at any minute.

'How's your job going, Mum?' Beth asked. 'Are they going to keep you on?'

Maggie felt a lump in her throat. Her daughter was being supportive.

'Hope so, darling,' she replied. 'I'm really enjoying it and the money's improved a bit already.'

She paused, waiting for Beth to do her 'let's go shopping and spend some of it' routine. But it never came.

'Must say you're looking very smart when you go off to work these days,' Beth continued. 'In fact, that black thing you had on today – wear that at the next parents' evening. It looked really groovy.' She smiled approvingly at Maggie. 'Oh, and you ought to get a briefcase,' she added. 'They're really cool at the moment. I want a job with a briefcase when I leave school.'

This was a slight barb at George. Beth was working harder and doing better at school than George, whose studies were a long way down his priority list. The fortunes of Southampton Football Club were much more important than irregular French verbs or the Abolition of Slavery Act.

Funny, Maggie reflected silently, George would normally have bitten back at his sister with some remark about briefcases not being for girlies. But he merely shrugged and carried on eating. She wondered just how much Garth's black moods affected all of them, not only her. The evening passed relatively peacefully. No arguments over the remote control, no rushing out of the kitchen to avoid the washing up. And both of them appeared to be up-to-date with their homework. Maggie felt quite blissful.

The kitchen clock ticked eleven. The kids were in their rooms, either asleep or, Maggie suspected, probably listening to their personal stereos under the duvets. No sign of Garth. She began to lock up the house and switch off the lights. Should she put the chain on the front door? No, that would only provoke another argument. She went upstairs, got herself ready for bed and snuggled down to begin the Patricia Cornwell. To her eternal shame, she couldn't remember the last time she'd read a book. But she was soon utterly gripped by Cornwell's world of police detection, forensics and pathology. One more chapter, she decided, and then she'd put the light out. She was so engrossed in Kay Scarpetta's latest case that she never heard the key turn in the lock.

Garth burst into the bedroom, giving her a terrible fright.

'I might have guessed you'd be up here, improving your stupid mind again,' he snarled, having caught sight of the book. His breath smelt very obviously of drink. 'I'm hungry. Get me something to eat.'

'Too late,' she replied firmly, having regained her composure. 'Kitchen's closed. You said you weren't coming home for dinner, so sorry, but I didn't leave anything out.'

To her relief, he stomped off downstairs. harrumphing as he went. Next thing, she heard faint sounds of yet another footie match on the television. As she finally drifted off to sleep, Maggie wondered why she didn't care where he'd been tonight or even whom he'd been with. So long as he left her in peace – in every sense of the word.

Chapter 16

With all her new-found knowledge, Maggie knew she had to make her mark as soon as possible. She'd made so much coffee to avoid the 'in crowd conversations' as she dubbed them that she was starting to have difficulty sleeping. She was also paranoid in case they thought she was some sort of caffeine head who needed a constant buzz to get her through life's long hangover.

Somehow Damien and Vanessa in particular seemed to lead rather glamorous lives that involved a great deal of eating out and staying in, but only if it involved dinner parties with smart London friends. There was a lot of talk of galleries, openings, previews and first night parties, and foodie chat which clearly didn't include the gammon steak, tinned pineapple and chips world that Maggie inhabited. Designer nosh was another area that Maggie knew she needed to bone up on.

She'd nearly put her foot in it one day by mentioning Thorntons when the chat had turned to truffles. She'd been able to laugh it off when it dawned on her that the discussion was about a company in Somerset who were apparently training dogs to dig them up as opposed to pigs. That had been a near miss. She'd have to be careful in future, or she could blow the whole thing.

Fortunately Vanessa inadvertently came to her rescue thanks to Patricia Cornwell, asking if she could borrow the book 'the nanosecond' Maggie had finished it. Maggie was able to enthuse about it genuinely, and seized the opportunity to give everyone a detailed insight into the plot. Afterwards, she remembered with a wry smile that the last crime novel she'd read had been in her teens, *A Murder is Announced* by Agatha Christie. That wouldn't have been greeted so enthusiastically by the Home Truths literati.

The world of stocks and shares was still proving a bit of a mystery, although Maggie was forcing herself to read Money Mail every week. Then she came up with a solution by pinching an idea from Stefan, who was forever checking his shares. She randomly chose a couple of companies from the FTSE, bookmarked them on her computer and occasionally flicked to see how they were getting on. Again Vanessa came to the rescue by endorsing her choice of an obscure oil company when they soared 23p one morning. Maggie didn't have a clue why but she beamed knowingly.

Meanwhile, the initial furore about Home Truths' rather brutal and controversial approach to flogging houses had begun to die down. Now that media interest had dwindled and the house-buying public had become used to a different way of doing it, things had steadied, although Maggie was still constantly amazed by just how many properties they were shifting compared to the bad old days of Farleys. She'd had one or two successes herself, taking a middle-aged couple to see 'the house with the unrivalled view of the stars, so rundown and roofless you can watch the Sky At Night without benefit of a telly'. Everyone thought it wildly overpriced for what was effectively a ruin. It had been on the market for over a year with a string of previous agents. But somehow it appealed to Maggie's couple, who told her they'd renovated several properties in the past. When she told them their offer of ten grand less than the asking price had been accepted, they hugged and kissed like teenagers on heat. Maggie felt a pang, watching them. They were clearly still very much in love, and obviously excited at their purchase. She couldn't remember feeling remotely like that with Garth around.

There was another subject looming that Maggie knew all the reading in the world couldn't cover up. Holidays. Vanessa was talking shopping in New York, Stefan appeared to be planning a golfing holiday in Portugal. For Damien, it would be a five-star somewhere or other. Even Fiona was muttering about Thailand or Sri Lanka early next year. She'd have to come up with some sort of answer as discussions were starting about booking leave.

'Don't worry about me. I tend to go last minute,' had been her initial response. She could always mention the kids' exams at some stage. That would bat it on a little further through the year. But at some point she'd have to come up with a lie, or a very good excuse. In the short term, the internet might come to her rescue again. She tapped in the names of some holiday companies. First up came 'Our lowest ever deal to the States – New York from £99'.

Her stomach lurched. Jack had gone to the States. She'd never known that until Freddie Chapple had come out with it. Perhaps he'd gone out on a 'lowest ever deal'. No wonder she'd never bumped into him. It was as if he'd disappeared off the planet. All the years she'd wasted subconsciously searching for his face, his distinctive walk, his firm shoulders, the mop of curly brown hair. The few times she'd returned to London she always scanned the crowds just in case. She'd been convinced that he still lived there somewhere, carving out a career in computers. Then there was the faint hope/fear that she'd bump into him in Weltham. But Jack had less reason than most people to come back to his home town. His parents had moved to Spain within weeks of his going off to college, and as far as she knew they were still there. What would there be to bring him back, other than to look up a few old mates and a gone-to-seed ex-girlfriend whom he'd dumped anyway? She gazed at all the flight destinations: Texas, Minnesota, Boston, Los Angeles, San Francisco. She wondered where, and when and why he'd gone. Without a word.

The slam of the front door said it all. Garth was in another of his black moods. He'd just lost two regular customers, he spluttered angrily, an old lady who'd gone into residential care and a couple who'd got one speeding ticket too many and decided it was time to move to France. He flung down a file on the kitchen table.

'I've got two grand more tax to pay than I thought,' he announced, grim-faced. 'That on top of the figures being twenty-five per cent down this year.'

Maggie felt a telltale gnawing in the pit of her stomach. She always worried about money. She'd often wondered if she'd lived a life of abject poverty in a previous life and starved to death. The thought of falling into the spiralling pit of debt and despair always got to her.

'Well at least my money's a bit better,' she tried to

console him. And herself. 'I'm over a hundred quid a month better off since I left Farleys.'

'Not when you're spending it all on improving books,' he spat back. 'I should be investing in some new kit at this time of year. A couple of rotary mowers and a new chain saw at least. The van's gone round the clock now so I should be trading that in. And the bloody income tax is due at the end of January.'

Maggie gasped in horror. Her extra hundred quid a month wouldn't meet that kind of outlay. She mentally cancelled Christmas. She'd planned to start putting up the decorations this weekend but the sight of tinsel would probably send Garth into virtual orbit.

She returned to stirring the cheese sauce for the lasagne, wondering what to say that might placate him. It clearly wasn't the night for arguing the case for improving her mind and therefore keeping her job. Then suddenly she had an idea. Would he bite her head off if she suggested it?

'I've been thinking—' she said.

'So I gather,' Garth snapped. 'These bloody books littered everywhere filling your head with unnecessary rubbish.' He went to the fridge for a beer, remembered he'd drunk the last one the previous night, and slammed the door shut again.

'Just let me make a suggestion,' she said, turning away to suppress a nervous half-laugh at his predicament. 'Your business needs a bit of marketing. Bit of a push.'

Garth swung back on his chair and shot her a mocking look.

'Yeah, right,' he snarled. 'I'll just ring up the local paper and take out lots of expensive advertising, get loads of clients and then get banged up in jail for not paying my tax bill. Or better still have no van left to get to them.'

'I'm not talking about spending heaps of money,' she said, trying to maintain a firm note in her voice. 'You just need to target your customers a bit. There must be loads of people round here who need some help with their garden but you're not reaching them. When did you last put out any leaflets? I can't remember.' She felt herself switching back into tougher Home Truths mode. She continued: 'Up to now, you've been relying on elderly people, but they're all dying off. You need new customers. And not only oldies, but people who want lovely gardens but are too busy to do them themselves. Think of all the people who tramp through Home Truths. Half of them have barely got time to inspect the properties, let alone do them up. I read a report last week,' she paused proudly, 'that said we're the hardest working nation in Europe. We work far longer hours and have fewer public holidays than any other country. So what does that mean? Less time to cut the grass and dig up the weeds. If you could target busy working people, you'd do much better. And they'd probably be prepared to pay more.'

Garth sat open-mouthed, not sure what to make of it. Maggie had never interfered in his business before. His mind raced. She was probably right, the silly cow, but he didn't want to admit it. Not just yet, anyway.

'So you tell me how I reach all these busy, filthy-loaded people without spending a fortune on advertising,' he said sarcastically.

'Well, I could ask at work if I could use their mailing list,' she replied. She stopped short. She hadn't meant to say that. She suddenly realised she'd never intended Garth to have any contact with her new colleagues, fearing it would be a collision course. She couldn't see

Garth, White Van Man with his *Daily Star*, mixing it with Silver Porsche Man. OK, it was selfish, but she could see it destroying the little bit of self-esteem she'd granted herself since she'd begun her brain update programme. What a ridiculous situation she'd just put herself in. On the one hand, using the Home Truths mailing list was possibly quite inspired, but on the other, putting Garth in the way of meeting Damien and co. would destroy her hard-earned credibility.

Garth solved the problem in his usual characteristic fashion.

'Wouldn't want to be associated with your arseholes and all that attitude stuff they shovel out,' he replied in a voice that implied 'subject closed'. He then rose to his feet and headed for the sitting room.

Maggie turned back to her lasagne. As she made up the layers of meat, sauce and pasta, she realised that she was rather relieved Garth hadn't taken up her suggestion. It was as though she were living a double life now. At work she was Maggie Fraser, sales negotiator in a new but fast-growing company. Finding her feet, expanding her horizons, broadening her mind. But at home she was Maggie Fraser, downtrodden wife and mother of two, providing constant supplies of clean clothes and plenty of chips. Garth, in his current bolshy frame of mind, would show her up.

She finally sprinkled the last of the parmesan cheese on top of the lasagne and popped it into the oven. Then she began clearing the kitchen table for supper. She picked up the file Garth had flung down, in order to lay out the plates. Annual accounts of Garth Fraser Gardening Services. She'd never bothered to look at them in the past but something compelled her to flick through the figures. Maggie'd never really read a balance sheet before and it took her a few minutes to work out what she was looking at. Incomings and outgoings all listed. The sums didn't make much sense to her, until two figures stood out. Entertainment and travel expenses were listed as more than five thousand pounds and Brenda's fee for doing the books was down as two grand. Maggie winced at the last one. Surely producing three pages of well-spaced figures didn't command that kind of fee? It wasn't as though Brenda was a city centre accountant with a posh office and postcode to maintain. She was merely a freelance book-keeper who worked from home. And an unqualified one at that. And that five grand figure. At first Maggie thought the travel meant running the van, until she noticed petrol, depreciation and servicing costs listed separately under motoring expenses.

Probably all just a tax dodge, she realised, suddenly feeling a bit naïve. If you don't claim it, then the tax man will grab it. Certainly Garth had not been lying when he said that there was no money this year to replace equipment and trade in the van. She shuddered at the horror of seeing it all in black and white. It served her right for taking a peek

Chapter 17

Christmas in the Fraser household was a muted affair. Owing to Garth's business crisis, Maggie'd thought it best to shelve her plans to chuck out all the old decorations and buy trendier ones. She'd resigned herself to dragging out the same tired old tinsel and silver balls, the artificial tree that was busily shedding its load of plastic needles, and the very threadbare Father Christmas that Beth had adored since she was a baby.

To avoid any possible confrontation with the now permanently stroppy Garth, she'd seized the opportunity to put up the decorations one evening when he'd announced he was going on to the pub after dropping Beth off at her end-of-term school disco. A reluctant George had been persuaded away from the television footie highlights to clamber up into the loft to bring down the familiar cardboard boxes. Then he and Maggie had set to work putting up the tree. George couldn't resist a dig at Beth's beloved Santa.

'Look how he's ageing,' he said sarcastically. 'His hair's falling out. He's not even fit for a charity shop.'

Poor old Santa's coat, once a resplendent red velvet, was rapidly losing its pile. Even his jolly plastic face now seemed to have a tinge of sadness as the flowing beard and moustache got thinner and thinner.

Mercifully the tree lights worked and soon the tree was up, lit and decorated in all its faded glory. They stood back to admire their handiwork. Still a magical moment, thought Maggie to herself, remembering how as a child she had longed for the day when the Christmas tree went up. It seemed such a blissful time, looking back, such soft focus excitement. No money worries, no responsibilities, no cares in the world, only the desperate hope that the lights would work and there'd be something Barbie-related in her Christmas stocking.

Duty done, George plonked himself down on a sofa to enjoy the widescreen highlights of the Southampton match once again. Maggie excused herself and returned to the kitchen to make a few mince pies and ice the cheat Christmas cake base she'd bought earlier that day. She'd done her food shopping very carefully in view of the ongoing financial crisis. Frozen turkey instead of fresh, the cheapest wine on offer and absolutely no nuts, chocolates or crackers. But she'd made herself buy her annual bottle of sherry to give the Christmas cake a bit of a kick, enliven a trifle or two and then be shoved at the back of the cupboard as usual. Only tonight she fancied a drink. Garth was down the pub enjoying himself, she thought, so why shouldn't she? She sat at the kitchen table, contemplating the golden liquid glinting in the small glass. Why was she suddenly overcome by a wave of depression? Perhaps it was the nostalgia of putting up the tree that had triggered it, together with the annual realisation that they were simply not a family who shared things in the same way that she had as a child. She felt a sudden guilt that she had failed to provide the safe, secure childhood for her own children that she had enjoyed.

Or, she told herself, perhaps she was feeling fed up at the thought of a week off work. Unlike the mean old Farley days, Home Truths had decided to shut up shop for the whole Christmas week with a bold proclamation in the window and on the website: 'Turkey and tinsel are not conducive to house buying, let alone viewing any of our more ridiculous properties. Come back in the New Year when we're all sober. Happy Christmas!' Even the no-frills turkey on the Home Truths logo was sporting a Santa hat and a scarf of red tinsel.

Naturally Damien, Vanessa, Stefan and Fiona thought shutting up for Christmas was a terrific idea. Maggie had nodded agreement along with the rest of them as they'd all raised a glass of champagne on the last afternoon. For them, a round of fun at endless glamorous parties. For her, a whole week of seasonal pressure, cooped up with Garth and the kids. And nowhere to escape with her newly rehabilitated brain.

Or perhaps her bout of the blues was the result of all the recent talk about Jack. His name seemed to have been coming at her from every direction. Each time she switched on the television, everyone seemed to be called Jack. Every movie starred Jack Nicholson or Jack Palance, every comedy show involved Jack Dee, every detective was played by Jack Shepherd. Even a neighbour who'd produced a baby last week promptly called him Jack. She emptied her glass and poured another without giving it a second thought.

No, it couldn't be the Jack problem, she told herself. After all, she'd managed to live without him quite happily for nearly twenty years. Well, not very happily actually, but she'd survived all right without him, thank you very much. They had a roof over their heads, food in the fridge and clothes on their backs. Everyone had all their arms, legs and faculties. Garth's business was ticking over. Well, no, actually it was collapsing fast by the look of that balance sheet. She was beginning to wish she hadn't looked at it. Oh, they'd manage somehow, she decided, taking a slug of sherry.

Her job was going pretty well. Except that she'd probably be rumbled before too long and then be thrown out on her ear. She could almost hear Vanessa giving her an appraisal at the end of her three-month trial.

'A very brave attempt,' she could almost hear Vanessa's rounded boarding school tones, 'but it's not quite hitting the spot, is it? You're just not quite focused enough for Home Truths. Sorry, Maggie, there's no easy way of saying this but we're going to have to let you go.'

Let you go, let you go, let you go . . . the words started ringing in her mind. Then she heard her own voice crying out in her head, 'No, I've let *myself* go. It's all my fault. I seem to have let everything go. My marriage is a disaster, the kids have been hell and it's my fault because I've just let them get away with it. Downtrodden old doormat, that's me. I've let things slip through my fingers. Even Jack got away . . . oh, damn and blast. Must delete that name from my brain. I'm just a stupid old woman who's just bloody tired because it's the end of yet another rotten, rotten year.'

She downed the rest of the sherry in one gulp. The accompanying shiver brought her to her senses. She looked up at the clock. Just nudging midnight. Clearly the pub was having a lock-in. She put the sherry bottle away in its usual spot at the back of the cupboard and headed upstairs to bed, hoping to be fast asleep before Garth came back. Praying he'd just leave her alone.

It was as if Maggie and Garth had made some imaginary Christmas truce. They managed to avoid any confrontation by simply adjusting their time clocks. If Maggie got up early, Garth lingered in bed. If Maggie mentioned she'd like to watch something on the TV that evening, Garth immediately remembered he'd arranged to meet so-and-so in the pub. And when she was in the kitchen cooking, he slumped in front of the TV. Yet there was an unspoken undercurrent to all this, like a time bomb trying to tick away on a rather flat battery.

Desperate to avoid an explosion over the actual holiday, Maggie drilled Beth and George on Christmas Eve, during yet another of Garth's pub outings, about behaving themselves over the long weekend. She also took the opportunity to knock some guilt into them about the financial situation. 'Don't moan about the lack of this and that,' she said firmly. 'There hasn't been the money for all the usual bits and pieces. Just be thankful you've got presents to open tomorrow morning. And for chrissake, don't give your father any grief. I don't think I can take very much more of his moods.'

That last bit caused tears to well up. Beth had been poised to come back with some suitably caustic reply when she spotted her mother's eyes a-glitter. She stopped herself and bit her lip instead. It clearly hit home with George too. He half gasped when he heard his mother talking in such terms and then stared resolutely at the table instead.

'How come Dad goes down the pub all the time if

we're short of money?' he finally asked quietly, eyes still downcast.

'Blokes' world,' Beth answered for her mother. 'It's that "don't do as I do, do as I say" thing that men trot out.'

'And what would you know, Miss Clever Clogs?' George replied, rising to the bait.

'What I know is that it's unfair on Mum,' said Beth, spotting a niche in the market and getting up to fling her arms round Maggie. 'She works hard all day and then comes home and works hard doing all the cooking and cleaning. But Dad just farts around doing a bit of mowing and then slopes off down the pub. Doesn't seem much of a deal to me. I won't be putting up with that when I get married.'

'Who says anyone would marry you?' George snapped. 'Not in that disgusting top you've got on. It should be taken away and shot.'

Clearly Beth's new pink swirly shirt from her Warehouse spree wasn't doing it for George.

'Hark at the fashion police,' she hit back, her voice rising with anger. 'Who'd put up with you and your disgusting habits? She'd have to be a complete moron to put up with wall-to-wall footie all the time. Or your collection of empty pizza boxes in that shit hole you call a bedroom.'

'Your room's worse than mine. I've seen all those minging plates and coffee cups everywhere and all your stupid clothes chucked around. Also it stinks. Like you. Did you know that? And one day you'll end up—'

'Trapped in some skanky house with a horrible bloke?' Beth finished for him. 'Not likely. I've seen what it's like for Mum, and—'

She stopped short. There was a hideous pause. Beth

realised she'd overshot the mark. Maggie silently got up from the table and left the room. She didn't want them to witness her tears, the tears of failure. This was her contribution to society – being a terrible parent to two unhappy children.

She went out into the hallway and caught sight of herself in the hall mirror. She glanced at her reflection and saw a complete stranger with a wild, forsaken look in her eyes, and a mop of untamed mousy brown hair with grey streaks starting to show through. Just for a split second, she saw a snapshot of herself as an old woman, lined and jowly, probably stooped and bearing a bleak expression of total hopelessness. Probably in pain, incontinent, completely gaga and stuck in some old folks' home being spoonfed tripe and onions for tea.

She climbed the stairs, her legs suddenly leaden with sheer fatigue. She didn't have nearly enough energy to wash her face or clean her teeth. Instead, she headed straight for bed, collapsing fully clothed on top of the duvet. Her head sank gratefully into the pillows. But instead of releasing the tears she so desperately needed to shed, she fell into a deep sleep. Too tired to cry, too tired for anything.

Half an hour later, Beth crept upstairs to see if her mum was OK. She was shocked to see Maggie still fully dressed and sound asleep on top of the covers. She went back down to talk to her brother. Another muted argument started up about whether to ring their father and tell him to come home.

George was of the opinion that his dad would simply get stroppy if disturbed and they'd had quite enough of that lately. But Beth took a different view.

‘Supposing there’s something wrong with Mum,’ she pleaded with him. ‘We’d never forgive ourselves.’

‘You’re hardly likely to get a doctor out on Christmas Eve,’ George observed. ‘No, she’s just tired. Just leave it. Anyway, it’s your fault. You shouldn’t have said that about Dad.’

Beth fell silent. For once, she knew her brother was right. But her conscience was weighing heavily. She went into the kitchen and dialled her dad’s mobile. ‘The Vodafone you are calling may be switched off,’ intoned the familiar female voice. ‘Please try later.’

She replaced the phone.

‘It’s Christmas Eve,’ she told no one in particular. ‘My Mum’s ill and upset, worried about money. And where’s my dad? Pissing it up the wall at the pub. Thank you very much, God.’

She rummaged around for the Yellow Pages that Maggie always kept in the kitchen, flicked through the pages until she got to the Public Houses section, and feverishly scanned down to the number for the Doghouse. Very apt, she thought. Best place for him. She dialled the number. It rang for ages and ages. Eventually a man’s voice answered, shouting to compete with the revellers in the background.

‘Garth?’ he queried when Beth explained what she wanted. ‘Garth Fraser? I’ll have a shout around, love, but we’re packed to the ceiling here, as you can probably hear.’

Behind him, choruses of ‘’ere we go, ’ere we go, ’ere we go’ were breaking out, competing with others joining in with ‘Do They Know It’s Christmas?’ being blasted out of the speakers. She could almost imagine the crowds packed in tight, swaying to the music as pints were passed – and spilled – over their heads. The wait seemed unending.

Eventually there was a rustling as he grappled with the phone. 'Still there, love?' he shouted over the din.

'Yes,' replied Beth anxiously. 'Is he there? Can you ask him to phone home?'

But his answer wasn't quite the one she was expecting.

'Sorry, love, no one's seen him for months. I've had a good look round, but he's definitely not in tonight. Merry Christmas! War is over! Ha ha!'

Not in their house, she thought to herself. No one's seen him for months? Didn't her father always make barbed jokes about being in the doghouse every time he went to the pub? Perhaps he'd changed his allegiance but still made the same joke. Beth tried to argue the case for her father, but she couldn't come up with any good excuses. She'd read too many problem pages in her magazines. When boys lied, they were usually up to something, and it was rarely anything good. Her dad was up to some sort of mischief but she wasn't about to tell her mum. Not in the state she was in.

Christmas Day passed relatively peacefully. The frozen turkey actually tasted pretty good and the homemade crackers that Beth and Maggie had put together one night out of kitchen paper cylinders, complete with tissue paper hats and handwritten jokes, went down well. Garth was quite subdued, probably from a colossal hangover, Maggie guessed. That suited her down to the ground. It cut down the sarcasm quota.

She'd slept a full twelve hours the previous night and felt much better for it. She was determined to get through the day without incident. Beth, who was on a massive guilt trip about her previous night's outburst, danced attendance on her. She was so relieved to see that her mum was OK that she did two solid hours of washing up without a murmur. After lunch, Garth retreated as usual to the sitting room where he proceeded to drop off to sleep and snore for Britain. George kept telling him to shut up as his snorting was interfering with Sky Sports' Christmas offerings. But at least with the remote control to himself he could do his favourite thing, which was to channel hop between Sky Sports 1, 2 and 3.

Eventually, all the dishes put away and the oven scrubbed down, Beth dismissed herself and went off upstairs to her room. Probably to ring all her friends for a gossip, Maggie thought enviously. She glanced at the kitchen calendar. Only a few more days and Pam would be back in circulation when Tom went off to his next posting. She really missed Pam's constant cheerfulness and ability to coax a laugh out of a crisis.

She tiptoed into the sitting room to see both Garth and George slumped on the sofas, sound asleep. The prized remote control had slipped from George's grasp and was lying on the carpet. She picked it up. Maybe she'd watch some television quietly. The luxury of being able to see something of her choice was too tempting to resist. As she scrolled down all the programmes, she thought back to the presents she'd been given. A couple of novels from Beth that she'd dropped hints about and a pair of gloves from George that she'd had to buy herself and give him to wrap up. The usual Opium perfume from Garth. She'd long since tired of it, but would never have dreamt of saying so, just in case it provoked yet another row. She and Pam had often joked about its being useful to have some in the house, just in case he needed doping down.

She went to the movie listings and started to scroll through them. All the usual Christmas offerings: *The Sound of Music*, *The Great Escape*, The *Wizard of Oz*. She'd seen them all countless times. She flicked on to *The Wizard of Oz* just in time to catch her favourite bit with the tornado, where the film transforms from black and white to colour and Dorothy realises she's no longer in Kansas. Maggie sat back to enjoy the magic once again, making sure the sound was low enough not to wake George or Garth. Judy Garland was soon dancing her way down the Yellow Brick Road in her red spangly shoes. Maggie remembered how, as a child, she had desperately wanted a pair just like them. They had seemed the height of sophistication. And then the magic came abruptly to an end.

'Oh no,' she uttered aloud and immediately clapped a hand over her mouth. The Tin Man – played by Jack Haley. How could she have forgotten? In her mind, she was back in Jack's tiny first floor student flat in Chiswick where they had spent so many evenings laughing at his namesake playing the Tin Man. She remembered how they used to buy popcorn from the newspaper shop below and watch old films on the telly because they couldn't afford to go to the cinema. How she used to wave the tin opener and threaten to open up his tin head and pull out his brain every time he forgot to shut the fridge door. How they'd laugh and laugh and how he'd tickle her in bed despite her protests. Then, after making love and more tickling, he'd fall into a deep sleep and she'd be left wide awake, stomach still in knots from laughing.

She hit the menu button and deliberately picked another channel, any old channel, anything to get away from thoughts of Jack Haley. An old repeat of *Property Ladder*. That would do. Might be useful for her job. She was soon watching Sarah Beeny remonstrating with a young couple who'd gone way over budget renovating a wreck of a cottage in deepest Devon. Thatch coming off in tufts, green mould creeping up the once whitewashed walls, no kitchen to speak of, and a bathroom so disgusting that it should have probably been shown after the 9 p.m. watershed on the basis that it would frighten the children, not to mention the horses. Lots of potential, though, once they'd cured the structural problems. The husband mentioned 'lowering the ceiling to get rid of those nasty beams' and 'installing recessed halogen lighting and painting the walls pink'. Maggie thought Sarah Beeny would implode at the idea. Then she watched her nudge him gently back to the idea that, having bought a traditional Devon longhouse, they should restore it as one, or they'd have wasted their money. This was all good learning curve stuff for Maggie. She felt a brief ripple of confidence go through her as she thought about her new job. How much she had achieved in such a short time, after all the years of steady decline at Farleys.

As the ad break came up, she glanced around at the sleeping bodies on either side of her. Much as she loved her kids, and oh how hard they were to love at times, she couldn't wait to escape back to work. As for Garth, she just felt dead inside, and almost hoped he felt the same about her. At least it would be mutual and guilt-free. The new-found feeling of being fulfilled and appreciated wasn't on offer at home, and never had been, as far as she could remember. Roll on New Year.

Since it was Christmas, all the commercial slots had

been taken up by holiday companies. Let's Go Travel were boasting their best offers yet, with prices slashed on Caribbean cruises, European short breaks and . . . flights to all the major cities in America. 'With the pound so strong against the dollar, there's never been a better time to make this the year of your American Dream.'

Maggie picked up the remote control and flicked away as fast as she could. Then she got up, padded out to the kitchen so as not to disturb the sleeping ranks, and headed for the sherry bottle. There seemed to be no escape from Jack bloody Haley.

Chapter 18

Beth couldn't contain her curiosity for very long. Over Boxing Day supper of cold turkey and ham and jacket potatoes, she spotted her opening.

Garth was busy opening a bottle of wine and struggling with the corkscrew.

'Hangover gone then, Dad?' she quizzed him.

Garth swore under his breath as the corkscrew slipped out of the cork and caught his finger. He shoved the finger in his mouth in an attempt to stem the flow of blood. 'What hangover?' he grumbled eventually.

'From the pub on Christmas Eve. You didn't touch a drop yesterday. Is this the hair of the dog?'

Maggie shot Beth a warning glance before firmly averting her gaze. This kind of baiting was the last thing she needed tonight. They'd managed to get this far through Christmas without a scene. Don't start one now, Beth, for chrissake. Just don't.

'You're far too young to know anything about the hair of the dog.' Garth appeared to be trying to keep his temper under control. 'OK, I had a bit too much on Christmas Eve, but that's my problem, not yours. And I have every right to go to the pub if I so choose.'

To Maggie's huge relief, Beth changed tack slightly. 'Of course. Sorry, Dad.' She smiled. 'I'm looking forward to going to the pub when I'm older. Bacardi Breezer, that's a nice drink. I had a sip of one at the school disco last week. One of the girls smuggled some in. Do they serve that in the . . . er . . . which pub is it you go to?'

Garth shot her a puzzled look. This was an unusual conversation coming from Beth. Her usual subject areas of choice were boy bands, lack of pocket money and how there was this lovely pair of hipsters in Mango which she really couldn't live without.

'The Doghouse, of course.' He inspected his finger to make sure the bleeding had stopped.

'That's a bit of a dump, isn't it?' Beth queried. 'Looks a bit scruffy on the outside. My mate Mo told me her parents have started going to that new Wetherspoons. They said it's been done up beautifully, with lots of shelves full of old books. And they do a cheap curry night on Thursdays.'

'Since when have you become an expert on local pubs?' George cut in, seizing an opportunity to rile his sister.

'I don't go to cheap curry night pubs,' said Garth scathingly. 'Or makeover themed pubs with shelves of pseudo old books. Not my scene at all. The Doghouse might be a bit of a spittoon but it's my local and I like it, thank you very much. Oh, and by the way, young lady, you shouldn't be drinking Bacardi Breezers at your age. And certainly not at school. Christ knows what we pay these teachers but you'd think they'd be on the case.'

Maggie sat in terrified anticipation, waiting for the inevitable eruption. But Beth had got her result and was now happy to defuse the situation as quickly as possible.

'Absolutely right, Dad.' She smiled at him. 'I think it's terribly wrong that there was booze at school. But the teachers can't search everyone. It's not fair to expect them to do that.' She deliberately took a mouthful of turkey. 'Mum, this is delicious. The best turkey we've ever had. In fact, I think it's the best Christmas I've ever had.'

She smiled benignly round the table. George rolled his eyes to the heavens as if to say, What a creep. To Maggie's relief, Garth took a slug of wine and got stuck into his meal. The subjects of alcopops, hangovers and the Doghouse weren't mentioned again.

The next couple of days passed in a whirl of endless cooking and television repeats. Because everyone was home all day, Maggie seemed to spend the entire time in the kitchen trying to make the turkey go as far as possible with cheap pasta and rice while the rest of them moaned about 'crap films on television'. She was just eking out the very last of the leg meat into a curry when the phone rang.

It was Pam, who'd just bid a tearful goodbye to both her husband and her son. Tom was going back to Gibraltar, while Mark was heading off to university early to prep up for a big exam. Maggie knew it was selfish to be pleased that Pam was back on the scene, but she couldn't stop herself breaking out into a smile. At last the sun was coming out from behind the clouds.

'So – how was Christmas?' Pam enquired.

'Jury's out,' said Maggie, checking that the kitchen door was closed before she continued the conversation. 'Well, we got through it and that's about all I can say. The kids have actually been very good, not much squabbling. And Garth gave himself a massive hangover as a result of

Christmas Eve which got us peacefully through Christmas Day.'

'You sound a bit defeated,' said Pam, ever observant. 'I can hear it in your voice.'

'Can't quite summon up the Home Truths attitude, if I'm honest,' Maggie conceded. 'I just want to get through the holiday without a row. Even if it means biting my tongue a few times. And I know what you're going to say—'

'That this isn't a long term strategy for a happy life,' Pam chipped in. 'OK, I'll let you off as it's Christmas. But come New Year, you've got to get back on that horse. Start laying down the law a bit, hon, otherwise you'll go under.'

Maggie didn't need a lecture just now, but she wasn't going to tell Pam that. She was just grateful to hear her voice.

'Anyway,' said Pam, changing tack. 'I've had the most marvellous piece of luck and it involves you. But I'm not going to tell you until I see you face to face. Otherwise you might find a way of wriggling out of it.'

Maggie groaned inwardly. This spelt trouble, she knew it. She still hadn't forgotten the seemingly endless ridicule from Garth about their day at Juicy Lucy's.

'Tell you what,' Pam continued cheerfully. 'Are you in tonight? Is old Garth Vader likely to be popping out to the next galaxy during the evening? Bet he will anyway, if he knows I'm pitching up. See you round eightish? OK?'

'Of course,' said Maggie weakly, realising how desperately she needed a decent adult conversation again. She was missing the banter at Home Truths and the challenge of keeping up with the culture chat. She wondered what Pam had in mind. She could guess from the preamble that it was going to be something controversial. Perhaps another day at Juicy Lucy's. Actually, she'd have jumped at that, now that she knew what it entailed and how marvellous she'd felt afterwards. No, clearly this was something more complicated. She just hoped it didn't involve money or give Garth another reason to turn himself into a weapon of mass destruction.

'Kenya? Are you kidding?' Maggie felt her blood run cold.

Pam's bombshell was that she'd won a holiday competition in a magazine. Two weeks in Kenya in a four-star beachside hotel, all meals included plus a couple of safari trips thrown in.

'And before you even mention stuff like drinks, we've each been given an allowance of two hundred pounds at the hotel for extras, like drinks, windsurfing lessons and so on,' Pam finished triumphantly. She'd even been to a travel agent to pick up a brochure showing pictures of the Paradise Palms Hotel on Diani Beach. It looked just like a scene from a Bounty bar advert. Ivory sand, coconut trees, turquoise sea. Paradise, in fact.

Maggie sat open-mouthed. She didn't know what to say. Her mind had gone a complete blank. Sensing this, Pam launched straight into a list of all the excuses she knew damn well Maggie would throw up.

'The kids will be at school, so that's not a problem.' She began ticking them off. 'You must be due for some paid leave from work now so that's not a problem. Garth will moan and groan but when he realises he can nip down the pub at will he won't see a problem. You can fill the freezer with ready meals so he can't moan about having to cook. You even mentioned everyone swanking on about travel at work so going to Kenya very neatly solves that little problem. They'll never know I won it in a competition. And Tom's away so he can't go. If you say you'll come, then that's *my* problem solved,' Pam finished triumphantly.

Typically, Pam had thought of just about everything.

'But I don't have anything to wear,' was Maggie's only contribution. 'I can't remember the last time I sat on a beach. I don't even possess a swimming costume any more.'

'Oh, we can soon sort that,' said Pam cheerily. 'Anyway, the clothes over there are dirt cheap so we can pick up a couple of cheap swimsuits and buy ourselves some nice sarongs when we get there.'

Maggie could feel a leaden lump forming in her chest. How on earth was she going to break this kind of news to Garth? It was all right for Pam to say he'd be pleased because he could go to the pub whenever he wanted. But Garth was bone idle. He expected full-on catering and cleaning services as of right and without question. She could just imagine the stack of two weeks' worth of plates and dishes when she got back. Garth never did anything around the house and she'd given up asking for help years ago because it only provoked another angry scene.

'I suppose I could get paper plates,' she said aloud by mistake.

Pam threw her head back and burst out laughing. 'The hotel's a four star so I think there's a good chance they'll provide china ones.'

'No,' said Maggie distractedly. 'Sorry, I meant here. It's just that . . .' She stopped, feeling embarrassed.

'Your lot don't believe in washing up,' said Pam,

realising what she meant. 'They still believe in Fairy Liquid, eh? Well, maybe it's time to blow the gaff on Father Christmas as well.'

Maggie nodded miserably. She was suddenly ashamed of just what a doormat she was. Pam was right. It was time they all had a taste of fending for themselves. Perhaps they'd appreciate her a little more. She'd never get an opportunity like this again.

'It would do me good,' she suddenly heard her own voice announce. 'I'll never have another chance like this. Yes, it will do me good.'

Pam clapped her hands in delight and produced a half-bottle of Moët from her handbag.

'Not chilled,' she apologised, giggling. 'Left over gift which I've been saving for this moment. I really must stop this bad habit of producing booze from my handbag every time I come round here.'

Maggie got up to fetch a couple of glasses. She noticed her hands were shaking as she took them out of the cupboard. She could feel her heart thump, thump, thumping in anticipation of dropping this little bombshell on Garth. But she must do it for all the reasons Pam listed. And, more important, for herself. For her self-esteem. For Maggie Fraser, stand-alone woman. Not Maggie Fraser, wife, mother, domestic slave and doormat.

'I'll have to find out if I can have time off work,' she said, suddenly panicking that this glimpse of paradise might be snatched from her grasp. 'We're a small office so only one person can go at a time.'

'The dates are flexible,' said Pam, as she removed the foil from the bottle and started unwinding the wire. 'The prize can be taken at any time up until the end of March.

I think mid-February would be spot on. I suggest that on Monday morning we both put in tentative requests for leave and then have a bit of a phone confab. That gives us plenty of time to dig out our flipflops and get our jabs sorted.'

'Jabs?' Maggie was taken aback yet again. 'What jabs?'

'Oh, sorry. That's the only bad news about the whole thing,' said Pam, trying to gloss over it. 'We'll need a few vaccinations, like yellow fever, typhoid, that kind of thing. Oh, and malaria tablets.'

Maggie gulped. She suddenly had visions of being attacked by swarms of mosquitoes in the middle of some huge African plain and being bitten to death. Or thrashing and delirious from an incurable fever in some filthy hospital.

'Leave it to me,' said Pam. 'I'll sort out a list of what we need.' Then she popped the cork and tipped the fizzing liquid into the glasses. 'I can't believe I talked you into this so quickly.' They clinked glasses, and she glanced at her watch. 'That really *was* quick! Funnily enough, I reckoned on much more of a fight.'

'You make me sound like an awkward old sod,' said Maggie, suddenly ashamed of all the barriers she'd put up. 'I am thrilled to be asked, ridiculously excited and just a little bit scared. Well, a big bit scared, if I'm honest.'

'What? About breaking the news at home?' Pam asked, searching her face for the truth.

'Partly,' said Maggie. 'It just seems such a huge adventure. Don't forget, I've never been further than France or Spain. And they're such a distant memory, my passport must have run out years ago.'

'And we're going south of the equator too.' Pam laughed. 'Seriously, Maggs, I understand what you mean.

I've been lucky in going to Hong Kong and the States a few times to see Tom, but I remember being a bit daunted the first time.'

Maggie fingered the brochure and reread the description of the hotel. It looked unbelievable. And here she was, agreeing to go. And it was all free.

She came back to her senses again. 'I haven't even asked you about this competition,' she said. 'What did you have to do to win?'

Pam laughed again and drained her glass. 'It was in one of my glossy mags. I had to answer a question and then I had to write no more than thirty words about whom I'd take on the holiday if I won it and why.'

'And who did you say?' said Maggie.

'You, you daft farthing.'

'Me?' Maggie sensed another shock disclosure.

Pam took in the white face. 'I just wrote something about a really good friend being slowly destroyed by her pig of a husband and that winning the prize would be her first step on the road back to self-esteem.'

Maggie sat there speechless.

Pam continued: 'Actually, you've already taken the first step at Home Truths. New job, new promotion. So our trip to paradise is a sort of consolidation and perhaps another step on the road to recovery.'

'God, you make it sound like the Priory.'

'Heavens, no. Not with all that lovely drinks allowance to get through. Oh no, we're going to eat, drink and be merry. And I thought we might really go for the fitness stuff too. Swim every day, walk along the beach, take in some rays and generally relax with a few good books and lots of laughs.'

'I'm counting the days,' said Maggie. A huge grin

spread across her face, and Pam beamed in delight . . . and relief.

First Monday back at work, Maggie bided her time, waiting for exactly the right moment to announce her news. A huge pile of post, hundreds of emails and a completely full answering machine were all there waiting for her. After a cursory round of 'did you have a nice Christmas' enquiries, everyone got stuck into the great catch-up. Not the appropriate time to mention holidays, Maggie decided. But her moment came at eleven o'clock when she'd finished making a round of coffee. It was time to draw breath for a few minutes.

'I wondered if I might book a bit of leave in mid-February,' she ventured as Vanessa stood in her office doorway, coffee cup in one hand, admiring a selection of antique rings on the other.

'Can't see a problem with that.' She glanced back into her office where the wall planner was. 'Stefan's back from Verbier by the seventh. No one else has booked in February so it's all yours, Maggie. Going anywhere special?'

This was Maggie's big moment and she wanted to milk it for everything she could.

'Kenya,' she announced. 'Just a bit of sun and sea to get me through the winter.'

'What a simply brilliant idea.' Vanessa nodded approvingly. 'Do you know, every winter I end up in Klosters with the same old gang, same old chalet, same old Glühwein, same second week in March. Just buy a different ski suit every year. It's all so predictable. I always think winter sunshine is really quite racy, don't you?'

'Oh, absolutely,' Maggie lied, trying to sound like an

old winter sunshine trooper. 'It feels somehow terribly naughty lying on a beach when everyone's grappling with burst pipes at home. Well, so long as they're not your own, of course!'

Everyone laughed. Oh, God, it feels good to be part of the set, Maggie thought to herself, slightly ashamed of her white lie. Oh well, maybe they all lie too.

At lunchtime, Maggie called Pam to report the good news.

'Great,' said Pam. 'I'll put in my leave request after lunch and keep you posted.'

By three o'clock Pam was back on the phone. 'All sorted and all booked. February the twentieth, flying from Gatwick. Scheduled flight to Mombasa, transfer to the hotel and then total effing paradise for a fortnight.'

Maggie found that the broad grin that had spread across her face simply wouldn't shift. She sat at her desk looking like a Cheshire cat as she flipped through her diary and added the word Kenya to the 20 February page. Then she ringed it twice, as if to remind herself. More like pinch herself. Tomorrow she must collect a passport form and get those dreaded jabs sorted. But tonight she must break the news to Garth. Until she'd got through that hoop, she couldn't even dream about packing.

Chapter 19

I'll tell him over dinner with the kids there, Maggie promised herself. She hoped and prayed that Beth would be supportive. Her daughter had been sticking up for her recently. She wondered whether to test the water with her first, but decided against it. It might look like collusion. George wouldn't care so long as some sort of food arrived in between football matches. No, it was Garth who'd explode, but perhaps he'd temper his explosion in front of the kids. Yes, she'd announce it to them all together.

It had been a long and tiring day back at work, she reflected, as she eased her old grey Ford Fiesta up on to the driveway in front of their house. As it spluttered to a halt, she glanced around the front garden. Admittedly it was January and not the most beautiful time of year for any garden, but theirs was in dire need of a good haircut. All the shrubs looked straggly even in their bare-branch state. The grass wasn't exactly neatly trimmed and in places it had given up the battle against moss, which mottled the lawn with huge patches of lurid green. And the few bulbs that had bothered to come up this year looked very forlorn indeed. Not much of an advert for a landscaping business.

Maggie realised that the whole concept of its being Garth's shop window had never occurred to her before. The front garden was just the front garden. Somewhere you parked the car before scurrying indoors as quickly as possible to get the dinner on the go. No wonder Garth's business was disappearing into the proverbial garden shredder.

Maggie's second realisation was that if she'd still been in the dreary rut that was Farleys, she'd never have thought of their garden as a sales pitch. The people at Home Truths, for all their sharp-suited cultural airs and graces, had honed up something in her head. If only Garth could hone up his as well, he'd probably have a decent business on his hands. Instead, all he could do was moan about old ladies who were nudging him down the garden path towards rack and ruin by having the temerity to book themselves into residential homes and therefore dispense with his services. He should be out there, finding new clients, getting himself a website, offering free estimates and at the very least tidying up his own front yard. Oh, and smiling. Going around looking and behaving like a clap of thunder wouldn't inspire anyone to book him to tend their roses. They'd want him to talk to their plants, not shout at them. Goodness, she had suddenly become a lateral thinker.

She locked the car, wondering why she bothered – no one would ever think of nicking it – and went indoors. She could hear Beth and George arguing about the television as usual but Garth was nowhere to be seen.

'Coming back later,' Beth informed her. '*Says* he's working late.'

Beth shot her mother a funny look, Maggie noticed. What was all that about? Maggie cursed him under her breath. This was the one day she wanted him home so that they could all sit down together to hear her bombshell announcement. As she chopped onions and browned the mince for a spaghetti bolognese, she began to wonder what to do if he didn't show up and she had to hold her news over to tomorrow. I have to tell him tonight, she told herself; I must get it over with tonight. The stress is just too much.

She could feel her heart thumping and her breath shortening. In her nervous state, she started to get rather clumsy. The tin opener got jammed on a can of tomatoes and then the top fell off the oregano pot and the entire contents fell into the pan. She hurriedly scooped out as much of the herb as she could, but the spag bol would be particularly aromatic tonight. Must calm down, she counselled herself. At this rate I'll need a hospital stay rather than a holiday.

Forty-five minutes later, it was ready to serve – and still no Garth. She couldn't keep the kids waiting. They'd clearly existed on sandwiches all day, judging from the pile of plates left in the sink. And crisps, according to the empty packets in the bin. They were probably high as kites on all the E-numbers they'd consumed. At least they'd be back at school later in the week.

'Grub up,' she called out through the open kitchen door. She started ladling the spaghetti on to plates. 'I don't suppose you want to wait for your father.'

'Dead right,' said George. 'I'm starving.' He'd spooned most of the meat sauce on to his pasta before Beth and Maggie noticed. They made him put most of it back.

'Remember there are four people in this house,' said Maggie.

'Three if you don't count Dad,' Beth chipped in.

There was that funny look on her face again, Maggie noticed. What was Garth up to? And what was Beth's game? She didn't much care about the first bit but she did hope that Beth hadn't somehow got dragged into it. So long as it didn't involve money. The last thing she needed was to discover that her husband was an inveterate gambler. Oh, the thought of that escape to Africa was becoming more alluring by the minute.

'Back to school for you two on Wednesday, then,' she announced with forced cheerfulness.

'Yeah, great, Mum,' George growled sarcastically. 'Thanks for reminding us. Can hardly wait.'

'Me neither,' said Beth without any enthusiasm whatsoever.

'Any thoughts yet on careers?' Maggie continued, trying to sound positive and get her mind off sun, sea, sand and coconut trees, not to mention an impending storm of tropical proportions.

'Well, I want to make loads of money and be able to buy whatever I want,' said Beth firmly.

'Bloody typical girl,' said George. 'And how are you going to make all this "loads of money" then?'

'I'm going to get a good job like Mum and work hard at it.'

Maggie felt a slight ripple of pleasure at that. To have become her daughter's role model was a bit of a turn-up for the books.

'And you, George?' she enquired. 'What do you have in mind?'

'I'm gonna be the king,' said George, smirking at Beth.

'I think they've got someone lined up for that,' said Maggie, laughing nervously. 'Dead man's shoes and all that. Or in the current case, dead woman's.'

'Or perhaps George means he wants to be Elvis Presley.' Beth was baiting him. 'Elvis Presley was called the King. I read about it the other week. He's dead but he had another hit not long ago, remember? They just remixed one of his songs and it went to number one. I think you'd make a great Elvis, George.'

George shot her a withering look. His sister never praised him. 'Whaddya mean?'

Beth started to laugh. 'Well, I think it would be great if you were dead. I'd like that because I could watch whatever telly I liked and get in the bathroom when I wanted to. And also if your records kept on making money, Mum and I would be able to go out shopping all the time.'

Excluding her father again, Maggie noted. She wondered if they'd had some big fall-out without her knowledge. Maybe that was why Beth was taking Maggie's side all the time.

'You'd have to put on loads of weight and wear one of those terrible white leather suits with all the studs,' Beth continued, taunting her brother. 'I think it would look really good on you.' George scowled at her but she took no notice. 'Anyway, Mum, how was your first day back?'

Once again, Maggie flinched. This level of concern was still new territory for her.

'Well, darling, it was a bit of a nightmare,' she said. 'We had nearly two weeks' worth of messages, emails and enquiries to get through. It's so much busier than when it was Farleys. We used to do very little between Christmas and Easter. But with this new firm, it never seems to stop. We must be selling ten times as many houses as before. I've got three houses to view tomorrow alone . . .'

She stopped. They all heard the front door bang shut. Garth was obviously home.

'Didn't wait for me then,' roared a familiar voice.

'You didn't say what time you'd be back.' Maggie tried to smooth things over. 'We were just all very hungry.'

She got up hurriedly to resuscitate the meat sauce quickly in the microwave. Garth went to the fridge, opened the door and shut it again. He'd forgotten there was no beer left.

'Been anywhere nice?' she asked as she began serving up his meal.

'Worked on a bit and then had a pint in the Doghouse on the way home,' he scowled at her. 'Any objection?'

'No, none at all,' Maggie replied as calmly as she could. As he took his first mouthful, the voice in her head kept nagging at her. Go for it, go for it. Any minute now the kids would have finished their meals and be itching to get back to the telly.

'Actually, while you're all here,' she faltered, her throat going suddenly dry, 'there's something I'd like to run past you. All of you.'

Not a flicker from Garth. He was far more interested in the food on his plate, attacking the spaghetti with his fork Typical, thought Maggie to herself, but I must plough on.

'You see, I've been offered the chance of a holiday. A trip of a lifetime. And I'd really like to go.'

Before Garth could clear his mouth to respond, Beth got in first.

'Fantastic, Mum,' she said, beaming very deliberately at George in the hope that he'd agree. 'You deserve it.'

'I wanted to tell you all together,' Maggie started to

gabble with nerves, 'because it obviously affects you all. I've managed to get the time off from work. They agreed that today. It's in late February so you two will be at school. I'll cook up lots of meals in advance but it means you'd all have to fend for yourselves a bit. Do your own sandwiches in the morning for school. Someone may have to do a bit of ironing, that sort of thing. I think it will do you all good, actually, and I know it will certainly do me a lot of good.'

She stopped and glanced round at them. Beth was now sporting an irritatingly false smile, while George looked annoyed. Garth shot her a glare as black as thunder. She noticed a muscle going in his neck.

'And just what good would it do me?' he thundered. 'Why should I have to do all that? I've a business to run. I don't have the time, and I certainly don't have the inclination or any intention of ironing.'

There was a hideous silence that seemed to last for ever.

Suddenly a voice piped up. It was Beth again. 'I'll do it. I'll do the sandwiches and the ironing. And if you make up some meals we can microwave then I'll do that too. Oh, Dad, let me. I want Mum to have a break. She deserves it.'

If Garth hadn't looked so incandescently angry, Maggie would probably have broken down and cried with emotion at her daughter's sudden rally of support.

'So who's behind this sudden holiday plan?' Garth's voice was now quiet and loaded with sarcasm. 'Oh, let me guess. This has the mark of your bloody friend Pam written all over it.'

Maggie couldn't deny it. 'Yes, Pam won it in a competition.'

'Pam won it in a competition.' The tone was venomous. 'And what is this holiday that you cannot afford to miss? That you can abandon your children for? A week at Butlins?'

'No,' said Maggie. 'Two weeks in Kenya.'

'Kenya?' Garth was back up the Richter scale again. Maggie wondered whether his voice would blow the windows out. 'Kenya? What on earth are you thinking of? You two silly women tripping off to Kenya? You must be bloody mad.'

George shoved his plate away and got up from the table. 'Get real, Dad. It's a top place for a holiday. If you'd been offered it, you'd have been off like a shot. Want your bags carried, Mum?'

Maggie smiled at him, grateful for the implicit endorsement.

'No thanks, darling, but I'll try to bring you back a little present.'

'And me, Mum.' Beth was straight in there, never wanting to miss a shopping opportunity.

'And what's this silly little escapade going to cost?' Garth continued.

'Nothing,' said Maggie, ignoring the sarcasm. 'Nothing at all. The prize includes all our meals and even drinks. We get two hundred pounds each to spend on anything we like around the hotel.'

Maggie had been anxious to impress upon Garth that it wasn't going to cost a penny. But it was the free drinks bit that got to him.

'Huh. You'll both be pissed as parrots and thrown to the natives.' He was livid.

'Don't be ridiculous,' said Maggie. 'We're going to take some water sports lessons and read some good books.'

Beth entered the fray again. 'Just think, Dad, you can pop down the Doghouse every night and when you get back I'll have one of Mum's lovely meals ready for you.' She flashed him an ear to ear grin. 'And you could take me and George to the new Wetherspoons on one of those cheap curry nights, to make up for us all missing Mum.'

'You're under age,' was all Garth could muster. The proverbial rug really had been pulled from under him. It was as if he'd had an information overload, being bombarded with data from all sides. To Maggie's surprise and relief, he suddenly appeared to capitulate. She'd been right. Thanks to the support from the kids, he'd rather abruptly caved in. Now she could really begin to believe the dream. Maggie Fraser, chief cook and bottle washer, was about to cut fast and loose from the sink. Maggie Fraser, not very successful wife and mother, was about to join the jet set – for a whole fourteen luscious days.

'I hope we're not having some fucking Shirley Valentine moment,' Garth finally snapped at her, when the kids had gone off to watch the television.

'Don't be daft,' said Maggie, as she stacked up the plates and cutlery ready to wash. 'I asked you, didn't I? I didn't leave a note on the kitchen door saying I'd gone to Greece.'

Although God knows I was sorely tempted, she thought in bed later that night. A fortnight on a sun-kissed beach. Her toes rippled at the thought of dipping them in the Indian Ocean. Even those two words, Indian Ocean, made her shiver with excitement. As Garth snored beside her, she lay wide awake and staring at the ceiling, far too excited to sleep. Garth hadn't exactly given it the green light, more the amber. But at least she was on her way. Her last waking thought was a mild panic that she didn't have a decent suitcase. And that certainly wasn't something she would be sharing with the people at Home Truths.

Chapter 20

'This is Captain Brian Freeman speaking. I'd just like to welcome you aboard our flight to Mombasa this evening. During the flight, I'll be giving you a progress report and some weather information when we get nearer to Kenya. Once we're airborne and I've switched off the seat belt sign, our inflight cabin services director and his team will begin a hot drinks service and give you information on meal times and movies during your journey. But in the meantime I'll hope you'll sit back, relax and enjoy your flight with us this evening.'

Sit back and relax? Some hope in these seats, thought Maggie. They're made for stick-thin models. It was so long since she'd been on a plane she'd forgotten how cramped the seating was. She wondered how on earth she was going to manage if the person in front wanted to tip his seat back even the tiniest bit, and nearly giggled at the thought of being pinned against the back of her own seat by the fold-down tray.

Suddenly the engines began to roar, the plane gave a shudder and then they were thundering down the runway. Maggie, sitting next to the window, found herself on the one hand marvelling at the speed at which they were travelling, given the size of the plane, and on the other with a huge lump in her throat at the idea of leaving her entire life behind for a fortnight. She felt her eyes prick with emotion, suddenly transfixed with fear that they'd crash and she'd never see Beth and George again. As the plane edged up into the air, she felt the rumble of the undercarriage disappearing into the belly of the plane. That was it now, no going back.

'Excited?' She heard Pam's voice in her ear.

'Bit emotional,' said Maggie, willing unexpected tears to stay in her eyes, rather than give the game away by trickling down her cheeks. They lapsed into a grateful silence. Maggie turned back to the window, watching the trees get smaller and smaller and the fields far below them turning into a vast patchwork quilt. Suddenly they were in cloud, and Planet Earth was gone.

Still fighting her ridiculous tears, Maggie turned her attention to the inflight magazine. She'd make herself read it from cover to cover with forced concentration to banish her emotions. It was crammed with snapshots of a jet set lifestyle that Vanessa and Damien obviously took to be the norm. An article on the big house-buying rush in France, with various commentators dismissing the south of France as overcrowded and 'so last year', tipping the Languedoc as the next Big Thing. She then moved on to a feature about buying shares in a vineyard and an account of Dubai's latest exotic skyscraper. Then there were the pages of reviews of what appeared to be the world's most expensive hotels and restaurants. Every tariff seemed to run into a vague four figures, on the basis, she supposed, that if you needed to enquire the exact price, you couldn't afford it. Nice life for the reviewer, she thought enviously. It also made a pleasant change to read glowing descriptions in which everything was talked up like mad by an army of invisible spin doctors, as opposed to the Home Truths philosophy of 'it might be a turkey but at least you know what you're buying'. It suddenly dawned on her that Home Truths was all about inverse snobbery. Perhaps that's how Vanessa and Damien justified it. After all, they clearly hadn't bought into the lifestyle of the lounge-dinette. That was just business, darling.

She was just getting stuck into a feature about Big Apple bus tours when lunch arrived. Again, Maggie had forgotten all about the obstacle course that was an airline meal. With no elbow room whatsoever, they were soon battling to get a scalding hot tin foil top off a container of chicken in a gloopy sauce with two small new potatoes and some very fed-up-looking green beans. It was surprisingly filling, Maggie noted. In her case, that was just as well, as the seat was so narrow that any over-indulgence would have put paid to further comfort.

As Pam, clearly a seasoned air traveller, nodded off next to her, Maggie kept squirming uncomfortably in her seat, reflecting on the past three weeks. It had been one long frenzy of shopping and cooking meals to put in the freezer, ironing for Britain and making lists of things that they all needed to remember. It was really only for Beth's benefit as she was the only one who seemed remotely interested in everyone's welfare during the coming fortnight. Maggie remembered once having the flu and being in bed for the best part of a week. Garth's idea of a nutritious and wholesome little delicacy to make her feel better had been a Cup a Soup.

She'd cooked chillis, lasagnes, cottage pies, chicken casseroles and steak pies, and also bought in some ready meals. Would anyone be bothered to read the instructions on the packet? Did anyone know how to work the microwave? She'd written them a note of explanation on that, together with big hints about vegetable peelers, just in case they remembered the concept of five portions per day. She'd even put a big Post-it note on the airing cupboard door to remind them where the immersion heater was.

Then there'd been the 'what to wear' dilemma. 'Half the clothes and twice the money' had been Vanessa's throwaway formula one day when they'd all fallen into yet another office discussion about holidays. Everyone, including Maggie who'd now learnt the game, had clucked in agreement. At least she didn't need much spending money with all the extras paid for as part of the prize. But half the clothes? She didn't have enough of anything to divide into two, especially not holiday wear. It was a good five years since they'd been camping in France and then it had been a rather rainy Whitsun in Brittany. So she'd scoured the sales and managed to buy a couple of swimming costumes, a cotton dress and a pair of cropped chinos left over from last year's summer sale, all hidden in amongst the winter jumpers and tweeds they were not trying to get shot of this time. She hadn't actually tried on the swimsuits, afraid that the sight of her sporting the beached whale look would put her off going altogether.

Pam, of course, would look marvellous as ever, having kept her figure with regular trips to the gym. Annoyingly, she had a real knack of wearing the right thing every time. Today, for example, she was in a navy velour track suit and top with a light cotton red and white striped sweater underneath. And she had a T-shirt, shorts and flipflops packed in her shoulder bag ready to put on at the other end where it would be hot. She'd suggested Maggie do the same but Maggie couldn't, in her wildest dreams, imagine experiencing any kind of heat in the middle of February. It had taken all Pam's persuasive powers to get her to leave her coat in the boot of the car at the airport car park on the grounds that she would definitely not be needing it in Mombasa.

Maggie thought back to the stress of waiting for her new passport to arrive, and having to borrow a decent-looking suitcase from a neighbour. Then there was the business of treading on eggshells where Garth was concerned. She'd steeled herself for the ultimate blow-up, mentally preparing herself on the drive home every night for a Vesuvian eruption she thought was inevitable. But apart from an odd gush of molten lava, Garth seemed to have kept deliberately out of her way. At least the permanently grumpy look didn't get any grumpier. Whatever his views on her going to Kenya, he kept them to himself. He didn't enquire where she was staying, or even wish her a good holiday. Just a gruff goodbye and a peck on the cheek, probably for the benefit of the kids. Perhaps he was jealous, deep down. Or maybe just plain relieved that she was away for a fortnight. Either way, she didn't envisage a Shirley Valentine scenario, where he'd suddenly turn up on the beach, begging her to come home.

Maggie also felt hugely guilty that she hadn't told him about the extra couple of hundred pounds she'd unexpectedly found in her paypacket just before Christmas. It had enabled her to buy the summer clothes and pay for the passport and all the jabs without rocking the financial boat. How sad, she reflected, that she had

had to keep quiet about it. Then she forgave herself with a timely reminder of how Garth occasionally played his sneaky game of suddenly announcing he was off to a gardening show at the very last minute so he didn't have to take her. Did that even the score? She wasn't sure.

After the second meal of the flight and a couple of glasses of wine, Maggie realised her guilty conscience was being jettisoned bit by bit. Already she could feel the stresses and strains of the past few months beginning to evaporate. And the wine had gone straight to her head. Despite the narrow seat and her aching legs, she finally managed to snatch some sleep. It was night-time and the cabin lights had been dimmed. As she drifted off, her head was filled with blissful thoughts of the Paradise Palms Hotel. She'd pored over the brochure pictures so many times in sheer excitement, not quite believing that somewhere so idyllic could actually exist and that she, Maggie Fraser, rubbish mother and generally boring person, could be going there for two whole weeks.

'This is the life,' said Pam, stretching out on her sun bed and flexing perfectly varnished toes. 'Doesn't come better than this, does it?'

Maggie nodded in agreement. Day two of their holiday and she was amazed how totally relaxed she felt. The journey from the airport to the hotel had been a terrible eye opener. She'd never seen poverty on such a scale. Everyone walking around barefoot, families living in small huts with straw roofs, a street market with shabby stalls boasting perhaps a couple of bananas, a small pile of rotten tomatoes or a couple of carved elephants. Yet everyone smiled toothily and waved as their small hotel transfer bus trundled past, swerving dramatically now and again to avoid the potholes.

It eventually dawned on Maggie why there was a constant flow of people walking up and down the road clutching huge plastic bottles. They were fetching water. It made her humbly grateful for what she had back home. She promised herself she'd never moan about the lack of a dishwasher again.

In contrast, the hotel was everything it had promised in those tiny pictures – and more. The rooms were arranged in two-storey rondavels set in beautiful tropical gardens. Theirs was on the upper floor for which Maggie was very grateful. Somehow in her bizarre logic, it got them up and away from the possibility of snakes and creepie-crawlies. She'd watched too many Bond films featuring the obligatory scene where a snake or a tarantula nips in through the window unnoticed and threatens to change the course of history by delivering a fatal bite to 007.

She was also cheered by the sight of a couple of seriously enormous women strolling around the hotel in swimming costumes, completely unfazed by their wobbling thighs and pendulous boobs. Their vast rivers of cellulite made her feel heaps better.

Hence, by day two, Maggie was feeling very happy with her lot. She could feel the sun seeping into her bones and easing away all the aches and pains of a wet and cold British winter.

'I'm really glad we decided to do nothing for the first two or three days,' said Pam, applying some tanning lotion to perfectly waxed legs. 'Here, turn round. I'll put some of this on your back. You don't want to go pink and end up sore.'

Maggie was following Pam's example and bypassing all the tempting croissants, rolls, bacon and eggs for breakfast, steeling herself to head straight for the huge slices of juicy water melon and pineapple and bowls of plain yoghurt. Fruit juice and no coffee. The original plan was to go for a brisk walk or jog on the beach every morning after breakfast and then lounge around the pool area and have a swim before lunch. However, the moment they left the hotel grounds – simply by stepping through a gate and on to the ivory sands – they were surrounded by locals who pestered them with sarongs, wooden carvings, and brightly coloured beaded necklaces and bracelets.

'We're too pale,' said Pam knowingly, laughing at Maggie's apparent distress. 'We're fair game – literally – because it's obvious we've only just arrived.'

Poor Maggie found herself standing there with bracelets on her wrists, beads round her neck and a carved black elephant being shoved in her face by a man chanting, 'Special price, mama. I give you special price.'

Pam took charge, calling a polite but very firm '*No*' to the crowd who had gathered around them and shepherding Maggie back through the gate as the hopeful traders reluctantly backed off.

'God, that was scary,' said Maggie. 'I thought we were going to have a fight on our hands.'

'Just their way of doing business,' said Pam. 'We have to respect that. In a few more days, when we've stopped looking like new kids on the block, they won't bother us quite so much.'

Maggie gazed back through the gate at the soft pale sands, the deep blue sea and the clumps of coconut trees that swept right down to the water's edge. It would be such a pity not to be able to sit there without being pestered. Now she understood why armed guards patrolled the hotel grounds night and day. It wasn't to protect the guests so much as to keep the beach salesmen away.

True to the competition's promise, there was an account to which they could sign their drinks, so every night they shared a bottle of wine and ended their meal with a Kenya Gold, a liqueur suspiciously like Tia Maria. Evenings at the Paradise Palms were just as idyllic as the days. So near the equator, night-time came quickly. Virtually no sunset, Maggie noted. The sun just dropped out of the sky without any preamble. Light, then dark.

Meals were served round the pool, with music provided by various African bands and singers who went on to entertain the guests throughout the evening. Maggie and Pam were beginning to love the evenings best of all. As well as savouring the cooking, mostly curries which they both loved, they found the entertainment sometimes awesome and sometimes downright funny. Maggie was mesmerised by a group of drummers who beat out the most fantastic rhythms and notes on their various instruments. Without any inhibition, they then toured the tables hardselling CDs to the guests. Every table bought one, Maggie noted, as she herself reached into her bag and produced the right number of shillings to buy hers. Perhaps the drums had a hypnotic effect that not only gripped your very soul, but got a hold on your wallet as well.

She also loved the dancers, who were often wildly energetic. The Flying Brothers and Sisters leapt and swooped with amazing abandon. Another troop performed a kind of African fly-swatting dance with huge whips that looked as though they'd been made out of zebra tails. The head of the troop, an elderly man with an ear to ear smile which revealed virtually no teeth, homed in on Maggie and dragged her up to join in.

As Maggie cheerfully copied the movements and swung the whip that had been shoved in her hand, she realised she really had left Maggie Fraser at home. Strangely, she felt no embarrassment whatsoever. There she was in her new cropped trousers and T-shirt, making people laugh with her efforts. When the fly-swatting dance was over, the elderly man took her by the hand and escorted her back to her table. Then, with another huge stumpy grin, he got down on one knee and proclaimed, 'Will you be my fourth wife!'

Maggie threw her head back and laughed uproariously. 'Sorry,' she said. 'You're too late. What a pity!'

'Your name?'

'Maggie.'

'Jambo Mama Maggie.' He shook her hand and bowed his head. 'Me. Jack. Have nice holidays.' With that, he returned to his troop for the next dance.

Maggie sat back in her seat. That bloody name again. It still haunted her. Pam, sensing a moment of distress, beckoned a passing waiter. 'Two more Kenya Golds please. Doubles.' Then she turned to Maggie. 'I checked our hotel account this evening,' she announced with a long face. 'Just to see how we were doing. It's really bad news, I'm afraid.'

That shook Maggie out of her moment of misery. 'Oh no, hon. What a pity. We could cut down on the Kenya Golds if you like. Or perhaps we should cancel one of the trips we've booked.'

'It's not that kind of bad news.' Pam burst out laughing. 'The bad news is that we're not spending *enough*! We're going to have to start drinking more. At this rate we're going to be leaving too many precious shillings behind, unspent. I think we should factor in a large G and T before dinner from now on.'

Later that night, with Pam sound asleep across the room, Maggie lay in her bed watching the room whizz around. Too much Kenya Gold, she decided. It's my own fault if I have a headache in the morning. She forced herself to drink a large glass of mineral water. Then she flopped back on her pillows, thinking about the African fly-swatting dance that evening with . . . Jack. That one syllable that was guaranteed pain. Where was Jack tonight? Did he ever think of her? Wonder where she was? Even here in the southern hemisphere, she couldn't seem to get him out of her mind.

Chapter 21

The following morning Pam suggested going into the village centre where a cyber café had recently set up.

'Just need to know that Mark's OK,' she said. 'Thought I'd send him an email. And with a bit of luck, he might have sent me one.'

Maggie was quite relieved. She too was anxious to know that the kids were all right and that Beth hadn't somehow blown up the microwave or burnt the house down. She'd thought about ringing them but she knew why she hesitated every time her fingers touched her mobile. She didn't want to risk Garth's picking up the phone. She knew the sound of his voice would send an inevitable shiver down her spine. With his lack of work at the moment, he could be home at any time. Having put several thousand miles between them for fourteen precious days, she wanted to keep it that way. An email to the kids would be much less stressful.

Hotel staff told them where to wait for the *matatu*, the local bus. Soon a clapped-out old vehicle, straight out of the fifties, belching fumes and creating a choking dust trail, staggered round the corner. Maggie looked at Pam and their hearts sank. It was full to bursting with people hanging off the sides and back and even clinging to the roof. It pulled up at the bus stop with a screech of brakes in a cloud of thick grey smoke. Maggie and Pam waited politely for people to get off, but no one did. Then Pam nudged Maggie and pointed up at the driver, who was beckoning them on to the bus, a grin from ear to ear.

'I think I'm a bit old to strap hang from the side of a bus,' Maggie half whispered as she attempted a forced smile at the driver.

'Me too,' said Pam, now regretting she'd come up with the idea.

They looked back to the driver who was now pointing specifically to his cab. Next thing they knew, hands were helping the pair of them squeeze into the tiny cab next to him and banging the rusty door behind them.

'No health and safety policy here then,' Pam observed, as they smiled at the driver while attempting to squeeze their limbs into the small spaces left. 'Must say Weltham council would make its buses pay if it ran them along these lines. I might suggest it when I get back.'

Mercifully the village centre was only two stops away. Just as well, Maggie thought, with a hot metal door handle burning into her back and her legs twisted into the most uncomfortable curl. The stench of body odour was overwhelming but, she reasoned, understandable. It was particularly hot and humid today and the people on the bus probably didn't have access to hot and cold showers, let alone deodorant.

Eventually the bus tottered into the village and ground to a halt, punctuated by another squeal of bare metal and a huge cloud of dust. The driver jumped out of the cab and then helped them down. They practically fell out into a heap on the pavement, their legs unable to support them after all the contortions. They promptly dissolved into fits of laughter. 'Bleugh. It was a bit ripe in there,' said Pam, recovering her composure and taking deep breaths of fresh air. When they'd finally straightened themselves out, and rubbed their aching limbs, they looked up at the little shop right in front of them. It had a display of brightly coloured T-shirts bearing the legend 'I Rode a Matatu' and featuring a cartoon of a bus crammed with people, just like the one they'd been on.

'Somebody here has a business brain,' said Pam, as they found themselves wandering in like robots, compelled to buy T-shirts for the kids.

They glanced around the small village square. The 'town centre', as the hotel staff had proudly called it, consisted of a few wooden huts with straw roofs. They soon found the cyber café. Judging by the small crowd milling around outside, it was the hottest thing to hit Diani Beach since . . . well, probably the midday sun.

'What did we do without email?' said Pam, as they finally sat down, side by side, rattling away on the keyboards, sending messages to their kids. 'Or the internet, come to that. It's amazing what you can find out. I found the answer to the competition that got us here through the internet. Hercule Poirot's London address. Took a bit of surfing but I got there. Saved having to plough through all my old Agatha Christies. And last year I managed to track down a distant cousin for my mum through a golf club website.'

'I gather Friends Reunited's pretty good for that stuff.'

'Actually, I've been tempted to sign up,' said Pam. 'Perhaps it's all to do with this turning forty lark. Trying to grab hold of what we've all lost. Why don't we sign up and add our names? It would be fun to see who gets in touch.'

Maggie firmly shook her head. 'Not for me.' What would she have to boast about in the Your Profile page?

'Oh, go on,' said Pam, the holiday mood prompting her to try out her powers of persuasion. 'It might be fun to meet up with all the old crew.'

'Don't forget,' Maggie reminded her, 'I had the pleasure of having Freddie Chapple turn up at the office not long ago. That was quite enough of a tiptoe down Memory Lane for me, thank you. He hadn't changed for the better, I can tell you. Same old awful teeth and pockmarks. And he's still wearing terrible pebble specs with big black frames. Obviously too short-sighted to choose anything half decent.'

'I'd like to find out what happened to Dave and his Morris Traveller with the phony royal connection,' said Pam wistfully. 'Remember? We talked about him at Juicy Lucy's.'

Maggie nodded. How could she forget? His boasts had been legendary from about the third form onwards.

'He' was such a bullshitter,' Pam continued. 'He actually told me once that everyone lies, but that it doesn't really matter since nobody listens.'

'Well, you did – for quite a while, as I recall,' Maggie teased her. 'You were very much in his thrall. Anyway, why on earth would you want to get in touch with him, after he put an ad in the lonely hearts column when he was still going out with you? It was a helluva put down.'

'Oh, nostalgia, I suppose,' said Pam. 'Or just curiosity. Bit of upper hand revenge. Do you honestly not wonder what happened to Jack and why he didn't turn up that night?'

'Of course I do.' Maggie gave a huge sigh. 'And I regret thinking about it every time I think about it. Just lately there's been a real spate of it. Everyone's either called Jack or talks about him. Even swotty Freddie Chapple seemed to know he'd pissed off to America.'

'Well, let's find out,' said Pam mischievously. She turned back to her screen and started tapping words into a search engine.

'Bugger,' she announced after a minute or so. 'What a shame he's called Jack Haley. I've tapped in his name and tried America, computers, computing and so on. And it keeps coming up with Jack Haley the actor.'

'Of course it does,' said Maggie somewhat bitterly. '*The Wizard of Oz* was his parents' favourite film. Jack Haley played the Tin Man, their surname was Haley so there was no contest. He had to be called Jack. God, I remember his mother telling me the story over a pile of ironing as though it were yesterday.'

Pam detected a wistful look in Maggie's eye. She was weakening. This was the first time in a long while that she'd not totally dismissed the mention of Jack out of hand. 'And what happened to his parents?' she pushed gently.

'Oh, they went to live in Spain just after Jack went off to university,' said Maggie. 'Some talk of running a bar somewhere along the costas. I think they'd run a pub for a while before Jack was born, so I expect they'd have the expertise to do very well. If they're still alive, that is.'

'They'd be easier to track down in Spain,' Pam continued lightly. 'There can't be all that many ex-pats living in Spain called Haley. Well, not as many Haleys as in England.'

Whether it was the sunshine, the relaxation or perhaps

the smidgen of a hangover from the previous night, Maggie turned back to her screen. Before she could stop herself, she called up a search engine and tapped in 'Haley and Spain'. Up came pages and pages of obscurity involving people called Haley and Spain, mostly chronic accounts of Haley family holidays on the costa del something or other. She scrolled down several pages and stopped. What a stupid idea.

Then, as if some unseen force were driving her fingers, they were back on the keys, typing 'Wizard of Oz and Spain'. Another pause and then up came another hotch-potch of entries, ranging from a poster of the film (*El Mago de Oz*) being offered for sale in Madrid at a vast price to DVDs on sale from a man in Benidorm who claimed to be a friend to the stars. She added the word 'bar'. No entries found.

Maggie forced herself to glance away from the screen and across the village square to where a man selling African instruments was literally drumming up trade. He was beating out a simple rhythm on a couple of small drums supported between his knees. She watched mesmerised as his hands flicked expertly over the animal skins to produce hypnotic music.

She tried to stay with him, concentrating on picking out the notes within the drumming in her head. But after a few seconds she was back staring at the screen again. This was madness, trying to track down Jack or his parents. But she couldn't stop. Her brain was whizzing. Think laterally, Maggie. If Jack's parents had opened a bar, what would they have called it? She tried 'Wizard' 'Oz' and even 'Jack' with 'Spain', 'Spanish' and 'Haley'. Nothing. She added 'bar' and 'pub'. That added simply pages and pages of possibles. But no probables. She must stop now. Her right hand reached for the mouse to click on the close button when she suddenly had a moment of inspiration. One last attempt, she promised herself, and then I stop this nonsense and walk away.

She typed in 'tin man' and then added 'Spain'. The computer paused for a few agonising seconds and then, suddenly, there it was.

> The Tin Man, bar in Puerto Pollensa, Majorca. British bar with a little touch of Hollywood. Guest beers, all day breakfasts, bar snacks including bangers and mash, Sunday roasts . . .

Maggie knew instinctively that this was it. If she'd had any life savings, she'd have bet them on it. As if stumbling across Pandora's mailbox, she clicked on the website address, frightened at what she might discover. With almost indecent haste, up came pictures of the Tin Man, downloaded in just a couple of seconds. There were exteriors of a typical Spanish bar situated down a sunny side street. The inside looked like a typical English local, plus a description:

> Enjoy the authentic atmosphere of a good British pub in Majorca's very best resort. Make it your local during your stay here in sunny Puerto Pollensa. Pasties and pies, and all your favourites, served up with chips and mushy peas.

The website included pages giving full menus and lists of beers, plus a selection of photographs of various groups of holidaymakers, all holding up beer glasses and smiling to camera. Maggie took a deep breath and clicked on to the Meet the Owners page. And there they were, Joe and Christine Haley, now white-haired, deeply tanned and barely recognisable, smiling broadly in front of a Wizard of Oz poster. She knew that poster well. Twenty years ago it had been in pride of place on a wall in the Haley dining room. And now here it was, the main feature of their pub. Beneath the picture was the full address, telephone number and email address of the Tin Man.

In a moment of madness, seated in a wooden hut in East Africa, she'd found out so much. One click and a message to their email address would probably elicit even more. Maggie suddenly felt as though she, like Dorothy, had stumbled upon her own Yellow Brick Road.

She got up from her chair and rushed outside, grateful for the sun, now high in the sky, fiercely beating down on her head. She glanced up at the sky, bright blue with tiny wisps of cloud, behind a row of coconut trees at the edge of the square which were gently rustling in the breeze. She remembered a friend who'd just lost her mother saying there was something magical about Africa, and that the sight of African skies had helped to ease her grief. It was certainly doing something for Maggie's emotions. They were jumping all over the place.

Maggie's head buzzed for the rest of the day. Pam, being very perceptive, guessed what was going through her mind and left her alone. After sending messages to the kids, they'd gone back to the hotel in a taxi, deciding that one *matatu* was quite enough for one day, and deliberately spent the afternoon quietly on sun beds by the pool. Pam was clearly devouring the book she was reading, flicking a page every few minutes. But Maggie just stared at the same page of her paperback over and over again. The words danced around but meant nothing.

In her head, she was making virtual tours of the Haley house all those years ago, remembering how the kitchen was laid out, how Mrs Haley made a really good Cornish pasty with proper beef skirt and turnip. The small neat garden out at the back, the greenhouse in which Mr Haley, a keen gardener, grew all his bedding plants from seed, the new bathroom suite which had been their pride and joy at the time, the dining room with its old-fashioned dark oak table and heavy chairs. And of course the precious film poster that had dominated the room. And the story of how they bought it for a fiver – a serious amount of money at the time – from the owner of a second-hand book shop which was closing down.

She remembered how Jack always snogged her passionately on the front doorstep just before he put the key in the lock, as if to say that'll have to last you for a while because my parents are at home. She and Jack had been of a generation which called each other's parents Mr and Mrs, with none of the familiarity of today's kids who cheerfully assume they can call their friends' parents by their first names.

She thought back to their first date, a drink in the snug at the Coach and Horses, long since demolished to make way for a road widening scheme. She'd agonised over what to order, asking for a Bacardi and Coke because it seemed so sophisticated. She'd made it last all evening because she didn't know how much money Jack had and didn't want to embarrass him by appearing to need a top-up. Jack had stared deeply into her eyes that night as they'd exchanged their first kiss in the pub car park. She'd never wanted it to end. She'd even found herself working out that the spot where they'd stood for the big embrace was now a traffic island. She'd thought about that moment every single time she passed it in the car and her stomach turned to jelly. Some days she took an alternative route to spare herself the pain.

So what was it that made him not show up that crucial night? She could merrily click on to the email address of the Tin Man website, she supposed. And then what? Write some cheery note to Mr and Mrs Haley. 'Remember me, Jack's old girlfriend who's now turned into a bit of a frump?' And what would they say? 'Oh, Maggie, how lovely to hear from you. Jack never stops talking about you. Here's his address and phone number. Oh, and don't worry about his wife and kids. They won't mind a bit you ringing up.'

And what would she say to Jack? 'What kept you? Why didn't you ring, you bastard?' To which he'd probably laugh, half cover the mouthpiece with his hand and tell his wife it was 'some old weirdo girlfriend from way back who's obviously lost the plot', make his excuses and promptly put down the phone.

Maggie lay back on her sun bed, admitting defeat with her book. She hadn't expected to come to Kenya to confront all these old demons. She'd come to try to escape them.

Chapter 22

The evening entertainment at the Paradise Palms looked promising. A troop of Masai warriors were due to demonstrate their singing and dancing by the pool. Then there was to be a fashion show, followed by a 'light-hearted cabaret act' from a duo tantalising entitled 'The Beautiful Miss Nancy and Mr Banana'.

'Sounds like a sex show,' said Pam. 'We can't miss this. I've a feeling we'll dine out on this one for years.'

Maggie wasn't so sure. Life with Garth didn't include dining out on anything. But life with Pam was always fun, and she knew her confidence had grown during the holiday in terms of doing things she'd once have dismissed out of hand. As she put on her winter-sale-Christmas-bonus floaty frock for the evening ahead, she reflected on the hilarious windsurfing lesson they'd had the previous day. Their instructor Benjamin had patiently explained the principles of the sport with their boards laid out safely on the sand. Then, wading out into just two and a half feet of water, they'd both attempted to stand up and find their balance. After two hours of honking laughter, Maggie had managed to travel about three feet before falling into the water yet again. Pam, who was much more lithe, had managed about nine before meeting a similar fate. The lesson had ended in hysteria when, as Maggie emerged from yet another ducking in the sea, a young lad had swum up to her bearing a carved wooden elephant and launched straight into a sales pitch.

But, as Maggie reflected tonight, putting on her mascara, she'd had a go, hadn't felt in the least inhibited or foolish. It helped not having the kids there to mock her. She certainly missed them but she didn't miss being sent up. What Garth would have made of it, she couldn't possibly guess. They'd never done silly things together, or had a go at something like windsurfing just for the fun of it.

She and Jack would have done, though. She remembered him taking her out on the Serpentine in London when he'd just started at university. Impulsively, they'd clambered into a boat and been pushed out into the lake before he made the announcement that he'd never actually rowed before in his life. They'd both laughed so much that they accidentally knocked one of the oars into the water and had to be rescued by the now very stroppy man who rented out the boats. They'd giggled at their own stupidity all the way back to Jack's student flat. Maggie found herself smiling at the memory as she applied her lipstick and looked forward to the evening ahead.

The hotel gardens by night never failed to make them gasp. Coloured lights hidden under the exotic cacti, shining down from coconut trees and lining the winding pathways gave the gardens a truly magical quality. As they walked towards the tables laid up for dinner, they noticed that a rope bridge had been rigged up across the swimming pool to create a catwalk for the fashion show. Tonight was African curry night and the aroma of coriander and cardomom hung enticingly in the air.

The Masai troop more than lived up to their billing. Dressed in their traditional red cloth, and wearing masses of coloured beads, they sang unaccompanied in the most incredible harmony. Their low soft voices rang out around the swimming pool, creating an electric atmosphere. Then the dancing gradually started as the singing gained in volume, with vertical leaps high into the air that would have put Nijinsky or Nureyev to shame. There was a long pause as the audience silently gasped at what they'd witnessed, and then everyone burst into rapturous applause and cheering.

The moment they'd finished, though, it was down to business in what Pam and Maggie had discovered was the typical Masai way. From out of nowhere, they each produced a somewhat incongruous sports bag and unpacked traditional spears and shields, beads and carvings, spreading them out on handwoven red cloths around the poolside and inviting, or rather gently insisting, that the hotel guests bought something. Pam and Maggie found themselves buying tiny beaded bracelets and not having the heart to barter for them. They were both rewarded with a free one.

'Clearly Buy One Get One Free isn't just the domain of Tesco or Sainsburys,' Pam remarked as they returned to their table, where poppadoms and chutneys had now been laid out.

'Well, at least that's my present for Beth solved,' said Maggie. 'I haven't a clue what to buy George, let alone Garth.'

'One of those nasty spears with the rusty tips would be perfect for Garth,' Pam joked. She picked up a chunk of poppadom and took a bite.

'Then I could go off into the sunset with the Tin Man,' Maggie said before she could stop herself.

'You could do a lot worse than that,' said Pam without a flicker, as she carried on spooning mango chutney on to her poppadom. 'In fact, I'd say you ought to at least give some thought to laying the ghost, now that you've got this far.'

'What do you mean?' Maggie recoiled, suspicious.

'Email his parents. Send a friendly note. They'll remember you with fondness, I'm sure. Make an excuse about getting in touch with old school friends. Enquire how Jack is and what he's up to. You'll probably find he's a fat old lardbelly living in some boring bit of middle America with a fat old lardarse of a wife and a gaggle of totally obnoxious children with awful names like Demi-Leigh and Madison. Then you'd heave a sigh of relief at the lucky escape you've had.'

Before Maggie could reply, a waiter arrived at their table bearing a tray of little dishes containing prawn, meat and vegetable curries, piles of fluffy rice, chapattis and nan bread. While he dished it all up with a flourish, Maggie's mind was racing. Was Pam right? Would Jack be a big fat American bore? Would it put an end to her anguish? Or would it upset her that she had spent so much emotion on the memory of a man who simply no longer existed?

'Just pour, please,' Pam told the waiter as he produced a bottle of red wine and two glasses. 'So what are you going to do?' she continued. 'Find out once and for all what happened that night, or be miserable for ever? Live your whole life mourning something that might have been crap anyway?'

'Dunno,' said Maggie defensively. 'Quite a lot of my life is crap anyway. She took a sip of wine and then forked up some prawn curry. 'This is absolutely delicious.'

'Yes it is, but don't change the subject,' said Pam firmly. 'Your life's been looking up lately. Since Juicy Lucy's, I've seen a gradual transformation in you, hon. Better job, more confidence, out of the ridiculous rut of Farleys. More respect from your kids, particularly Beth, who's been very supportive lately. You've sharpened up your wardrobe . . . oh, and by the way, have you looked in the mirror lately?'

Maggie looked at her quizzically, mouth full of curry.

'There's a very good-looking woman in that mirror,' Pam continued. 'You look like you've lost at least a stone since we've been here – that's in just ten days of healthy eating, exercise, and above all *fun*! Fun is slimming, it's relaxing and it suits you. So does the golden tan.'

Maggie put down her fork. 'Actually, come to think of it, I did notice this morning that my trousers weren't so tight.'

'It's not just the trousers.' Pam was warming to her theme. 'You're getting back to the Maggie I knew at school. You were always a laugh a minute. That's why you always had lots of boyfriends. Everyone, including me, wanted to be your friend. You had a wonderful confidence and optimism about everything. You saw good in everyone. You always had time for people. Made them feel special. That's why the Jack thing screwed you up. He treated you appallingly and you, not surprisingly, couldn't cope. Everyone came to you with their problems, but you couldn't share your problems with anyone.'

Maggie nodded sadly. That last bit was certainly true. She'd gone into a black hole after Jack disappeared. Thrown up her secretarial job in London and come running home to Weltham, only to find that virtually all her friends had simply moved on.

'I just couldn't bring myself to talk about it to anyone,' she murmured. 'Not even you, hon. Just saying the words "we've broken up" set me off into another crying session.'

Pam refilled their glasses. 'I do remember you were very distant for a very long time,' she recalled. 'You just wouldn't talk about it. I assumed you'd recovered when you married Darth Vader. Of course, I didn't realise it was a rebound job. I personally think the bastard has very nearly destroyed you, along with the rest of the cast of *Star Wars*. For what it's worth, I think the timely demise of Farleys has been the making of you.'

'Oh, God,' Maggie sighed. 'You're probably right about the rebound thing. But then hindsight's easy, isn't it?'

To Maggie's relief, the tannoy came to her rescue with an announcement that the fashion show was starting up on the catwalk across the pool and of course all the outfits were on sale in the hotel boutique if they wished to purchase. Suddenly all the underwater lighting came on, with coloured spots trained on the rope bridge. Across it came a stream of long-limbed lithe African girls, their hair in braids and decorated with beads. In what was almost a ballet, they moved and swayed to the rhythms of the music, modelling a range of dresses, shorts and tops, skirts and sarongs, all in vibrant limes, oranges, lemons and turquoises.

'Far too bright for English skins,' Pam observed. 'Although we could get away with it now, with our tans coming along.'

'Couldn't imagine wearing that to work,' said Maggie wistfully, as a beautiful yellow and black dress with frilled neck and hemline and a matching turban sashayed past. 'It looks great on her, but it would be a tad ridiculous at Home Truths on a rain-lashed day with me traipsing clients round one of our really seedy properties.'

They'd finished their curries and were now consulting a huge menu of ice creams.

'You're right about the job thing,' Maggie continued reflectively. 'Even I've noticed that I've gained a bit of strength and confidence through it. Yet at Christmas, when I was stuck at home, I reverted to being a mouse. Anything for a quiet life. I went through hoops not to have any rows. Just couldn't help it.'

'But you're back up there again now,' said Pam, 'and I hope this holiday has helped. I don't think three months ago you'd have dreamt of even mooting the idea to Garth, let alone started packing.'

'I wouldn't have missed it for the world,' Maggie replied simply.

They sat back in their chairs to enjoy the rest of the fashion show and await the arrival of 'The Beautiful Miss Nancy and Mr Banana'. Clearly, from the number of superlatives in the billing, they were the equivalent of the Beckhams in Mombasa.

An hour later, they were wiping their eyes from laughing so much. Despite the mega build-up, the beautiful Miss Nancy was anything but. She was a big girl, to put it politely, who merely did a wiggling dance in a circle round the tables. Everyone waited for something to happen but nothing did. As the drummers drummed away, the wiggling just went on and on. As a result, when she'd finished, she got a roar of applause from an audience who'd decided it was all a huge joke.

Then came her companion. Mr Banana turned out to be Kenya's answer to Wayne Sleep, a tiny live wire of a man who leapt about energetically to no real purpose. He then picked up a hand mike and insisted on getting as many people up on the dance floor as possible to teach them 'Diani Beach's latest dance craze'. This consisted of a bit of rather basic line dancing involving the unpeeling of a banana. After several rehearsals, with Mr Banana leaping about and shouting instructions with great gusto, he pronounced them ready to go. At this point he produced a huge basket of mouldy bananas and invited the 'volunteers' to take one in order to do the dance. Along with everyone else, Pam and Maggie gingerly picked up their fruit. 'Somebody or something beat us to it,' Pam remarked. The fruit was so black and rotten it was practically crawling.

'Videos ready?' he shrieked at the crowd. 'Then go, go, go.'

The chorus, including Pam and Maggie, duly went through their steps, unpeeling their bananas as instructed by their tiny tutor, and gradually it dawned on all of them what the grand finale was to be. Suddenly everyone was exchanging panicky looks that said, 'How on earth do we get rid of the bloody banana?' Pam and Maggie were by now laughing so helplessly that they practically tripped over their own feet. By the time they'd reached the end of the dance, everyone was on the verge of hysteria. The ever enthusiastic Mr Banana interpreted all the laughter as a huge sign of success. He and Miss Nancy took endless bows as the applause went on and on, people wiping their eyes on their napkins as they cheered and clapped.

'No wonder they were given such a build-up,' said Maggie. 'We're all hysterical and the hotel thinks it's provided something really top notch.'

'A triumph of cheek over substance,' Pam agreed. 'Nancy and Mr B must think that everyone who comes on holiday here is a bit clumsy. I reckon we all managed to "accidentally" drop our bananas. What a brilliant piece of marketing. So bad everyone laughs, and so it becomes good.'

'Bit like Home Truths in reverse.' Maggie was still wiping her eyes. 'We say the houses are crap and everyone refuses to believe us, so they feel compelled to take a look and find out for sure. That was brilliant! I don't think I've ever laughed so much in my life.'

'Or at least,' said Pam, 'since . . . well . . . you know who.'

Chapter 23

Suddenly it was all over. No more *matatu* trips to the cyber café, no more Mr Rotten Banana and the not-quite-so-beautiful Miss Nancy, no more lazy dinners on warm evenings around the hotel pool, no more snorkelling over coral reefs, no more breathtaking glimpses of baobab and acacia trees set against African skies. Now it was just a dream, reduced to a memory and a few photographs.

Maggie gazed sadly out of the window as the plane nosed into the air, leaving the tall sweeping coconut trees, the ivory-white sand and the deep blue sea with its fabulous rolling waves far below. There would always be a little bit of her heart left behind on Diani Beach. She'd never known a fortnight whizz by so quickly. It was goodbye sea, sand and sun, hello Sainsburys and the kitchen sink.

She wondered how the kids would react when she got home. Pleased to see her, she hoped. But Garth? He wouldn't be the remotest bit interested and would probably dismiss her photographs without even bothering to look at them.

'Oh, Mum, you're looking fantastic.' Beth ran to greet her and flung her arms energetically round her.

'Have you missed me?'

'Not half.' Beth grinned. Then she suddenly looked embarrassed, indicating the kitchen with a swift tilt of her head. 'Nobody helped,' she said bitterly. 'I've done my best but it's endless. All that cooking and washing up. You've no idea how much there was to do.'

Maggie burst out laughing at the irony of that last bit but decided not to comment. The mere fact that Beth had clearly done her best against the odds was enough. They went into the kitchen and the sight she'd expected was there to greet her in glorious technicolor: a pile of dirty plates so high it practically created an eclipse of the kitchen window.

'At least I fed the ungrateful bastards every day,' Beth apologised. 'Sorry, Mum, but I just couldn't keep on top of the washing up. I did them lunch today and they did their usual. Which was to run out of the door as they were chewing the last mouthful.'

Maggie hugged her daughter again. This was the best bit about coming home. 'Don't worry, darling. I know you've worked hard. Let's have a cup of tea and then we'll get to grips with this lot, shall we? Now tell me, how is George and where's your father?'

'George is round at Simon's house watching the footie. Simon's team is Chelsea and they're playing Southampton this afternoon, so whatever the result one of them will be furious.'

'And your dad?'

'Oh, pub as usual,' said Beth dismissively. Then she deliberately changed the subject. 'Mum, you must be knackered. That long overnight flight and then driving back home from Gatwick.'

'I managed to sleep a bit on the plane,' said Maggie.

'But I expect I'll collapse later on. Let's get that kettle on and attack those dishes. Then I can drop off to sleep without any guilty conscience.'

Beth was clearly relieved that she was home. Maggie wondered just how beastly Garth and George had been to her but she was too tired to push it just now. What she did need, though, was an inkling of Garth's general mood so she could psych up to the unpleasant prospect of seeing him again.

'So how was Dad while I was away?' She shot Beth a piercing look. 'Truthfully?'

'Bit stroppy,' Beth confessed. 'Just the usual, really. I was rather glad when he kept disappearing off.'

Oh, tell me about it, Maggie thought to herself. The tea really hit the spot and gave her enough energy to get through at least some of the dishes. Then Beth helped her carry her case upstairs where she confronted a linen basket so full of clothes and towels that it could have filled the bath next to it. What would they have all done if she'd been in hospital for several weeks? Answer: exactly the same, she suspected.

As she began to unpack, she was suddenly hit by a wall of fatigue. She managed to retrieve Beth's beaded bracelets, carefully wrapped in tissue paper, before she felt herself slipping into unconsciousness. She flopped on the bed, fully clothed, her head hit the pillows and she was gone. Much later, when it was dark, she was half woken by the sound of someone coming into the bedroom. It was Garth, judging by the grunting and cursing. She was aware of a faint whiff of beer on his breath. Her last thought was that at least they'd got through her first day back without exchanging a word. That meant he'd probably never mention the holiday at all. As she drifted off once more, she realised that they'd probably never have sex again.

As Maggie had expected, Garth made no enquiry whatsoever about the holiday. He merely muttered his thanks for the bottle of Scotch she'd bought him at the Mombasa duty free shop. Over Sunday lunch, George asked a couple of questions about the weather and whether there were any 'fit birds' at the hotel, and then launched into a long tirade about yesterday's tragedy of Southampton's slaughtering at the hands – or rather feet – of Chelsea football club.

The rest of the day passed in an endless toil of catching up on two weeks' worth of washing and making a stab at the ironing. Shirley Valentine probably came back to exactly the same thing. Maggie comforted herself, which was why the film very sensibly ended in Greece.

The prospect of getting back to work and routine was suddenly quite appealing, especially as it included avoidance of Garth. Picking up yet another load of washing, she caught sight of herself in the bathroom mirror. Well, the glorious tan was still there, if a tiny bit faded from jet lag. And she'd definitely lost weight. She hopped on the bathroom scales. Just under a stone lighter in a fortnight – and that was with her clothes on. She made an instant resolution to take a power walk every lunchtime from now on.

'Gosh, you look absolutely fantastic!' The reaction was instant and raucous. Damien, Mr Too-Smooth-To-Move, became uncharacteristically animated when he caught sight of Maggie.

'You look soooooo good,' he crooned, before dashing

back outside to remonstrate with a new traffic warden who was about to slap a ticket on his Porsche.

Even Vanessa, who tended to be more interested in her own pronouncements than those of her fellow workers, asked several questions about the trip. Mostly about the hotel, location and service, and, more important, the pedigree of the guests. Maggie had once heard Vanessa braying down the phone to a Sloany friend, rather tellingly pronouncing someone 'NQOCD'. Fortunately Fiona had been on hand to quietly translate this as 'not quite our class, darling'.

Maggie decided not to regale the office with what she considered to be the most fascinating aspect of the trip – visiting a Masai village and being covered in thousands of the flies that swarmed round huts traditionally built out of branches and animal excrement. She also decided to give a miss to the fantastic tale of two fat women on the beach who sold brightly coloured sarongs in exchange for clothes: she and Pam had dug out all their old T-shirts and flipflops at the end of the holiday and triumphantly swopped them for two beautiful sarongs. That was definitely NQOCD. Instead, she stuck rigidly to the G and T aspects of the trip, throwing in words like exclusive, luxurious, five-star, and so on. Everyone nodded approvingly.

With the pleasantries about the holiday dealt with, it was back to the grindstone. Maggie logged on to her computer and checked her email. Two hundred unread messages. She groaned as she began wading through them and trying to get her brain into gear. Several particularly dreadful flats and houses had apparently found new owners to love and restore them, but generally business had been quite quiet. Now, of course, they were gearing up for the Easter rush. There was a note to all the staff from Damien, dealing out a sharp message that post-Christmas figures hadn't been what he'd expected and they'd better pull off something good over Easter or else. 'Or else', Maggie assumed, meant no bonuses, or, worse, job losses. She shuddered momentarily, reminding herself of their financial state at home. Garth's lack of communication on all fronts lately meant she had even less of an idea of how his business was doing. That one time she'd actually taken a peek at the books had sent her reeling in shock. She'd never had any real notion of what Garth earned other than that it apparently provided a roof over their heads and paid some of the bills. She seemed to spend all her salary on food, providing Beth and George with what they needed, running her car and generally plugging the gaps.

Given the recent stilted atmosphere, this was definitely not the time to start asking Garth how much money he made. His reply would probably be unprintable but, she guessed, along the lines of 'Why the sudden effing interest? Mind your own effing business', followed by a vicious reference to her swanning off on an exotic holiday and then a long diatribe, blaming her sudden curiosity on Pam.

She was just dealing with the final emails and thinking about making some coffee when up popped an email from Pam:

> Hi honey. Crap to be back, isn't it! Right now, could do with a nice swim and laze by the pool followed by a large G and T. Must catch up later in the week and swap photographs. Also have

some interesting news. But refuse to tell you until we meet up. Love Pam x

Maggie shuddered. Pam's interesting news sounded very suspicious. She hoped it wasn't another line of inquiry about Jack. She'd left all that stuff firmly behind in Kenya, she'd promised herself. It was merely a holiday aberration, a moment of foolhardy curiosity, a case of the sun going to her head and affecting her judgement. Just like all those holidaymakers who stagger off planes from the Spanish costas clutching stuffed donkeys or sporting gondoliers' straw hats from Venice. It had seemed a fun idea at the time.

She'd reply later on when she'd made the coffee. As she went out to load up the machine, she reminded herself how coffee making had always been her device to avoid the culture/holiday chat in the office. Now at least she could hold her own amongst the office glitterati and literati. She'd managed to read three really cracking books on holiday too, so she could chip in with them when the conversation inevitably got back to the Booker, the Turner or Damien Hirst's latest dead animal.

Back at her desk, the coffee too hot to sip yet, she turned back to her screen and, before she could stop herself, tapped in the website address for the Tin Man. Just to make sure she hadn't imagined it, she reassured herself. Just to see if it was still there and not accessible only from Mombasa.

Sure enough, the picture of a tanned and smiling Joe and Christine Haley reappeared. Maggie took a sip of coffee, and before she'd even thought about it she'd clicked on to the page of photographs showing happy, mahogany-tanned customers, all enjoying a pie and a pint at the Tin Man. Now she couldn't stop herself, clicking on the pictures to enlarge them, looking for the familiar face with the laughing blue eyes and the soft brown hair. There were a couple of candidates for Jack but, as they were half obscured by other happy drinkers, she couldn't be sure. She must stop this. But she couldn't. Her brain refused to halt her errant fingers on the mouse, click click clicking away. More possible sightings, but she couldn't be sure it was him. Had he aged? Got wrinkles? Liver spots? Had he gone grey? Lost his hair? Teeth?

'Right, Maggie.' Vanessa's cut-glass accent came booming out of her open office door and straight through Maggie's reverie. 'I've got to go out now to a regional branch meeting so I've set up a couple of properties for you to view this afternoon, get you back in the groove. One looks rather dreary and frankly in need of a good steam clean. The other's a piece of pretentious nonsense. I apologise for the second one, but we all thought it best if you took the instruction.'

That sounded a bit loaded, Maggie thought to herself as she watched Vanessa's departing chalkstripe-suited back. Was this the office punishment for going off on holiday, to get landed with some ghastly, difficult client?

She looked at the first file. A dreary semi in a dreary road on the south side of Weltham, with nothing to be said for it. Nowhere near a good school, or a shopping centre, and not even on a bus route. Just very handy for aircraft noise and set slap bang in the middle of a flood plain. Now that would be a challenge.

Then she looked at the other one. The address, Ashleigh Manor Road in Cravensborne, rang a vague bell. Probably an unmemorable house on a nothing-to-say-about-it estate. It was clearly going to be a rather bland afternoon, but she might as well get back into routine as fast as possible.

Maggie did her power walk at lunchtime, as she'd promised herself. But there was no contest between Weltham High Street in the grey March drizzle and a leisurely swim in the Paradise Palms pool.

As she headed for the first house of the afternoon, she reflected once again on the Tin Man pub and how she'd unwittingly played detective. Just a fluke, she decided, and definitely not something to pursue. Yet there was no reason why she couldn't send Jack's parents a jolly email, say she'd come across their website and enquire after their health. But how would anyone 'stumble' on the Tin Man pub in Puerto Pollensa? She could tell a slight porky and say that Home Truths were looking to expand to foreign commercial properties and she'd been asked to do some research into British type pubs in Majorca. But was that a sufficiently stumble-worthy excuse?

Mercifully, the silly fantasy had to stop as she'd now pulled up outside house number one. Vanessa's dreary description was probably being kind. It had absolutely nothing going for it at all. Character completely lacking, damp well up the dull brick walls, paint peeling off the front door, window frames gently rotting. Jungle of a front garden. Even the gate was half hanging off and the three steps up to the front door were broken. No wow factor here. She knocked on the door. It was immediately answered by a tall and gangly man she judged to be in his late thirties. He wore scruffy jeans and a fleece, and sported several days' worth of stubble. He rather epitomised the house, Maggie thought to herself. No wow factor there either.

As he showed her round he made no attempt at any

conversation, other than grunting about a quick sale and mentioning a price that Maggie knew nobody with any grip on their sanity would pay. They went upstairs, the floorboards squeaking rather ominously. Three bedrooms but only two with any sort of furniture in them. Maggie soon spotted the reason. Above the empty room was a not inconsiderable hole in the roof. It had clearly been there for some time because the rain had gradually brought down the ceiling plaster so you could gaze up at the sky. Maggie looked up through the hole to see a small flock of geese flying nonchalantly overhead.

'How long ago did the tiles slip?' she asked the owner.

'Dunno,' was his surly reply.

'You do know that at Home Truths we describe the properties we take on in very honest terms,' she ventured, knowing that Vanessa and Damien would expect her to have a field day over this unexpected bonus for birdwatchers. 'You might not like how we describe your property when you see it in print. We tend to say outrageous things because it really does sell houses.'

'Just get shot of the fucker then,' said the man gruffly.

'I don't think we'll achieve the price you mentioned,' said Maggie, ignoring his swearing, 'but I think we could sell this quickly for you if you're prepared to drop fifteen per cent.'

She almost jumped at the sound of her own confidence. She knew it was just the sort of house that Home Truths adored having on its books. Simply disgusting, with huge faults that could be described in gloriously slutty detail. Maggie could still not quite get over the fact that although Home Truths was run by people like Vanessa, Stefan and Damien, with their taste for the high life and mixing it with the right people at the right parties, they were entirely happy to do business at the bottom end of the market.

The man with the stubble grunted his reluctant agreement over the price and Maggie headed out of Weltham to drive the eight miles to Cravensborne, where she was to meet the owner of 57 Ashleigh Manor Road, a Mr Gerald Bryan. She was still racking her holiday-befuddled brains as to why Vanessa had said they thought she'd be the best person to deal with this property.

Fifteen minutes after leaving the hole in the roof, she was parked outside the other extreme: a positively over-smart detached house on a rather pseudo gated estate. Clearly someone keen on topiary had been tending the garden. The front boasted several neatly clipped box hedges and immaculately shaped yew bushes.

The front door, guarded by two standard bay trees in brass pots, bore a brass plate giving the house a name: Ashleigh Manor. Rather a cheat considering the address. Perhaps Mr and Mrs Bryan had a wicked sense of humour. But somehow she suspected not. Already she sensed a house in which everything had been done, overdone and done again, just to be sure. As the door opened, she realised she was right. Greeting her was a middle-aged man with short grey hair swept back military style. He was totally overdressed for a visit from an estate agent, in a double-breasted navy blazer with gleaming brass buttons, grey flannels, highly polished brogues and a blue and white striped shirt with a bright red cravat. Maggie was utterly fascinated by the cravat. She'd never come across anyone who actually had the chutzpah to wear one. He was either a friend of Dorothy or one of those ex-military 'I'll wear what I bloody well like' types. The latter, Maggie decided.

'Come in, come in,' he announced briskly. He looked about forty going on sixty. Maggie glanced quickly around the hallway. Totally overdone, with terrible paintings in elaborate gold frames and a half-moon mahogany table polished to the point of erosion. He ushered her into the sitting room, where a baby grand piano had been squeezed into a corner and was groaning under the weight of an army of photographs in highly buffed silver frames.

'Lovely piano,' Maggie commented. 'Do you play?'

'Oh lawks, no,' he said, in a tone that indicated it was a ridiculous question. 'But jolly useful for photographs and resting the odd cocktail, eh?'

Maggie nodded, trying to look as though she agreed. They sat down on opposite chintz sofas near the fireplace, a symphony of mock marble with a huge brass screen. She got her file out ready to go through the basic Home Truths introductory pitch. She couldn't help but notice a magazine rack neatly stacked with back numbers of *Majesty* magazine, *Country Life*, *Horse and Hound*, and *The Lady*. Clearly true blue royalists, so she'd better not make any remarks about Prince Charles's latest scandal or take the mickey out of the Queen.

'Wife rather upset about selling the house,' Mr Bryan continued, in his brusque military manner. 'Doesn't want to be part of this, if you understand me.'

'Of course,' said Maggie soothingly. 'People buy and sell in all sorts of different circumstances. All we try to do is get your house sold as quickly as possible for the right price.'

'Exactly. Exactly.' He rubbed his hands together and

then adjusted his cuffs, Prince Charles style. 'Tried it low key with a couple of other agents but not a snifter. Got to bite the bullet now and be shot of it. So called in you chaps.'

She glanced round at the windows. wildly overdressed with elaborate royal blue velvet curtains complete with swags and tails. They'd have looked fantastic in a Victorian house with high ceilings and the proportions to take such a dramatic effect, but here in this rather poky four bedroom detached they were completely over the top.

'Taken a bit of a hammering on the stock market,' Mr Bryan harrumphed by way of explanation, adjusting his cravat. 'Not to mention Lloyds.'

Why didn't he go the whole hog and insist on calling himself Major, Maggie wondered. And why don't I buy the Lloyds name bit either? Lloyds names don't live on housing estates, unless they're terribly ex-Lloyds names, surely. They began a tour of the house, Maggie putting notes into her dictaphone.

'Dining room in here,' continued 'the Major', opening a door into a tiny room into which a huge mahogany table had somehow been crammed. Must have been a flat pack, thought Maggie with amusement, as she counted ten high-backed chairs squeezed round it. How guests managed to get themselves seated must be a feat of engineering in itself. Maggie looked up at the ceiling, half expecting to see some sort of winch. Instead she found herself gazing at a huge and incongruous glass chandelier. On the table were three enormous silver candelabra.

'Lovely room, eh?' said 'the Major' wistfully. 'Had some wonderful black tie dinners in here.'

Maggie turned away to stifle a laugh. The concept of

a whole pile of pseudo aristos turning up in full evening dress to squeeze themselves into this tiny dining room was just too ludicrous for words. She could imagine women in long dresses having to crawl on all fours across the table to manoeuvre themselves into their seats.

'Wonderful, I'm sure,' she replied, trying to keep a wobble of laughter out of her voice. She nearly lost it again when they went into the kitchen to find a couple of elderly corgis slumped and snoring in a basket in the corner. She half expected 'the Major' to fling open the fridge door to reveal bottles of Malvern water, Cristal champagne and the entire range of Duchy Originals, just in case Her Maj or Fergie called by.

The tour continued with Maggie desperately trying to keep herself in control. It was rather like a Tardis, she decided. Ordinary four-bedroomed detached estate house on the outside, Sandringham crossed with Balmoral on the inside. She rushed through the measurements as fast as she could, said goodbye to 'the Major' and fled to her car.

As she sat in the driver's seat, out of sight of the house, she burst out laughing. It had been one of the most pretentious piles of rubbish she'd ever seen. She put her key in the ignition. Then she stopped herself from turning on the engine. In her efforts to contain her secret amusement, she'd forgotten that Vanessa had made a point of sending *her* to view this particular property, but now it occurred to her again to wonder why.

Then, in one glorious moment, it suddenly dawned on her. The *Majesty* magazines, the corgis, the ridiculous dining room, the black tie dinners, the 'Major' who'd taken a hammering on the stock market. Of course! Why hadn't she thought of it before?

Who was the most pseudo royal family aficionado she'd ever known? Answer: Marina. Bitchy Marina Bryan who'd been sacked by Home Truths. That's why they'd sent her. And, of course, that was why Her Maj wasn't at home. Clearly Marina's losing her job had rocked the fortunes of the 'royal household'.

Chapter 24

'Be your very own Mrs Bouquet. Practise keeping up appearances in this totally pseudo four bedroom detached "manor house". All the cachet, but not so much of the council tax. Lovingly polished and buffed to Buckingham Palace standards. Chintzy sitting room that would appeal to any wannabe Windsor. Posh velvet curtains (royal blue, natch) and chandeliers included in the price. Play at being Hyacinth in the bijou dining room for those smart occasions, or entertaining weekend house guests. Minor health warning – it's tiny so only suitable if you have very thin friends. Kitchen fully equipped for your domestic staff. Good sized hall for leaving riding boots, headscarves, Barbours, shotguns, fishing rods etc. Highgrove style organic garden to rear affords enough privacy to talk to your plants without being spotted by the neighbours. Drive big enough for a Bentley, but might have to reverse out. Easy commuter distance for RAF Brize Norton, Ascot, Henley etc. Corgis regrettably not included in the sale.'

Maggie clicked save, print and then sat back in her chair. God, that was cruel, but Marina deserved it. She thought back bitterly to the day she'd bumped into her in the café and how bitchy she'd been. She also pondered on how much she herself had changed since that time. Not only had she sharpened up her brain considerably, but gone were the days when she'd be seen out in a tatty old track suit and no make-up. She looked back at what she'd just written. A few months ago, such catty remarks would never have entered her head either. The Home Truths ethos was certainly contagious. She must summon a bit more strength at home, too, in dealing with Garth and the kids. Her new attitude was already doing Beth and George a power of good, both at home and at school where they were getting better marks. But Garth was just as surly and evasive as ever.

She turned her attention to writing up the other house.

'If you're a fan of *The Sky At Night*, then this one's definitely for you. Unique views from this three-bedroomed pile of ****. Thanks to an act of divine intervention (and probably a few winter gales), nature has provided your very own black hole – in the roof. Who needs Patrick Moore when you can literally lie back in bed and look up at the stars? This house is a born again virgin. It's been untouched for years. Needs fit young stud (with cement mixer) to put a telltale smile back on its face. Bearded Bohemian owner will consider all way-out offers, man.'

Maggie doubted very much that the bearded Bohemian would even read the details. So long as they got shot of the house for him, that was all he was interested in. She added the room dimensions and printed it all off. Then she put the two files on Vanessa's desk for approval. She still suffered a quiver of nerves every time she awaited a verdict. Vanessa, in full dramatic flow on the phone, waved a bejewelled hand in acknowledgement while she clinched what appeared to be a deal involving a cocktail party.

'Perfectly ghastly man . . . no, darling . . . all sorted . . . done deal . . . totally gorgeous . . . yes, darling . . . eight-ish . . . marvellous . . . will Rupert and Lulu be there? Fantastic . . .'

Maggie waved a silent goodbye and went out for lunch. She was meeting Pam for a quick sandwich so that they could compare their holiday photos. And there was the small matter of Pam's mysterious news. That filled Maggie with slight trepidation. Pam's little bombshells tended to live up to their hype.

They met at the photo shop, collected their precious envelopes and then went to the rather dreary baguette bar next door which was known more for its speed than its style.

'Not exactly the Paradise Palms,' said Pam, glancing around at the tired-looking tables and faded dark red paint. Perched on wobbly stools, they got the food order out of the way as quickly as possible so that they could get to the business they'd come for: leafing through their holiday memories.

'Oh, God, it brings it all back' said Maggie, after a minute or two of wistful silence. They swapped envelopes and another silence ensued.

'Oh, look,' said Pam, rather deliberately, Maggie thought. 'There's you at the Cyber Café, just as you found the Tin Man website.'

Maggie stared at the picture. There she was hunched over the keyboard, looking intently at the screen. Oh, God, here we go again. Maggie began to panic. She was still somewhat ashamed of her recent little foray on to the internet, just to check that the Tin Man website was still there. Thankfully the baguettes and coffee arrived at that moment so the photographs had to be put away.

'So what's the big news then?' Maggie asked tentatively, wondering whether it was better to stick to the Tin Man or risk the unknown – which might be something worse.

Pam shot her a perceptive look and laughed. 'Nothing for you to worry about. Just my own insatiable nosiness. Fuelled, I suppose, by the Tin Man episode, I've had an attack of curiosity. I've found out what happened to Dave Gregg.'

Maggie looked at her blankly for a second or two.

'Dave the bullshitter,' Pam reminded her. 'Dave the Rave who put an ad in a dating column in the local paper when he was still going out with me.' She broke into a grin from ear to ear. 'He got his comeuppance!' She stopped to take a huge bite out of her baguette.

'Well, go on,' said Maggie. 'I'm on the edge of my seat – literally. This bloody chair is wobbling like mad.' She bent down and levelled the uneven leg with a folded-up tissue. By the time she'd done it, Pam was ready to spill the beans.

'I logged on to the Friends Reunited website when we got back from Kenya, clicked on our old school year and added my name. Saw a few familiar names. But not Jack, just in case you're beginning to panic.' She deliberately took another mouthful just to keep Maggie on tenterhooks. Then she continued: 'Didn't think any more about it until I got an email this morning from Dora. Remember her?'

Maggie winced. Isadora Fielding was one of the biggest gossips in the class, and a first class bitch in the making.

'If you remember,' Pam continued, 'Dora answered Dave's ad, along with half the women in town. When she realised who it was, she couldn't wait to spill the beans to me, the cow. That's how I found out. I wasn't best pleased at the time, but she did do me the most enormous favour in the long term.'

Maggie found herself immediately transported back to Weltham Grammar, remembering how they all used to cram into the tiny sixth form girls' common room. Many tears had been shed in that room by Pam, who'd been devastated and also deeply humiliated by the whole incident. Dave had been her first big love affair, and she'd lost her virginity to him, which made the humiliation and the loss even more painful.

Lonely hearts ads had only just started being featured in newspapers and were generally viewed as being only for the truly desperate, i.e. plug ugly. Dave had covered himself in glory by giving out his phone number in the ad. He'd been either too mean or too stupid to pay extra for a box number for replies.

'Well, guess what happened to him!' Pam announced triumphantly. 'Actually, you'll never guess. He went to prison.'

'Prison? Bloody hell,' Maggie gasped a little too loudly, which immediately engaged the interest of the surrounding tables. She and Pam instinctively moved their heads together to continue. 'Did he post that little bombshell on Friends Reunited?'

'No, you daft berk. Didn't I tell you that I heard vaguely back along that he'd gone on the knock? The old routine of in for a penny, out for a pound. Dora seemed to think it caught up with him and that he got done for handling stolen goods as well. So he ended up doing a stretch.'

'Is he still inside?' Maggie was absolutely riveted.

'No. Dora thinks he's on the straight and narrow now and – wait for it – thought he might have set himself up as a life coach.'

'A life coach? Well, he'd have plenty to draw on, I suppose.' Maggie chuckled at the thought of it. Then she looked suspiciously at Pam. 'Don't tell me you're going to track him down?'

'Already have.' Pam tapped her nose, pausing again for another bite from her baguette. 'He's got a website. I thought I might send him an email. What do you think?'

Maggie couldn't imagine anything more appalling. Other than sex with Garth. The memory of that horrible drunken night still haunted her. 'Don't you think that it might backfire?' she suggested. 'He might read into it the idea that you still care about him. If his ego is still the size of France, he'll be spilling over into Belgium and Germany.'

'Nah,' Pam answered knowingly, 'not after all this time. I just feel I'd like to square things with him. Right between the eyes.'

Maggie looked horrified. 'You're not suggesting you're going to go round and beat him up, are you?'

'No, just wind him up a bit. Write to his website and let him know that I know he went inside and what a complete plonker he is.'

Maggie retreated to her coffee cup. This was dangerous territory. I promise not to look up the Tin Man website ever again, she silently vowed to herself. But she knew in her heart it was a promise she wouldn't – and couldn't – keep.

Back at Home Truths, to Maggie's enormous relief, Vanessa was waxing lyrical about her descriptions of the

Sky at Night and the New Balmoral, which had already gone online.

'I read it out to Damien,' she proclaimed expansively, 'and he was positively honking with laughter.'

The concept of Too-Smooth-To-Move Damien honking at anything, other than a tractor blocking the road, was too bizarre to contemplate.

Maggie thanked her – and someone up in heaven – for the praise and hoped it meant that her job was a little more secure in the light of Damien's veiled threats regarding sales figures. Another pile of emails and messages greeted her, including one from the Bearded Boho asking her to ring him. Her heart sank. Had he already seen the website and rung to complain? She'd become quite hardened to the initial abuse from sellers, but just now her head was buzzing too loudly about the Dave Gregg life coach revelation to cope with someone ranting about their less-than-flattering house particulars.

She scanned the list of emails. Two listed Sky at Night as their subject. Phew! They were both requests to view the house. At least she'd be able to ring Boho with some good news. And in record time, too. The details could only have been online for an hour at the most.

She rang Boho to impart what she thought he'd consider good news.

'Too effing cheap,' he growled ungratefully. 'That's why they're snapping it up.'

'But you wanted a quick sale,' Maggie protested, with a 'some-people-are-never-satisfied' note in her voice. She'd picked that up from Stefan who used it to great effect when people complained at the size of their mortgage ('but we always try to avoid that word') repayments.

Boho whinged on for a few minutes and then suddenly capitulated, agreeing to some viewing times for the prospective buyers. Maggie whizzed through the rest of her emails. Pam, she noted, had already got back to her desk and sent her a note with Dave's life coach website address. She might not be able to resist looking at that later on.

She got Boho off the phone with 'sorry my other line's ringing, even though I don't have one' consummate ease. She'd never had the confidence or attitude to do that at Farleys.

She knew she should have rung the interested parties straight away but she couldn't resist it. She tapped Dave's website into a search engine.

The result was instant and hilarious. She'd never have recognised him from the photograph on the home page. All the curly black hair and thick black-framed specs were gone. Instead, a rather well-worn face with short grey hair had taken its place. And curiously, or perhaps to avoid association with his prison record, he'd reversed his name. The David Gregg she'd known at school had become Gregg David, Life Coach to the Stars.

The accompanying blurb was hilarious. Clearly being a life coach was a profession that needed neither qualifications nor government appointed regulator. It merely required cheek – in industrial strength quantities.

> Do you see yourself as an innocent bystander on the sidelines of life, peering at the world through a distorting mirror? Are you on the roller coaster whose brakes have just failed? Are you tumbling down the waste disposal chute of life? In short, are you out of control? Then let Gregg David, Life

Coach to the Stars, help you find the answers, pick up the reins and fix those brakes.

She wondered whether Pam would actually carry out her threat and exact her revenge. Knowing Pam, she probably would.

She glanced around the office. Vanessa had gone for the day, Stefan was at another branch and Fiona had just gone out on a viewing. For once, she was alone. She made herself dial the numbers of the two parties interested in the Sky at Night. As soon as she had them both booked in for viewings later in the week, she made herself a cup of tea and sat back down at her desk. She took a deep breath and began typing . . .

Dear Christine and Joe, This is probably a bolt out of the blue but I stumbled across the website for the Tin Man and thought I'd drop you a line . . .

Chapter 25

'Remember Randy Old Luke?' Pam's voice was bursting with excitement. Maggie braced herself for another onslaught of misplaced nostalgia.

'How could I forget?' she replied. Another gobby ex-boyfriend of Pam's who'd cheated on her rather publicly. 'You bumped into him in a pub snogging another woman, as far as I recall.'

'Yep, and spent a lifetime wishing I'd slapped the pair of them.' Pam was laughing. 'Well, I've tracked him down.'

Oh, God, thought Maggie, another Friends Reunited triumph. 'So what's the idiot up to? Let me guess. He was always very mouthy. Don't tell me he's joined the wonderful world of life coaches as well.'

Pam started laughing so loudly that Maggie had to hold the phone away from her ear. Eventually she calmed down. 'I've not only tracked him down but I've heard his voice.'

'I must say, hearing Luke's voice isn't high up my wish list but I do appreciate it might be part of yours. Go on. Put me out of my utter misery.'

'He's a DJ,' said Pam. 'Works on one of the tiniest radio stations in the country.'

'How on earth did you find that out?' said Maggie, astounded. 'Not nasty Dora mixing it again by any chance?'

'Nope,' Pam replied. 'Just persistent and tenacious research. Actually it was easier than you'd think. There aren't many Luke Godalmings around. Especially when the words Bonkers FM come up next to it. It just had to be him.'

Maggie wasn't convinced. 'You can't be certain it's him, surely.'

Pam burst into fits of laughter once again. 'Remember, I told you I heard his voice. I looked up Bonkers FM's website. All radio stations have them, these days, plus you can hear what's on air. I looked up when his programme was on and listened to a bit of it through the computer last night. He does one of those sad late-night phone-ins for loonies. You know the sort of thing: bit like a radio version of a drop-in centre for drop-outs.'

'You're not getting out enough,' said Maggie drily. 'When's Tom's next bit of shore leave? You need a calming influence.'

'Oh, don't be a spoilsport,' said Pam. 'It's only a bit of fun. And I get so bored in the evenings sometimes. Anyway, I'm thinking of phoning in for a laugh. In fact, why don't we do it together one night? Phone in and wind him up a bit.'

Maggie groaned inwardly. Pam's wild ideas too often turned into reality.

'Sorry, hon, gotta go,' she said hurriedly, seeing a streak of silver metal whizzing past the window. 'Damien's just drawing up outside.'

Later that afternoon, Maggie couldn't resist having a quick peek at the Bonkers FM website. Sure enough, there was a picture of Randy Old Luke, grinning inanely. Now virtually bald and sporting a rather unattractive earring, he had supplemented his picture with a biog that bore no resemblance whatsoever to his earlier life. There were grandiose statements about 'being destined for a career in the biz-that-is-called-show' and 'knowing from his earliest childhood days that he wanted to entertain'. He'd done that all right, the infamous night in the appropriately named Sour Grapes where Pam caught him out. Even Maggie had to admit she was curious enough to want to hear his radio show.

'I'm popping round to Pam's for a couple of hours,' she announced to Beth and George. 'Don't stay up too late. Take my advice and make sure you're in bed before your dad gets back from the pub.'

Beth shot her mother a meaningful look. Surely her mother wasn't at it as well, saying she was going somewhere and being somewhere else. 'Why are you going round there?' she asked suspiciously. 'She usually comes here.'

'Oh, thought it would make a change,' Maggie replied hastily. 'Also, to be truthful, your dad's not Pam's greatest fan. And besides, you two have got exams coming up. A bit of peace in the house would do you good. Why not crack on with that revision?'

Beth pulled a face. Britney and Boyzone hadn't needed French verbs to get to the top of the charts. But she knew her mum was right.

'One day you'll realise it was worth it, working hard at school,' Maggie told her daughter. 'Reeling off all the Westlife hits in the correct order won't get you a job in a few years' time.'

She kissed her daughter on the forehead, put on her coat and slipped out of the door. This was madness, she reflected, as she started up her car and headed for Pam's house a couple of miles across town. Yet in no time at all she was sitting with Pam in front of a computer in Tom's little downstairs study, clutching a huge glass of Merlot and listening to the inane output of Bonkers FM. Luke's show was due to start at 10 p.m.

Luke's voice had already come up in a trailer promising 'late night fun and games, and conversation for night birds'.

'I bet we don't get through,' said Maggie sceptically. 'There must be loads of people trying to get on the show.'

As always, Pam was undeterred. 'I bet not,' she said. 'We hadn't heard of Bonkers FM until the beginning of this week so on that basis I can't believe Randy Old Luke is exactly broadcasting to half the nation.'

They sat glued to the screen, listening to the station's output and laughing at Luke's photograph.

'I'd never have recognised him,' said Pam. 'How the mighty have fallen. And in his case, there's been a bit of follicle descent too.'

'Just coming up to ten o clock and that means time to join Luke Godalming for his late night fun and games here on Bonkers FM. We're all bonkers here,' shouted someone over an Ibiza type dance number.

Up came a brash signature tune and the unmistakable voice of Randy Old Luke, gobby as ever, with a rather pseudo transatlantic drawl added for good measure. 'Welcome to the best late night show in the land. Thanks for joining us here on Bonkers FM. We're all bonkers here.' Luke proceeded to drawl his way through a rundown of what was coming up on the show. Great music, time checks, fun and games, time checks, weather, time checks, competitions, presumably a few more time checks . . .

'I'm going to enter the competition if I know the answer,' said Pam, who clearly had thought this out. 'When it's time to call in, I'll take the phone in the other room and you can carry on listening here.'

They each took a huge slug of wine as if for Dutch courage.

'Now here's a number from one of my favourite song writers,' Luke drawled on, 'sung by simply one of my all time favourite singers.' Up came Frank Sinatra singing 'New York, New York'.

'Anyone would think he knew them all personally,' said Pam sarcastically. 'I'm going to try to pull off a little trick someone told me at work.'

'What's that?' Maggie was instantly suspicious.

'Well, apparently on some radio stations, when they start a new competition and people ring in, they're put through to the programme researcher who asks them in advance what they think the answer is,' Pam explained. 'The researcher then lines up a few calls from people they know will give the wrong answer, so that it spins the whole thing out a bit longer. Otherwise the competition's over too quickly and they have nothing left to fill the programme with. Think about it, Maggs. When did you last hear the very first person on the phone winning the prize?'

'Hmm, you have a point. So what's your plan?' Even as the words left Maggie's mouth, she realised it was almost an unnecessary question.

'If I get through, I'll give the wrong answer to the researcher, and hopefully the right answer to Luke on air.

So then I win the competition and get to talk to him. I heard him have quite a chat with last night's winner.'

Pam explained that she'd picked up this snippet from one of the guys in her office who worked for hospital radio. He'd told her that the really small radio stations had virtually no budgets and therefore very few listeners, so they relied heavily on phone-ins from their regulars.

'So, as soon as the competition question comes up,' she continued, 'assuming we know the answer, I'll beetle into the other room and get on the phone.'

They sat back in their chairs and took another sip of wine while Sinatra finished his rendition of 'New York, New York'. And then, the minute Ol' Blue Eyes had left the 'city that doesn't sleep', up came Luke's irritating drawl with the competition question.

'OK,' said Pam. 'Now let's see if we can beat the system.'

'George W. Bush is the president of the United States,' Luke continued. 'What does the W stand for?'

'That's easy,' Maggie and Pam chorused in delight. 'It's Walker.'

'Right,' said Pam, rubbing her hands. 'I'm going to phone in and say it stands for Dubya and spell it out. Say I saw it in the newspapers.'

'That's brilliant. You're wasted at the council.' Maggie had always envied Pam's quick-wittedness. 'Good luck. This is so exciting, I'm shaking.'

'I've got goosebumps,' Pam admitted. 'This bit of revenge is long overdue.' With that, she disappeared into the sitting room next door.

Maggie remained in front of the screen, listening to Luke crooning on about tonight's big prize, which was a Bonkers FM tea towel plus a rollover prize from the previous night, a Bonkers FM egg cup. She was beginning to see what Pam was talking about. This was the very thin end of the radio wedge.

'We're all bonkers here at Bonkers FM. Some mad, mad prizes on offer tonight but no winner so far. Bert just now thought George Bush's middle name was Walton. Mixing him up with the Waltons, eh, Bert? And Annie thought it stood for Wisconsin. Wrong! Then we had Dean who thought it stood for wan— hey, let's not go there, Dean. Now I've got Pam on the line. So Pam honey, here's that million dollar question one more time. What does the W stand for, in the name of the President of the United States of America?'

'Hi, Luke,' Pam's voice came through clear and calm. 'I think it's Walker.'

Luke, clearly expecting the Dubya answer, was already in 'I'm sooooo sorry that's the wrong answer' mode.

'Oh no, that's the wr . . . ight answer!' he managed. Suddenly the inane chatter was sounding ever so slightly strangulated. A tinny fanfare of trumpets hastily followed. Maggie could just imagine him already thinking, 'Shit, how on earth do we fill for the next hour or so?'

'So it's a big well done to Pam,' Luke had recovered his composure, 'and a Bonkers FM tea towel and egg cup are on their way to you. Poptastic congratulations to you, my darling. Stay on the line, Pam. You're listening to Bonkers FM. We're all bonkers here. Is there anyone you'd like to say hello to?'

'Oh, yes, please,' said Pam. 'I'd like to say a big hello to all the people I was at school with.' She then reeled off half the names of their old class, excluding Luke himself.

Luke clearly didn't make the connection at all. 'That's

just fantastic,' he drawled on. 'Now tell me, while we're on the subject of George Bush, have you ever been to the United States?'

'Yes, I have, actually,' said Pam.

'Oh, do tell.' Clearly, with the competition now down the tubes, Luke had lots of time to fill. She briefly outlined a trip to New York she'd been on with Tom before Mark was born. This was music to Luke's ears because it gave him the opportunity to do the big swank about *his* time in New York. It consisted of a whopping fib, Maggie suspected, about DJ-ing in some trendy Manhattan club.

'What a fantastic experience,' Pam crooned. 'You've obviously had an amazing life.'

Luke couldn't resist the prompt. 'Well, that certainly was one of the many high spots so far. Along with Bonkers FM. We're all bonkers here.'

He lapsed into his jingle at every opportunity, and then proceeded to talk through a few more 'high spots' in his star-studded career, referring to the 'biz' whenever he could, and dropping names and places to PhD standard. All mention of his previous life as Pam and Maggie knew it had been conveniently deleted. According to Luke, he'd grown up practically next door to Duran Duran and half the cast of *EastEnders*.

'Gosh, that's all sooooo interesting,' Pam gushed. 'Can I share my most interesting moment with your listeners?'

'Of course,' replied Luke, clearly grateful that he had an articulate listener for once who was helping him out of a hole.

'I was about eighteen at the time and going out with a guy. Funnily enough he was called Luke, same as you. Probably what reminded me.'

Completely unsuspecting, Luke gave a deep throaty laid back type of laugh. 'Lot of us about,' he drawled. 'Do go on, Pam. You've got the nation gripped here on Bonkers FM. We're all bonkers here.'

'Well, he was a cheat and everyone warned me but I was too stupid to take any notice,' Pam continued warmly. 'I really liked him, although you know, Luke, how love is a bit blinkered when you're young.'

'Certainly do, Pam. Go on.'

'Well, eventually I caught him out. He was sitting in a pub near where we lived, snogging this other girl. Everybody knew about her, except me.'

'Oh, Pam, that's terrible. Luke was now offering up fake sympathy. 'So what did you do?'

Pam laughed. 'That's the trouble, Luke. I didn't do anything. I just walked away. I suppose I hoped that perhaps it was some horrible mistake and that he'd come back to me.'

'And did he, Pam?' said Luke, clearly hoping for a heartwarming ending to this unfolding tale of love and loss.

'No, he didn't, Luke,' Pam replied. 'And my big regret is that I didn't go up and bang their heads together.'

'Sounds like they were already headlocked.' Luke was now oozing oily charm and mentally wondering whether to start a late-night heartache spot on the show, as this story was going so well.

'Hey, you wanted your revenge, Pam,' he continued encouragingly. 'That's perfectly understandable. But I thought you said this was the most *interesting* moment in your life. It sounds more like a sad one to me.' Then he abruptly broke into jingle mode again. 'Stay tuned, people. Pam here is telling us about her most interesting moment. Perhaps *you'd* like to phone in with *your* most interesting moment in a moment. Ha ha. Stay tuned to Bonkers FM. We're all bonkers here. So, Pam, what happened after that? You have the entire country hanging on now, you know.'

Maggie could sense Pam psyching herself up for the kill.

'Well, Luke,' she continued, her voice tightening, 'it all happened twenty-two years ago, but amazingly I've tracked him down.'

'Brilliant! Isn't that just the most amazing thing, bonkers people? She's tracked him down. And . . .'

'I discovered that he was working on a local radio station, running a late-night phone-in. Bit like yourself, Luke, on Bonkers FM.'

'Mad people, mad music. Bonkers FM – we're all bonkers here.' It still hadn't dawned on him!

'In fact, Luke, *this* is my revenge. This is my most interesting moment. You were that person. You cheated on me and I've spent years wanting to get my own back. So you can stuff your Bonkers FM tea towel and egg cup up your bonkers arse, which was rather spotty as I recall . . .'

'Start spreading the news . . .' Frank Sinatra's voice suddenly came back, hastily cutting Pam off.

Pam came through to the study, wiping away tears of laughter. 'He always did talk as though he had a firework up his bum,' she said, collapsing into a chair in hysterics.

Chapter 26

Dear Christine and Joe, Can't believe the coincidence but I was doing some research on British pubs in Spain (I'm a negotiator at an estate agency) and stumbled on your website. I don't know if you remember me but I used to be a friend of Jack's at school and worked in London for a while when he was at university. Just couldn't resist sending you a note . . .

This was about the tenth draft Maggie had written. It was the wording of the connection with Jack that she couldn't get right. 'I used to be a friend of Jack's' was hardly a credible euphemism for 'we were madly in love for ever and then he disappeared'. The other bit she got stuck on every time was the reason for writing. It was all very well to say she couldn't resist sending them a note but they were bound to wonder why. Because I am enquiring after your health? Those tans in the photograph look a bit overdone, and perhaps you should consider a higher factor sun cream? Because I write to everyone I think I might have vaguely known over the past forty years? Or because I never got over your son and want to know where he is and what he's doing?

Then there was the required sentence about her own life. At one end of the spectrum was 'I'm married to a wonderful man, and together we have created an idyllic life in our beautiful home with our two happy and gifted teenage children'. Or, at the truth end of the market, there was 'I'm stuck with an unsuccessful piss artist and two sometimes bolshy children as we slip-slide our way slowly into the pit of debt and despair, following a lifetime – so far – of underachievement'.

And what about the hidden message she wanted to convey? 'Your son was the love of my life. I've never stopped loving him and missing him, and the hurt and pain of his sudden departure will go with me to my (probably early) grave.'

And what would be their reply? That's if they bothered to reply. The putdown version would probably be: 'Oh yes, we remember all Jack's girlfriends with great affection. He's doing terribly well, you know. We're so proud of him, running his own computer business in Los Angeles and living in a beachside house in Malibu. Our daughter-in-law couldn't be more exquisite and their four beautiful children are destined to be high flyers in law, finance, medicine and acting.'

The perfect reply would, of course, describe Maggie as the 'daughter-in-law we'd always hoped for. Jack talks about you constantly and is terribly unhappy in America. Meeting you again would change his life and rescue him from the treadmill of his lonely existence in the Californian sunshine.'

Then what? In her idle daydreams, Maggie had never risked getting as far as some life-changing scene at an airport. Far too scary. And besides, she had Beth and George to think about. No, this was just a tiny fantasy that had grown out of proportion and needed to be filed under Past Mistakes. It was all right for Pam to track down old rotters and see them off, but she had real reasons to despise them. Where Jack was concerned, their parting was still a painful mystery.

As she tidied up her desk, ready for another viewing session, she suddenly found herself thinking about Jane Eyre. As part of her continuing campaign to keep up with the chat in the office, she'd taken to delving into some of the classics she'd never got round to reading at school. Charlotte Brontë's most famous novel had been at the top of her list of should-have-reads. Jane Eyre got her man. Even plain little Jane Eyre, the downtrodden governess, finally came up trumps. OK, his mad wife had to burn down the house and blind him first but they'd managed to get it together at the end. Maggie had felt warm salty tears trickling down her cheeks as she read the scene of their bittersweet reunion.

Nope, she told herself, stacking up a bunch of files, it would definitely not be like that with Jack. He'd probably be a cigar-toting, overweight loudmouth with a brassy wife and loud fat kids, boasting heaps of dollars and stock market killings. Or, almost worse, he'd be the same lovely guy with the soft blue eyes and the wicked grin. The cheeky sense of adventure, the ability to light up a room and make everyone feel they were special and valued. He'd probably be successful but modest, hardworking and a wonderful family man. As a result, he'd have perfectly behaved kids and a lovely wife who probably looked and cooked like a dream, and thrived on his love and encouragement.

I have got to stop this, she told herself. This is a waste of good thinking time. This is a fantasy. This is not real life. This could get painful.

And just to spite herself, she had another look at the draft email to Christine and Joe Haley and added the words 'you both look so well and haven't aged a bit. I recognised you immediately'. Must stop this, she told herself yet again.

'I've tracked down a couple more,' Pam announced over lunch the following Saturday. As always, Pam looked amazing. Today she was wearing a pair of beige combats and a cream T-shirt with a black suede bomber jacket.

If I lost another stone and a half and had a tummy tuck and a face lift, I might be able to get away with that, thought Maggie sadly. Her power walking was certainly toning her up but the weight wasn't shifting as fast as it had in Kenya.

'Tracked down a couple more what?' she asked suspiciously. 'More dodgy life coaches or graveyard DJs?'

'No, just people from our class,' Pam explained. 'Dora knows it all.'

'She always was the most horrendous gossip,' said Maggie. 'I'm afraid I never liked her.'

'Me neither, but I had another email from her this week and she seems to know what happened to just about everyone.'

'Including Jack, I suppose,' said Maggie, bracing herself for the bald facts at last.

'No, before you start panicking again,' replied Pam swiftly. 'Only that he went to the States, which we know already. But she knows what happened to Rick.'

Maggie gasped. Two decades and more rolled back.

Rick Churston, an intriguing combination of brains and an obsession with old bangers, had been one of her first boyfriends when they were still at school. She'd always suspected that Dora had tried a few times to steal him from her, which probably sowed the seeds of their mutual mistrust and dislike.

'Apparently he's a top barrister,' said Pam. 'Specialises in employment law.' Maggie went white. Pam laughed. 'You look like you picked out the winning lottery numbers but forgot to buy the ticket.'

Maggie hastily regained her composure. 'No, it's not that. He was just an early pash but it was a baptism of fire. I trusted him about as much as I trusted Dora. But it's amazing how people turn out. I shouldn't be surprised really. He was terribly clever – one of those irritating people who never seemed to do any revision but always got top marks. I hope he's driving a better car these days.'

Rick was the first in his year to have a car, a battered old Triumph Herald, sprayed a vile custard yellow, which he insisted on driving to school and parking in the staff car park. Everyone knew when Rick had arrived, thanks to its rattling exhaust and screaming fanbelt.

'We can only hope,' said Pam, raising her eyebrows at the memory. They paused while their warmed goat's cheese and dressed herb salad was plonked down in front of them.

'And no, I don't want to go and see him perform in court,' said Maggie, anxious to scupper any attempt by Pam to have some fun along the lines of her encounter with Bonkers FM. 'Rick didn't humiliate me in the way that Luke did you. Or David Gregg or Gregg David or whatever he calls himself these days.'

'True,' Pam agreed. 'You were a bit luckier than me in

that respect. I did go through it a bit with those two, didn't I?'

'You got the luck in the end, though,' said Maggie with a slight tinge of envy. 'You're really happy with Tom and Mark's doing well at university.'

Pam shot her a sideways glance. 'And how is Darth Vader at the moment?' She could never quite hide the dislike in her voice.

'Oh, we keep out of each other's way as much as possible now,' said Maggie. 'It's funny, I was only thinking that the other day. We're managing to avoid each other quite successfully. It's so much better that way. I can't remember the last time we sat down to a meal together. It must be weeks ago. I cook for the kids and then leave him some of it to reheat. He's either out working or in the pub or God knows where.'

'How's his business?' Pam asked, with another piercing look.

'Don't know,' said Maggie. 'We don't discuss it. I'd almost rather not know. Today he's at a gardening festival . . . allegedly.'

'Why allegedly?'

'Because I don't trust him any more,' said Maggie. 'I'm certain the business is going down the tubes but he's in some sort of denial. He doesn't seem to be making any effort to save it. He's obviously totally disorganised because we get a regular trickle of stroppy phone messages from people who were expecting him to cut their grass that day.'

She outlined her attempts to help him market himself, starting with tidying up their own garden. She explained how she'd suggested setting up a website, targeting the streets with larger plots, having leaflets printed, and even displaying some in the Home Truths branches for anyone needing a garden tarted up for a quick sale. But Garth had ridiculed all her suggestions and studiously ignored her advice.

'Who pays the mortgage?' Pam asked bluntly.

'He does,' Maggie replied. 'Or at least I hope he does. I must say I have had the odd nightmare about that.'

They paused while their plates were cleared away. Pam decided to change the subject.

'Must enter some more holiday competitions,' she said brightly. 'I still lie in bed dreaming about the Paradise Palms.'

'Me too,' said Maggie. 'And I don't restrict my dreams to bedtime either.'

Dear Christine and Joe, What an incredible coincidence! I couldn't resist writing, having stumbled across your website during some research I'm doing on British pubs in Spain. I'm Maggie Berry, by the way. If you remember, I used to go out with Jack all those years ago. I'm a negotiator at an estate agency and we've been looking at the possibility of setting up a foreign commercial arm, hence my research. Realised it must be you, given the name, the Tin Man. I still remember the Wizard of Oz poster in your dining room.

Anyway, I thought I'd send you a quick note to say hello and that you both look fantastic in the photograph on the website. Life must be treating you well. I'm fine, enjoying my job and I now have two teenage kids to keep me busy! Do remember me to Jack.

If ever I'm in Majorca, I'll come and see you.
Best wishes, Maggie.

Maggie's finger hovered over the send button. She read the email again. There was one blatant lie which was the line about the foreign commercial arm. And another lie by omission. No mention of Garth. But then, people don't have to compartmentalise themselves these days by stating whether they're married or divorced. Actually, the foreign business was actually a genuinely good idea. She'd been constantly reading about Brits selling up and leaving Rip-off Britain to run gîtes in France, or bars in Spain. Even the *Weltham Gazette* had begun a tiny foreign section on its property pages, and knowing Vanessa and Damien they'd want to be at the forefront of anything.

She re-read the email again and again. It was harmless enough. A family friend from the past, getting in touch out of polite interest, she told herself. It was *not* a cynical attempt to find out what had happened to the love of her life, bounce back into his world and snatch him away from his nearest and dearest, just because she herself had made a mistake in her choice of partner – or was it? Was she actually being nosy, curious or obsessive? Would this lead to more pain when she read the reply full of glowing reports about Jack's wonderful life in the States?

She reread it yet again. Oh dear, she spotted three more fibs. The discovery of their website wasn't 'an incredible coincidence' at all. It was the result of her sun-befuddled brain's doggedly surfing the internet in a tiny cyber café. Nor was she ever likely to be in Majorca. Fat chance of that, unless Pam came up with another competition win. And it wasn't a 'quick note'. She'd been tinkering with it for weeks.

Once again her middle finger hovered over the send button. Should she or shouldn't she? God, this was like the movies, with the whole audience wondering whether she would go through with it, yet subconsciously knowing that there'd be no point to the film if she didn't.

I'll toss for it, she thought, rummaging in the top drawer of her desk where she often kept some car parking change amongst the pens, staples and paperclips. She couldn't find a single coin.

If the phone doesn't ring in the next twenty seconds, I won't send it. An ominous silence.

OK, it all hinges on the next phone call. If it's a time waster, I won't send it.

Maggie sat almost paralysed at her desk now, waiting for her phone to ring. She could hear Vanessa's muffled tones through the office door, clinching yet another big deal amid plans for a shooting weekend. Fiona and Stefan were out with clients. Outside in the street, a young couple were clearly having a heated argument, judging by their body language, as they peered at the property details in the window. Probably first time buyers shocked at the prices, she judged.

Come on, phone, ring. Put me out of my misery once and for all. But the phone refused to play ball.

Oh, stupid game, she finally decided. She got up and went out to the tiny kitchen to make some fresh coffee for herself and Vanessa. It was just beginning to drip through into the jug amid the telltale hissing when she heard her phone ring. She dived out of the kitchen, and, in an almost rugby style swerve, grabbed the receiver.

'Home Truths,' she almost barked down the phone.

'Maggs? It's me. You sound under pressure. I'll ring back.'

It was Pam. Maggie hit the send button before she could stop herself.

'I've done it! I've done it!' she screamed excitedly down the phone.

'What on earth are you on about?' Pam was the voice of concern.

'Emailed the Tin Man,' Maggie said breathlessly. 'I was playing this game with myself about whether to send it or not. And I decided that if the next call was not a time waster, I'd hit the button. And it was you.'

Pam roared with laughter so loudly that Maggie had to hold the receiver away from her ear for a second or two.

'Oh, Maggie, you are a basket case.' Pam was still laughing. 'So it was all down to one phone call, eh? Well, I'm glad I'm not a time waster. And I'm *really* glad you've sent it.'

An unexpected wave of relief came over Maggie. She hadn't realised she'd feel like that. It was as though there'd been a problem and now it was off her desk. It just left the small matter of waiting for a reply.

Chapter 27

Donning a pair of wellies and some rubber gloves, Maggie tried to remember the last time she'd done any gardening. Garth had always grudgingly done it, muttering and cursing about it being a busman's holiday. But he hadn't touched the garden in months now and it looked like a jungle. Not exactly a great shop window for a burgeoning garden services company.

Maggie couldn't bear to see the mess any longer. All the spring bulbs had been and gone without so much as a whisper, fighting for recognition amongst the dandelions, overgrown lawn and straggling shrubs. She decided to give everything a serious haircut. After an hour of wielding a pair of rather blunt and rusty shears, she'd managed to fill three refuse bags with clippings. Then she dragged an old Flymo out of the garden shed and plugged it in. After a bit of a splutter, it whirred into action. The grass was so long in places that the poor motor kept cutting out. As a result, it took her nearly an hour to cut the lawn.

She stood back to admire her work, wiping away beads of perspiration with a grimy hand. It certainly looked better. From beneath that canopy of weeds, and in some corners some seriously indigenous brambles, something neater and tidier had emerged. Rather like me, she thought. A bit frayed round the edges but a little nip and tuck would do wonders.

As she stood in the watery sunshine, still catching her breath, she wondered yet again just what Garth was up to with his business. No one in their right mind would have guessed that this house belonged to a professional gardener. It would be like discovering that your bank manager couldn't count beyond ten or that your favourite author had never mastered joined-up writing.

She must somehow tackle Garth about the mortgage. That throwaway comment from Pam had hit home. She was now, it seemed, paying all the day to day bills: food, phone, electricity and gas. Not to mention the kids' needs. The council tax and mortgage repayments were supposed to come out of Garth's account. She had a shrewd idea he simply lobbed the statements straight over to Brenda the book-keeper, perhaps too afraid to read them properly.

Ah well, at least the exercise this morning had done her good. Sweating at least twice a week was essential for a healthy heart, she'd read recently. Let's hope it cancels out the total stress-out I'm feeling about money.

Tomorrow was Monday and she was counting the hours until she could log on and see if— She stopped herself yet again. This idle thinking about Jack might have been entertaining on holiday, but now it was well out of order. It felt, well, almost adulterous somehow. There was something in her subconscious that had stopped her from giving out her hotmail address. When Joe and Christine replied, they'd be writing to her at Home Truths. That's, of course, if they replied at all.

'And they won't,' she said aloud, as if to remonstrate with herself. How would they react to her note? For a start, they'd be loyal to Jack. Perhaps they even knew the reason why Jack didn't turn up that night. Maybe they were pleased – even relieved – it had all ended. She could imagine them discussing it. 'Well, she was hardly a catch . . . it was just a teenage thing that wasn't going anywhere . . . oh, don't get me wrong, Maggie was a nice enough girl, but . . . whereas our Jack was always going to be a high flyer.'

Oh, shut up, you silly woman, she told herself. If they reply, then that's lovely. If they don't, for chrissake have the sense to leave it alone.

At nine o'clock prompt, Maggie was behind her desk, feverishly tapping her log-in name and password into her computer. Up came nearly thirty inquiries from the website, mostly about a new property, or rather a ruin, which had gone on the market that weekend at a knockdown price.

'Knockdown or knock it down. That's up to you. Nothing whatsoever to commend it, except the price. Big snag – constant pong of fat from the fish and chip shop opposite. Suit enthusiastic DIY-er with low cholesterol levels. Or greedy builder looking for a fast buck – and fast food virtually on site. No need to bring your own sandwiches.'

Maggie scrolled up and down in despair. Nothing from the Tin Man. What a fool she'd been to send her note. She forced herself to concentrate on the emails enquiring anxiously about Knockdown. Mostly first time buyers, she guessed, utterly desperate to get on to the property ladder somehow, no matter how lowly the rung.

‘Lots of interest in that ruin opposite the chippie.’ She got up and put her head round Vanessa’s door. ‘Shall I organise a group site visit?’

‘Good idea,’ said Vanessa. ‘It’ll save us a lot of time. Half of them won’t realise that what they’re interested in is a dump, so best get the agony over *en masse*. Incidentally . . .’ She handed Maggie last Saturday’s edition of the *Weltham Gazette* and tapped the relevant page. From a quick glance, Maggie could see it was full of photographs of Spanish villas and apartments. ‘Don’t want to get pipped at the post on this. What do you think about us taking on some foreign properties? You’re at the sharp end here with the punters. Do people mention France or Spain when they’re enquiring?’

For a nano-second, Maggie was transfixed with fear that she’d be forced to ring up Joe and Christine Haley and actually pick their brains on this one. Served her right for fibbing in that email.

‘Yes, a few of them do,’ she stumbled, trying to regain control of herself. ‘But I think for most of them it’s more of a wish-list type of thing. You know, the “if only” types. If only we didn’t have the kids, schools, our parents, our jobs to think about stuff. Whether they would translate into genuine inquiries, I don’t know. But maybe we should explore.’

Then she suddenly remembered an article she’d read several weeks ago in the *Sunday Telegraph* about relocating to France and Spain.

‘Of course, we’d need to offer some specialist advice.’ She began plundering the details. ‘There are a lot of tax and pension implications, plus all those weird French inheritance laws that go back to Napoleonic times. I’m sure most people are fazed by it when they delve beneath the surface. We'd need to set up a handholding service, I think, because most people just don't have the language skills or the confidence.'

Me neither, she wanted to add.

'Absolutely right.' Vanessa beamed at her. 'I stagger around Verbier quite happily but that's only to the extent of ordering a few cocktails, shopping and complaining about the ski lift. Ploughing through a sale contract would be a different matter.'

'Probably the easiest way would be to tie up with a reputable French or Spanish agent,' Maggie suggested, 'and offer to market their properties here for a split fee.'

Where had that come from? She'd just made it up. And here was Vanessa, in complete agreement.

'Exactly what I was thinking. I don't think my people in Verbier would be much help. For our kind of clientele,' she rolled her eyes momentarily to heaven, 'we probably need to think about the most popular holiday areas, the costas, the Canaries and maybe the Côte d'Azur. Do you have any contacts we could plunder?'

What Vanessa was really saying was that *her* friends were too posh to be of help to the lower end of the market.

'Might have,' said Maggie, now wishing this whole conversation would go away. 'I'll have a whizz through my Filofax.'

'Marvellous, darling! I'll mention it to Damien when he's around later on. He's been bending my ear about expanding. It would make our lives much more interesting than dealing with that ghastly little heap opposite the chippie.'

Maggie went back to her desk and began setting up a group site visit for the 'ghastly little heap' . Apart from the

Tin Man aspect, she had to admit to herself that the idea of having some connection with France or Spain did seem very glamorous. Not that she'd probably see any of the action, but it would be fun taking calls and wafting through endless details extolling the virtues of Tenerife, St Tropez or even Benidorm. She could envisage a whole new clientele of Division Two footballers' wives click-clacking on their Jimmy Choos in and out of the office.

She began replying to all the punters interested in the ruin, offering them a choice of site visits on two afternoons later in the week. She was amazed at the quick response, some replying almost by return click. Clearly there was a huge market for something this cheap – and, by definition, with immediate vacant possession. She could imagine the much cheaper properties in France or Spain, which came with the promise of a sunshine lifestyle, would probably disappear even faster.

The morning whizzed by, with another ten phone calls expressing interest in the ruin. What was it about total wrecks that the English seemed to be so drawn to? She'd read in that *Sunday Telegraph* that Brittany in particular still had plenty of ruined barns all ripe for renovation and that the French, for some reason, didn't share the same passion.

Exhausted from the phone bashing and trying to sort reasonably equal numbers for the two site visits, Maggie went out for her lunchtime power walk The early May sunshine was really invigorating. She glanced up at a cloudless blue sky. She could completely understand why people wanted to up sticks and live abroad if they thought they would get many more days like this one. Maybe it was something she could do herself when the kids had left home. Be the Home Truths representative in some lovely little Breton town. They'd visited Vannes once during a camping holiday years ago and she'd fallen instantly in love with its twisting cobbled streets, the medieval wash-houses down by the river with their roofs and floors bowed incongruously over the centuries, the exquisite flower beds next to the old ramparts, the bustle of the flower and honey market and the smart cafés with their tables and chairs spilling out into the streets in front of the marina. Garth, she noted to herself, was not part of this snapshot.

Back at the office, there were more emails and more phone calls about Knockdown. She just couldn't believe how much interest it was generating. More people had responded to her note about the site visits. There simply wasn't enough parking nearby to accommodate more than twenty cars per visit. She'd have to organise another couple of visits next week. Those whose emails had arrived after lunch, would have to be offered the next week appointments, she decided. And suddenly there it was – tucked in amongst all the messages entitled Knockdown – a message from the Tin Man.

Maggie felt the colour drain from her face. Her hand was shaking as she grasped the mouse to double click on the message. The words swam on the screen and she had to read the message twice before she could make proper sense of it.

> My dear Maggie, How absolutely delightful to hear from you! Of course we haven't forgotten you and often wonder what you are doing. We moved to Spain twenty years ago, before the days of email, and so we lost touch with a lot of people. Also, setting up a business in Spain was

incredibly hard work in the early years, but we finally got to grips with the language which helped. We take life a bit easier now we're older. Just wish we saw Jack and his family a little more often. He's based in Massachusetts these days so we don't get to see as much of them all as we'd like.

Promise you'll come and visit us if you're ever on the island. And if we can help on the property side, then just get in touch. We have some good friends who are estate agents whom we could highly recommend. Glad to hear you're doing so well. Jack will be pleased to hear your news.

Fondest regards to you and your family,
Christine Haley (and Joe of course. He's behind the bar).

So there it was, the reply she'd hoped for. But not the result. She'd wanted to hear Jack was unhappy, divorced and pining to come home to England (and her). What she got was the picture of someone who had definitely made his life in the States, and of course the key word, 'family'. She felt a stab of pain at that. What did it mean? Clearly he must have kids but did it mean 'wife and kids', 'wife, kids and wife's huge family' or even 'ex-wives one and two, plus wife and various kids along the way'? Then there was the last bombshell. 'Jack will be pleased to hear your news.' Would he? Or would he think what a lucky escape he'd had from the girl he'd sensibly dumped?

She forwarded the email to Pam with a note asking what she thought. Back almost immediately came a phone call.

'What a lovely note,' said Pam encouragingly. 'Really friendly, and a genuine invitation to visit or phone. So you've clearly not been painted as some Cruella de Vil type character.'

'It's worse than that,' said Maggie before she could stop herself. 'Home Truths is thinking of expanding into France and Spain. So my little fib about the research has become a reality. Vanessa wants me to find some reputable estate agents.'

Pam burst out laughing. 'Ha ha,' she roared, 'serves you right. Well, you'd better get on the phone to them immediately, then. They've got all the answers waiting for you.'

Oh, God, Maggie groaned inwardly. Not today. Can't face that today. It's far too soon. I'd have to psych up to that. Maybe tomorrow.

Driving home that night, Maggie resolved not to phone but to write them a polite email and pray that they'd come up with a name and phone number for their agent friends. But as she pulled up in front of the house and admired its newly shorn garden, she realised once again how much everything depended on her job. With Garth's business and general whereabouts now shrouded in mystery, she really had to capitalise on what she'd achieved at Home Truths. Yes, she'd make that call tomorrow. If it meant more Brownie points at work then she'd grit her teeth and do it. This wasn't about Jack any more, this was about survival.

Next day Maggie waited until she was alone in the office. She'd already typed out a kind of prompt script with the exact phrases she wanted to say. 'Happy enough', 'married a long time', 'kids growing up and away', 'really come alive with this new job'. She dialled the number of the Tin Man. It connected immediately, which slightly unnerved her. A series of long continental ring tones followed. Five more and I'll hang up. One, two, three, four . . . it was answered by a woman with a thick Spanish accent.

'Buenos dias. Teena Mana.'

Maggie took a deep breath and asked in her most businesslike voice if Christine Haley was available.

'Si si. Un momento.'

The phone went down at the other end. Maggie could hear muffled calls for Christine amid a background noise of bottles clanking and general kitchen activity. Then she heard an English female voice getting louder and louder as its owner approached the phone, saying, 'That Worthington will need changing in a minute . . . Paco, can you get that done before the lunchtime rush . . . no, the potatoes haven't arrived yet . . . they've promised around twelve . . . the tables in the back bar need a good polish . . . Hello, Christine Haley speaking.'

Maggie's voice got stuck in her throat. Christine Haley repeated her name. If Maggie couldn't get any sound out, Christine would hang up, thinking it was some crank caller. Maggie tried again. Her voice seemed to have got stuck halfway down her throat.

'Hello, er, Christine.' It seemed strange calling her that after years of 'Mrs Haley'. 'It's Maggie. Maggie—'

She'd been prepared to go into a long introduction about the email and the offer of help with the property agent friends. But Christine was straight on to the case.

'Maggie,' she exclaimed. 'How lovely to hear from you. I was only telling Joe last night about your email. You obviously got mine, then.'

Maggie was momentarily overwhelmed by this easy

welcome. 'I did and I hope you didn't mind me ringing,' she said cautiously. 'Is this a good time to talk?'

'Oh, it's mad here all the time.' Christine laughed her familiar throaty laugh. 'We're supposed to be semi-retired now but that's a joke. Actually we're a bit short-staffed this week so I'm doing more than I normally would.'

They lapsed easily into a chat about how the Tin Man bar came about, all the trials and tribulations, Spanish planning laws, drains and so forth, with Maggie bracing herself for the inevitable mention of Jack. And then it came.

'Of course, if you remember, we moved here just as Jack was finishing at university.' Christine was in full flow now. 'I remember feeling terrible that we had somehow abandoned him in London, but the opportunity to buy the bar came up and we grabbed it with both hands. It was long before the days of emails and cheap flights, so it was a major step for us. We felt horribly guilty, upping sticks and leaving him behind.'

I wasn't exactly nuts about him abandoning me either, Maggie thought to herself. She must get Christine off that subject and on to the purpose of the call. Yet there was a bit of her that ached to talk for hours about Jack and hear every painful snippet about his life.

'Anyway, I don't want to take up too much of your time,' she prompted them both. 'Just wondered if I could take you up on your kind offer and talk to your estate agent friends.'

She briefly outlined the idea of Home Truths' providing a marketing arm in England in return for a cut of the commission fees.

'Oh, I'm sure they'd be interested in that,' said

Christine. 'Anyway, nothing ventured, nothing gained. There are an awful lot of Brits crawling around Majorca these days, trying to buy places. We read about your property prices so we can see why. But be warned. They're really beginning to rocket here too. Mind you, a lot of the house hunters haven't a clue what they're getting themselves into and I know our friends deal with a lot of resales. People come out here thinking life will be one long holiday. The sun shines, the wine flows and now, thanks to satellite telly, they can even watch *EastEnders*. And then what? They miss their friends and their families. They miss the rain, the fog and the seasons. They miss Marmite, a quick flutter on the Grand National and a chicken tikka masala. We came out here to work, which was vastly different. Anyway, hark at me carrying on! Joe still says I talk too much. Bear with me for about thirty seconds while I get that phone number for you.'

She put the phone down. The background noise of clanking bottles continued, mingled with some faint guitar music. Maggie could almost sense the cool atmosphere of the bar, with all the shelves being restocked with beer for the long day ahead. Meanwhile, in the street outside, the sun was probably beating down and blistering the paint off the shutters.

Christine picked up the phone again. She dictated a number and assured Maggie that their friends Duncan and Elaine were terrific and would certainly be able to help. Maggie was very relieved to hear they were English.

'Now,' Christine continued cheerily, 'you must promise me that if you come over to Majorca to set this property thing up, you'll come and see us.'

'Of course.' Maggie tried to sound convincing. 'Listen,

thanks again for being so helpful. I'll let you know if anything comes of it.'

'I insist. It's been lovely to talk to you, Maggie. Joe and I were saying last night how fond we always were of you. I probably shouldn't say this,' she lowered her voice slightly, 'but we were terribly sad when it didn't work out between you and Jack.'

'Er, yes, well, it was one of those things' was all Maggie could come up with. For a whole second, she willed herself to ask if they knew the reason why it hadn't. But the words just wouldn't come out. They probably didn't know anyway, or if they did it was virtually guaranteed to cause her even more pain. Whatever the reason, it was all now firmly in the past. Except that sometimes, like now, the pain was very much in the present.

'Anyway,' Christine continued, diplomatically filling the sudden gap in the conversation, 'it was a long time ago. But we've often thought of you and wondered what happened to you. So it was really lovely to hear after all these years. I hope you didn't mind, but I forwarded your news to Jack. We don't get to speak to him very often because of the time difference. I'm certain he'll want to get in touch.'

Maggie found herself muttering a stunned goodbye, replaced the phone and stared at it for ages. 'I'm certain he'll want to get in touch'? What was that all about? She rang Pam and relayed the gist of the conversation.

'I've opened up a right can of worms here,' she finished, whipping herself up into a nervous frenzy. 'I can't believe I've managed to get myself into this mess. From a garbled throwaway a few months ago from old Freddie No Mates that Jack was doing something in the States, I not only track down his parents and their business, but am now about to chat up their friends with a view to a business arrangement and what's worse can expect – or not – an email from Jack any day.'

Pam laughed unhelpfully.

'So do you think he'll get in touch?' Maggie continued, her voice still shaking from the conversation with Christine.

'Oh, yes, I do,' said Pam. 'If he'd cast you as some kind of Lucrezia Borgia his parents wouldn't be tripping over themselves to say how pleased they were to hear from you. So you're in with a chance.'

'What do you mean, in with a chance?'

'Oh, you know, they still like you very much.' Pam hastily back-pedalled. 'They still regard you with great fondness. If they thought you'd hurt their son and been a cow, they certainly wouldn't be giving you all this help.'

'I suppose not,' said Maggie. 'But the hurt's on my side. Although maybe they don't know that. Maybe . . . oh, I don't know any more. I'm maybe-ed out. What if he replies?'

'We'll share a good meal and a lot of wine and talk about it,' said Pam brightly.

'I thing we ought to do that *before* he replies. *If* he replies.'

'You know he will.'

'Do I?'

'Yes. I'd bet money on it.'

Chapter 28

Maggie didn't sleep a wink that night. She tossed and turned, her mind picking over and over the conversation she'd had with Christine Haley. She'd been really friendly and helpful. But then, why shouldn't she? Whatever happened between Maggie and Jack twenty years ago, it clearly no longer mattered to Christine and Joe. Of course it didn't, because it clearly didn't matter to Jack either. If he'd still felt anything for her, would they have been so helpful? Yes, probably, because she'd always remembered them as being a very outgoing, friendly couple. Anyway, why on earth would Jack pine for *her*? He was the one who hadn't turned up and just disappeared off the planet. If it had been a big deal for Jack they wouldn't have replied to her email, let alone come up with all the other stuff about insisting she visit them and forwarding her email to him. And why on earth would Jack want to hear her news after all these years? He'd clearly moved on. Moved on big time, in fact. Gone to make his life and probably his fortune in America. If he wasn't interested enough when she was Maggie Berry, he sure as hell wasn't likely to be riveted by Maggie Fraser. Twenty years older, two stone fatter, way off course in the fashion stakes –

and life stakes, come to that, although making a brief comeback recently with better job, improved brain and a mini-makeover thanks to Pam. But it was hardly a hold-the-front-page success story.

Garth, snoring noisily beside her, seemed like a stranger these days. Thank goodness, there hadn't been a reprise of that awful night. But now she couldn't even remember the last time they'd had anything resembling a conversation. Probably because they had nothing to say, and avoided any occasion on which they might have to say nothing. She was rather grateful for that. Her mind was now full of thoughts about the Tin Man, and Christine's forwarding her email to Jack; wondering if he'd reply. What Garth did from nine to five was his business. Although when it came to his business, Maggie was certain he wasn't taking much care of it.

She'd noticed recently that he insisted on snatching up the post the moment it hit the hall floor. Was she just being paranoid or was it because there were creditors' letters making final demands? She lay on her back in bed, staring at the ceiling by the faint light of the street lamps outside. Was she imagining all this? Or was he concealing the awful truth about their financial situation and just going to the pub to blot it all out?

He stirred, muttering under his breath in his sleep. She caught the now familiar whiff of beer. She'd have to tackle him about money soon, yet her mind just kept coming back to Jack.

She rolled on to her side, desperately trying to sleep, but it was hopeless. Her mind was racing, formulating, reasoning, searching for solutions and motives. But there were no answers because she didn't have any facts. It was all based on a polite conversation with a woman she hadn't seen for over twenty years. Eventually, she must have drifted off, only to be woken almost instantly, it seemed, by a flurry of alarm clocks.

Pam had cooked a massive pot of boeuf bourguignon, which she served up with new potatoes and lashings of butter. The wine was already open and two large glasses had been poured.

'Smells fantastic,' said Maggie, taking off her coat and sitting down at the kitchen table.

'It's good for me to do this, as I don't bother much when I'm on my own,' said Pam, looking effortlessly casual as always, in cropped jeans and a crisp white cotton shirt. 'I'll freeze what's left and shovel it down Mark when he comes home next week. Try to be a good mum for once! How are your two, by the way?'

'Oh, bearing up. Unbearable sometimes,' said Maggie. 'They're better than they used to be, I must say. I think it's finally dawned on them that Garth is giving me a rough ride, one way and another. Beth in particular has been very supportive lately. Really helping me around the house without being prompted. George isn't quite in that league, but they're not squabbling anything like as much as they did. There's a bit more homework going on too. It's a relief, I can tell you.'

'Probably growing up a bit and seeing old Darth Vader in his true light,' Pam remarked, taking a sip of wine.

'You're probably right,' Maggie conceded, 'but that's pretty difficult as we rarely see much of him in daylight these days. He just creeps home late at night from the pub. I can't remember the last time he was there with us for a meal. Seems to have made an art form of avoiding us all. Sad in a way, but I guess we probably all prefer it that way. Neither Beth nor George has said anything, although I get a few knowing looks from Beth. At least I'm not accused of being a sad old alcoholic any more, if they see me with a glass of last Christmas's sherry in my hand. I'm getting a bit of a sympathy vote these days.'

'And so you should,' said Pam, ladling out the beef with a flourish. 'There were times when I was sorely tempted to come round and box their ears, the way they used to carry on.'

'Yes, I know,' said Maggie, hanging her head in shame. 'To be honest, I blame myself. I let everyone treat me like a doormat, just trying to keep the peace. I think the job at Home Truths has been an incredible catalyst in that I've had to be much tougher at work and have tried to apply the same principles at home. Too late for Garth, who can't stand my new-found "flippin' attitude" as he calls it. But the kids are definitely better. There's much less squabbling over the remote control. Mind you, that's helped enormously by Garth's not being around and lording it over the television.'

Pam smiled knowingly as she spooned potatoes on to their plates. 'Must be a relief for them,' she said, 'knowing they can come home to some peace and quiet and not a war zone.'

'Yep. I feel a lot sharper in my head, too. In fact since that day at Juicy Lucy's. I'm sure that was the start of it. I feel I'm almost back to the days when I was seeing Jack. As you keep reminding me, I was much more confident then. That is, of course, until he didn't turn up. It was all downhill after that.'

'You mentioned him first,' said Pam triumphantly. 'I was having a private bet with myself as to how long it would be until the subject came up.'

'OK, OK.' Maggie sighed. 'I can't stop thinking about this and I've been lying in bed at night, trying to turn little snippets of nothing into hard-blown facts. In fact, I almost don't want him to reply. Well, not for a while, anyway. I'm somehow enjoying the fantasy of the anticipation. When, or rather if, I get an email from him, the reality will probably be harsh.'

'And what do you think that harsh reality will be?' Pam enquired.

'Oh, you know, the all-American family living the all-American dream. The family group all hugging and smiling, flashing expensively whitened teeth and practically dressed in the Stars and Stripes.'

Pam laughed as she took a slug of wine.

'Oh, dear, your mind has been working overtime, hasn't it? You make them out to be like the Osmonds. What do you honestly think he'll say in this email? Eh? "Dear Maggs, How lovely to hear your news. Have a nice life. Love Jack" or "Dear Maggs, Have missed you for ever. Please forgive me and come over immediately. Your air ticket's in the post." If he did that, I'd certainly be counselling you not to go.'

Maggie had to laugh. 'OK, I'm being paranoid.'

They began mopping up the bourguignon sauce with chunks of ciabatta.

'I think he'll write,' said Pam finally, 'but his reply will be somewhere in the middle. Polite, friendly and non-committal.'

She got up from the table and headed for the fridge. She opened the huge door and brought out a glass dish.

'Banoffee pie,' she proclaimed. 'In honour of Mr Banana and the Beautiful Miss Nancy. Bananas and toffee filling. Very sweet, very calorific, very scrummy.'

The subject of Jack wasn't mentioned again.

It was one of the most gruelling weeks she'd known at Home Truths. There had been no let up in the calls, the viewings, or the emails, Maggie reflected, driving in on the following Friday morning. This week had been non-stop with hardly a moment to draw breath, yet the constant expectation of an email from Jack had been almost unbearable.

Fiona had been off sick for half the week, so Maggie'd really had her work cut out for her. In addition, she'd started making inroads into a possible French/Spanish connection by ringing Christine's estate agent contacts. They'd turned out to be every bit as helpful as Christine had promised, having set up their agency around the same time that the Haleys were launching the Tin Man. Maggie guessed they'd all probably shared many an evening of celebration and commiseration over a few bottles of Rioja as they'd struggled to get their businesses off the ground. Like the Haleys, Duncan and Elaine had worked hard, learnt the language and never regretted the move. Now, she guessed, they were in semi-retirement too as they referred Maggie to their manager, a local Spanish chap called Jose-Maria who, they assured her, spoke excellent English. In principle, they liked the idea, particularly the no-holds-barred Home Truths approach, saying they felt it would weed out the time wasters.

'They leave their brains on the plane,' Elaine told Maggie. 'They totter in here, sunburnt and sozzled after a day on the beach and a night on the sangria. They don't really know what they want to buy, have no idea of their budget and then expect us to ferry them round everything from a tiny flat to a two million pound *finca*.

It never occurs to them that we'd rather deal with serious clients.'

The arrangement was that Jose-Maria would email her a list of properties currently on their books and Maggie would forward a sample of the Home Truths details. Then, presumably, Damien would go out to Spain to strike up some kind of deal.

Vanessa nodded ongoing approval and asked to be updated the following week. She was embroiled in some huge negotiations with a builder who was in danger of going belly up as his estate just wasn't shifting.

'Those places are so tiny you couldn't swing an anorexic dormouse in them,' she'd told him loudly on the phone for all to hear. 'I don't know who you had in mind when you built them, but clearly they're for people who don't cook and possess no clothes whatsoever . . . first time buyers? Rubbish . . . they're more like starter cupboards, darling.'

So Maggie cracked on with the French and Spanish connection on her own, glad to have too much to do. But her eyes rarely strayed far from the top left hand corner of her screen, where the new emails alerts popped up.

She'd tried contacting some French estate agents but copped out of ringing them, suspecting that Vanessa's 'cocktails only French, darling' was probably much better than she portrayed, and consequently reluctant to have her own stumbling efforts overheard. Instead, she wrote some polite emails, craftily translated via an internet translation website for which she thanked God on an hourly basis. At least her letters looked reasonably businesslike.

She'd already had a couple of promising replies, which had boosted her confidence. At least they'd understood her attempts at French and been sympathetic to her grovelling apologies for her lack of linguistic skills. This was all helping her 'keep-my-job' campaign in the event of any cutbacks. Everytime she considered that possibility, she shuddered in terror. And then glanced again at that top left hand corner.

She'd spent all week making more silly bets with herself. If the awful man with the acne makes an offer on the 'darkest flat known to man' – at least nobody else would have to suffer his zits – then Jack will reply. If the phone doesn't ring for a whole ten minutes, then I'll hear from him. If I do an extra big power walk at lunchtime, there will be a message when I get back. But there was just cyber silence.

By late Friday afternoon, Maggie was becoming quietly distraught. Deep down, she'd been hopeful that he'd write, buoyed up by Christine's comments and Pam's optimism. Even just a short note to be polite. Simply hello, brief news, goodbye would have been something. But nothing.

How stupid am I, she said aloud to herself as she drove to a viewing. The last job of the week – 'A roof over your head – just. Welcome to Bodger's Castle' – and then she was going home.

She switched off the car engine and waited for the clients, yet another young couple desperate to get on the property ladder. She glanced in her rear-view mirror and wiped away a stray tear. How had she managed to get herself into such a stupid state?

The couple duly arrived and shuddered at what they saw. 'Amateur night out, I'm afraid,' she apologised to them, as they plodded through the half-finished kitchen and unplastered sitting room. 'But it's got potential.' She hated that word and always felt ashamed about using it as it seemed such a cop-out. Unfortunately it applied to many of Home Truths' properties.

As they tramped around the dismal house, their faces got longer and longer. This could be me, Maggie thought miserably, when we're forced out of our house and have to downsize. She couldn't summon up the energy to talk the place up or suggest ways of improving it. What potential could this house possibly have?

'We'll have a think and let you know,' said the chap. 'Would they take a lower offer, say ten grand less? There's a lot to do here.'

'Definitely worth a punt,' said Maggie sympathetically. She didn't actually have a clue. It was one of Fiona's properties and she hadn't spoken to the owner personally to gauge his mindset.

'I just want to have a quick chat with my dad,' said the young man. 'He's better at DIY than me. Can I ring you at the office in, say, fifteen minutes?'

'Sure,' said Maggie. Bum, she thought. It was just past six o'clock and she'd intended going straight home. But once again the job cuts scenario hove into view. Another offer this week would be good for her sales figures. 'I'll be there until six thirty.' She looked at her watch. Another chance to check her email too.

The couple said their goodbyes and promised faithfully to ring her one way or the other within half an hour.

Maggie drove back to the office and parked defiantly on Damien's preferred spot on the pavement outside. Surely she'd get away with it at this time of night. She unlocked the office, switched on the lights and sat down at her desk. She logged on to her computer and immediately opened up her emails. Ten more messages but none from him. She ran her fingers through her hair in despair at her own stupidity. The betting was moving on to a new, more negative phase: if he doesn't reply by such-and-such, he won't reply at all. The goalposts were moving back and back. She wondered at what point Pam would concede defeat too. Maybe mid-week next week?

The phone rang, making her jump slightly. 'Good evening. Home Truths, the no-frills estate agent. Maggie speaking. How can I help you?'

It was the young chap ringing back as promised with an offer on Bodger's Castle of fifteen thousand less.

'I'll pass that on to the owner and come back to you,' said Maggie, checking that all the contact details were in the computer. 'I've got your mobile number and I'll be in touch as soon as I hear back.'

She replaced the phone. Might as well do it now, even if it meant leaving a message. She dialled the owner of Bodger's Castle, a Mr Carling who, she noted, had obviously got the hell out of it and now lived up country. She was all ready to leave her message and then flee.

To her slight annoyance, Mr Carling answered the phone. Maggie politely passed on the offer and launched into her standard spiel about the property's needing a lot of work done on it and how it was difficult for first time buyers as building work was rather an unknown quantity when you are on a strict budget.

Mr Carling suddenly cut through her speech.

'OK, I'll take it,' he said resignedly. 'I could do with the cash as I'm doing up my new place and want to get a move on.'

Maggie shuddered at the thought of his launching himself on yet another disaster zone. Then she thought of the young couple and how pleased they'd be. And finally she thought about her own survival. She put down the phone and punched the air.

'Yes, yes, yes!' she announced to herself as she dialled the young man's mobile to tell him the glad news. Every sale still gave her a huge buzz.

She could have sworn he was nearly crying with delight when she told him. At least she'd made someone happy. She was just about to log off her computer and get the hell out of there when her attention was distracted in two directions. To the left, an incoming email warning had popped on to the screen. To the right, a traffic warden was standing across the street looking at her car.

The email address began with j.haley . . . oh, my God, it's him. Meanwhile, over the road, the traffic warden was whipping out his pad. Maggie leapt off her chair, was out of the door and across the road in seconds.

'I'm so sorry,' she gabbled. 'I've just come back to help a young couple get an offer accepted. Bodger's Castle, we call it . . . it's a tip . . . but the owner has just agreed a big discount and I was just telling them the good news.'

She was certain none of that made any sense to the traffic warden. She could feel her heart thumping in her chest. She certainly didn't need a fine at the moment.

The warden hadn't yet put pen to paper. He glanced at her sternly. 'You work for that idiot with the Porsche?'

'Yes, I do,' said Maggie, wondering if this were a good thing or a bad thing in the warden's eyes. She vaguely remembered something about Damien's doing some kind of shady deal with one of the wardens but sensed it was best to keep quiet.

Suddenly the warden smiled. 'Listen,' he said kindly. 'I've got a daughter who's just married and I know how difficult it is for these kids to get started. I haven't started writing out this ticket yet so I'll let you off. Just this once. But move the car. Now.'

'I'll have to phone the owner back first and then lock up,' said Maggie, desperately wanting to read that email straight away.

'Hmm,' said the warden. 'Look, I'll tell you what. I'll stand here looking stern. You nip back in and sort it out. You've got two minutes, starting now. OK?'

Maggie nodded and rushed back into the office, her heart thumping. I can read the email while I'm ringing Mr Carling, she thought. Suddenly the thought of a ticket didn't matter quite so much. After all, the rewards were beginning to stack up. A sale of a difficult property and an email from Jack.

She deliberately made herself dial Mr Carling first and then opened up the email just as he answered the phone. The words stayed a tantalising blur as she conveyed the news that the deal on Bodger's Castle had been clinched.

'I'll be writing to both parties on Monday with details about solicitors and so on,' she said, trying to read Jack's note at the same time. She hit the print button with her spare hand. She'd have to read it in the car. She glanced at the traffic warden outside. He was tapping his watch.

She logged off, grabbed the sheet of paper out of the printer, flicked off the lights, crashed the door shut and locked it.

'Thanks.' She beamed at the traffic warden. And then, impulsively, she planted a big kiss on his cheek.

'Don't often get that sort of treatment in my job.' He laughed. 'Now don't do it again. The parking, I mean, not the kiss.'

Maggie leapt in the car, Jack's note still tantalisingly

unread and stuffed in her handbag. She drove off to the nearest lay-by and pulled in. Her hands shook as she unfolded the piece of paper.

Hi Maggs, So sorry . . .

Maggie burst into tears.

Chapter 29

'Hey, this Saturday lunch lark is becoming quite addictive,' said Pam, as they sat down in Weltham's first foray into Spanish tapas. It was all brown leather furniture, terracotta pots of huge palms and Gypsy Kings music thumping away in the background. They paused to glance at the menus, which had about forty different tapas to choose from.

'God, this is a bloody novel,' said Pam, putting the folder aside. 'No wonder the Spanish stay up half the night, getting through this lot. Anyway, I'd rather read your email first.'

Maggie bent down and fished it out of her handbag. Pam inspected the piece of paper carefully as she unfolded it.

'I see this has been well used,' she said teasingly. The paper was already greying and curling at the corners from much reading and rereading the previous night. 'Won't last the weekend. You'll have to print off another one on Monday.' Maggie had already outlined the traffic warden scenario.

'You're the one with all the foreign connections these days,' Pam went on, indicating the menu. 'You order up while I read this long-awaited missive. I'm sure you know the contents off by heart.'

Maggie groaned as she took a half-hearted look at the list. Thankfully it was all translated otherwise she wouldn't have had a clue. *Merluza*, she discovered, was hake. *Pollo*, reassuringly, was chicken. She'd have to bone up a bit if she ever went to Majorca and dropped in on the Haleys . . . oh, stop that. She pulled herself up short.

Pam read and reread Jack's note as Maggie now watched her face, searching for clues. Pam was right. She did know it off by heart. She could almost hear Jack's voice saying the words.

'Hi Maggs, So sorry not to have replied sooner but been away on business and only just got the message from my folks. Amazing that you came across their website – it's a good one, eh? It's designed and maintained by my company. Don't know what Mom told you but that's what I do these days. Learnt the trade and then set up my own business ten years ago and I'm still here, so must be doing something right. Started out in California but much too artificial. So we now live on the East Coast, near Boston. It's not exactly a tea party though. The traffic is terrible. People actually say, "Shall we walk, or do we have time to take a cab?" Great city though. Recommend it if you haven't visited. So you're a realtor! Bet you're really good at cutting a mean deal. And hey, two kids. I've got two as well. Better go, haven't seen them all week. Stay in touch. Jack.'

'Wow,' said Pam, sitting back in her chair when she'd finished.

'Wow what?'

'That's amazing.'

'What's amazing?' Maggie was getting slightly agitated.

'The power of the internet,' said Pam in a mock reverent tone. 'Just awesome.'

Maggie couldn't bear this. She knew Pam was teasing her. 'We know about the blinking internet. We use it everyday. We even used it to track down some of your old flames. What do you make of the letter?'

'More important,' said Pam, shooting her a meaningful look 'what do *you* make of it?'

Maggie laughed nervously. 'Me? Oh, I've analysed it to death. And come up with nothing at all.'

'Do you know what I make of it?' said Pam. 'I think it's polite, it's friendly and it's non-committal. Exactly as I predicted.'

'Yes . . . and?' Maggie prompted.

'There are some interesting omissions in this piece of evidence, my lord,' Pam continued, now affecting the air of a high-flying barrister. 'I should like to draw the court's attention to the lack of a mention of a wife. Of course, it's there in implied terms, as in "now *we* live on the East Coast", as opposed to express terms, in which case the precise name of said person might have been helpful to the court.'

'Cut the crap,' said Maggie impatiently.

'Oh, all right.' Pam sat back in her chair, resuming her normal voice. 'He might be widowed. You hadn't thought of that, had you? But it's not the sort of thing people tend to bung into a first note. Or he could be widowed with girlfriend, or divorced. Or divorced with girlfriend. Or, let's face it, even married with girlfriend. But he's hardly going to give you that kind of scenario in a first letter.'

'You say first letter,' said Maggie. 'Do you think he'll write again?'

'Only if you write back.'

'Go on. What else do you think?'

'Interesting that his company created the Tin Man website. We could find out a bit about that, if there's a credit somewhere. Don't quite understand why a man who runs an internet design company doesn't access his email for a week. But perhaps that's his polite way of excusing the delay. Perhaps he didn't want to reply too quickly just in case . . .'

'Just in case what?'

'Oh, just in case he appeared too keen,' said Pam, with a grin. 'You're not going to reply immediately to this, are you? It's the same principle. It would betray some sort of desperation.'

'What about the end bit?'

'I think he gets out of it rather well. We just about learn he has kids and there's a good reason to sign off. What did you expect? "Love, kisses and sexy snogs from across the pond, Jack"?'

'No,' Maggie sighed. 'Wish he had, though. But there's something I need to ask you. Do you think getting in touch with your ex amounts to, well, a kind of adultery?'

Pam roared with laughter. 'Depends on your definition. The Bill Clinton version of events with Monica Lewinsky takes it to the max. What was it he said? "I did not have sex with that woman"? In the States, not all intimate acts count, apparently. But I know what you're saying. Searching for Jack has been rather like chucking a few extra logs on the old fire of passion. Fanning old flames is a dangerous game. Some people would say it's adultery of the mind. But I'm pretty sure it's the best fun you've ever had with your clothes on.' She looked at her watch. 'We've been here half an hour now,' she tutted.

'They should rename this place Mañana. Perhaps that's when you get served.'

They looked round for any waiting staff to flag down. They all appeared to be in the kitchen.

'They're probably having lunch,' said Maggie. 'God, I'm starving. All this emotional nonsense is burning up the calories. I've lost nearly five pounds so far this month.'

'Thought so,' said Pam. 'You're looking great. Better than I can remember.' She handed back the precious note.

'That's the one shame about email,' said Maggie, as she stuffed it back in her bag. 'You can't analyse the handwriting.'

'No,' said Pam, 'but even I could hear Jack's voice in that text, despite all the Americanisms. I expect that occurred to you too.'

'It did,' said Maggie, tears suddenly welling up. 'It was as though twenty years had rolled back, just like that.'

The rest of the weekend was dominated by Maggie's next dilemma: how and when to reply. She deliberately threw herself into a guilty frenzy of housework, scrubbing the kitchen from top to toe and then cutting the front lawn. Now she'd got the garden straight, she was determined to keep it that way. Some of the shrubs that she'd chopped back so severely were already responding with new growth. Maggie loved this time of year. In fact, she loved May more than any other month. Bulbs over, not quite geranium time. Centre stage for azaleas, rhododendrons and a huge red paeony that she utterly adored.

Garth's comings and goings were still mystifying her. He'd gone out on Saturday morning in his van, muttering about a job on the other side of town. But Maggie noticed when he came in later that evening that his hands were spotlessly clean. No grime under his nails, no pile of sweaty clothing flung down near the laundry basket. Perhaps she should follow him, find out what he got up to. But the truth was, she had neither the energy nor the interest. The less she saw of him, the better. And if he was playing away, she no longer cared. She'd begun to admit to herself recently that she hoped he was, on the basis that at least it would spare her any more enforced sex. Everything at home was so much more peaceful without him. She decided to do a barbecue for the kids on Sunday afternoon if the fine weather kept up.

Every now and again, thoughts of Jack stopped her in her tracks. She wondered what he'd be doing right now. Probably taking his angelic children and their film star mother to a theme park for the day, or entertaining friends to a hog roast in the grounds of their lavish clapboard New England home. She knew very little about Boston, apart from the famous Tea Party incident that Jack had alluded to in his email. She'd read somewhere that it was near Harvard university and had a lot of bookshops. No wonder Jack liked it there. He was always a bookworm.

What on earth was she going to say in her reply? She'd need to echo the tone of his message, she decided. Upbeat and non-committal. She'd talk up her job a little bit, and as Jack hadn't mentioned his wife she didn't need to mention Garth. She'd start drafting it on Monday and then send it on Wednesday. This had been Pam's advice: wait at least five days before replying. Of course, once she'd sent it, the whole agonising process of waiting for a reply would begin all over again. She wasn't sure her nerves would stand it.

She dragged the barbecue out of the shed and

inspected it for rust. It certainly needed a good scrub down. Another job to keep her mind off everything.

Monday brought the usual rush of inquiries from weekend web surfers. Maggie was eternally grateful that she didn't have to work on Saturdays. From the weekend team's handover note she received every Monday morning, it seemed half the town's nutters came out house hunting.

A couple of particularly terrible flats had found new owners at the weekend so that was good news. And Vanessa was fulsome in her praise for Maggie's shifting Bodger's Castle so effortlessly. In between all the catching up, Maggie kept sneaking a look at Jack's email again on screen, just to make sure she hadn't somehow imagined it. There it was, now copied into Maggie's private file for eternity.

She'd just finished the initial paperwork on the Bodger's Castle sale when up came an email alert from the Tin Man.

> Hi Maggie, Heard you've made contact with Elaine and Duncan. Sounds very promising. They seem very keen on the idea and told me about your company's unusual approach. So I've just taken a peek at your Home Truths website. Funniest thing I've read for ages. Well done. Do you write all that yourself? Heard from Jack at the weekend and he said he's making contact with you. Hope this finds you well and don't forget to come and see us when you tie up the deal.
>
> Best wishes, Christine (and Joe who's out shopping).

Maggie forwarded the note to Pam. 'Well, they're certainly very pro you,' was Pam's response. 'Looks like our next girlies' holiday could be in Puerto Pollensa.'

Maggie shuddered slightly at that last remark. Pam's throwaways had a habit of becoming reality, with Pam dragging her kicking and screaming into submission. She wasn't sure she was ready now – or ever – to meet Jack's parents again. That was just a little too close for comfort. She'd been able to cope with email and even a phone call, but turning up in Majorca? That was another matter.

She couldn't stop herself from replying, though. There was something irresistible about receiving an email from someone who really had earned their place in the sun. She could close her eyes and envisage the Haleys' idyllic lifestyle: cheerfully running their bar, enjoying the fruits of their labour, sitting on their sun-kissed balcony overlooking the bay, surrounded by soft mountains behind. She'd seen the pictures on the website. She permitted herself another quick visit to the Tin Man online and another quick gander through the photographs. Now, of course, it didn't matter if Vanessa or Damien caught her looking at them. This was all part of her French and Spanish research . . .

She clicked her way through the now familiar photographs, once again scanning the crowds of deeply tanned and happy Tin Man punters, glasses held aloft, just in case Jack was amongst them. Then she suddenly remembered that Jack's company had created the website. She started looking for a credit, or some kind of clue. There it was at the very bottom of the Contact Us page. She'd never scrolled down that far before. 'This website was designed by The Tin Man Inc.' Of course it was bound to be called that. Maggie almost kicked herself for being surprised. And there it was. Another irresistible invitation: to click on the company website.

Up came a very glitzy animation with the very latest whizz-bang graphics, an impressive list of clients, news releases and a rather cheesy mission statement. Jack was chief executive and appeared to head a team of around twenty people, mostly designers and production staff. Maggie had been hoping for a photograph but clearly Jack had decided that demonstrating what they could do was far more important than a row of company mug-shots.

She wrote a short reply back to Christine and Joe, admitting that yes, she did write some of the website and that yes, negotiations with Elaine and Duncan were progressing well. She also assured Christine she'd take up their offer if she was in the area. Like hell . . .

Later on she'd start drafting a reply to Jack. She'd gone over and over in her head what she wanted to say and what she *really* wanted to say.

Chapter 30

In the end, Maggie virtually copied Jack's email. She decided to keep the same length, tone and amount of information.

> Hi Jack, How lovely to hear from you. It was such a fluke, finding your parents' website in the course of my research. They sound really well and happy. They've been very helpful in putting me in touch with some estate agent friends. Very impressed with their website. Hope you gave them a discount. I'm afraid I've never been to Boston but I think you'll find that the traffic's just as bad here these days. A new speed camera is born about every ten seconds. Really love my job as a "realtor" as you put it. This is an estate agency with a difference as you'll see if you take a look at our website. Maggs.

She found it difficult ending with just 'Maggs'. It seemed a bit cold and abrupt but what else could she put? 'Fond regards', 'best wishes', 'sincerely'? However, she thought her last line was a stroke of genius. It might just provoke a reply. She clicked 'send' to stop herself thinking about it any more. That was it, out into cyberspace and another waiting game begun. She promised herself not to start the betting game again . . . unless she didn't hear back within a week. But that's a bet in itself, you silly woman, she remonstrated.

The best news of the week was that Ashleigh Manor, aka 57 Ashleigh Manor Road, quasi-royal residence of Marina and Gerald Bryan, aka Her Maj and the Major, had finally found a buyer. With Fiona still off sick, Maggie had no choice but to make the call herself. She flinched slightly when Marina answered the phone in a rather strangulated voice. When Maggie announced who she was, Marina proceeded to pretend to be the cleaner. Maggie then had the great delight of saying pompously that it was a personal matter and that she couldn't discuss it with anyone but Mr or Mrs Bryan, and promptly hung up. Ten minutes later 'the Major' rang to be told details of the offer. He accepted immediately. God, they must be desperate, thought Maggie, as the buyer had offered twenty thousand less than the asking price.

Maggie wondered idly whether they'd throw away all those back copies of *Country Life* and *Horse and Hind*, as Marina always pronounced it, before they moved out. She announced the good news to Stefan, who'd just swanned in through the door and begun his usual routine. With a flourish, out came the name plate on the desk, as usual, followed by the ceremonial clicking of the briefcase and the unveiling of the laptop.

'Oh, Balmoral?' He laughed. 'Thought it might go soon. Just come up with a super little package for the couple buying that one. Yes please. Tiny splosh of milk and no sugar. It's been a long day.' Maggie headed out to the kitchen to make coffee. She was continually fascinated that he still never uttered the word 'mortgage'. A bit like people who go through hoops not to mention 'cancer', instead calling it the Big C, or just 'it'. Or society tarts whom Sunday newspapers always described as party girls, or alcoholics whose epitaphs always hinted that they 'lived life to the full'.

'Richard, the Halifax surveyor, told me about it,' Stefan continued. 'Just had to go and see it for myself. Talk about pseudo. And to think we employed Her Maj here for a time! I do remember Vanessa saying she was all headscarf and no tiara.'

Maggie chuckled out in the kitchen. It still amused her that Marina had got her comeuppance. She came back out with two large strong coffees.

'Thanks, doll.' Stefan gave her a half-wave of acknowledgement as he cranked himself up into Big Deal Mode for another bit of financial wizardry.

Maggie went back to her desk to get the paperwork started on 'Ashleigh Manor'. It would give her a great deal of pleasure to sign her name at the bottom over the job title 'Negotiator'.

She was just about to add 'Sold subject to Contract' against it on the website when up came another message from Jack. She gasped audibly. That was a bit quick. Far too quick.

> Ha ha. Your website is a hoot. It's so wonderfully eccentric – could only happen in Britain. Have been laughing aloud at some of houses. Especially the mini royal residence and the sleep-is-a-goal flat over the disco. Sadly it would never work over here. Americans just wouldn't appreciate the humour. We talk everything up and up and over the top. Thanks for a great chuckle. Jack.

Maggie's heart sank. The word chuckle brought back instant memories. Jack had such an infectious laugh that people joined in even if they didn't know why. If something struck him as really funny, he'd often giggle for ages. Then, hours later, he'd remember the joke or the situation and the chuckling would start all over again. She remembered the time when they— oh, stop it, Maggie. Get a grip.

She reread his message. It was a lovely reply but what now? She suddenly felt rather flat. This was all a bit of an anticlimax. She'd found Jack – and yet she hadn't found Jack. This was someone she once knew, who now lived in another continent. Did she really want to get into a ping-pong match of jolly but banal emails? What was the point? And more important, could her nerves stand much more? She forwarded Jack's note to Pam at the council, hoping she'd come up with some pithy observation.

Pam replied immediately, suggesting a quick drink in a wine bar after work and delighted to have an excuse not to go home too early to an empty house. They met an hour later in Grape Expectations just round the corner from Home Truths.

'Told the kids I'll be home in half an hour,' Maggie warned her. 'I'm running a nagging campaign at the moment, getting them to do their exam revision. George is in the middle of his GCSEs and, predictably, he's regretting he didn't work a bit harder. We've had quite a few scenes.'

'Hell, isn't it?' said Pam. 'Seems like yesterday Mark was doing his.'

They picked a quiet corner and sat down. Maggie found herself suddenly quite tearful. She steeled herself not to cry by taking a huge slug of wine. Crisp and cold, it hit the spot.

'I just feel incredibly flat all of a sudden,' she said. 'I suppose it was always going to end up like this. The man I would have crawled over hot coals for is now just some disembodied emailer.'

'I understand,' said Pam simply. 'It's the kind of friendly note you'd expect from any old mate, rather than the Big One.'

'I don't know what I thought it was going to be like, but I never quite expected this. I suppose I wanted an explanation, an apology, or at least some kind of cataclysmic reaction. Not bland chatty notes.'

'Still hasn't mentioned the wife, though,' Pam observed with a small smile. 'And he did reply very quickly.'

'Let's just not go there,' said Maggie. 'I'll write back at some point but I must stop getting myself into a tizz about it all.'

'The trouble is,' Pam continued, 'that the discovery is much more fun than the aftermath, as Pandora probably found out. I mean, we had a great laugh giving old Bonkers Luke a run for his money on that terrible radio phone-in. And as for Dave Gregg – sorry, Gregg David, life coach to the stars – that's just too wonderfully ridiculous for words. Also, those relationships ended very publicly. It was easy for me to get seriously angry about them. But in your case, Jack just didn't turn up that night. End of story.'

'And I was left waiting hours, days, weeks, months – oh, probably years – to find out what happened. And although I've now tracked him down, I still don't know.'

'There's one other big difference,' said Pam. 'My exes did me a huge favour. They were total prats and I went on to meet Tom. Happy ending. Jack left you hanging out to dry and you ended up with Darth Vader.'

Maggie nodded silently and picked up her bag. It was time to go. 'At least the Force isn't with us quite so much these days,' she said drily. 'It does make life so much easier when he's up the pub.'

'And you don't have to remember to put your Life Saver on charge,' Pam grinned.

Next day, Maggie caved in. She wrote Jack a bland little note back saying she was pleased he'd enjoyed the website and – hot off the press – she was sorry to report that 'Balmoral' had just been snapped up. Was he still interested in the sleep-is-a-goal flat over the disco? She signed off saying they were frantically busy with the Whitsun bank holiday coming up.

And that must be the end of that, she decided. Draw a line under it, move on. Concentrate on what you have. Two healthy kids and a good job. Shut up and be grateful. Except that she'd left the front door of the sleep-is-a-goal flat wide open for further response.

The French and Spanish connections were coming along reasonably well. Some agents backed off immediately when they saw the style of Home Truths but a few were definitely intrigued. They were all, without exception, English-speaking agencies so perhaps they appreciated something of the British approach to humour. After all, the idea was to attract British clients anyway. From Maggie's point of view, that made it easier to deal with them. She'd had been able to start phoning them without fear of being rumbled as a complete idiot when it came to languages. Now, with Vanessa's permission, she'd been giving them some commercial information, including the impressive statistics on how quickly Home Truths shifted properties. And also just how quickly they sold the more awkward or blighted places that would have stuck fast, given a more conventional approach.

'Give me a full report when you're ready,' Damien had commanded during one of his brief Porsche-on-the pavement calls. 'If it looks promising, I might even ask you to make some of the preliminary visits yourself.'

This threw Maggie into a flat spin. She, Maggie Fraser, going to France and Spain, setting up commercial deals? She suddenly felt terribly gauche. Her previous ventures abroad were a bit thin on the ground apart from Kenya. Hardly a good basis on which to become an international deal broker. The thought of Christine and Joe's help seemed like a lifeline. At least they'd be on her side and able to translate if necessary. Now that the heat had gone out of the kitchen where Jack was concerned, maybe she could make that visit after all, without feeling awkward in any way.

'*Un helado y dos cervezas, por favor*.' Maggie was repeating the phrases aloud in the car, trying not to be spotted by fellow motorists. She'd decided that a smattering of Spanish was her new goal, just in case she did make that trip to Majorca. So she'd invested in a Spanish crash course with tapes that she could play in the car. So far she could order an ice cream and two beers, find a good local restaurant and ask the way to the post office. Whether she'd understand the replies was another matter. But at least she was having a go. The next section was to be all about times and dates, followed by something intriguing entitled 'General Difficulties'.

I bet they don't list any of mine, she thought to herself. Moody, absent husband, exam-stressed kids, bizarre job –

oh, and ridiculous mid-life crisis hankering after an old boyfriend who'd dumped her twenty years ago. She had a quick peek at the difficulties. They were much more down-to-earth problems like punctures, plane delays and slug-in-my-lettuce situations.

She kept thinking about the Tin Man bar and imagining a life in almost permanent sunshine. On the surface, an idyllic existence. But the reality was probably hard slog for relatively small return, together with the stress of taking a huge risk at the start. Setting up a few links with agents was a doddle compared to that. Especially as everyone seemed to speak English. Nevertheless, Maggie had a terrible fear of looking a fool if she had to make the trip. So she shoved in another tape and began the endless repetition of phrases about buying maps and stamps and asking for information on train times.

Fiona was still off sick so her workload was ending up mostly on Maggie's desk. For the past few days, Maggie had been coming in half an hour earlier to attack the paperwork before the phones started ringing. She glanced through her diary today. In addition to the never-ending inquiries, there were three viewings in the morning alone, and then after lunch a group visit to a piece of land with planning permission on the edge of town. She and Vanessa were having to compare diaries to make sure there was at least one person in the office all the time. Maggie got the distinct impression that Vanessa was running out of patience over Fiona's prolonged flu. It was beginning to impact on her social life. A couple of high-powered lunches had been noisily cancelled so that she could help Maggie to man the office.

The morning viewings overran before they'd even

started. The first couple, who'd arranged to see a 'buy-to-let so awful it will bring out the Rachman in you', had turned up twenty minutes late. They then proceeded to rubbish every room in the flat at great length. Maggie'd learnt that this was often a sign of genuine interest so she rang her subsequent viewings to beg a slightly later start. Property number two was one of the all time stickers. It had been with Home Truths for months now and was heading for the record books. There was nothing particularly wrong with it, just another terrace in just another street, but somehow it never quite made it to the top of anyone's wish list. As usual, the rather brassy woman viewing it decided it was her 'fall-back situation'. Just like all the others before her.

Maggie was just setting off to the third property, a disastrous barn conversion, when she got a call on her mobile from the first couple. They wanted to see the awful flat again as soon as possible. Bang goes my lunch hour, she realised. Think bonus, think job security. It would be a sandwich in the car and then straight to the block viewing in the afternoon.

So it was a very weary Maggie who staggered back into the office just before five, dreading the mound of paperwork and phone calls to return.

'Well done, darling,' Vanessa cooed from her office. 'You've probably shifted that ghastly barn conversion *and* the Rachman flat. I've just passed on sensible offers on both. And they're cash buyers, too.'

Maggie collapsed in her chair, exhausted from her efforts. She tried to look pleased.

'So glad you're back,' Vanessa continued smoothly. 'I think I've made a bit of a pig's ear of our website. I've managed to screw it up, trying to update some prices.

You're much better at all that uploading stuff than I am.'

Maggie concealed a huge sigh and thought bonus again. 'OK,' she said. 'Give me the bumph and I'll sort it out before I go home.'

Next thing, Vanessa emerged from her office, carrying two glasses of champagne. She offered one to Maggie.

'Well done, darling.' She raised her glass. 'There's cause for a celebration. I've just had the figures through. You're the top negotiator out of all the branches for the last quarter. Beaten everyone else hands down.'

Maggie was almost too exhausted to be stunned. 'Gosh,' she said, managing a weary smile. 'I had no idea.'

'And you've shifted some complete dogs' breakfasts too,' Vanessa continued. 'That barn conversion, for example. Disaster area, only suitable for the completely unhinged. Yet you probably got a buyer today. I told the owner he should be pretty ruddy grateful.'

They sipped the champagne, Maggie still stunned at the news.

'Oh, by the way,' Vanessa continued, her face becoming more serious. 'Just thought I'd better let you know. We fired Fiona today.'

Maggie gaped in horror. 'Oh, no. Why?'

'Quite straightforward really. Nice girl, but she's simply not delivering. And we can get rid of her now before it gets too complicated. Saves us all from something totally ghastly like an industrial tribunal.'

'Oh, gosh,' was all Maggie could muster. Her mind started buzzing again. She'd been working flat out since Fiona had been off sick. Was this the way it was going to be from now on?

'Will you replace her?' she finally managed.

'Yes, but probably in another role.' Vanessa had a

twinkle in her eye. 'I'm going to discuss this with Damien, naturally, but I thought I'd sound you out first. It seems to me it would be better if we had someone in the office all the time. Answer the phone, deal with the emails, update the website. That would free you up to do what you do best, which is get out there and sell. So I'm thinking of hiring an assistant for you, rather than another negotiator.'

An assistant? Maggie suddenly felt the weight of the entire branch on her shoulders. Then she reassured herself that Vanessa would still be looking after the top end of the market, negotiating with builders on new sales. She just hoped her sales figures weren't some kind of lucky fluke. Perhaps Vanessa's finding herself somewhat grounded since Fiona's absence had been a factor in this new idea.

Maggie muttered grateful thanks and finished her champagne. Vanessa went back into her office to collect her bag and briefcase.

'Don't stay too late, darling,' she beamed as she opened the front door. 'Go home and celebrate your success. Get that husband of yours to take you out for dinner.'

'What a good idea,' said Maggie, laughing inwardly. Fat chance of that.

Vanessa paused to fumble for her car keys. 'Oh, nearly forgot. A chap called Jack rang you about an hour ago. Sounded American. Wouldn't leave a number. Said he'd ring again. Have fun, darling.'

The door clicked shut. Maggie sat at her desk, her head in her hands. It was all too much for one day.

Chapter 31

'*¿Puede usted recomendarme un restaurante?*' Maggie was stationary at traffic lights, asking her car stereo for handy hints on eating out in Spain. '*La carta* is the menu, *la cuenta* is the bill,' she reminded herself out loud. 'I am not going to think about this phone call. It's merely a fluke. There are probably hundreds, if not thousands, of Americans called Jack who might want to buy rubbishy properties.' And they could all have got her name from the website. It was just a coincidence and she wasn't going to give it another thought. End of story.

'*Una tortilla española y una ensalada mixta*,' she intoned, forcing her mind back to ordering from the menu. '*Y vino blanco, por favor.*' Yes, that's what she needed when she got home. A great big glass of wine. She'd stop at the off-licence on the way. The post-Christmas sherry had long been polished off. She'd read recently that British career women were drinking at alarmingly high levels to help cope with the stress in their lives. Did that mean she, too, was heading down the slippery slope to alcoholism? Career women? She'd never thought of herself as one, but maybe now she was. Stress?

Yes, she could certainly tick that box. Well, if being a career woman meant having the odd glass of wine at home, that was OK by her.

She pulled up outside Grapes To Go and nipped in for a cheap bottle of Frascati, as advertised in the window. Clearly someone had over-ordered as the shop was stacked from floor to ceiling with the pale yellow bottles. As she was getting back into her car, she saw Garth's van roar up the street in the opposite direction. Thank God. She heaved a sigh of relief. He's clearly out for the evening as usual. This was one night she really didn't want to have to deal with him.

Maggie got home to find George in a foul mood. GCSE English Literature, his last exam, hadn't exactly been a funky experience, apparently. But at least he was prepared to talk about it.

'I had revised, Mum. Honest,' he told her, 'but I just picked the wrong bits.'

Maggie tried to conceal a huge sigh. 'What came up?'

'Some crap about *The Mill on the Floss*.'

'You sound surprised. That was one of your set books.'

'Yeah, but I couldn't get on with it. So I just hoped the other stuff would come up. You know, sort of balance of probabilities.'

How like your bloody father, she thought to herself. That could have been Garth talking. Sheer wonderment that the very thing he knew might happen but hadn't prepared for came to pass. Like the inevitability of his old ladies' going into residential homes and therefore not needing any more gardening done. They were hardly going to defy nature and get any younger.

'Never mind, darling,' she said, taking in George's distressed and tired face. 'It's not the end of the world. I was crap at English Literature too but I've somehow managed.'

'You write all that mental stuff for the website, don't you?' said George, cheering up a bit. 'I told my mates about it. They think you're really clever and funny.'

Already emotionally frazzled, Maggie almost burst into tears. It was the first time George had ever paid her that kind of accolade. The endorsement of George's spotty friends was somehow up there with the Oscars. She pulled herself up. Crying with emotion wouldn't win her any more Brownie points. And it certainly wouldn't help George in his current predicament.

'Tell you what,' she continued with forced jollity, 'I've had a terribly long day today but I've also had some good news at work. Why don't we three go out for a meal and celebrate the end of your exams?' She called up the stairs to her daughter. 'Come on, Beth. Get your glad rags on. We're going out for a meal.'

'It'll take her an hour to get all that muck on her face,' said George sarcastically. He'd been ribbing Beth recently over her experimentations with eye make-up.

Fifteen minutes later, Beth emerged in a denim mini skirt and a bright yellow top, sporting strange panda-like eyes. George opened his mouth to make some caustic remark but Maggie stopped him with a meaningful look.

'You look great, Beth,' she announced firmly. 'Now come on, let's go. Where do you fancy eating?'

'McDonald's,' said George.

'KFC,' Beth waded in.

Maggie could sense a half-hearted fight brewing. 'Shut up, the pair of you,' she intervened swiftly. 'I'll decide, as it's my treat. Get in the car. We'll go on a mystery tour.'

Averting the usual fight about who sat where in the

car, she told them both to get in the back. There were audible moans when she drew up outside Café Rouge.

'Just for once,' she hissed, 'let's enjoy something which didn't end its existence in a bap.'

To her surprise, they both shut up and meekly went inside. The evening was a huge success, which Maggie put down to being in a proper grown-up restaurant, being treated like adults. She told them about her triumph at work and they both seemed thrilled for her, almost relieved, Maggie detected. She wondered if this were down to her own paranoia. Or perhaps they'd already guessed that something was up regarding their father's business and that she was becoming the main breadwinner. Probably too frightened to ask, Maggie surmised. But then, so was she.

Beth tucked into a salmon steak in a creamy dill sauce and even George pronounced his filet mignon and frites the best chips he'd ever tasted.

'Even better than Burger King,' he declared.

'Praise indeed.' Maggie laughed. 'We'd better send a message to the chef.'

As Maggie clambered into bed later that night, she reflected on what a wonderfully grown-up evening they'd had. And on the fact that she'd managed not to think about Jack for three whole hours. She then fell straight into a deep dreamless sleep.

On Monday morning, as she'd half dreaded, half hoped, there was another email from Jack.

> Hi Maggs. Tried to ring you on Friday but you were out there selling! Won't be able to try again this week as I'm working in California and the

time difference is antisocial. Reason I called – I'm in London in a couple of weeks' time, meeting some potential clients. Don't know if your work ever takes you up to town but wondered if you fancied meeting up for a quick drink or some lunch? See that sleep-is-a-goal flat has gone. Keep up the good work! Jack.

So that was what the phone call had been all about. Maggie thanked her lucky stars she'd been out. At least with email, she could have a think, have a confab with Pam and consult Mystic Meg before she composed a reply.

She reread his note and then forwarded it to Pam, her heart still hammering in her chest. What on earth was she to do? This had disaster written all over it. It was all very well for Jack writing jaunty notes and suggesting a jolly meet-up, but for her this was an emotionally racking experience and the culmination of twenty years of mental agony.

She went to answer the phone, thanking her lucky stars that, because of Californian time zones, it wouldn't be Jack. As she tried to speak, she realised her throat had gone quite dry. The shock, she supposed.

She cleared her throat, apologised profusely and dealt with the call as briskly as she could. Another query about a tiny bungalow 'well and truly stuck in the sixties. A symphony of formica, pop art wallpaper and heaps of brown and orange.'

She kept glancing at the corner of her computer screen where the new email alerts appeared. She'd hoped for something from Pam, but she must be away from her desk. Eventually, amongst the Monday morning glut of calls from sellers complaining about the bluntness of their property descriptions and time wasters hoping for a snoop around a posh property, came a call from Pam.

'Strewth, Maggs,' she spluttered, 'just got your email. Sorry, been taking the minutes of the world's dreariest committee meeting. Thought I'd expire from boredom. Is that a cause of death? Maybe I'm starting a new trend. Anyway, re Jack. You have to go. You must lay this ghost. Get this whole thing sorted out. I won't discuss it. All I'm prepared to do is talk about what you're going to wear. And I'll look up the train times for you. But that's it.' She hung up.

Some friend, Maggie muttered aloud. She'd been hoping for an indepth discussion, the whys, the wherefores, the whatevers. But Pam clearly wasn't having any of it. She suddenly felt rather hung out to dry, like a line of weekend washing.

During her lunchtime power walk, she decided to work out the pros and cons on her own. As she pounded the pavements, she tried to list positive reasons to meet Jack. Lay the ghost, find out why he never turned up, catch up on old times, have a day out in London. The cons list included discovering some horrible truth, not liking him any more, realising she'd wasted twenty years on meaningless emotion . . . oh, and the outrageous cost of the train fare.

She began to go over all the old ground yet again, the endless conjectures about why he never showed up. Met someone else, couldn't bring himself to dump her face to face, had landed fab job with lifestyle to match that didn't include her. At least this way she'd find out once and for all. By the end of the walk she couldn't believe she was actually veering towards acceptance.

*

Maggie managed to wait two whole days before replying.

> Hi Jack. It would be lovely to meet up. Let me know your dates in London and I'll try to juggle my work around your visit. Yes, the disco flat went for a snip, but we do have a 'grow your own mushrooms in this dark basement Dickensian hovel' in the same price range. Maggs.

'Juggle my work' wasn't quite a lie, she appeased her conscience, just implying that he wouldn't necessarily be the only reason she was in London. If their meeting was a disaster, it would also give her an excuse to glance at her watch and rush off to 'an appointment'. Memo to me, she mentally dictated: must take large handbag that gives impression of Filofax, notebook, pens.

She was secretly pleased that Jack found the website amusing. He was obviously logging on regularly. It made her feel less guilty about her almost daily ritual visit to the Tin Man bar and Tin Man Inc. websites. She found herself rereading Jack's emails, trying to analyse every word and turn of phrase. It reminded her of English Literature exams at school, just like the one George had messed up. Instead of simply reading the books, the loathsome Miss Small – who moonlighted in the English department since the call for Latin was not what it had been – analysed them to death, barking at anyone who deigned to laugh and belittling anyone who failed to come up with the correct answer. Under this treatment, any possible enjoyment of the books gave way to a kind of confused stupor.

Clearly Jack was sounding her out on a meeting before coming up with specific dates, she decided. She was playing the same game now, agreeing in principle but reserving a get-out clause if she decided to cry off. But Maggie already knew she wouldn't. She was overcome by a feeling of inevitable destiny. She'd have to go. She didn't have any choice. It was no longer the meeting that bothered her, it was managing the empty feeling that would inevitably follow. They'd chat about old times and old friends, she'd tell him about her life, he'd tell her about his, he might even explain why he never turned up. Might even apologise. Then he'd say a cheery goodbye, with or without a peck on the cheek, and fly back to his life of 24/7 sunshine and success, wondering what he ever saw in her.

Except, she reminded herself, that at least he'd be seeing a more presentable Maggie than he might have done a year ago. She was now a rather more successful mother of two, commanding a respectable wage, holding down a good job and, even she had to admit, scrubbing up a lot better of late. The weight loss had given her more confidence. Shirts had been tucked into skirts for the first time in many a long year, nails were now always varnished, clothes more imaginatively put together.

With Vanessa out on one of her long power lunches, Maggie picked up the phone and dialled Pam's number, hoping for a proper discussion about developments now that she'd come to her decision.

'OK, I'm going to meet him,' she announced. 'What do you think I should wear?'

'Yippee,' Pam yelled so loudly she might as well not have used the phone. 'Gosh, I didn't think you'd do it, Maggs. Well done. Good decision. Now, clothes. Let me think . . .'

'I've implied that I'll be up in London on business so it will have to be a bit office-y looking.'

'Good, that's easy then. You've got lots of nice things to put together now. Not black. Too funereal and too safe.'

'Very slimming, though,' Maggie chipped in. She'd already mentally decided on black trousers and top.

'But it's summer,' said Pam. 'Go for a bit of colour. Not too bright, but something memorable. How's your bank balance? I feel a Saturday trip to the shops coming on, don't you?'

Maggie groaned. She should have known it would come to this.

'Not sure I can afford anything,' she said, the worry about whether Garth was still paying the mortgage never far from her thoughts.

'Tell you what,' said Pam, undisguised excitement in her voice. 'I'll come over Saturday morning, we'll have a root through your wardrobe and then pick up what you need after that.'

'So long as it's not more than a fiver.' Maggie laughed. 'I took the kids out to Café Rouge to celebrate my sales figures the other night. So that's my fun over for this month.'

'Oh, don't worry, we'll sort you out,' said Pam confidently. Clearly this was now Pam's *raison d'être*. 'Besides, if you have to go over to Spain soon on this business link-up, you'll need something smart but summery. Can't wear black in Spain, honey. Everyone will mistake you for someone's elderly granny.'

Pam did it every time, Maggie thought to herself. Always came up with such a definitive reason that she couldn't say no. She was totally wasted at the council.

*

'Not linen,' Pam was rifling through Maggie's wardrobe the following Saturday morning. 'Looks great just off the ironing board, but it'll be creased to death after sitting on the train . . . also you need to have most of the interest above the waist as you'll be sitting down in a restaurant most of the time. No point in having a fab skirt with lots of interesting embroidery detail shoved under a table . . .'

'You've been watching too many makeover programmes,' Maggie teased her.

But Pam was undeterred. She continued her rummage amongst the hangers. 'Aha,' she finally exclaimed, 'this is more like it. Might be able to do something with this.' She pulled out a long voile skirt with a tiny pattern in deep blues and turquoises on a cream background which Maggie had bought in a sale but never worn, regarding it as a mistake.

'Don't have anything to go with it,' she protested half-heartedly.

'No problem,' said Pam, shoving it unceremoniously into her bag. 'We'll take it with us.'

Soon they were heading for Top Shop, to Maggie's huge embarrassment. 'Beth will probably be in here,' she muttered in a vain protest.

Pam knew exactly where she was heading. She made a beeline for the knitwear, and was soon holding up the skirt against a row of pretty beaded cardigans. Within seconds she'd found what she was looking for, in exactly the right shade of deep blue to match the skirt.

'That colour really suits you. Go and try those on.' She propelled Maggie towards the changing rooms, shoving two sizes of the cardigan into her hands. Maggie offered up a silent prayer that it wasn't a communal arrangement.

'The 12's much better than the 14,' Pam pronounced when Maggie emerged for a rather nervous twirl. 'Makes for a more fitted shape. It can be an early Christmas present.' Before Maggie could protest, she snatched the cardigan out of her hands and marched off in the direction of the till. Maggie couldn't remember the last time she'd bought a size 12.

Next thing, they were in Monsoon, Pam sifting knowledgeably through the sale racks until she found a simple cream silk top with four rows of top-stitching round the V neckline. This time Maggie insisted on paying. She looked anxiously at the ticket. Thank goodness the item had been substantially reduced.

They then collapsed over a cappuccino in the Costa coffee shop next door for a discussion about their purchases.

'I think this is a perfect look' said Pam, spooning up the froth and chocolate. 'The skirt's lovely and fluty at the bottom so you can wear some pretty heels to emphasise it. The cardigan is a kind of jacket substitute so it's softer yet still quite businesslike and the hint of cream silk underneath is soft and sexy and great for your skin tones. Makes you look as though you have a lovely light tan. Plus I've got just the most perfect beads to pull it all together.'

'You're talking like a bloody magazine.' Maggie laughed. 'But seriously, I am relieved about this. I really want to look my best, and also I want to be comfortable. I'd hate him to have the satisfaction of going away thinking what a lucky escape he'd had from an old bag lady.'

'There's no chance of that, honey.' Pam smiled. 'You're looking great these days. I know you've got lots of stress with Garth and everything, but it's a great fat buster.'

Maggie took Pam's advice and wore the outfit to work on Monday just to make sure it was comfortable. Never wear new clothes to somewhere important, Pam had counselled. Perhaps that was why divorce rates in Britain were rocketing. Brides felt so ill at ease in their meringues the first time round, they divorced and gave the frock a second, more comfortable outing. Maggie glanced at her reflection in the glass as she unlocked the office door. She was really pleased with it, except for her shoes. She'd dug out a pair of navy sandals she thought would work, but they just didn't give the finished outfit the pizzazz she'd hoped for. A pity, but a quick look at her bank account online ruled out any further purchase.

She admitted to a silent tear that there wasn't the hoped-for reply from Jack waiting for her, with his London visit dates. A black cloud of disappointment began to descend on her.

She was halfway through the usual Monday morning mountain of messages when Vanessa emerged from her office in a cloud of Chanel No. 5. Maggie got up instinctively to make some coffee.

'Yes please, darling,' said Vanessa, 'and I've got some good news for you. Damien's just confirmed a very generous bonus for your sales figures *and* a pay rise. You'll get a letter confirming it tomorrow.'

New shoes after all, was Maggie's first guilty thought, rather than a restock of the freezer. The fates really are steering me to this meeting, if it actually happens. She was now plagued with doubts. Perhaps Jack had had a domestic crisis or maybe he was too busy enjoying a sexy reunion with his wife after a week away in California. She tried to shut that concept out of her head. Should she email him again? No, leave it. Just cheer yourself up by buying some shoes at lunchtime anyway.

She spotted them almost immediately. The perfect pair, strappy blue beaded suede sandals with a slender heel, were an outrageous ninety-eight pounds. She couldn't possibly justify them, not even with her bonus. Not if, and she was steeling herself for this, she was about to take over some of the mortgage as well as all the bills. She was just gazing longingly into the window at the shoes when a young blonde sales assistant popped her head out of the doorway.

'Fab, aren't they?' she said. 'Look I'm not supposed to tell you this, but our dragon of a manager is having another of her two-hour lunches. Sales starts tomorrow. Everything in the window's at least a third off, including those shoes. Come in and try them on. If you like them, I'll put them by for you.'

Maggie followed her into the shop like a programmed robot. She tried on the shoes, which, of course, felt as comfortable as slippers. The assistant pronounced them 'completely gorgeous' and said how beautifully they showed off her slim ankles. Then she quietly put the shoes back in the box, put a finger to her lips and then stowed them under the counter.

'See you tomorrow,' she whispered conspiratorially. Maggie walked back to work on air, exhilarated at having found the perfect shoes and being envied her slim ankles. She'd never thought of them as being anything other than ordinary. But when she caught sight of herself in a shop window, yes, she supposed they were looking quite good these days.

Somehow this was all going too well. First a bonus, second the perfect shoes, and now even a tip-off about a discount. All she needed now was a specific date from Jack. How ironic that he'd suddenly gone quiet on her. Surely the phone call and the email weren't for nothing.

She knew that if he were to reply today it would not be until late afternoon because of the Boston time difference. At six o'clock she gave up imagining excuses for him, got in her car and drove home, feeling tired, miserable and rather stupid.

Next day there was still nothing. At lunchtime she went to claim her shoes, but not even the sight of them being wrapped in tissue paper could cheer her up. Isn't it just typical, she thought. They're the most beautiful shoes in the entire world and now I don't have an occasion to wear them.

I'll wear them to work she resolved. Give Vanessa a run for her money in the footwear stakes. That's what I'll do, she thought, trying to justify the most expensive shoes she'd ever bought.

The email was waiting for her the next morning. Full of apologies, one of his kids had been ill, the trip to London had nearly been postponed, but now it was back on. He mentioned three days at the end of the following week. Maggie was taken aback. Suddenly it seemed too soon. Too looming.

Still no mention of his wife, she noted, when she'd calmed down a bit. She glanced through her diary. Yet again, the fates were conspiring. The end of next week had no viewings booked in so far. She decided to take Wednesday, Thursday and Friday off. Wednesday to get ready. Thursday the day itself. And Friday for tears, regrets and recriminations. She'd better ask Vanessa if she could take some leave.

'Of course, darling,' Vanessa exclaimed expansively. 'You're owed tons anyway. But there's one condition. I must know where you bought those utterly gorgeous shoes.'

Maggie smiled and told her. She edited out the bit about the sale, though.

'Doing anything particularly wonderful while you're in town?' Vanessa enquired, assuming Maggie was spending the whole time in London.

'Oh, a bit of shopping, the usual stuff. Visiting old haunts. I worked there for a while after I left school.' Maggie babbled on. 'Meeting some old friends for lunch . . . actually, can I ask your advice?'

'Friends' sounded more innocuous than the singular. It raised questions, like what type of friend. Maggie was certain that if she told Vanessa she was meeting an old boyfriend whom she was probably still nuts about, Vanessa would have been fascinated, started fanning the flames and recommended a good divorce lawyer at the snap of her rouge-noired fingers.

'My mind's gone a blank on anywhere to eat,' she continued, hoping she wasn't blushing at the fib. 'I think we'd all like somewhere smart and busy. Just in case we run out of things to say.'

'No contest,' said Vanessa immediately. 'Too late to book the Ivy so it has to be Joe Allen. Just off the Strand. Nothing much to look at from the outside but downstairs in the basement it's all brick and mirrors and theatrical bits and bobs. Lots of thesps go in there. If the conversation lulls, you can always celebrity spot. It's open all day, too, so if you're having a marvellous time you can just carry on through to the evening.'

Maggie gulped. She hadn't envisaged that kind of scenario.

'Anyway, you're the techie one round here,' Vanessa continued. 'They're bound to be on the web.'

Maggie thanked her profusely and immediately took a quick peek at the Joe Allen website. She forwarded a brief update email to Pam.

'Perfect,' Pam came back on the phone. She was too excited to confine herself to email. 'Just the right ambience, with lots going on. Sounds like a good celebrity hangout. Yummy menu too, and he'll be paying so don't bother to read the prices. And it's open all day so you can stay there all evening if things go well.'

'Funnily enough, that's what Vanessa said,' Maggie observed. It was almost as though the pair of them were fellow conspirators.

Chapter 32

The departures screen at Weltham station announced that the train for London Paddington would be arriving on time. Maggie glanced up beyond the flaking paintwork of the station roof at the bright blue sky. Yet again, someone's up there making this too easy for me. The outfit, the bonus, the shoes, the time off work. Even her unruly hair had been brushed into relative submission. Everything had fallen into place too smoothly.

She stood on the platform clutching her briefcase and a couple of magazines. She'd nearly picked up a copy of *Private Eye* but thought better of it. It had been Jack's favourite and they'd often read out extracts in funny voices to each other, sitting up in bed. She didn't want him to think she had any recall of their more intimate moments. Too much of an emotional giveaway.

She found a seat in a quiet carriage, switched off her mobile phone and tried to settle back to some meaningful features in *Marie Claire*. Women were doing fantastic voluntary work in Sudan, a new breed of women philosophers, a woman surgeon who'd pioneered an unusual thumb operation, it was all ground-breaking stuff. But the words just spun round and round. She craved a cup of coffee but with the train rocking and rolling she was terrified that she'd spill some of it on her cream silk top. In the end, she pulled out a copy of *Heat* magazine and flipped idly through the pages, trying to engross herself in a fashion round-up on this year's Cannes Film Festival. Page after page of sun-showered beauties in more or less the same sparkly dresses. Strappy top, cleavage and split to the thigh. It was almost a uniform in different colours. Most of the actresses she'd never heard of and probably never would again. This was their day in the sun, and then what? Was it better to have had the excitement of that media exposure and then watch it all disappear? Or never to have had it in the first place? Bit like love. She sometimes envied people who appeared to cruise through life without apparently experiencing any great passion. Just sitting contentedly on the sidelines of life. Presumably they didn't miss white-water rafting down the River of Love.

That's what had screwed her up about Jack. The passion, the stomach going topsy turvy at hearing his voice on the phone, the thought of being in his arms, the laughter over silly things like reading out their horoscopes and pretending to follow the advice. Sunday mornings in bed with tea, toast and the papers. Sunday afternoon sex amongst the toast crumbs. Trying to cook up a Caribbean meal for ten on two hot plates for his birthday. Attempting to pass it off as home cooking until someone found the Tesco Jerk Chicken Sauce jars in the bin. Queuing for cheap tickets for the Proms and pretending to be Swedish when asked who was conducting.

Maggie shivered and tried to blot it all out. She glanced at her watch. Two hours and counting . . . she felt like a patient about to undergo a major operation. Another hour on the train, and then she might risk a coffee at one of the places on the station where it would be safe from spills. Then a quick tart up in the loo, queue for a cab. Another quick tart up in the cab and then The Meeting. One o'clock was the agreed time, with a table booked in Jack's name. One ten was when Maggie intended to pitch up. This was not a case of being fashionably late. She just couldn't bear the idea of being there first, waiting and waiting, like the terrible night he never showed

Now she was at Paddington, the train having arrived dead on time. She carefully sipped her coffee, noticing that her hands were shaking. She'd told Gareth she was going to London on Home Truths business, which was slightly true. After all, it was thanks to Jack's parents that she was now pursuing the Spanish/French links for the company. His total uninterest had made her guilt much easier to bear. She was beginning to see how easily people could fall into adultery. When the person at home doesn't care about you any more, it's human nature to seek out someone to fill the gap.

She inspected herself in the loo mirror. Her hair had reverted to its usual rebellious self. She gave it a violent brushing but couldn't quite recreate the earlier success. Skin rather pale, she thought, regretting she'd hadn't factored in some time to catch a few rays in the garden.

The taxi queue was much too short. At this rate she'd get to Joe Allen far too early. Even the traffic seemed to be flowing quite swiftly for London. Rather than be delivered to Joe Allen's door in Exeter Street, she took a snap decision and asked the cabbie to stop in the Strand. She could then walk up and down a bit until her designated time. She gazed into jewellers, men's outfitters and even the Boots window. One or two people openly stared at her. There was nothing very riveting about a massive Buy One Get One Free poster for deodorant. The state of the nation's armpits didn't warrant two whole minutes of attention. The sun, now high in the sky, was burning through her cardigan. But she couldn't take it off. The outfit depended on it. She'd forgotten just how dusty and stifling London could be in the summer. The air just hung, as if barricaded in between the tall buildings. She wished now she'd headed around the corner for the Thames and the chance of a cool breeze off the water. But her watch told her that time had now run out.

She walked back towards Exeter Street. Jack was just a couple of minutes away. By now she felt hot, sweaty and very nervous, her heart thumping away as though she'd just been called to the dentist's chair. For a few seconds, she flirted with the idea of running away. Leaving him in the lurch, just as he'd done to her. But her feet weren't listening to her heart. They just kept on going, as if driven by some invisible and fateful force. Having got this far, she might as well go through with it.

She'd fantasised about this moment so many times over the past week. In her dreams, she had intended to alight straight from an air-conditioned taxi on the dot of 1.10 p.m., cool as a cucumber, and then sweep confidently through the entrance. Instead, she felt like a darn good hose down and a large gin and tonic.

'Table booked for Haley,' she told the greeter.

'He's here already,' was the response. Her heart skipped yet another beat. At least she wouldn't be the one left waiting this time. She followed the man as they descended into the mercifully cool basement. Despite her nerves, Maggie loved the place immediately. On the brick and mirrored walls were playbills, posters and bits of theatrical memorabilia, interspersed with signed photographs from grateful and famous diners. The place was full to bursting with a high buzz of excited conversation. She'd read that this was the place to be seen if you were an in- or out-of-work actor. Raw ambition was certainly on the menu. Snippets of conversation as she passed by the tables confirmed the agony of stardom. 'Looked marvellous in the part but we couldn't hear a bloody word' . . . 'Disastrous, darling! He's only had two days' filming since *Titanic*' . . . 'Trouble with her lines not unconnected with vodka' . . . 'Not surprised it's coming off, the reviews were shocking' . . . 'Isn't that Patsy Kensit over there?' Waiters in long white starched aprons streamed up and down, bearing huge white plates dotted with tiny, beautifully arranged morsels.

The journey seemed to go on for ever, twisting and turning round the tables to avoid the enthusiastic elbows of gesticulating diners. Finally, the greeter moved slightly to the left and ushered Maggie past him to the next table. A man immediately stood up to greet her with a broad smile. A man she didn't recognise. A complete stranger.

Horrified, Maggie stood there, completely frozen to the spot, and wondering if this were some horrible mistake. Some chatroom pervert who'd passed himself off as Jack and lured her to London and God knows what else. She stared at the man, six feet tall, slim and tanned, with very short brown hair speckled with grey. He was wearing a cream linen jacket, a casual light blue shirt and dark blue trousers. Silver, square-framed glasses perched halfway down his nose.

'Maggie.' He held out his hand. She held out hers in automatic response. Their hands stayed clasped for just a moment longer than a conventional handshake. 'Good to see you,' continued the stranger, in a strange Transatlantic drawl. 'You haven't changed a bit.'

They sat down. Maggie still couldn't speak. She stared at the man as though he'd just flown in from Mars. She and 'Jack' had made this arrangement on email so she hadn't even done a voice check.

'Clearly *I* have,' the man continued, with a nervous laugh. 'Maybe this will help.'

He removed his glasses and smiled again, revealing a row of perfect white teeth. That made it worse. Jack's teeth were never that perfect. Very white but a bit higgledy-piggledy. She looked into his eyes. Deep blue with a little sparkle, and then, as he smiled, they crinkled up in the way that she'd always remembered. And his earlobes . . . yes, they were unusually long, just like Jack's. She used to stroke Jack's 'luscious lobes', as she called them. With a jolt, she realised it *was* Jack.

'You're looking at me as if I'm an alien,' Jack continued. There it was again, that way his eyes scrunched up when he was teasing.

'Sorry.' Maggie finally found a voice. 'How very rude of me. Good to see you, Jack. You haven't changed a bit either.'

She groaned inwardly. That was a ridiculous thing to say, given the silence and her open-mouthed shock.

'Not quite quick enough!' Jack laughed. 'I don't believe you, but it doesn't matter. Tell you what. Let's order and then we'll start this whole thing all over again.'

He's making huge efforts to break the ice, she thought, and I'm not helping him one little bit. Come on, Maggs, you've waited twenty years for this moment. Don't throw it away in a stunned silence.

'What a good idea,' she said, forcing a smile and wishing her voice didn't sound quite so strangulated. Her throat had gone dry and appeared to have taken delivery of a huge lump. She could already imagine her lonely journey home, kicking herself for blowing the whole thing so spectacularly. Too nervous and shocked to speak, she'd have to confess to Pam.

'Well, I'm going to have . . . oh, dear, can't decide between the sea bass and the lamb cutlets,' Jack announced, obviously determined to keep some sort of dialogue going.

'Oh, I was thinking about the sea bass,' said Maggie. She wasn't at all. She couldn't even read the menu properly, her hands were shaking so much. It was just a meaningless piece of cardboard with all the words on it dancing around distractedly.

'Tell you what,' Jack continued, unabashed. 'You have the sea bass and I'll go for the lamb and then we can swap if you don't like the look of yours.'

That last bit gave Maggie a jolt. She'd completely forgotten that that's what they'd always done, on the few times they could afford to eat out. They always ordered different dishes so that they could swap, or compare, They even did it with takeaways.

'OK,' was all she could manage. Come on, Maggie, come on, she urged herself. You've got to do better than this.

Jack summoned a waiter to give their order. 'And we'll check out the Caesar salad to start with,' he added, looking at Maggie for confirmation.

She nodded. 'But please don't wave a cucumber

anywhere near it,' he continued. 'As I recall, Maggie, you were never a fan.'

He smiled at her again. She nodded dumbly, amazed that he remembered. She'd always hated the slimy feel of cucumber, not just for its taste, but because she was convinced it made her burp. She'd forced herself to eat some the first time she was invited to Jack's parents' for supper, too shy to say she didn't like it. Sure enough, the climax of the evening was a resounding burp which, mercifully, Joe and Christine had found very funny. All cucumber was good for was treating swollen eyelids. She made a mental note to pick up a large one on the way home. There would be a lot of crying before the day was out.

Jack poured her a glass of white wine from the bottle already on the table. 'Well, here's to us, meeting up again after all these years. I hope you don't mind me ordering it before you got here. Dry white OK?' They touched glasses, Maggie afraid that hers would shatter into thousands of pieces, like her nerves.

'So tell me,' she began, desperate to contribute something to this already downward-spiralling conversation. 'I want to hear all about your life in Boston.'

'OK,' said Jack, 'so long as you give me a snapshot of your life too. I'm dying to hear more about this estate agency . . . see, I've remembered not to say realty.'

'That's a ghastly word.' Maggie managed a small laugh. 'Anyway, you first.'

Interestingly, Maggie noted, Jack chose to begin his tale in America. He skipped the bit where they split up and his reasons for going to the States, and instead fast-forwarded to landing a job with a website design company just as the dot com business was taking off. As he talked, Maggie allowed herself to gaze at his face, her eyes roving over his features again and again. Bit by bit, the old Jack, the Jack she'd consigned to memory, was merging into the new Jack sitting opposite her. She could see now why she'd been so thrown by his appearance. It was all to do with the shape of his head. The old mop of wavy light brown hair that she'd loved running her fingers through had given way to a stereotypical American cropped look. She hadn't realised that under all the hair, his head was rather square. The short cut didn't suit him at all, she decided. Yet out of this strange robotic head, the familiar blue eyes danced and twinkled as he talked. His hands hadn't changed either. She glanced at the long bony fingers, the same strong nails with their prominent half-moons. No rings.

Jack had now reached California, describing how phony and threatening he found it and how the endless sunshine made him miss the seasons. Hence the move to Boston.

'What's Boston like?' she said, not really wanting to know. She wanted him to tell her about his family set-up, but there was still no word on the subject. 'Everyone who's been there says it's really groovy.'

Jack threw his head back and laughed. 'Jeez, Maggs. Haven't heard anyone say that word in years. Groovy.'

'Stop taking the mick,' Maggie scolded him. She was at least relaxing a little. The searing pain in her shoulders, the lump in her throat and the faint beginnings of a migraine were beginning to subside. Probably helped by the wine.

'OK, Boston,' Jack began. 'It's the cradle of American history, a city of spires and statues, beautiful parks and loads of bookshops. The Bull and Finch pub – that's the home of the TV series *Cheers*. It's a walking city. Just as well, as the standard of driving is appalling. People don't like to signal. They think it gives away their strategy.'

'Where's your office?' Maggie prompted, still grateful not to be saying much. She knew exactly where his office was. She'd visited Jack's company website so many times they must have been wondering why they'd racked up so many hits recently.

'It's very central. We're near Quincy Market, which you'd adore.' Jack was warming to his theme. 'It always reminds me of Covent Garden, just round the corner here. In fact, I thought we might have a walk round there later, if you have time before your meeting.'

Oh, my God, thought Maggie, I'm not ready for any 'later'. I thought it would be a quick lunch and then goodbye till next time/for ever.

'Oh, yes, my meeting.' She'd half forgotten her get-out clause. 'It's not till later. Tell me more about Boston.'

'Quincy Market and the Faneuil Hall are real tourist traps. Loads of flower stalls, street entertainers and food. It's great for al fresco eating. We always send visitors there for coffee and bagels as part of the tour.'

Maggie was desperately curious to know whom the 'we' referred to. Did he mean his office team or his family set-up? She must pluck up the courage and ask about his personal life at some point, or she'd be kicking herself into the next century.

She took a deep breath to begin edging towards that subject area when fate intervened yet again in the form of their waiter, returning with caesar salads and a very phallic-looking pepper mill.

'So tell me about your family?' she said as brightly as

she could. She'd at least be able to cover her reaction by pausing on a mouthful of lettuce.

'Well, you probably know how the folks are better than I do,' Jack said, with another heart-stopping grin. 'I don't get over to Spain to see them as often as I'd like. Kids in high school. Big exams coming up. Caroline's sixteen and Jack Junior is fourteen. And Betsy, my wife . . .'

Maggie felt a huge stab of pain go straight through her heart.

'. . . has a huge and very close family so there are an awful lot of family events. Americans love anniversaries. They're constantly hatching, matching and despatching.' He rolled his eyes to indicate that there were too many such happenings.

So there *was* a wife. Jack wasn't a divorcee or a widower. Unless Jack was married with a bit on the side, every one of Pam's theories had just been blown out of the water. Maggie wanted to get up and run away right there and then.

Jack promptly dived into his salad. Was that because it looked irresistible, or was he keen to get off the subject? Maggie knew that in her present state of agitation, no theory that she conjured up would have any reasonable basis whatsoever. It was now her turn. Her soliloquy carefully practised daily in the car – 'My life in half a dozen brief sentences' – went straight out of her head.

She started with Farleys and outlined the circumstances of its dramatic evolution into Home Truths. She noticed that she sounded much more confident when she was talking about work. She then went over the official version of events to explain how she came across Jack's parents' website, in the course of setting up a French and Spanish connection. It wasn't a blatant lie; she'd already forgiven herself. It was merely a reversal of timing. Still avoiding any mention of home life, she talked about still being friendly with Pam. Jack seemed keen to hear about life in Weltham and old school friends.

'Remember Freddie Chapple?' she asked.

'Vaguely,' Jack replied. 'The class swot in the Brains from *Thunderbirds* specs?'

'That's the one. He came into the office a while back enquiring after a really tatty house. Still just as spotty. And just plain weird. It turns out he wanted to buy *back* his parents' old house. How spooky's that!'

'No change there then.' Jack laughed. 'What about the rest of them?'

Maggie was tempted to tell him about Pam's late-night phone call to Luke at Bonkers FM and spill the beans on David Gregg, ex-con, and now reinvented as Gregg David, life coach. But she had already promised herself she wouldn't. It would expose their little game of tracking down old flames. Jack might then go away wondering if that was what this meeting was all about. She couldn't risk his thinking that, even if it was true.

'Most of them seem to have disappeared off the face of the earth,' she said instead. 'Or signed up with Friends Reunited. That's been a big craze here in recent years. Pam signed up and immediately got an email from Isadora Fielding. Much to her regret. She was always bad news, that girl.'

'Oh? Why's that?' Jack asked, a little over-hastily, and then took a slug of wine.

'Dora was a terrible minx,' said Maggie, the wine now suddenly kicking in. She could hear her voice sounding uncharacteristically bitter but she couldn't resist having a pop at Dora, even after all these years. 'Dora was always stirring things and telling fibs, just to wind people up. She was really clever at it too, top of the Premier League. It was Dora who tipped Pam off about David Gregg's ad in the lonely hearts column in the *Gazette*, while she was still seeing him. And then proceeded to tell half of Weltham. Remember that?'

Jack nodded vaguely.

Maggie continued, now warming to her theme: 'I remember she was really horrible to one poor girl in the lower sixth. What was her name? Cecile Walters. Gosh, haven't thought about her in years. Dora told Cecile that she was fed up with being groped by Cecile's boyfriend and could she ask him to stop it. Cecile believed Dora and promptly finished with him. Whenever there was trouble, Dora was always somehow involved, usually lurking around in the shadows—'

Jack was suddenly red-faced and choking. He waved his hand to indicate it was only a minor problem and then picked up his napkin to wipe his mouth.

'Sorry about that.' He finally recovered. 'That salad dressing just hit the spot a bit too violently. Do tell me more about Dora. I didn't realise she was like that. I thought she was just a bit of a pathetic creep around the teachers, actually.'

'Oh, it was all part of the act,' Maggie replied. She was very tempted to add that she always thought Dora fancied him but pulled herself up. That kind of remark might bring them back to the fateful night and she wasn't quite ready for that. Perhaps she never would be.

'Anyway, you haven't told me about your kids yet,' Jack prompted.

Ah, here was the difficult one. Did she paint a picture of an idyllic home and a life which she had managed perfectly well without him? Or did she tell it like it was, a loveless existence on a shoestring with two only recently reformed teenagers? And run the risk that he'd merely pity her? The last thing she wanted was pity from Jack. She wanted to walk away from this with her head held high and her pride intact. She didn't want him to have the satisfaction of knowing that he'd had a lucky escape, made a better life with someone else. She didn't want him recounting to friends over bloody bagels and sodding coffee in his beloved Quincy Market that he'd 'met up with an old flame who'd really let herself go'.

Besides, this was supposed to be a fun lunch between old friends, not a Relate-style counselling session. At least that was how it had been billed. So far it just wasn't going according to plan.

Chapter 33

'Well, I'm married.' She finally got there, at the pudding stage. She couldn't stop a ridiculous little laugh. 'My husband runs a gardening business.' She stopped herself from inserting 'not very successful' into the sentence but couldn't inject much pride into her voice. 'And I've got two kids. George's just finished his GCSEs and Beth's a couple of years younger. They've run me ragged over the years with their squabbling but I must say they've been a lot better lately.'

Jack shot her a curious look 'GCSEs? What are they? I'm so out of touch with the education system here now.'

'Like our old O levels and GCEs. If George gets good enough grades, he'll go on to the sixth form and start his A level courses next term. Mind you, judging by the panic scenes we've had at home and the lack of revision, I have my doubts. Kids, eh?' She raised her eyebrows.

What am I on about? she thought to herself. I'm telling him my kids are at each other's throats and that they don't bother to work. This isn't exactly painting the picture of a huge success story. Pride and dignity, Pam's final key words of advice, kept coming back into her head. Pride and dignity. Pam would be well impressed with her. With one master stroke, she was being disloyal to her own children and portraying herself as a not terribly brilliant mother. Jack would be hotfooting it back to his American dream in Boston as fast as he could, heaving sighs of relief to be back in Betsy's sensible – and probably annoyingly slim – arms.

She took another slug of wine, knowing she'd regret all this. Her head was swimming with emotion, heightened by the alcohol. She'd gone from tense nerves to slightly pissed nerves. She couldn't believe how much she'd drunk. They were now most of the way through a second bottle and Maggie kept trying to stop herself from drinking any more, but picking up the glass had become a kind of prop. A way to stall the conversation, or buy a few seconds to collect her thoughts.

The tales over the bagels in Quincy bloody Market would now include 'she's evidently a terrible mother, and I know I shouldn't say this but she's well on the way to a serious drink problem'.

She put her glass down and looked up at Jack. He was gazing at her intently. Almost frighteningly. What was he about to say? Even in her slightly hazy state, Maggie was bracing herself.

'So how old is George?' he almost demanded, the familiar blue eyes narrowing.

'Sixteen,' said Maggie. 'Beth's fourteen. Roughly the same ages as your kids.' And there the similarity probably ends, she thought bitterly. She could imagine his two perfect children: tanned skins, perfect manners and that all-American schmaltz you see on their sitcoms.

'Are you sure?' Was she imagining it, or had Jack raised his voice a natz just then?

'Well, I was there at the birth, so I think I should

know.' She half laughed, trying to make it into a joke. 'Pretty horrific, actually. I never intended to have any more, not after that! Twenty-four hours of solid agony. But then Beth came along and she was a lot easier . . .'

Why the hell was she giving him this boring trivia? Most men weren't the slightest bit interested in maternity details.

A waiter loomed between them and presented Jack with the bill. He immediately whipped out a credit card. Oh, my God, thought Maggie, panicking, this is nearly over. He's going to go and I still haven't found any answers to my questions. Maybe I've just answered them all myself. Maybe Jack foresaw in me what I turned out to be, A Woman of No Substance.

They both stared at each other, almost like the strangers they'd been at the start of this silly idea.

'I'm sorry, but . . .' Jack started.

'What?'

'OK, I'm sorry but there's something I need to know,' Jack began again. Were his hands shaking slightly? 'I probably have no right to ask but I'll ask anyway.'

Maggie braced herself yet again. Surely it was the other way round. There were things *she* needed to know.

'Were you pregnant when we split up?'

Maggie's face immediately answered his question. She reached for the glass again. She was going to regret this later on. Was that it? Jack had left her because he thought she was pregnant? Had she wasted all these years of mourning on a guy who fled because he thought he'd got her up the duff? She certainly hadn't thought of that one.

'No of course I bloody wasn't.' Even she heard the anger in her voice. 'Is that why you disappeared? You thought I was pregnant and you ran away. And you came here today hoping to hear about the child you think you fathered but never met. I'm sorry but that's disgusting.'

Several tables abandoned thespian talk and tuned in, shunning the showy arrival of several cast members of *Holby City*, in order to hear the next instalment of Jack and Maggie.

'And just how did you get to hear about this phantom pregnancy?' she continued, trying to lower her voice. 'Why didn't you ask me? After all, wasn't I supposed to be the mother?'

Clearly agitated, Jack wrung his hands, those long bony fingers she'd loved so much. She wanted to throw her wine all over him and sock him in the jaw. Bollocks to dignity, sorry Pam.

'But I wasn't the father,' he said quietly. 'I was told you were pregnant by somebody else. I came round to your flat and saw his car parked outside. So I walked away. Well actually I ran away. I saw an ad for cheap flights to Los Angeles, found a bloke in the pub that night to take over my flat. Next day I went to the airport with what I could cram into a suitcase and basically hung out there for a couple of days until the flight. I just couldn't face the prospect of running into you with Rick in tow.'

'Rick? Who the hell's Rick?' Maggie noticed the restaurant was now spinning around her. She wondered how much more shock she could take.

'Rick Churston. The guy you went out with before me.'

'What on earth has he got to do with it?'

'Well, clearly nothing, as I am just realising.' Suddenly the all-American tan had faded from Jack's face. Was there just a hint of a tear in those familiar blue eyes?

Nothing was making any sense to Maggie. Like a robot, she reached down for her bag. Jack took this as a sign that she was leaving. A look of panic started to creep across his face. Their fellow diners registered undisguised disappointment that this fascinating drama was about to draw to a close. Would they be denied the final denouement before the tragic couple left to go their separate ways?

'I don't know what you're on about.' Maggie stopped herself for a second to swallow a sob. 'All I know is that you didn't turn up that night and I spent years and years yearning for you, wondering where you were, what had happened. And now I've just realised that I wasted my time. The Jack I knew wouldn't have run off like that.' She tried to get up, but her legs wouldn't let her.

Jack grabbed her arm across the table. A ripple of renewed interest spread around their neighbours. Were they going to get that end-of-episode cliffhanger after all?

'At least, Maggie, let me tell you what happened from my side,' he pleaded, his fingers turning her skin white as he tried to restrain her. 'Just hear me out. Please.'

'OK.' That was the first sensible thing she'd said this afternoon. He relaxed his grip slightly. She might as well hear the whole ridiculous story and then get the hell out. She could then spend the rest of her life quietly kicking herself for moping over such a spineless bastard.

'If you remember, we'd had a bit of a tiff,' said Jack, his voice calming slightly. 'I can't actually remember what it was about, probably you going on about me being late all the time. Anyway, we hadn't seen each other for a few days and I was coming round to your flat that night to try to make the peace. I was having a pint or three, sitting outside the Argyll Tavern. Remember we used to go there sometimes, just up from the Palladium. Well, I bumped into Dora.'

Maggie felt a sharp pain in her chest. Not that bloody cow Dora again. Whenever there was trouble, Dora was somehow always the common denominator.

'She'd driven up to town to do some shopping. We got chatting. I hadn't seen her since we all left school so it was quite nice to go over old times. I'll be honest, I'd had a bit too much to drink and I told her that you and I had had a bit of a bust-up. Looking back on it, she did come on to me rather blatantly. She was all tits and sympathy. Then she let slip that you'd been seeing Rick again on the side for quite some time and that she'd heard that you were pregnant. I was flabbergasted and at first I didn't believe her. But she seemed to know so much about it, including how you'd confided in her that you were going to finish with me, go ahead with the baby and marry Rick. There was loads of detail and I thought you two were friends so I suppose I began to believe it. She kind of clinched it by saying something along the lines of, "Well, when you go round to her flat tonight, I bet you'll see Rick's car parked outside." So I did.'

'And?' Maggie sat frozen in her chair.

'Sure enough, there it was. I remembered it from Weltham Grammar School days. He drove that old yellow Triumph Herald. You couldn't mistake it.'

Maggie nodded sadly. Rick had been one of the first in their class to pass his driving test. His parents had promptly bought him the car for his eighteenth birthday. It broke down nearly every day and became a regular feature in the school car park.

'Well, if it was his car, he certainly wasn't visiting me. And no, I wasn't pregnant and no, I hadn't been seeing him on the side. You can believe me or you can believe Dora.'

Jack looked at her, his face a picture of agony. They both sensed there was nothing more to be said. They got up from the table without saying another word and began walking towards the stairs. The stairs that would take them up to the street outside and their final goodbye.

They stepped out into the street. The sweltering hot sunshine had gone, replaced by ominous dark clouds and the beginnings of a summer storm.

She turned to face him. Jack's face looked as thunderous as the sky.

'Maggs, I've made a horrible mistake,' he began, his voice shaking uncontrollably, 'which I will regret for the rest of my life. I can't even begin to ask your forgiveness. I want to stand here and take you in my arms and love you to death. But I can't. I'm not worthy of you.'

'We both have other responsibilities now . . .' Maggie tried, aware that she was slurring her words.

'I came here to catch up with an old friend, talk over old times, wish her well.' Jack was mumbling almost to himself and gazing at the pavement. 'But then I find that I had inadvertently treated her in the most appalling fashion. I couldn't possibly expect to be a friend of hers now. And now I look at her and I realise that I made the most terrible mistake. I want to kiss her and hold her. But if I do that, I'm lost.'

'Look, Dora was always a shit . . .' Maggie's voice faded away. Jack had turned tail and was walking, almost running, down the street. A hunched figure of misery, he'd soon disappeared round the bend, probably heading for a cab in the Strand. Maggie made to go after him, but the alcohol, combined with her suede sandals, made speed impossible. By the time she reached the Strand, all she saw was yet another posse of cabs hurtling off at the change of traffic lights.

The heavens delivered what they'd promised. A monsoon suddenly hit the dusty pavements and beat relentlessly against the shop windows. Maggie stood in total despair, watching the line of black cabs disappearing up the Aldwych as a roll of thunder crashed almost overhead.

Chapter 34

Maggie had no idea how long she walked up and down the Strand. Her clothes were soaked through and clinging to her skin. The dust combined with the downpour had ruined her beloved suede shoes. The beautiful turquoise was now mud-spattered and barely recognisable.

She'd half-heartedly searched for Jack, scanning faces, shoulders, cream jackets, anyone around the six foot mark. But she knew in her heart that he'd gone, whisked away in one of that posse of cabs, to who knew where. A business meeting, his hotel, Gatwick, Heathrow? She wandered aimlessly around Covent Garden, past the Theatre Museum, past the crowds of hopefuls outside the Theatre Royal, sheltering from the rain as they queued for last minute tickets, back again past the stalls, searching the faces one more time. She seemed to be the only person walking. Everyone else was scurrying to get away from the incessant rain, jostling with umbrellas, leaping aside from puddles. At least no one had time to take in her tear-strewn face. She found herself back in the Strand, still looking, still hoping, still crying. Exhausted, distraught, and very, very pissed. What had that all been about? Dora, pregnancy, Rick Churston, yellow Triumph

Herald? She tried to piece together what she thought she'd heard but none of it made any sense at all.

Suddenly she was back in front of the Boots two-for-one deodorant window. The feeling of déjà vu brought her to her senses. She fished out her mobile phone. Ten missed calls. She flicked through the menu and found that Pam had rung, left messages, and texted her.

She rang Pam's number, wondering if she'd actually have any voice left. Her throat was tight and burning. Her head hurt all over and her wet clothes were starting to make her shiver.

'Thank goodness.' Pam's voice sounded like a brief ray of sunshine down the phone. She took in the whole situation from the tone in Maggie's voice. 'OK, honey, just get yourself to Paddington, ring me from there to tell me what train you're on and I'll pick you up this end from the station. Stay at my place tonight. I'll speak to Beth. Don't worry. They'll be fine.'

Maggie found herself nodding inanely instead of speaking. Thank goodness for Pam. She caught a glimpse of her swollen face in the Boots window reflection. It would take more than cucumber to cure that lot. The vision that stared back at her of a red-eyed, bedraggled and soaking woman was so horrendous she decided not to inflict it on tube passengers. Besides, she might not be able to stop crying in front of them. At least, if she caught a cab, she could blub away in the back without the driver's seeing her. She walked to the kerb, still holding on to a ridiculous hope that Jack had secretly followed her and might leap out of one of the shop doorways, or even be in the taxi waiting for her. No, you stupid woman, that only happens in films. A cab pulled up. The driver appeared not to notice her stricken face. She got in and slammed the door behind her. As the cab pulled away, she looked behind her, watching the Strand with its shiny pavements and scurrying people get smaller and smaller until it disappeared. Soon they were heading along the Marylebone Road towards the Paddington turnoff. This really was the final farewell to Jack.

Pam's house felt like a wonderfully safe haven to a refugee. Maggie was huddled on a sofa in a bathrobe, clutching a mug of comforting tea. She'd enjoyed a warm, scented bath and her clothes were already spinning round in the washing machine. Pam was busily spraying the turquoise sandals with some kind of industrial-strength cleaner and gently buffing them up with a small wire brush.

'I'll get these gorgeous shoes back to life if it takes all night,' Pam announced. 'Now, how about a sandwich or a bowl of soup? I think you could do with something inside you to bolster you up.'

'I want to talk about it,' Maggie whispered. 'I'm so confused, I need to get it all out, if you don't mind.'

'Food first,' said Pam firmly. She was itching to know what had happened but felt Maggie needed something solid inside her first. She disappeared into the kitchen to make a tuna sandwich. Maggie glanced round the sitting room. Pam's taste was minimalist and calming, very easy to maintain if you don't have kids or husband around very much. She admired the room's clean lines, pale blue leather sofas, chrome and glass coffee table. Plasma screen telly, Tom's pride and joy. Shelves backlit to display strategically placed pieces of coloured glass. Even the fireplace had colour co-ordinated pebbles arranged on the hearth. She thought of the shambles and clutter that was her house and shuddered. How long would it be her house? She shuddered once more, thinking about the money situation.

'Right,' said Pam, emerging from the kitchen with a tray. 'Here's your sarnie and a big glass of water. Let's get you rehydrated and minimise the chances of a hangover tomorrow.'

'What did you tell the kids?' Maggie asked.

'Oh, I just told them the truth. That you'd had a really heavy day and I'd decided to give you a bit of pampering,' said Pam with a warm smile. 'I told them how hard you'd been working and that you needed a bit of TLC.'

'It was certainly heavy, all right,' said Maggie, trying not to cry again. Just the thought of Jack made her feel waves of hysteria coming over her once more. 'I really do need to talk to you about it.'

Pam gave her a piercing look. 'OK,' she said simply. 'Just a few headlines will do for now. There's the tissues if you need them.' She indicated a box of Kleenex on the table nearby.

Maggie took a deep breath and began her tale. The frosty start, the total lack of recognition, and how nervous she was.

'It all went suddenly downhill when I told him about George,' she continued. 'Jack wanted to know how old he was. Then he finally came out with this bizarre story about why he never turned up that night.'

'I hope he made it a good one,' said Pam wryly.

'Good? Huh, it would almost make a movie plot. We'd had a bit of a tiff and not seen each other for a few days. I do remember that, obviously. Which was why I was waiting so anxiously to see him that night. Well, apparently, earlier that day he bumped into Dora . . .'

'Oh, God.' Pam put her head in her hands. 'Not bloody Dora again. I might have known. Trouble with a capital D.'

'Exactly. Well, apparently Dora told him I was pregnant by Rick.'

'Rick? Rick who?'

'Exactly what I said. Rick Churston. Yes, and wait. It gets even more ludicrous . . .'

Maggie stopped to wipe her eyes, tears beginning to trickle softly down both cheeks. Pam put a hand on her arm.

'Go on,' she said gently.

'Well, Dora said she knew all about this "pregnancy" and promptly told Jack that I'd been back with Rick for months. Apparently she trotted out all sorts of girlie details.'

'I can't believe Jack just swallowed that,' said Pam. 'He was much too smart for that.'

Maggie took another tissue in readiness. 'Well, this is where that little bitch played her trump card. She said to him, something along the lines of if you don't believe me, go round to Maggie's flat and you'll see his car outside. Remember that ghastly custard yellow Triumph Herald that used to conk out everywhere?'

'How could I forget? It broke down in the entrance once and kept most of the staff trapped in the car park.' Pam laughed at the memory of the ghastly Miss Small, red-faced and fuming at being stuck at school until the AA man turned up like an angel of mercy. 'Anyway, so what happened then?'

'Well apparently Jack went round to my flat, saw a yellow Triumph outside and concluded the worst. That car was a really bad spray job. There couldn't have been many custard yellow Heralds in the world. It's just too coincidental. God knows what Rick was doing there. He certainly wasn't visiting me. I hadn't seen him since we all left school. But apparently the bottom line is Jack saw the car, bought the story and ran away to America.' Maggie collapsed in tears and grabbed another handful of tissues.

Pam waited patiently while her friend recovered some of her composure.

'You don't think,' she began gently, 'that this is just a convenient story for Jack to get himself off the hook, do you? I mean, nobody can prove the car was there or not. And let's face it, we'd never get the truth out of Dora. She can't even spell the word, let alone attempt any sort of grasp of its meaning.'

'I *do* believe him.' Maggie sobbed quietly and then blew her nose. 'He was so distressed when he realised what had happened that he suddenly came out with all this stuff about making a horrible mistake and not being able to ask me to forgive him. And then he mumbled something about wanting to kiss me and then he ran off down the street.'

'And then you walked up and down the Strand in the pouring rain,' Pam finished for her. She got up and put a comforting arm round Maggie. 'You poor, poor baby,' she murmured. She sat thinking for a few moments, taking in what Maggie had told her. And then it suddenly dawned on her.

'Jack didn't lie to you, Maggs. He went there in good faith. And the car outside *was* Rick's yellow Herald. Except that he didn't own it by then. He sold it just after we left school.'

Maggie looked puzzled. 'I don't remember that,' she whispered, her voice now wobbly with tiredness.

'Of course not,' said Pam. 'You'd gone off to London with Jack, but I remember what happened to that car. He sold it to Dora.'

Maggie was too tired to see what Pam was getting at.

'When Jack went round to your flat, he saw what he thought was Rick's car,' Pam explained triumphantly. 'It was the same car all right, but by then the owner was Dora. So it was dead easy for her to taunt him about Rick and all that pregnancy stuff. All she had to do was to find out your address, which she probably got off Jack, drive round there, knowing that's where he was heading, and then park the car as near as she could to your flat.'

Maggie nodded resignedly. This was all too much to cope with.

'Of course, Jack didn't know what a total effing cow Dora is,' Pam continued. 'Let's face it, it took us years to find out about some of her nasty little shenanigans. But who could have guessed she'd stoop so low?'

A few weary tears began their descent down Maggie's red raw cheeks.

'I'll get some cucumber for those eyelids,' Pam offered.

'Not more bloody cucumber.' Maggie managed a half-laugh. 'Funnily enough, Jack remembered I hated the stuff.'

'You haven't heard the last from Jack,' Pam said wisely.

'Oh, yes, I have,' Maggie replied as firmly as she could. 'I can't go through any more of this. That was one goodbye too many.'

Chapter 35

There was a tap on the bedroom door. Pam came in with a smile and a cup of tea. Maggie looked at the alarm clock next to her bed.

'Eleven o'clock,' she muttered. 'Why aren't you at work?'

'I'm skiving,' said Pam cheerfully. 'I decided to go sick so I could look after you. You need a bit of TLC today. Anyway, I can't remember the last time I was actually off work ill, so it's time I was. I'm having one of those duvet days I read about.'

'That's very naughty but much appreciated,' said Maggie gratefully.

'It's the very least I owe you. I feel incredibly guilty about all this. It was me who kept fanning the old flames. Egging you on to meet up with Jack. Press-ganged you into that cyber café in Kenya, made encouraging noises and even chose your clothes. I should be had up for contributory negligence.'

'Rubbish,' said Maggie, propping herself up in bed. 'I was the one who fired off the email to his parents and then agreed to meet him. At least I now know why he never showed up that night.' She took a sip of tea and sank back against the pillows.

'I'm considering paying Dora a visit,' said Pam, 'but only if you say so.'

Maggie shook her head. 'Nope,' she said, 'please don't. It would only please the bitch to think that her little plot caused so much long-term trouble.'

'She probably won't remember it anyway,' Pam agreed reluctantly. 'Merely one little porkie in a lifetime of pies. Pity, though, as I'd have liked to settle my personal score with her about Dave Gregg's lonely hearts ad. I think she managed to tell everyone in town so that my humiliation was complete.'

'In that particular instance, as you said yourself, she did you a favour,' Maggie observed.

'Yes, Maggs, but the point is it didn't seem like it at the time. The whole town knowing the bloke you're going out with is advertising in the local paper for a new bit of substitute skirt.'

Maggie took another sip of tea. 'Unfortunately she hasn't done me any favours in the long term either,' she said, thinking about Garth and how much their never brilliant relationship had deteriorated recently. 'Guess I'll have to get up in a minute, go home and face the music.'

'Oh, stay here all day,' Pam offered. She was feeling desperately guilty about the whole thing. 'I'll do us a spot of lunch, we can sit out in the garden and then I'll run you home later on when the kids get back from school.'

'Oh, that would be lovely,' Maggie replied, giving in immediately. A few more hours cocooned away from trouble seemed like bliss.

*

Maggie could somehow smell trouble, even before they'd rounded the corner into her road. Garth's van was parked on the drive. Unlike him to be home at four o'clock in the afternoon, or in daylight, come to that. She said a brief goodbye to Pam and put her key into the front door with trepidation. Garth was sitting at the kitchen table with paperwork strewn all over it. He had his back to her, his head in his hands.

'Are you all right?' she asked unnecessarily. Slowly he turned towards her, his face bearing a strange expression she'd never seen before. An expression of total despair. She saw he'd been crying. That makes two of us, she thought.

'What's wrong?'

Silence.

'Garth, I can't help you if you don't tell me,' she said softly, feeling a sudden strange compassion for him which felt alien to her.

As he lit a cigarette, she noticed that his hands were shaking uncontrollably. He had difficulty connecting the end of his cigarette with the flame from the match.

'My business has gone bust,' he finally announced. 'The bank has pulled the rug from under me today. Owe my suppliers, can't pay them. Couple of bad debts. Bingo. All gone.'

Like a robot, Maggie walked over to put the kettle on, blood rushing in her head and making a strange whooshing sound in her ears. She needed a few desperate seconds to take in what he'd just said. The very thing she'd suspected and dreaded had finally come to pass. And yet it was still a shock.

Garth waved a shaking hand across all the paperwork on the table and then slumped back in his chair. This wasn't the time to remind him that he hadn't marketed his business properly, kept his own garden in order, or sought new customers, and certainly wouldn't have found them in the pub.

She put some tea bags in a pot. 'Look, the kids will be home in a minute,' she said. 'Let's put on a brave face, wait for them to collapse in front of the telly and then have a look at the problem.'

A key in the door signalled their immediate arrival. Too late to muster brave faces and normal 'How was school?' mutterings. Beth and George clattered through the door, dropping their school bags on the hall floor with a thud, and charged into the kitchen to raid the fridge as they always did. And then stopped dead in their tracks. Was it the shock of seeing their father home at this time of day, or confronting both parents in the same room, sporting white faces and very red eyes?

Beth let out a sob before bolting upstairs to her room. George, looking horribly embarrassed, muttered something and disappeared into the sitting room. Seconds later, the sound of Sky Sports with the volume turned up seemed to ricochet around the house. They probably think we're splitting up, Maggie thought. Oh, God, that would be the easy option. She turned to Garth, who was shakily lighting another cigarette from the butt of the previous one.

'Right,' she said, picking up some of the paperwork. 'What's the extent of the debts?' Garth just shook his head in response, tears trickling down his face and settling on his beard.

It was worse than she'd thought. Much worse. She sifted quickly through the paperwork to discover that three suppliers were now pressing for payment through the courts and the mortgage company had applied for a repossession order which had already been granted. Garth had clearly been concealing the letters from her although, she noticed, they were addressed to the pair of them. They were about to be homeless. In less than a fortnight.

'Why on earth didn't you talk to me about the mortgage arrears?' she asked pointlessly. She was tempted to add that it obviously didn't matter to him as he appeared to have moved out to live at the pub anyway. An argument now would just fudge the whole thing. She needed to think straight and act quickly, but first she needed some reassurance and some good advice.

She picked up the phone and dialled Pam's number. Garth opened his mouth to protest but she shook a warning finger at him to shut him up. For the first time she could remember, he just sat there dumbly, like a turkey gazing hopelessly at the December page of the calendar. She outlined the problem to Pam.

'Get on to the mortgage company to see if you can renegotiate,' said Pam. 'This kind of thing happens all the time. Mortgage doesn't get paid, usually the wife hasn't been told because hubby grabs the post. I once worked with a girl whose husband had regularly spent their mortgage money on gambling. He then "solved" the problem by taking out a pile of loans in their joint names by merely forging her signature. Then guess what? He gambled that lot in the hope of winning back what he'd lost. At least you haven't got that to contend with.'

'I hope not,' said Maggie, making a mental note to grill Garth about any other loans.

'What about Home Truths?' Pam continued. 'Do they do preferential rates for staff? Why not see if you can extend the loan over a longer period? After all, you've lived in your place for a long time. You must be some way through the repayments.'

'Brilliant idea,' said Maggie. 'I should have thought of it.'

'Maggs, you've just had a big shock,' Pam said gently. 'Nobody's expected to think straight after what you've been through. And all this on top of all the other stuff.'

Pam was right. Thoughts of Jack were gone, paling in significance compared to this. She dialled Stefan's mobile number. Late Friday afternoon, he'd probably be in some chic wine bar, quaffing champagne to celebrate another successful week of wheeling and dealing. Would he hear his phone amid the inevitable guffawing and glass clinking? Fortune smiled for once. Stefan answered almost immediately.

Without any preamble, Maggie outlined the situation. The bank had foreclosed on her husband's company and their home was now in jeopardy. She roughly outlined the figures involved on the mortgage. She could almost hear him wincing as she mentioned the M word. True to form, it didn't register in his reply.

'I'm sure we could sort out a fantastic package to suit your needs.' Stefan went straight into work-speak. 'You're a good oppo, Maggie. We could base it on your salary as your husband's seems a bit, er, variable. And don't worry, darling, I can lose the commission fee somewhere and the rest will be on mates' rates. You'll have heaps of equity to play with. Tell you what, I'll make sure I'm in your office first thing on Monday morning and we'll touch base and work out some ball park figures.'

'Thanks heaps, Stefan,' said Maggie, almost crying with gratitude. 'Just one thing – I'd rather you didn't tell

Vanessa and Damien about this. It's a bit embarrassing.'

'Wouldn't dream of it, darling,' he said. 'If they're around on Monday, I'll produce the figures and give it a different surname just to give you an idea of the repayments. Pick another surname so you know who I'm talking about, just in case we need it.'

'Haley,' said Maggie, before she could think properly.

'OK. Figures for Mrs Haley then,' said Stefan. 'Consider it done, darling. Have a great weekend.'

That night, Maggie went through Garth's business paperwork, bit by bit, debt by debt. Just as she had dreaded, he hadn't done anything remotely like a full week's work for nearly a year. Even she could spot that he'd spectacularly under-estimated on a couple of big jobs, with the materials costing nearly eighty per cent of the price. She couldn't understand how he'd managed to attend so many gardening trade shows when he seemed to begrudge spending anything on new equipment. The repair costs on one ancient hedge trimmer alone could have paid for a new one twice over by now. This was madness. She kicked herself over and over again for not being more forceful with him about marketing and advertising.

The sums owed to the suppliers were way beyond her means, but if she received another good bonus at the end of the month she might be able to make them some paltry offer and see if it would be accepted on a 'better-than-nothing' basis.

By the end of the evening, she'd reluctantly concluded that even if she sorted everything financially, Garth couldn't carry on running the business. He'd made too many wrong and expensive decisions. And, fundamentally, he was probably too lazy. The early years had been easy, with plenty of work, but now that regular customers had died or moved or were tightening their belts, he hadn't had the motivation to go out and bring in enough new business. He'd be much better working for someone else. Told where and when to turn up rather than merely contribute to his favourite pub's coffers.

It was strange having him in the house. Admittedly he was now snoring on the sofa, but she couldn't remember the last time he hadn't spent the entire evening in the pub. There were no prizes for guessing why he'd taken to such heavy drinking. He'd taken the bloke's route of blotting out the inevitable collapse of his business.

Her head now ached from all the shock and her eyes were strained from more maths in one evening than she'd done since she'd left school. She couldn't wait to get to bed, fall into some oblivious stupor, wake up in the morning, and discover that it had all been a horrible dream. To lose Jack yet again was awful enough. But then to come home to the collapse of your husband's business and the possible loss of your home . . . At least she had so many problems now, she could take her pick. Maybe this was her punishment for harbouring those now ridiculous yearnings for Jack.

She was just wondering whether to leave Garth on the sofa for the night, or wake him to get him up to bed, when the phone rang. She glanced at the kitchen clock. Past eleven. It might be Pam, perhaps, just making a last minute check that she was OK. She got up from the table wearily and dragged her aching legs over to the phone.

'Hi. Is that Maggie?' said a vaguely familiar female

voice. The background noise made it difficult to hear. Someone ringing from a very noisy pub.

'Yes. Who's this?' said Maggie weakly.

'It's Brenda. Is Garth there?' Brenda, Garth's book-keeper, sounded somewhat the worse for drink. Understandable, perhaps, Maggie supposed, since a source of her work had just dried up.

'He's asleep. Can't it wait until the morning?'

'No, it bloody can't,' came the unexpected reply.

'Look, I'm sorry about this business,' said Maggie, fading fast and wishing Brenda would go away. 'But I only found out tonight. It's been quite a shock.'

'So he finally told you, then,' Brenda snarled down the phone. Maggie was taken aback. She didn't need to be that nasty. Brenda must have lots of other clients on her books. Surely it wasn't the end of the world for her.

'Yes he did,' she said, wishing Brenda would get off the phone. She'd obviously been on the pop all night so probably wouldn't remember the conversation in the morning anyway. 'Look, why can't you ring back tomorrow? I'm sorry, but I'm about to go to bed.'

'You don't sound all that pissed off,' Brenda continued. It was clearly a karaoke night in the pub and the crowd in the background were launching into a tuneless chorus of 'Lady In Red'.

'Yes, I *am* very pissed off about it, but I can't do anything until Monday.'

'Monday? Why Monday? What's Monday got to do with it?' Brenda started to laugh maniacally.

'On Monday I'll be trying to sort out some of the problems with the bank and making offers to the suppliers.' More hysterical laughter. Maggie wished she'd just shut up. 'Look, Brenda,' she continued wearily, 'I'm going to put the phone down in a minute but I just wish at least one of you had told me about this mess. It's all water under the bridge now.'

'He hasn't told you, has he! Typical of the bastard!' With that, she hung up.

Chapter 36

It took Maggie a further hour of sifting through the accounts, bills and letters. Then she made a couple of phone calls to check rail fares and room rates and soon had her answer. The people who took her calls must have wondered why some mad-sounding woman would want a rough estimate of last year's room rates at Holiday Inns in Birmingham, Manchester and Exeter in the middle of the night. She gasped when she realised how cheap Ryanair flights were to Dublin. Especially if they were for one person – not two.

So Garth and Brenda had been having an affair. And Maggie had never suspected. She sat at the kitchen table, gazing at the evidence in front of her, the clock sounding strangely noisy when it chimed 2 a.m. All the garden shows, trade exhibitions and conferences Garth had insisted on attending. She thought back to the times when she'd found tickets in his pockets to various events such as Chelsea and Hampton Court and his habit of mentioning them at the last minute. She always thought it was to avoid the hassle of having to take her, or the kids: George always hoping to be dropped off at some

Southampton footie match en route, Beth clamouring to go shopping in whichever town or city the event was taking place. Now she could see why he did it. In order to take Brenda. No wonder the figures claimed against tax for travel and hotels were so enormous. Clearly it wasn't just his books she'd been looking after. And he hadn't been tending just her roses either. They'd been having a glorious time on expenses, using garden shows as an excuse. Unfortunately the expenses had come out of the business, and now that the business was gone the party was well and truly over. Hence Brenda's rather drunken call tonight. Perhaps Garth had dumped her earlier in the day, her usefulness now over.

Maggie sat back in her chair and found herself almost laughing. Not much else left to lose, she thought. My husband's been having an affair for possibly years and I don't really care. I'm not even upset, just pig sick that I was too stupid to see what was going on under my nose.

She tried to remember how long Brenda had been working for Garth. It must be at least ten years, she figured. She vaguely remembered meeting Brenda's husband once. A tall burly bouncer type who went rather well with Brenda's big and bouncy platinum blonde barmaid look. No mention had been made of him for years. Perhaps they'd split up and Garth had provided comfort. He'd clearly just run out of that particular commodity, judging by last night's phone call. Well, perhaps they'd now both got what they deserved.

When Maggie's head finally hit the pillow, she was too weary to sleep. She tossed and turned, confused by the fact that her life had gone topsy turvy in forty-eight hours. She lay in bed, staring at the ceiling rose, the faded pattern on the curtains dimly lit by the street lights outside. She noticed a small spider busily working away at its web around the lampshade above the bed. He seemed to have a nice life, a relatively untangled web compared to hers. No hassle, no stroppy letters from the bank, just a bit of effort to set up the web and then sit back and wait for lunch to arrive. As the dawn chorus started up in the garden, she began to prioritise the tasks that lay ahead.

Monday would be mortgage day, with Stefan already on the case. Thank God for Stefan. Trying to save the roof over their heads was the most important task.

Reassuring the kids. She'd have to tackle that as quickly as possible over the weekend. But what to tell them? 'Your Dad's having an affair'? 'We might lose our house'? They were too old to be fobbed off with some excuse. She'd have to be honest. Well, sort of.

Dealing with Garth. Had he really dumped Brenda? Would she bounce back into his life once the hangover had cleared? Or would she cut her losses now that the perks were gone for good? The latter option might be tempting with his angry wife and his mortgage company both baying for his blood.

Maggie was surprised at how completely unemotional she felt about the whole thing, how coldly calculating, how almost mildly amused she was. Perhaps she should think about a divorce and leave the pair of them to sort it out between themselves.

And then of course there was Jack. Well, actually there wasn't Jack at all. He'd run away for a second time and there was no point in chasing after him. Any tears she might have shed had suddenly dried up. No point in spending them on a wimp. She had much greater problems to deal with than Jack Haley.

Maggie rose at seven. There was nothing to be gained by just lying there, staring at the ceiling. Sleep had more or less evaded her. She'd only managed fitful snatches as her mind whizzed round again and again over the matter of Brenda and Garth. She kicked herself yet again for not spotting all the telltale signs. She'd get to the bottom of that one today if she could.

She shoved on an old dressing gown and went downstairs. Garth was still spark out on the sofa, mouth wide open and snoring. He'd obviously dribbled during the night because there was a huge wet patch on the cushion near his mouth. She wondered whether Brenda found that particularly attractive.

Back in the kitchen, the previous night's paperwork was still spread out on the table where she'd left it, a poignant reminder of what she had discovered. Not just that the business had gone to the wall, but that Garth had been bonking his book-keeper.

She made the inevitable comforting cup of tea and wondered if she could possibly ring Pam at this hour of the day. Yes, she decided. It didn't get more emergency than this.

'Sorry it's so early, but I need your help,' she announced apologetically. She told Pam what she'd discovered and outlined her plan. 'Do it, do it,' Pam immediately urged. 'It's brilliant. What have you got to lose?'

'That answer's easy. Absolutely nothing.'

Maggie waited until 8.30 before she made the call. She made sure Garth was still sound asleep before she dialled the number. Then she had a quick shower, shoved on a pair of jeans and a cotton shirt, made herself coffee and waited. Bang on 9.30, the doorbell rang. She prayed the kids would have their usual Saturday lie-in until at least eleven. She glanced into the sitting room as she marched purposefully down the hall. Garth was still comatose.

'Come in,' she said grimly.

Brenda, in tight black trousers, leopardskin top, spiky heels and half a ton of jewellery, swept in petulantly through the door. Maggie almost struggled for breath as she found herself downwind of the thick cloud of Dior's Poison that enveloped Brenda. For a brief instant, she envied the woman her chutzpah. She'd come out of her corner of the boxing ring, fighting for her man, whereas Maggie knew that if the situation had been reversed she'd have sloped away in tears.

She ushered Brenda into the sitting room where, without ceremony, she shook Garth's arm to wake him.

'Brenda's here,' she announced gruffly. Garth opened an eye and promptly shut it again. Was this a drunken nightmare? Was that Brenda sitting in their sitting room with Maggie?

'Come on, wake up, Garth, for goodness' sake.' Maggie found herself in brisk work-mode. 'We can't wait around all day. You've been having an affair with Brenda for the past . . .' She looked at Brenda for the answer.

'Seven years.' Brenda completed the sentence without any trace of remorse. God, she was bold as well as brass.

'And I've only just cottoned on to it,' Maggie continued. 'Bit slow off the mark but that's my fault. Now, as I am about to renegotiate our mortgage on Monday, I need to know whether you're leaving or staying. Not that your salary will be taken into account, seeing as you don't have one. Or rather, the pair of you managed to spend it.'

Garth opened both eyes and then shut them again. Perhaps he'd now caught a whiff of the Poison and could no longer doubt who was in the room.

'What the fuck . . .' he started.

'Exactly so,' Maggie retorted, her Home Truths persona thankfully kicking in. 'I've invited Brenda round here so you can decide, right here and now. Her or me. Quite simple.'

Brenda nodded firmly, her huge hoop earrings clanking in agreement. Clearly her hackles – as well as her bleached blonde highlights – were up too.

'Now sit up straight and make a decision,' Maggie ordered as if she were addressing a naughty schoolboy. 'We don't have all day.'

Garth dragged himself up into an upright position on the sofa. He looked a picture, unshaven, his clothes all creased and his black and grey hair dishevelled after a night on the sofa. There was a nasty whiff of stale fags and beer on his breath. Maggie began to pray he'd rush off into the sunset with the over-perfumed Brenda, and leave her in peace. At least the house would smell a bit more pleasant.

Garth began to rise unsteadily to his feet.

At that moment, Beth chose to appear at the door of the sitting room. No one had heard her coming down the stairs. Maggie wondered for a moment just how much she had overheard.

'Pooh, what a terrible smell—' Beth stopped and her mouth dropped open as she took in the scene. Her father looking like a tramp, brassy Brenda whom she probably hadn't seen for years and clearly didn't recognise, and her mother with an implacable expression on her face.

'I don't know what you're all on about,' Garth muttered, his exit now blocked by Beth.

'Mum, what's going on?' she asked, with a frightened look.

'Be with you in a minute,' said Maggie, shooting her daughter a knowing look that said, 'Get back to your room, it's horrible in here.' Beth didn't need a second telling. She dutifully turned tail and scurried upstairs.

'Now look, Garth,' said Brenda, keeping her obvious anger in check, 'you've spent years telling me you couldn't leave her and the kids. Now she doesn't want you, so what are you waiting for?'

Garth sank back into the sofa, confused by all the drama going on around him.

Maggie glared at Brenda. '*She* didn't say that. *She* – or rather I – merely asked my husband to decide who he wants to be with, his wife and kids or his bit on the side. Although admittedly he's not much of a catch now, is he? Thanks to the pair of you,' Maggie shot Brenda's considerable cleavage a venomous look, 'the business has gone tits up.'

They exchanged angry looks and then both turned to confront Garth.

'I don't know what you're all on about,' he repeated, slumping back on to the sofa.

Once again Maggie took control. 'I think you do, Garth,' she said. 'You two have been cooking the books in more ways than one. Shagging and spending for years, by the look of it. All these Have-It-Away days have killed the business and probably lost me and my kids our home. Well, frankly, Garth, since you seem incapable of making any kind of decision, I'll make it for you. You're welcome to her. Take yourself, your tarty mistress and your debts with you, out of that door. Right now.'

Pam would be proud of me, Maggie kept thinking. This whole scene seems so unreal. This isn't me speaking. It was like watching a Hollywood film in which she'd somehow landed the major part.

Garth merely waved a dismissive arm in their direction. 'Can't you both just shut up? You wake me up, the pair of you, demanding some sort of decision. I can't think straight—'

'Well I can,' Brenda snapped, her bright red lips pursed in anger. Clearly the bouncer husband had passed on a few tips. She took two steps towards Garth, bent forward slightly and punched him hard, full across the face where he sat. Wedged into the corner of the sofa with nowhere to dodge, Garth took the full force of the blow. Brenda's bling blinged fingers certainly made their mark. Blood began oozing from his face as his hands flew up to stem the flow. He sat there groaning. The two women stood looking at each other. Neither went to his aid.

'Well, goodbye then,' said Brenda, calmly picking up her studded leopardskin handbag, as if it were all in a day's work. 'You're welcome to him,' she told Maggie with a smirk of pity. 'Can't believe I've just wasted seven years on a wuss.' She turned back to Garth, who was now making whimpering noises as the blood spilt through his hands. 'Just one final thing, Garthie darling. You're crap in bed. Sorry, but all these years, I lied. Thought I'd better confess. Had to fake it. You were rubbish. Don't worry. I'll see myself out.'

The front door banged emphatically shut. Maggie stood frozen to the spot, staring at Garth, feeling merely pity and disgust for him. The blood was dripping on to his shirt. Brenda had certainly hit the spot. Maggie's only concern was that it might stain the sofa and be difficult to shift. Prospective buyers might be put off, thinking the house had been the scene of a brutal murder. She went out into the kitchen and phoned Pam.

'It backfired,' she announced quietly. 'Brenda socked him one and left. I think I'm saddled with him.'

'Bloody hell,' said Pam, privately wishing she'd been there to see Garth getting his just deserts. 'How do you feel about that?'

'Confused, and faintly disappointed, if I'm honest,' said Maggie. 'I thought he'd grab the opportunity and go. I suspect I'm the lesser of two evils. And much cheaper to run, judging by the amount of money they've got through on their fun trips. I've got to stay, even if it's just for the kids' sakes. I must put up with it at least until they leave home.'

Pam didn't agree with that last bit, but made a quick decision that this wasn't the moment to nudge Maggie in the direction of a divorce lawyer.

'At least if Brenda is really off the scene, he won't be spending so much money,' she suggested, grasping at straws of comfort.

'There isn't any left to spend,' said Maggie. 'It's not just the question of the mortgage to sort out; there are heaps of debts. And now the champagne has finally gone flat, Brenda realised that Garth without all the shagging in swanky hotels wasn't so much fun after all. Her parting shot was that he was crap in bed and that she'd been faking her, er, appreciation all these years.'

Pam couldn't resist laughing.

'I quite admired her, actually,' said Maggie. 'She probably told Garth more home truths in a couple of minutes than I've managed in two decades. Trouble is, she can skip off into someone else's trousers and expense account tomorrow. Meanwhile, I'm stuck with the bastard and all his baggage.'

They rang off, after Pam had offered beds for the weekend for Maggie, Beth and George if they needed a refuge.

Maggie walked down the hallway, pointedly ignoring the sitting room, and went upstairs to talk to Beth. She was surprised to find her sitting on the end of George's bed, watching football on television. She'd obviously been crying. George, still in bed, looked stony-faced.

'There's no easy way to say this,' said Maggie simply as she sat down on the bed next to Beth, 'but there's no point in me trying to hide it from you. You're both too old to be fobbed off.' She drew a deep breath. 'Your dad's been having an affair with the woman who came round this morning. It's all over now but she smacked him round the face before she left. Quite hard, actually. No, don't worry' – their mouths had dropped open in shock, the colour draining from their faces – 'he's going to be fine, but sometimes these things happen. They've been spending a lot of money and your dad's business has gone bust. I know it's a lot to take in but I think I can sort things out for all of us. And I know that you'll support me.'

Beth regained her composure first. Maggie half expected them both to rush downstairs to see how their father was. But to her surprise, they stayed resolutely put. Beth shot her mother a very intent look.

'We knew about it, Mum,' she said. 'Well, sort of suspected it. All those times Dad said he was going to the Doghouse for a drink. We found out one night that he never goes there. I rang them once to give him a message when you weren't well, but they said he hadn't been in there for months and months. The next day I made a point of asking him where he'd been, and he said the Doghouse. So we knew he was up to something.' Beth bit her lip. 'We should have told you, Mum, but we didn't want to upset you. You had enough on your plate.'

'Yeah, sorry, Mum,' George added apologetically. 'Why did the woman turn up this morning?'

'I think your dad dumped her last night when the business collapsed,' Maggie explained. 'She phoned up very late ranting and raving, so I called her up this morning and invited her to come round, so we could sort it out once and for all.'

'Gosh, Mum, that was brave.' Beth was suddenly wide-eyed. George, too, looked impressed. 'So what happened?'

'Your dad didn't appear to be capable of making any decision so she thumped him and left.'

'Well, he's in the doghouse as far as I'm concerned,' George announced firmly. He got out of bed and put his arms round Maggie. Not to be outdone, Beth held her mother's hands. 'Don't tell me off for swearing, Mum,' George added, 'but Dad's been an effing bastard to you.'

'All right, I won't this time,' Maggie whispered, suddenly fighting the tears she'd held off for so long. 'I'm sorry, I've probably said too much.'

'No you haven't,' said George. 'We'd kind of guessed. By the way, what's that terrible smell?'

'Brenda's perfume.'

'Well it's bloody awful,' said George, wrinkling his nose.

Maggie glanced at her kids, supportive and strong for her. Through her tears, she managed a small smile.

They'd suddenly grown up. If this morning's confrontation had achieved anything, it was the miraculous transformation of her children into responsible and loving human beings. Garth might be crap in bed, as Brenda so deftly put it, but at least his kids had turned out all right.

Chapter 37

Two months later. The first September nip in the air and a flurry of dead leaves on the grass heralded the end of the summer and that depressing 'nothing is for ever' autumnal feeling. As Maggie logged on to her computer, she gazed at her desk calendar – a Spanish phrase per day – and realised just how much she wanted this year to be over. To draw a line under twelve months of pain and loss.

Today's phrase – *¿Dónde está la parada de autobús más cercana?* – asking directions to the nearest bus stop, was now as *superfluo* as all the others she'd carefully mastered. The once hoped-for trip to Spain had, in the end, been undertaken by Vanessa, quietly tipped off by Stefan that Maggie wasn't in any fit state to do the deal. There had been nods and winks about 'trouble at home' but one look at Maggie told the entire story without need of words. She looked a broken woman, coming vaguely alive during working hours when she had a purpose and a goal, but sinking under the familiar black cloud as six o'clock and going home time approached.

Maggie was glad to bow out of the Spanish experience. She'd at least been spared what would have been the terrible ordeal of meeting up with the Haleys at the Tin Man, doing business with their friends and setting up the property connection. She was vastly relieved not to have heard any more from the Haleys since her fateful meeting with Jack. Either he'd told them about the London encounter and they were being loyal to their son, or perhaps they felt bad about the way Jack had treated her and now felt that keeping in touch would be inappropriate. Nor had she heard from Jack. No apology, no explanation. Just complete cyber silence. As the weeks had gone by, Maggie had been grateful for one less thing to deal with, one less problem to solve, one less decision to make. She had had too much else to contend with at home.

Thanks to some spectacular number crunching, Stefan had produced some manageable figures on a renegotiated 'repayment plan', based on her salary alone, so she'd been able to save the house at the eleventh hour. He'd even recommended a solicitor who helped her renegotiate with Garth's debtors. To her amazement, nearly all accepted her feeble offers of settlement. Just as well, because her performance at work hadn't reached the dizzy heights of the spring bonus. The housing market had slowed down anyway, amid city rumblings of an interest rate hike, but even Home Truths' alternative approach to shifting everything 'from the posh to the pits', as Damien once succinctly put it, couldn't quite buck the trend. There wouldn't be any bonuses for some time to come.

The stress of nearly losing their home and now counting every single penny had taken its toll on Maggie. She couldn't remember the last time she'd had a good night's sleep. Post-Brenda, Garth had now installed himself in the tiny spare room, and true to form they hadn't discussed it at all. But then, they never had that type of conversation.

Yet even with the entire bed to herself, sleep evaded her. One particular weekend, money had been so tight that the kids volunteered to turn out their bedrooms for the local car boot sale. Thanks to them cheerfully flogging all their out-of-favour CDs, DVDs, clothes, shoes, books and magazines, Maggie had been able to do a supermarket run. She knew she was now through the worst, but the scars wouldn't heal for a long time to come. She seemed to be permanently tired and often went to bed at nine with a book. For several weeks she'd been stuck on page 346 of a Jilly Cooper novel, unable to concentrate yet unable to sleep.

She often thought back wistfully to the spring. She'd been riding high, buoyed up by the trip to Kenya, excited at playing a huge part in the Spanish business deal, renewing acquaintance with the Haleys, and then, of course, there'd been all the nervous excitement about meeting Jack. It was all so very different now. With the benefit of hindsight, she realised how ridiculous an idea that meeting had been, only ever destined to end in tears.

Here in the office, she was surrounded by tempting details of villas, *fincas* and *apartamentos* on glorious stretches of the Spanish costas. She could even have visited them, and now been able to talk first hand to excited prospective buyers about the heady smell of the oleander, waxing lyrical about the heat of the sun, the gentle lapping of the Mediterranean on soft white sand, the joy of sipping a glass of ice cold sangria whilst nibbling at some delicious mouthful of something or other at the local tapas bar. She could have actually tried out her Spanish, and found her own way to that wretched nearest bus stop.

She picked up the phrase-a-day calendar, gave it one last defiant flip and then chucked it in the wastepaper bin under her desk. Enough was enough, she decided. Roll on the next four months and an end of this terrible year. At least today she was meeting Pam for a quick lunch, their first proper get-together since the Brenda crisis. She had kept resolutely silent as Tom had been home on shore leave and Mark had been back during the university vacation. It was Pam who would need cheering up today, as she was always upset for the first few days after he'd gone.

As Maggie waded through the overnight emails, she encountered some good news. After nearly six months of effort and about thirty viewings, one of their most depressing properties had, at last, found a buyer. 'This immensely dreary one bedroom flat has lots and lots of serious attitude. So handy for local transport, it's slap bang next to a railway line. Would suit the hard of hearing, shift-working trainspotters or people who party a lot and need a cheap crash pad.'

Maggie noted with delight that she'd been the negotiator who'd shown the prospective buyer round the flat. He hadn't struck her as a party animal or an anorak but the offer was good and she knew the seller would be deeply relieved. That would earn her a few much needed Brownie points as well. Somehow the morning whizzed by after that and soon it was time to meet Pam.

'God, Maggs, you've lost even more weight,' Pam exclaimed as they airkissed in the street outside the new French crêperie that had just opened up.

'Not for the right reasons,' Maggie replied ruefully,

admiring Pam's white Capri pants, pale green shirt and pair of fabulous matching green wedges. At this rate, she thought, even I might be able to wear look-at-me clothes like that one day. 'But it's great to be able to slide into all my clothes without the buttons complaining.'

They picked a table outside under the blue and white striped awning so they could watch the passers-by, Parisian style.

'Last of the summer sunshine,' said Pam as she plonked her sunglasses on top of her blonde hair and surveyed the menu, 'so let's enjoy the last of the summer wine.'

They ordered smoked salmon and crème fraîche galettes and two glasses of dry white wine. Suddenly it felt like back to normality for Maggie.

'So, update me,' said Pam, settling back in her chair, glass in hand. 'How's Darth Vader? Still fighting the Force?'

'Well, at least he's been forced to fight for something useful for a change,' Maggie managed to joke. 'Seriously, he's been in this job for a couple of months now and seems to be making a go of it. Having said that, working piece-rate for his rival was a bit of a dent to his pride, but frankly he didn't have any choice. No business and definitely no Brenda. I also think he believed I would throw him out.'

'And did that cross your mind?' Pam gave her a piercing look that took in the lacklustre hair and the bags under her eyes.

'No, to be honest. My mind kind of lay down and died a while back. But I discovered that the kids had a very firm word with him along those lines. Beth let slip the other day that she and George had actually threatened him that I had a divorce lawyer lined up if he didn't get a job sorted out. I think the general message was, "Everyone else in this house is working hard. Why can't you?" I gather George put the boot in further, with a remark about spending far too much time at the pub, throwing money down his throat instead of being at home. That must have hit home, coming from his sixteen-year-old son.'

Pam clasped her hands in delight. 'Those kids of yours have really come up trumps,' she said. 'When I think back to how they used to squabble all the time, and—'

'And I played the part of the willing doormat.' Maggie completed the sentence. 'Yes, I look back and realise they were vile because I allowed them to be vile. Garth included. At least all that's changed.'

'And how are things between you and Garth?' Pam enquired.

'Uneasy truce,' said Maggie, taking a sip of wine. 'We're a bit like parallel lines, really. Running alongside each other but never crossing. We have nothing to say, which suits me fine at the moment. He's in the spare room now and he also knows he's in the doghouse. Bit ironic as he spent months telling us that's where he was every evening. Now we know he was probably tucked up between Brenda's double-Ds.'

'And any more appearances from Big Brenda?'

'Not even an encore, let alone a hint of cleavage. Although she did leave her mark on Garth's face for ages. Those rings must have had flick knives concealed in them. Apparently he told one of the neighbours he'd been clawed by the cat. George heard about this and promptly put them right. Told them (a) we don't have a cat and (b) the wounds were inflicted by Dad's bit-on-the-side. Dare say the whole street knows now.'

'And how do you feel about that?'

'Couldn't care less, frankly,' said Maggie with a weary sigh. 'I'm just so disgusted about the whole episode, mostly because I never cottoned on to what was happening. Thinking back now, I quite admire Brenda in a way. Apart from wearing her perfume as if it were an anti-mugging device, she stuck with her man for a long time and came out fighting for him. Then, when she realised what a waste of space he was, she did a kind of hit and run, quite literally. She's probably got a better life now and I'm the mug who's bloody well stuck with him.'

Pam had to bite her lip. She desperately wanted to persuade Maggie to do what Brenda had done. To cut her losses with Garth and run, but she still felt guilty about the whole Jack business, blaming herself for nudging Maggie too enthusiastically in his direction.

Maggie continued. 'I know what you're thinking: that I should get out of it. I know I should have done. I've stayed for the kids, but day by day I'm finding out more and more that they hate and despise him for what he did. And, I suspect, for what he *is*. A selfish, self-centred, self-opinionated pig. I really wish he'd gone off into the sunset with Brenda. But I feel I've lost the moment. Missed my slot. I'm just very, very tired.'

'Perhaps for now.' Pam couldn't resist. 'But nothing's for ever, hon. One day when you're feeling a bit stronger, you might make the changes. But you're probably right – you've been through too much at the moment to cope with any more. No news, I take it, from the Tin Man contingent?'

'Nope, thank God. That's it with the Haleys. Today, *mañana* and all the rest of them.'

The galettes arrived, which prompted Pam to

announce the good news that Mark had done well in his end of term exams and was on target for a first. And that Tom would be home for Christmas. Then it was suddenly time to go back to work.

Somehow the rest of the day went with a zing. The black clouds of the past few months had just parted briefly to reveal a tiny piece of blue sky, Maggie decided.

'We're all kinda concerned about you,' said Don, putting his beer down on the bar counter and shooting Jack a look that took no prisoners. 'You just look haunted, day after day after day.'

Jack stared intently into the bottom of his glass, saying nothing. They were having an end-of-a-long-week beer in their favourite bar opposite Quincy Market. Late summer tourists, who'd just done the Boston Heritage Trail, were now flocking around the flower stalls, brandishing cameras as the traders did brisk business amongst the office workers fighting through the crowds to snap up weekend flowers for their wives or girlfriends.

'The business is just fine,' said Don soothingly. 'Everything's ticking along. We've got enough contract work from California alone to keep us going for months, without seeking new clients. Staff are happy. We're on target for another good bonus at the end of the year. What's eating you, buddy?'

Jack sighed and drained his glass. He indicated to the bartender that they'd each like another. 'Oh, I don't know.'

'Look,' Don continued gently. 'Is there some kinda problem you need to discuss? Is it Betsy? The kids?'

'Yes and no,' Jack replied unhelpfully. He reached for his wallet, took out a ten dollar bill and laid it on the counter.

'Ever since you came back from England, you've been

worried about something. You've become more and more preoccupied as the days have gone by. Look, if you don't want to talk to me, that's fine. But there's a really good shrink near here that my sister once went to. I could give you his card.'

Jack took a slug of the fresh beer, put his glass back on the counter and let out a huge sigh.

'OK, Don,' he said finally. 'You're my best buddy as well as my business partner. I'll tell you but it's totally confidential. Not even my folks know the whole story.'

Don nodded in agreement.

'I went to England to set up some business, as you know,' said Jack, staring at the bar counter, 'but I also went for another reason. There was something in my past that resurfaced. Something very special that I had lost. I went back because I had no choice. It was just so compelling . . .'

'A woman?'

'Yep. Betsy knows nothing about this, of course.'

'Of course.' Don nodded.

'Her name's Maggie. We were at school together, we went to London together and then we broke up. She's the reason I came to the States. She went back with an old boyfriend, or so I thought, and I've never gotten over her.'

'So why the sudden interest again?'

'I just needed some answers. I wanted to see her face one more time and see how I felt. Perhaps somehow find a way to move on.'

'And?'

'It was terrible. Worse than terrible. We met for lunch. Turns out it was me who left her. I'd been spun a complete web of lies by one of our so-called school pals. Told she was pregnant by this previous boyfriend. I couldn't believe it so I went round to her flat and sure enough, his car was parked outside. So I ran away. Grabbed my shiny new graduation certificate and a clean pair of jeans, and got the first plane out of Heathrow.'

'Were you sure it was his car? Didn't you check it out?'

'Didn't need to. Bright yellow Triumph Heralds aren't exactly thick on the ground.'

'What about Maggie? What was her version of events?'

'Well, this pregnancy bit was all news to her. As far as she was concerned, I just didn't show up and she never heard from me again. She's married now and got a couple of kids, virtually same ages as mine.'

Don drained his glass and ordered two more beers.

'Jack, these things happen. Right people, wrong time, wrong people, right time. I'm sure this Maggie's moved on, just as you have.'

Jack followed suit and finished his beer. 'That's the problem, Don, I haven't moved on. I feel like such a doofus. I'm living a lie with Betsy. Her family just does it for me. They're loud, they're rich and they never stop having parties, barbecues, family get-togethers, anniversaries, you know all the American happy holiday stuff. No disrespect, buddy, but I'm still English in some ways. I like a quiet life when I'm not at work. I love my kids, I love my work and I love Boston.'

'You've left Betsy off that list,' Don observed quietly.

'Yeah, I guess I have,' Jack replied. 'Oh, God, Don, she's a case of one shopping mall too far. And she does my head in with her constant need for a retailing fix and her obsession with being, as she puts it, "fashionably late". Sometimes we're so late at these endless parties that we almost arrive the next day. I hate parties anyway and I absolutely hate being late.'

Don contemplated the crowds outside, still milling around the market.

'Are you sure you're not just having a bit of a mid-life crisis?' he enquired gently. 'Most guys go through these phases. Marriage is a tall order, you know. And this Maggie is probably happily married now. You mentioned she had a couple of kids. If you were to get it together, there's four kids mixed up in all this mess.'

Jack suddenly looked a picture of despair. 'I'm well aware of that, Don. But over that lunch, we suddenly realised what had happened over this pregnancy lie business and everything just fell away. We were back to how we were, how we should have been. We should never have broken up.'

He put his head in his hands.

'Then what happened?'

Jack straightened up and looked at his pal. Don detected a trace of tears in his eyes.

'I felt my whole life rushing past me. It was like a great big blur. I knew that if I stayed a moment longer, I'd stay for ever. And that wasn't fair to my kids, her kids or Maggie herself. Or even Betsy. So I did it again. I left her. I got up and I left her.'

Don heaved a deep sigh. 'That was three months ago,' he said quietly. 'And you still feel the same?'

Jack nodded.

'In that case, you could start by apologising. See what she says in response.'

Jack shook his head and took another gulp of his beer. 'Why should she bother to reply to me? I've effectively left her twice now. I don't deserve a reply, let alone another chance.'

Don drew a deep breath and looked Jack in the eye.

'OK, I'll give it to you straight. Sometimes, Jack, life throws up something good; once, maybe twice if you're very lucky. Maybe by the third time you've gotta push your luck. Wasn't my place to say this before but I've always thought Betsy wasn't right for you. Too wrapped up in her own big and expensive whirl. And just the sight of her enormous mother brings me out in zits so God knows what it does to you. You've often said you never see your kids either. They're always being whisked off to tennis lessons, dance classes, parties, family stuff. Seems to me you make the money and they all go off and spend it. Her family's loaded anyway. Follow your heart. But remember. I'm your buddy, not your stockbroker.'

Jack put his head in his hands again. 'Thanks Don,' he mumbled. 'I'll give it some thought.'

Don shot him a perceptive look. 'Sounds to me like you've been doing that for some years now.'

Chapter 38

Dear Maggs, I don't know how to apologise for what I did. The shock of what really happened between us just got to me. I can't believe we broke up over such a terrible and wicked lie. I've spent the last few weeks wondering how I could have treated you so badly. Is there any glimmer of hope that you might at least forgive me? Do hope to hear from you but I know that I don't deserve to. With love and in hope, Jack x

Maggie read the email and immediately hit the delete button. She then went to her trash and with a defiant stab of her finger deleted it from there too.

In hope, she muttered to herself bitterly. Some hope. I can't take any more of this. It's not meant to be and it never was. He just wants me to appease his conscience by hitting the reply button and saying 'Of course Jack I forgive you' and then he can tick that box and skip off happily back into his Boston sunset. I'm fed up with being nice to everyone, accepting their apologies and sweeping up after their crises. It doesn't pay to be nice. It didn't do my marriage any good and it certainly wasn't much help to my kids. I am no longer nice. End of story.

She got up and wandered out to load up the coffee machine. She must perk herself up a bit as she had an afternoon jam-packed with viewings of five really terrible flats. The client was a rather formidable chap called Chris Burrows, a professional landlord and frequent dealer with Home Truths. He knew exactly what he was looking for and could see beyond the damp, the decay and, in some cases, the nasty pong. But he was a tough negotiator and didn't take any prisoners. Maggie was always rather scared of him and reassured herself by making sure her mobile was within fingertip reach just in case. At least it would take her mind off Jack's email.

She came back to her desk with a large black coffee, wondering whether to email Pam about this latest bombshell. She decided not to, unable to face the thought of any more discussion about Jack. Pam's well-meaning plot to get them together had well and truly backfired. No, she'd save what little energy she had left for coping with the formidable Mr Burrows. She needed an offer this afternoon to make this month's figures look a bit more respectable. She made another silly bet with herself. If I get a sale this afternoon, I'll tell Pam. If not, I won't.

Mr Burrows strode into Home Truths on the dot of two, as he always did. In his late fifties, tall and tubby, with thinning hair and a permanently red face, always dressed in the same old cheap, shiny suit, he had practised the art of using his weight and size as a bullying tactic. She could imagine all his tenants being far too terrified to ask for the return of their deposits when they moved out.

'So are we ready then?' he boomed condescendingly.

He always addressed Maggie as if she were a recalcitrant schoolgirl. 'Have we found our car keys at the bottom of our stupid handbag?'

'Yes, Mr Burrows,' said Maggie, already fingering her keys and the mobile phone in her jacket pocket. She loathed these afternoons. They reminded her of the bad old days at Farleys.

'You look different,' he proclaimed as they walked round the corner to where her car was parked. 'Been ill?'

'No, just lost weight,' she replied. She waited for the inevitable bite back.

'Well, it suits you,' he announced, to her slight surprise.

They headed across town to the first flat. As usual, Mr Burrows was straight out of the car and crawling all over the grimy one-bedroomed horror. He was too mean – and probably too experienced by now – to employ a surveyor, so viewings with him often took ages. He looked at every nook and cranny, examined every cupboard hinge, and if he could have squeezed his fat girth up any chimney, he wouldn't have hesitated.

Maggie knew from past experience that the less said the better. She wandered round the flat in silence, wondering how anyone could have let it get in such a state.

'It's a fucking tip. Asking price is far too high.' This was Mr Burrows's habitual opening gambit once he'd done his inspection. Then he beamed at her, showing a row of crooked and discoloured teeth.

Maggie almost recoiled in shock. She couldn't remember Mr Burrows ever doing anything remotely like smiling, so she'd never seen the ghastly teeth before. Obviously he was too mean to see a dentist.

'Could get this cleaned up fairly quickly,' he announced briskly. 'I'll offer five thou under. That's it. Take it or leave it.'

Maggie winced again. She couldn't believe her luck. She was fairly certain the desperate sellers would accept the offer.

'Right, woman, get a move on.' Burrows was off again. 'Let's see the next pile of shit. Two buys in an afternoon would be a record, even for me.'

He loomed over her in his usual bullying way. It made Maggie's flesh creep but she tried not to show it. Strewth, she thought to herself, if the seller accepts Burrows's offer, I really will have to tell Pam about Jack's email. Maybe I'll extend the bet. Burrows has to buy two flats this afternoon before I tell Pam.

The bet looked as though it was off after they'd visited the second flat, which Burrows pronounced as 'the biggest pile of crap' he'd ever seen in his life. This was standard Burrows-speak so Maggie couldn't really be disappointed. She'd just become mildly excited at the prospect of clinching two sales in one afternoon for the same buyer. That would be a record, even for Home Truths.

She felt the familiar old energy and adrenalin rush of chasing a deal. By the time they'd pulled up outside the third flat, she was firing on all four cylinders and determined to give old Bullyboy Burrows a run for his money.

'Now this one's a real slag heap,' she announced, taking a leaf out of his book. 'No one in their right mind would want to buy this, let alone rent it out.'

'Hang on a minute,' he roared, in a manner that probably passed for approval, 'I'm supposed to say that. You're pinching my lines, woman.'

They galloped round the flat, with Mr Burrows clearly thrown because Maggie had changed tack. Instead of the usual poking at walls and floorboards with a biro, the Burrows way of conducting a 'survey', he had finished within ten minutes. Maggie's heart sank. This normally meant no go.

'Knock off a couple of grand,' he bellowed at her as they stood in the filthy remnants of a kitchen, 'and I'll take it. Sod the other two places. I've spent enough today. Run me back to your office and I'll wait while you get on the phone to the owners.'

Maggie was flabbergasted. And ecstatic. She allowed herself a brief, heady moment imagining a small bonus.

As luck would have it, Damien and Stefan arrived at the office just as Maggie was passing on both acceptances to Mr Burrows.

'She's good, this girl,' Burrows boomed at Damien. 'Just bought two flats in under an hour. Must be a record. Bloody good show. And I'll need a bit of finance from you, laddie.' He thumped Stefan's desk so emphatically that the accountant's beloved name plate bounced. With that, he strode out of the office, banging the door. They heard him starting up his rusty old pick-up and roaring off down the street.

'Brilliant,' said Damien, giving Maggie an approving smile. 'I know he's a pain in the arse but he's just become our best customer. Champagne, I think. Go in and raid Vanessa's fridge.'

Maggie went into Vanessa's office. Even though she was away on holiday in Thailand, there was still a whiff of Chanel No. 5 in there.

They were soon toasting her success. 'It might be a no-frills estate agency,' said Damien, 'but the staff deserve a little pat on the back from time to time. Well done, Maggie. Two pits beautifully despatched.'

Stefan gave Maggie a conspiratorial wink as if to say, 'It can only get better.'

Maggie paid out on her own bet and rang Pam to tell her about Jack's sudden apology.

'Took him bloody long enough,' was her friend's surprisingly terse response. 'Do forward it to me so I can have a read.'

'Nope,' said Maggie firmly. 'We're not doing any more psychoanalysis. It's deleted and before you ask me, no, I'm not replying. Why should I accept his apology? It's twice now that he's left me. I know New York was so good they named it twice, but I'd like to know what you call a bastard who's left you twice.'

'Certainly not the Big Apple.'

'More like the Big Rotten Apple.'

'Fair enough.'

'You look terrible. Have you heard anything?'

'Nope, not a word. It's three weeks now.'

'Hey, listen, pal, you waited three months to apologise. Can't blame her for making you sweat.'

'Maggie wouldn't do that. She's not the type. Doesn't play games.'

'Wanna go for a beer, talk about it?'

'Nope. Not tonight. Gonna sort a few things out with Betsy.'

'That sounds ominous.'

'We'll see.'

'In that case, you might need that beer tomorrow night.'

*

'You are looking so much better,' said Pam over Saturday lunch at the crêperie. 'You seem a lot more energised.'

'Yeah, I do feel as though I've turned a bit of a corner,' said Maggie, 'and it's all thanks to shifting those two flats to the revolting Mr Burrows. The kids have been absolutely smashing through all the money business, especially selling half their stuff. I couldn't believe they did that. It's all helped to bring back my confidence.'

'Well, it suits you,' said Pam enthusiastically, noting the brighter eyes, shinier hair and healthier skin tone.

'I'm even coping better with Garth,' Maggie continued. 'He's still creeping around doing an impression of a scalded cat and we still don't really speak, other than essentials in front of the kids. I think he's frightened to open his mouth in case I ram something into it.'

'Bet that's tempting. How long do you think this situation will go on?'

'For ever, as far as I'm concerned,' said Maggie firmly. 'He seems permanently ensconced in the spare room now.'

'But that can't last, surely?'

'No, of course it won't,' Maggie conceded, 'but it'll do for now. I know the marriage is all over bar the paperwork and I'm sure it's only a question of time before he reverts to his old habits. He'll be back up the pub and head down some new bit of cleavage before too long. I know it sounds lazy, but I just wish he'd leave. It's true I'm feeling a bit stronger now, but I simply don't feel I have the energy to go through a divorce. So I'd rather he left me, you know, just pushed off into the night. It would be so much easier somehow. Do you think that's a cop-out?'

Pam shook her head.

'I wouldn't mind betting,' Maggie continued, 'that once he's got a bit of money in his pocket again, Bouncy Brenda will be back on the scene.'

Pam stirred her coffee and gave Maggie one of her no-nonsense looks. 'Now I want to do something for you today,' she announced. 'I want to buy you something lovely to wear to show off that fab new figure.'

Maggie opened her mouth to protest.

'Shut your mouth, hon.' Pam put up a warning finger. 'We're off to buy you some Capri pants like mine. You said how much you liked them and the green shirt. They'd look great on you. I checked in Next and they've still got them in your size. I won't take no for an answer and also it's to make me feel less guilty for persuading you to meet up with . . . well, let's not mention his name.'

'You can't keep doing this for me,' Maggie protested. 'Every time I hit some kind of crisis, you whip me into a shop and buy me something. I feel terrible that I can't reciprocate.'

'Oh, rubbish,' Pam retorted. 'You'd do the same for me if the situation was reversed. You know you would.'

'Yes, of course I would. But we can't have the same outfit.' It was a feeble protest as she was secretly excited at the thought of a treat after so many months of penny-pinching.

'Oh, we'll just draw up a roster to wear them on different days,' Pam replied triumphantly. She'd already bought Maggie a pair of the green shoes to complete the outfit, in the hope that someone up in heaven would forgive her her trespasses in advance, for the email she was now planning to send on Monday.

'Don? It's Jack. Fancy that beer tonight?'

'You sound a bit better, Jack. Things calming down in your head?'

'Well, kinda. Just a ray of hope.'

'How were things with Betsy the other night?'

'It was painful, real painful. But I think it was more painful for me than for her.'

'Really?'

'Yeah. There's an irony here. I keep torturing myself about whether I'm committing adultery in my head. By simply wanting to be with someone else. But I suspect Betsy's already crossed that great divide some time ago. I sense she is actually seeing someone else.'

'Two wrongs don't make a right, Jack. What about the kids?'

'Oh, they're fine. Except that they're caught up in this endless family thing. You know what Betsy's mother's like. It seems to be some relative's anniversary or birthday every single day of the year and that means they have to be involved in the celebrations. I love my kids to bits, but I've never felt they belong to me. I always feel I'm the provider rather than the nurturer. I'm the doormat they wipe their boots on, despite the fact that I pay for the doormat and the boots. That make sense to you?'

''Fraid so, Jack. Seeing as we're being frank, I might as well say I've watched you over the years working your butt off for your family. Yet your family are never at home, except in a crisis.'

'Is it that obvious?'

''Fraid so.'

'Tell me, Don, whaddya think about me setting up something more permanent in Europe?'

'You're the bossman. But I'd say it's an obvious direction for us, and you, being English, are the obvious guy to do it. But is this what I think it might be? Is this the ray of hope you mentioned? Has she accepted your apology?'

'Don't know yet. But I'm working on it.'

'Don't take offence, Jack, but I hope this ray of hope isn't just a figment of your imagination.'

'No, Don, it's not. I've suddenly acquired an ally. Well, several allies actually.'

'Add me to that list then, buddy.'

'Already have.'

Chapter 39

Maggie decided to have a lie-in. It was Saturday after all and she'd really put in some hours this past week. Also, the house was blissfully deserted. Without the general rumblings of the washing machine, Sky Sports and the latest boy bands, she could actually hear the birds singing their hearts out in the garden.

Beth was on a sleepover at a friend's house and not due back until teatime. George had already gone off to play in a school football match. She'd heard all the usual accompanying clattering around the house as he located his kit and then did his ceremonial banging together of the boots in the back garden to get off all the dried mud from the last match. George believed life was too short to wash football boots, especially since Maggie refused to do it for him any more.

Garth had muttered something cryptic about being offered some overtime today so he'd left the house two hours before. Maggie lay back against her pillows, savouring the peace. She could only truly relax when Garth was out of the house. Their conversations had become more and more minimalist and she'd noticed how they'd both skilfully avoid being in the house together alone. It meant they could keep postponing the inevitable conversation involving the D word.

Her thoughts drifted back to how things were before the Brenda bombshell. Then, she'd have just accepted Garth's overtime explanation at face value. Now she had her suspicions he was back to his old tricks. The difference this time around was that her suspicions were coupled with high hopes that Brenda or Brenda Mark Two might snap him up and leave her in peace. Garth had been left in no doubt as to what she and the kids thought of him. The leaving would be much easier this time.

The clock showed half past ten. This must be my longest lie-in since I had the kids, she reflected. No Saturday lunch with Pam today. Pam was having to entertain her dreaded mother-in-law, down from London on a short-notice visit.

'You will be home all day in case I need you to come round and bail me out?' had been Pam's desperate request. 'I'll be over to yours with a large bottle the minute – no, make that the second – she's gone.'

Pam found her mother-in-law rather intimidating. She was convinced that the woman went around like a hotel inspector checking for dust the moment her back was turned. And she had to keep a running tab on all the ghastly vases and pictures Tom's mother had inflicted on them, so she could whip them out of the attic and back on display for the day.

'Garth's working all day, so I'm definitely in,' had been Maggie's reply. 'I've got tons of housework to catch up on. Come round as soon as she's gone. It'll give me an excuse to stop.' So Maggie's plan for the day was to shove on an old track suit, whip round the house with the vacuum, do the washing and maybe even get to the bottom of the ironing basket. Then she'd have a good old soak in the bath and look forward to Pam's arrival. With a bit of luck, Garth might see Pam's car and stay away a bit longer.

Soon the sitting room and kitchen were looking a lot more respectable. She decided to complete the job by giving the windows a good clean too. She was just fishing out some vinegar and old newspapers, one of many tips passed on to Pam by the ghastly mother-in-law, when the phone rang.

It was Pam. 'I'm on my way,' she announced breathlessly.

'Blimey, that was a short visit,' said Maggie, glancing up at the clock. It was only just after 2 p.m.

'What are you wearing?' said Pam, in a rather strange tone.

'Old tracky bottoms. Why?' Maggie enquired suspiciously.

'Get tarted up. We're going out.'

'Where?'

'Never you mind. Tell you what, you can have the turn to wear the Capri pants and the green shirt. See you in fifteen minutes.'

Oh well, at least the windows were saved from a fate worse than vinegar. Maggie dutifully raced upstairs and under the shower, washed her hair and got dressed as fast as she could. She wouldn't get her hair dry or any make-up on in that time, but she could do that after Pam arrived. She wondered if there'd been some horrible bust-up with the mother-in-law.

She was just doing up the buttons of the green shirt and admiring its softness once again when she heard a car honking maniacally in the street below. Beep, beep,

beep. She grabbed a brush to sort out her wet hair and went over to the bedroom window to see what was going on. Its incessant beeping was already becoming annoying.

She couldn't actually see the car from her window as it was obviously several yards up the road, hidden by a bend. But it seemed half the neighbourhood had already beaten her to it anyway. Some were already at their garden gates, others peering through curtains as the mystery car horn kept going. Beep, beep, beep. Some lunatic who'd had a couple of bevvies too many in the Doghouse, she guessed. For one terrible moment, she hoped it wasn't Garth, flipping his lid over the frosty situation at home. The neighbours would enjoy that one, having heard all about Brenda, the cat who clawed his face.

She went back to the mirror to finish getting the wet tangles out of her hair. Suddenly the doorbell started ringing. Again and again. What on earth was going on? Then she heard Pam's voice shouting through the letter box.

'Maggs, where are you? Come on down. Be quick.'

She shoved her feet quickly into the beloved pale green wedges and stumbled downstairs as fast as she could, brush still in hand. She could see Pam's outline through the glass front door. Clearly there was some kind of emergency going on. In her haste, Maggie fumbled with the latch. Eventually she got it open. Pam stood on the step, looking flushed and breathless.

'Are you all right, hon?' Maggie was immediately concerned. Pam was normally the picture of calm and chic. 'What's happened? Tom's mum give you grief?'

'No, no. Come out here, Maggs. Come out into the street.'

'But my hair's wet.'

'Oh, don't worry about that. Come out into the road. Now.'

She grabbed a protesting Maggie's arm and propelled her down the path to the road. Pam's hand was digging into her arm, which seemed strange. But they were moving too fast for her to protest. When they rounded the hedge, Maggie could finally see what all the commotion was about. A small crowd had gathered around the mystery car which was still honking its horn.

'Here she is,' Maggie could vaguely hear people saying. 'Maggie's here now. Let her get through.'

The crowd parted slightly and Maggie found herself being pushed through the gap. This was suddenly surreal. Everything went temporarily out of focus. Through the haze, she found herself standing in front of a bright yellow . . . omigod . . . Triumph Herald. She shivered, feeling her wet hair beginning to drip down her back. At the calm centre of the blur, the noise and the sea of expectant faces, sat Jack in the driver's seat. His face was implacable, his hand still pressing the horn robotically.

'What the hell . . .' She couldn't finish the sentence. The crowd's patter ceased, the car horn stopped. All the commotion of the last few minutes simply drifted away. There was an awful silence. It seemed to last for ever.

Puzzled, Maggie turned back to Pam, who was still standing right behind her, her faced clenched with nerves. She turned back again to see Jack getting out of the car and walking towards her. She could see his hands shaking. He opened his mouth to speak. Nothing came out. She opened her mouth. No sound either.

Pam finally found her voice and stepped forward

between them. The crowd all leant forward, anxious not to miss anything.

'This is all my doing,' Pam said, her voice wavering. Maggie looked at her darkly. Pam never wavered over anything. Pam was strong, determined and wise. Pam was the tough rebel from school. So why was she trembling?

'This is my doing. Jack wants to apologise in the only way he could think of,' Pam stammered. 'You might never forgive *me* for this, Maggs, but I hope you'll forgive *him*.'

Maggie's mouth still wouldn't move. She felt like a goldfish taking in water.

'Come on, Jack,' urged one of the crowd, now craning their necks to see what was going on. 'Say sorry, whatever it is you've done.'

'Yeah, come on, Jack,' shouted another, clearly picking up the plot. 'Get it off your chest, mate.'

'Yeah, go for it,' yelled another.

'She'll forgive you,' added someone else.

Maggie finally managed to move her lips. 'The car . . . what's this car doing? What are you doing here?'

Eventually one of Maggie's neighbours leant into the car passenger seat, brought out a bouquet of red roses and shoved them into Jack's hands.

'Go on, for chrissake,' the neighbour yelled, 'say sorry. Get it over with. It's getting nippy out here and that poor girl will catch her death with that wet hair.'

That did the trick. Suddenly Jack found his voice. 'Maggie, I beg your forgiveness. Please. I'll never leave you again. Please take me back.'

He handed her the flowers. She stared at them as if they were triffids from outer space.

'Aaaaaah, go on, have him back!' the crowd urged.

Clearly they'd all got the measure of Garth's bad tempers and permanent scowls over the years. 'Give him a break. Go on, love.'

Jack, encouraged by the crowd, started to explain. 'I thought that if I turned up in a yellow Triumph Herald, you might realise how much I need you to forgive me.'

Pam, regaining a little bit of confidence, chipped in: 'He had to track one down and have it sprayed specially.'

Maggie gazed at her. How on earth did Pam know all about this?

'Why aren't you in B-B-Boston? What are you doing . . .'

'Back in Europe for good,' said Jack emphatically. 'No baggage. Just me. Setting up another arm of the company, but only if you'll help me.'

'Oh . . .' Maggie was still in a blur. 'You want to offer me a job? I couldn't possibly . . .'

'Look, I'll explain all this.' Pam had suddenly found her nerve. 'Maggie, blame this on me. You can hate me for the rest of my life. I'm prepared to risk our friendship but I know that you and Jack are meant for each other. Always were.'

The crowd ooohed and aaahed in appreciation. Then they bent forward even closer so as not to miss the next instalment.

Pam continued: 'When your marriage virtually packed up over the Brenda episode and all the debts, I emailed Jack's parents at the Tin Man in Spain, told them the situation. They replied immediately saying they'd always thought you were the one for Jack. And more important, they could then tell Jack he was in with a chance.'

Jack took up the tale. 'My marriage has been in denial for years and years but it took meeting up with you to make me realise what I'd missed out on. Then I discovered that my wife has been dallying with her personal trainer for quite some time and is only too delighted to see the back of me.'

'W-w-what about your kids?'

'Oh, they'll be fine. And I'm sure they'll come over and visit us during their vacations.'

'Us?'

'Us. Please, Maggie. I can't let you slip out of my fingers again. We've wasted twenty years. Please say you'll be with me, on whatever terms you choose. Only so long as it's for ever.'

'Aaaaah,' went the crowd.

'But my kids . . . I can't just . . .'

'Pam says your kids have really stuck by you through all this terrible time. I can't wait to meet them. Please say you forgive me and then we can at least sit down and talk things through.'

'Good idea,' shouted one of the crowd. 'Hurry up and say yes, love. It's starting to rain.'

Maggie found herself and Jack being propelled up her garden path and into the house. Ridiculously, she was relieved to remember that at least she'd cleaned up the sitting room.

Pam followed them in and stood on the front step with a gesture that indicated 'show's over now, folks' to the crowd, who scuttled obligingly away as the heavens finally descended.

'I'll put the kettle on,' she said diplomatically and shut Maggie and Jack in the sitting room.

Maggie flopped into the nearest sofa, her knees finally buckling under her. Jack was now down on one knee in front of her, still begging her forgiveness.

'One look at you in that restaurant was enough,' he said, pleadingly.

'But I didn't even recognise you.' Maggie managed a laugh. She paused and took a long lingering look at him. 'Do you . . . do you think . . . do you think you could grow your hair a bit longer? I used to like it when it was longer and slightly wavy.'

'Does this give me hope?' said Jack, visibly encouraged. 'Of course I'll grow it longer. Any way you like. Look, I don't wanna bombard you, Maggs, but what would your kids think about moving to Spain?'

'Strewth,' said Maggie, taken aback yet again. It was all too much to take in. 'You *are* bombarding me. Why Spain?'

'Well, the folks are trying to retire. I've spent the past twenty years missing them. They never got on with Betsy and her ghastly family, hence we never saw much of each other. So I wondered if we might make a fresh start over there. What would your kids make of that?'

'You'd have to ask them,' said Maggie, still dumbfounded. 'They'll be back in an hour or so.'

She started to laugh. And laugh and laugh, until it hurt.

'What's so funny?' Jack was suddenly anxious.

'When I was setting up the Home Truths connection with Spain, via your folks, I started to learn Spanish. You know, two beers and an ice cream please, and directions to the nearest bus stop. But in the end I never went over there. After our disastrous meeting at Joe Allen, I came home to find out that this house was—'

'I know all about it. Pam told me the whole story.'

'Pam seems to be up to her neck in this. What else did Pam tell you?'

'That I still had hope. That you might find it in your heart to love me again.'

'I never stopped,' said Maggie simply. She hung her head and started to cry. Jack got up from the floor and took her in his arms. At that moment, Pam appeared at the door with a tea tray. She promptly went away again.

They sat on the sofa, Maggie, feet tucked under her, curled in beside him, his arm round her, his hand stroking her hair. Just as they used to in the old Chiswick flat, watching Bogart movies.

'Can I ask you something?' Jack finally spoke again.

'Of course,' said Maggie, wondering for a moment what Garth would make of it all when he came back later on. And knowing that she didn't actually give two hoots.

'What made you decide to try to find me again?'

Maggie thought for a second or two. 'Well, it all started at Juicy Lucy's.'

'Juicy Lucy's? What the hell is that?'

'It's a health club. And Pam's to blame yet again.'

'That girl's got a helluva lot to answer for.'

They both laughed.

'Well, to cut a long story short . . .'

'No, don't, Maggs. I insist on hearing the long version. We've got all the time in the world.'

NAILING HARRY

Jane Blanchard

The strut of a peacock, the libido of a rabbit and the morals of a skunk. Meet Harry Hampton, office super rat and boss from hell.

Harry specialises in stealing other people's ideas, sacking staff he doesn't like and claiming credit where credit isn't due. After surviving another round of reckless redundancies, four female workers decide they've had enough of Harry's game. It's time to bully off, to show this womaniser just what women are capable of.

And they're not the only ones to reach breaking point over Harry's antics. His much younger, beautiful wife Val also wants her revenge – and she's determined to make it as public as she possibly can . . .

GETTING IT!

Jane Blanchard

WANTED – Fun people for the TV challenge of the decade! Do you love shopping? Do you want non-stop excitement? Then join *Getting It*, TV's newest and most exciting shopping channel . . .

When Fran and Stella see the advert for a new TV station, they don't believe they have a chance of landing a job. But after lying about their ages and enduring the interview from hell, somehow they're in. Goodbye routine, boredom, drudgery. Hello lights, camera, action.

Except the glamour is rubbing off Getting It before it even hits the TV screens. Instead of being a glittering success, the station accidentally becomes cult viewing. As one disaster follows another, the audience tunes in for the bloopers rather than the bargains. The station sucks like the Super Suck vacuum cleaners the presenters are failing to sell. Fran and Stella discover they're getting it (fame, that is), but for all the wrong reasons . . .